Praise for the novels of

CARLA NEGGERS

"Carla Neggers is one of the most distinctive,
talented writers of our genre."
—Debbie Macomber

"Neggers delivers a colorful, well-spun story
that shines with sincere emotion."
—*Publishers Weekly* on *The Carriage House*

"Tension-filled story line that grips
the audience from start to finish."
—*Midwest Book Review* on *The Waterfall*

"Suspense, romance and the rocky Maine coast—
what more can a reader ask for? *The Harbor* has
it all. Carla Neggers writes a story so vivid you can
smell the salt air and feel the mist on your skin."
—*New York Times* bestselling author Tess Gerritsen

"A well-defined, well-told story combines with
well-written characters to make this an exciting
read. Readers will enjoy it from beginning to end."
—*Romantic Times* on *The Waterfall*

"Neggers's brisk pacing and colorful
characterizations sweep the reader toward a
dramatic and ultimately satisfying denouement."
—*Publishers Weekly* on *The Cabin*

Also by CARLA NEGGERS

BREAKWATER
THE WIDOW
DARK SKY
THE RAPIDS
NIGHT'S LANDING
COLD RIDGE
THE HARBOR
STONEBROOK COTTAGE
THE CABIN
THE CARRIAGE HOUSE
THE WATERFALL
ON FIRE
KISS THE MOON
CLAIM THE CROWN

CARLA NEGGERS

Cut and Run

MIRA

MIRA®

ISBN-13: 978-0-7783-2419-5
ISBN-10: 0-7783-2419-2

CUT AND RUN

www.MIRABooks.com

Printed in U.S.A.

For Joe, Kate and Zachary—
and special thanks to Bill and Aunt Dini.

Prologue

Delftshaven, The Netherlands

Alone in her small dressing room, Juliana Fall took a handful of ice chips and rubbed them on her cheeks and the back of her neck. She was so unbelievably hot! But it was her own fault. She'd left her long, pale blond hair down and had chosen a dress of heavy winter white silk—and the tiny seventeenth-century stone church had been her idea. It was packed with people. Her manager had fought her choice for weeks. *Why* make her Dutch premiere in a church with limited seating capacity when she could have had the Concertgebouw in Amsterdam? Was she crazy? No, she'd said, just adamant. She'd refused to explain that the church, in the old Delftshaven section of Rotterdam, was the one in which her parents had been married. It was the truth, but it sounded too sentimental for a rising international star in the highly fickle, competitive world of concert pianists.

Even at twenty-three, she was scrutinized not just for how she performed, but for what she wore, said, did—for everything. Already she was being touted as the most beautiful pianist in the world. One critic had raved about "her dark emerald eyes, which fill with passion even as she gives her trademark distant smile." If only he'd paid as much attention to her interpretation of the Mozart sonata she'd performed.

She laughed, wondering what he'd say if he could see her smudged mascara and the sweat that had matted her dress to her skin and dampened her hair.

"Juliana?"

Johannes Peperkamp smiled sheepishly from the doorway. He was her uncle, a balding, gentle old man, tall and all bones inside his ill-fitting suit, with a big nose and a permanent soft, sad look in his blue eyes. He was sixty-six but looked eighty. Until that afternoon, he and Juliana had never met. He'd taken the train from Antwerp, where he was one of the world's preeminent diamond cutters, and had taken his niece into his arms as if he'd known her all her life. He'd told her he owned all her recordings and liked to listen to them at dawn, when it was quiet. What a change from his younger sister! Wilhelmina Peperkamp was a stout, difficult woman. She lived in Delftshaven, one of the few sections of Rotterdam not demolished by the 1940 German bombings that had led to the capitulation of The Netherlands and the long Nazi occupation. Aunt Willie had been so annoyed at Juliana's ignorance of Dutch that she'd refused to speak English for their first thirty minutes together. Catharina, Juliana's mother and the youngest Peperkamp by thirteen years, had sat in quiet humiliation. She must have known—Juliana certainly did—that she was the one being criticized for not teaching her American daughter Dutch.

Juliana recovered from her surprise at seeing her uncle, and the indignity of being caught rubbing ice on her face. But she reminded herself that he was family. "Uncle Johannes, hello, what're you doing back here?"

"I've brought you something," he said in his own excellent English.

Juliana winced. Now? She had fifteen minutes to pull herself together for the second half of the concert. She snatched up a hand towel as her uncle withdrew a small, crumpled paper bag from inside his jacket. What was she supposed to say? The Peperkamps mystified her, and she wondered if her idea for a family reunion had been a good one after all. She'd already had to accept the mediocre instrument, the lousy acoustics, and, although the church was sold out, the comparatively small audience. But now the Peperkamps themselves were proving to be quite a handful. Her mother was obviously ill at ease with her older brother and sister, whom she rarely saw, and hadn't had much to say since arriving in Rotterdam the night before. And Aunt Willie was impossible. After getting off to an inauspicious start with her niece, she'd snored through most of the first half of the concert.

And now this.

Johannes thrust the bag at her. "Please—open it."

"But, I…"

She couldn't bring herself to argue. Her uncle looked so eager, even desperate. Unprepossessing as his gift seemed, it meant a great deal to him, and with the death of his wife, Ann, a few years ago and no children of his own, Juliana guessed he was a lonely man. For the first time, she felt the weight of being the last of the Peperkamps. She could indulge him.

With the towel around her neck, she stuck her hand in the bag and pulled out a heavy object wrapped in faded purple velvet. Her uncle's water-blue eyes glittered as he urged her on. She unwrapped the velvet. In a moment, she held in her hand a large, cool rock. But her pulse had quickened, and she lifted her eyes to her old uncle, licking her lips, which had suddenly gone dry.

"Uncle Johannes, this isn't— Tell me this isn't a diamond."

The old man shook his head solemnly. "I can't do that, Juliana."

"But it's too big to be a diamond!"

"It's what we call rough. It has never been touched by a cutter's tool."

Juliana quickly wrapped up the stone and stuck it back in the bag. For four hundred years, diamonds had consumed the Peperkamps. They'd entered the trade in the late sixteenth century when Jewish diamond merchants had fled the Spanish Inquisition and arrived in more tolerant Amsterdam. The Peperkamps were Gentiles. Why they'd taken up one of the few trades open to Jews—and dominated by them, even today—remained a mystery. But it wasn't one that interested Juliana. She considered diamonds ordinary and bland. Even ones like the Breath of Angels, which her Uncle Johannes had cut and was now in the Smithsonian, bored her. An exquisite stone, everyone said. She supposed it was, for a diamond.

"I'm flattered, Uncle Johannes, deeply flattered. But this must be a valuable stone, and I just can't accept it. It would go to waste on me."

"Juliana, this is the Minstrel's Rough."

"The what?"

A look of anguish, but not surprise, overcame the old man. "Then Catharina has never told you. I've often wondered."

She listened for a note of criticism of her mother in his tone, looked for it in his expression, but saw none. Perhaps he knew as well as his niece that Catharina Peperkamp Fall rarely discussed the first twenty-five years of her life, the years during which she'd grown up in Amsterdam, with her daughter—or anyone else. When Juliana had complained to her father about her mother's reticence, Adrian Fall had nodded sympathetically, for he too had been shut out from so much of his wife's early life. But he said that it was Catharina's past, not Juliana's or his.

"She won't approve of my telling you now, even less of my giving you the Minstrel," Johannes Peperkamp went on heavily. "But I can't let that stop me. I have a responsibility to future generations of our family—and to past generations."

Juliana was beginning to question whether she should take her uncle seriously. Was he just a crazy old man? And what she was holding just a hunk of granite? But he seemed so intense, and his guttural accent lent a mysterious quality to his words. She said carefully, wiping her jaw with a corner of the towel, "I don't understand, Uncle Johannes."

"The Minstrel's Rough has been in the Peperkamp family for four hundred years. We—your family—are its caretakers."

"Is it—" Her voice was hoarse, her hands trembling as they never did when she performed. "Is it valuable?"

He smiled sadly. "It used to be that any Peperkamp could have identified what you now hold in your hand. On today's scales, Juliana, the Minstrel is a D grade, the highest grade for a white diamond. Few are one hundred percent pure and colorless, but the Minstrel comes as close as any rough can. In the business, we call it an ice white."

"What will happen when it's cut?"

"If it's cut, Juliana. Not when. For four hundred years we've guarded the Minstrel's Rough from that very end. Surprising, isn't it? A family of diamond cutters protecting a rough from their own tools. We've had four centuries to study this stone, and should it ever have to be cut, we know its secrets. I have markings, which I will teach you. They will tell a cutter precisely where to strike in order to preserve weight without sacrificing beauty. But you must understand: the value of the Minstrel lies not only in what it will be when cut, but also in its legend."

"Jesus, Uncle Johannes. What legend?"

"In 1581, when the Minstrel's Rough first came to the Peperkamps, it was the largest uncut diamond in the world—and the most mysterious."

"But that was a long time ago…"

"Not so long. The Minstrel's Rough is still the largest and most mysterious uncut diamond in the world."

Juliana's heart beat faster than it ever did when she had preconcert jitters. "Why mysterious?"

"Because its existence has been rumored for centuries, but never confirmed. What you are holding, my Juliana, only Peperkamps have seen for four hundred years. No one else can prove it exists."

"Uncle Johannes, I don't even like diamonds."

"Your mother's influence," he said gently, and smiled. "I understand, but it doesn't matter. In each generation, one Peperkamp has served as caretaker for the stone. In mine, it was I. In your generation, Juliana—"

"Please, don't."

He took her hand. "In yours, there is only you."

Johannes Peperkamp returned to his seat in the wooden pew beside his two sisters. What a trio they made. At fifty-one, Catharina was still as slim and pretty as a girl, her eyes dark green like her daughter's, but rounder, softer, and her hair still as pale blond as it had been forty years ago when her big brother had whisked her out on the canals to go ice skating. Johannes wished she would smile. But he understood: she was protective of Juliana, afraid he or Willie would let something slip about a part of their shared past that she'd never told her daughter. And he already had, hadn't he? The Minstrel's Rough, however, had not been a slip. He'd planned what he'd tell Juliana for weeks but had always hoped she'd already know, that her mother had long ago related the story of the Minstrel.

He should have known better.

Averting his eyes from those of his younger sister, guiltily sensing the fear in them, Johannes smiled briefly at Wilhelmina. Ah, Willie. She'd never change! She was as plain as ever with her stout figure and square features, with her blue eyes of no distinction and her blondish hair, never as pale and perfect as Catharina's, now streaked almost completely white. She was sixty-four years old and didn't give a damn if she were a hundred.

Willie might have approved of his visit backstage with their niece, but, never one to hide anything, she'd have insisted he tell Catharina. How could he? How could he explain his ambivalence, the duty he felt to generations of Peperkamps coupled with the horror he felt at what the Minstrel's Rough had come to mean to his own generation—to Catharina and Wilhelmina, to himself? Their father had passed the Minstrel on to him in 1945 under circumstances even more difficult than those Johannes now faced. How could he ignore the responsibility with which he'd been entrusted? He'd had to give the stone to Juliana. There was no other choice.

You could have thrown it into the sea, Catharina would tell him again, as she had so long ago.

Perhaps he should have listened to her then.

And Willie—dear, blunt Wilhelmina. She'd make him tell Catharina and then she'd make him tell Juliana everything, not just what he'd wanted to tell her. *What you are holding, my Juliana, only Peperkamps have seen for four hundred years. No one else can prove it exists.* They were the words his father had told Johannes when he'd first seen the Minstrel as a boy.

Now they were a lie.

Yet what did it matter? The past was done.

Juliana returned to the makeshift stage and smiled radiantly at her audience, and Johannes felt a surge of pride and admiration. After the shock he'd given her, she'd composed herself and began the second half of her concert with the same blazing energy, the same flawless virtuosity, as she had the first half.

Within minutes Catharina elbowed her older sister in the ribs. "Willie—Willie, wake up!"

Wilhelmina sniffed. "I am awake."

"Now you are. But a minute ago your eyes were closed."

"Bah."

"No more snoring. Juliana'll hear you."

"All right." Wilhelmina sat up straight in the uncomfortable pew, for her a major concession. "But all these sonatas sound the same to me."

"You're hopeless," Catharina said, but Johannes, at least, could hear the affection in her voice.

If the past had not been what it was, thought the old diamond cutter, feeling better, Juliana never would have been born. She's our consolation—Catharina's, mine, even Willie's. And now, through her, not just the Peperkamp tradition but the Peperkamps themselves would continue.

One

Len Wetherall settled back against the delicate wrought-iron rail in front of the Club Aquarian, enjoying the sunny, cold mid-December afternoon. He was a people watcher, and there was no place better to watch people than New York. Here, for a change, he could do the watching; he wasn't always the one who was watched. He was three inches shy of seven feet tall, an ex-NBA superstar, black, rich, and a man of exquisite taste and enormous responsibilities. He knew he didn't blend in on the streets of SoHo any more than he did anywhere else. But here no one gave a damn.

People were moving fast, even for the city. Len watched a pink-haired woman in a raccoon coat swing around the corner, covering some ground. She had on red knit gloves and red vinyl boots, and her mouth was painted bright red. Her eyes—

Len straightened up, buttoning one button of his camel wool overcoat. Her eyes were the darkest emerald green, and he'd recognize them anywhere.

"J.J. Pepper."

When she spotted him, she grinned, her teeth sparkling white against her bright lips. Even in the harsh afternoon light, her eyes were as mysteriously alluring as everything else about her. She came right up to him, stood on her tip-toes, and he bent down and planted a kiss on her overly madeup cheek. His wife, Merrie, couldn't understand why J.J. wanted to paint up her hair and face like that. "She must be a real light blond underneath that colored mousse she uses," Merrie had said. "And I'll bet her skin's perfect. Why would she want to cover up all that?"

Why, indeed? But Len had learned not to ask J.J. Pepper too many questions. She'd just give him one of her dazed looks, as if they weren't operating on the same planet, and avoid a straight answer. He'd asked her once how old she was, and she'd said, "Oh—around thirty." Like she was making herself up. The colored hair, the vintage clothes, the gaudy makeup, and the rhinestones were all a part of her look. They were what she wanted other people to see. Her package. During his fifteen years with the Knicks, Len had listened to everybody's ideas about how he should be packaged. He'd learned the hard way just to go on and be himself. J.J. would learn, too, sooner or later.

J.J. Pepper had first glided into the Club Aquarian that spring. The place had been open just one year, and already it was one of the hottest nightclubs in New York. Len had opened its doors shortly after his final season as a power forward with the Knicks. His original dream had been to start up his own down and dirty jazz joint, but if nothing else his years on the basketball court had taught him who he was and, maybe more important, who he wasn't. Down and dirty wasn't his style, and he wasn't a purist about jazz. He liked to mix in some popular, some soft rock, some easy classical, turn the musicians loose, and let them do their thing. He wanted his club to have a little polish, a certain cachet. Tall ceilings. He wanted it to be the kind of place where people could have a good time, wear their best clothes, be their best selves.

Looking at J.J. the first time, he didn't think she'd fit in. She'd had on one of her nutty outfits, a thirties dress and lots of rhinestones, and had plunked herself down at the baby grand, like, hell, baby, I *belong* here. Right then he'd known she had it, never mind the crazy lavender hair and the feeling she wasn't quite on the level with him.

She'd started to play, stopped after a few seconds, and turned to him. "Did you know this piano has a muddy bass?"

"That right," he said, noncommittal.

"I'll compensate today, but you should have it looked at."

"Sure, babe. I'll get right on it."

Before he could pull her little butt off the bench, she'd started to play. Then he didn't want to stop her. He'd just stood there, listening. Her technique was awesome. He'd never heard such sounds come out of that piano, damned muddy bass or no damned muddy bass. But she didn't let go; she held on tight to all the notes she had memorized. He could feel something there inside her, waiting to get out. And when it did—man, he wanted to be there. The walls'd be shaking.

She played three tunes and stopped. She turned around on the bench and looked up at him with those pink-and-lavender streaked eyes for his verdict. She didn't seem winded or nervous. Len had the feeling that if he told her she wouldn't do, she'd just shrug her nice round shoulders and walk off, ego intact.

"Not bad, J.J." A fake name, he decided. Who the hell would call a kid with eyes like that *J.J.?* He didn't believe the Pepper, either.

"Thank you," she said, polite, but not what he'd have called relieved. She knew she was good.

"You need to let yourself go, put some heat into what you're doing."

She frowned, smacking her plum-colored lips together. "Improvise, you mean?"

"Yeah, improvise." He thought, bub, what're you getting yourself into? But then he heard himself say, "You can play the early crowds, some lunches if you want. I'm looking for somebody to do Sunday brunch, if you're interested. We sometimes bring in a classical pianist. You know any Bach and Beethoven?"

"I'd prefer to stick to jazz and popular. When would you like me to start?"

"Tomorrow night."

"I can't start tomorrow night."

"Can't?"

"I have a previous commitment."

"You playing another club?"

"No."

She wasn't going to explain. "What about Sunday?"

"You want to open me with a brunch?"

"Yeah. Earl Hines you're not, babe."

Those high, sweet white cheeks of hers got red. "Okay, Mr.—"

She'd forgotten his damn name. "Wetherall," he supplied, deadpan. "Len Wetherall."

She'd never heard of him. Took her two weeks to figure out who he was. Told him she followed hockey, not basketball. He'd dropped the name Wayne Gretzky, but she'd just said, "Who?" It had been another one of those little inconsistencies. They all added up to a big fat lie, but Len had decided if J.J. Pepper ever wanted to level with him, then he'd listen.

Until then, he'd let her be whoever she wanted to be.

"Hey, sweet cheeks," he drawled now, giving her a slow grin. Her eyes were done up in a glittery gold. "Good to see you. How was New Zealand?"

For a second she looked as if she didn't know what he was talking about, as if she'd forgotten she'd walked out on him four months ago to go mountain climbing in New Zealand. Then everything clicked and she laughed. "New Zealand was terrific."

He'd have believed she'd been to Yakutsk just as well. "Bring me back a sheep?"

"Postcards."

Where'd she pick up postcards? Not in New Zealand, for damn sure. "You ready to play?"

She gave him a wide smile, and this time there was relief in it. "Sure."

"Then get in there. Later you can tell me about New Zealand."

"Be glad to."

The glint in her eyes told him she was having a grand time lying to him. But inside, the late-afternoon crowd and the baby grand piano were waiting, and she seemed glad to see them both.

The Dutchman smoked a cigar as he stood alone on the park side of Central Park West at Eighty-first Street. Across from him on one corner was the sprawling Museum of Natural History, on the other, the prestigious Beresford. From his vantage point, he could review the two entrances to the Beresford on Eighty-first Street as well as the one on Central Park West. Doormen in green uniforms with gold braid were posted at each entrance. They didn't worry Hendrik de Geer; if he needed to, he could get past them. For now, he was only observing.

He saw the woman in the raccoon coat step out of a yellow cab on Eighty-first, a wide, busy street that cut through the park. She said something to one of the doormen and was permitted to go inside. Her hair was pinkish blond. At first Hendrik had assumed it was a trick of the sunlight, but he soon realized he was mistaken and that, indeed, her hair was pink. She had left the Beresford a few hours earlier. He'd waited for her, smoking in the cold. He had to see her once more, to be sure.

He was sure now. She was Juliana Fall. He had seen her smile and her eyes. She could be no one else.

All at once the cigar tasted bitter. It was a Havana, his only extravagance. Johannes Peperkamp had given Hendrik his first cigar when he was still just a boy, and he'd choked on the smoke and vomited, embarrassing himself in front of the older friend he'd so badly wanted to impress. Hendrik had long since stopped worrying about trying to impress anyone. All that interested him was survival. His judgment of character and his ability to size up a situation were quick and accurate, and over the years those abilities had helped him stay alive. As he grew older, he found himself becoming increasingly dependent on his instincts. He could rely no longer upon the physical strength or the quickness of youth—or with his whitening blond hair and age-toughened, wrinkling skin, on its appearance. What he had was experience. Instincts.

His instincts now were telling him to run. He would need only to disappear, as he had many times in the past. It was a particular skill of his. He could do it.

He threw down the cigar and stamped it out with the heel of his boot. Then he turned around and walked through the stone gate into the park. My instincts, he thought, be damned.

Juliana Fall, aka J.J. Pepper, let the hot water of the shower rinse the last remnants of the pink mousse from her hair, and it felt as if a part of herself were being sucked down the drain. *You're not J.J.!* Yes, but wasn't J.J. real? Hadn't Len kissed J.J. on the cheek and hadn't the crowd at the Club Aquarian applauded J.J.?

J.J. existed. She was an aberration, perhaps, but she did exist. She had even taken over an entire bedroom in Juliana's sprawling, elegant apartment. It was decorated twenties-style, and the closet and drawers brimmed with vintage clothes and jewelry from between the two World Wars. J.J. fare. Juliana seldom was seen in anything but the latest designs from the collections of top designers.

Stepping out of the shower, Juliana wrapped herself in a giant soft white bathsheet and towel-dried her hair. In the mirror, she looked like herself again—blond-haired, pale-skinned, every bit the world-famous concert pianist. But her mind hummed with the chords of Duke Ellington, Earl Hines, and Eubie Blake. Her autumn European tour—she hadn't stepped foot in New Zealand—was to have driven J.J. Pepper from her system, exorcised her, because J.J. was not a part of her but something that had possessed her.

At least that was what she'd told herself. But twenty-four hours back from Paris and still suffering jet lag, she was dressed in a thirties green satin dress and off to the Aquarian. She'd expected, hoped, dreaded Len would tell her to get lost. He hadn't. He'd told her to play. And, by God, had she!

She'd had a good time.

A hell of a good time.

J.J. Pepper was back, and Juliana Fall didn't know what to do about her. Tell Len the truth? Tell *herself* the truth? That she, Juliana Fall, was the pink-haired, free-spirited, jazz-playing J.J. Pepper?

She went into her own bedroom and put on a simple white Calvin Klein shirt, a straight black wool skirt, and a raspberry wool jacket. J.J.'s raspberry boots would have matched the outfit, but she chose instead her black Italian boots and passed over the raccoon coat for her black cashmere. She was having dinner tonight with Shuji, and if there was one thing Eric Shuji Shizumi would never understand, it was J.J. Pepper. Shuji was a phenomenal pianist, a wild, intense, impatient genius who exhausted audiences with his thrilling performances. He was forty-eight, and in his long career, he'd taken on only one student: Juliana Fall.

"And if he finds out about J.J.," she said aloud as she waited for the elevator, "he'll lop off your head with one of his authentic Japanese short swords."

He'd threatened to do the same for transgressions far less serious than playing jazz incognito in a SoHo nightclub.

Halfway to the lobby, she remembered she was still wearing J.J.'s gaudy rhinestone ring, which she snatched off, dropped into her handbag, and tried to forget.

The Dutchman had walked across Central Park, ignoring the falling temperature and the lightly falling snow. Children on the plastic things they now used for sleds laughed as they passed him; he ignored them, too. He crossed Fifth Avenue and continued along East Seventy-ninth to Madison and up several more blocks, until he came to a little bake shop with white-trimmed window-panes. Inside, the display of Dutch wooden shoes filled with chocolates and tiny gifts made it look as if St. Nicholas had already been there. *Sint Nicolaas.* Hendrik hadn't thought of him in years.

Catharina's Bake Shop the sign read in simple delft-blue letters. The Dutchman lingered in front of the window. Small round tables covered with delft-blue cloths were crowded with customers, laughing, happy customers indulging themselves with hot chocolate, silver pots of coffee, china pots of tea, fat cream puffs, perfect tarts, and trays of scones, tiny sandwiches, assorted jams, and cheeses. Glass cases were stocked with good things to take home, and smiling white-aproned waitresses bustled among the customers.

For the first time in more than forty years, Hendrik de Geer felt himself swelling with nostalgia. He had to blink away hot tears—him! A couple hurried past him, and when they opened the door, he heard the tinkle of a little bell and smelled cinnamon, nutmeg, anise, butter, and fresh coffee.

It was almost more than he could bear. They were the smells of his youth, and he choked with emotion, unable to hold back the memories.

He didn't venture inside. He shoved his cold hands into the pockets of his cheap overcoat and stared through the window, watching a couple torture themselves over which cake to choose. The chocolate or the buttercream? If only his choices were that trivial.

A woman appeared behind the glass case, and for a moment Hendrik thought her radiant smile was directed at him. *Catharina*...he wanted to cry out to her.

But the sight of him would only bring her pain, and he stepped back so that she wouldn't be able to see him out on the street, alone in the dark. She spoke to the couple, and he watched, marveling at how little she'd changed. Even now, in her late fifties, there was something so captivatingly fresh and innocent about her. Her wispy white-blond hair was braided on top of her head like some long-ago Dutch queen, but without queenly arrogance, and she wore a turquoise knit dress beneath her apron. She had a strong chin and nose, almost too strong, but her dark green eyes were round and soft and exactly as Hendrik remembered.

She helped the couple choose the chocolate cake and wrapped it herself, and when the Dutchman heard the tinkle of the little doorbell as they left, he was halfway down the block.

Choices. What nonsense was this about choices? He had no choice. As always he would simply do what had to be done.

Eric Shuji Shizumi had lit a cigarette over coffee—a bad sign. He was demonically good-looking, a wiry man with sharp features, longish fine black hair touched with gray, and probing black eyes. He was notoriously single-minded. Born in San Francisco, he was *sansei*, third-generation

Japanese-American. But his earliest memories were of a
concentration camp in Wyoming, something he never discussed, never permitted to be printed in his program notes.
He could have married a dozen times over, but it was the
piano that possessed his soul and consumed his life—and,
some said, Juliana Fall. She had heard the rumors but had
always dismissed them. She knew Shuji at least as well as
he knew her, and whatever had bonded them together for
the past twenty years, it wasn't sex and romance. Their relationship was volatile and incomprehensible. In their own
way, they were devoted to each other, but neither had
shown any inclination to marry, either each other or anyone else. Shuji was no longer formally her teacher, but she
was still widely described as his sole student and continued to rely on his advice and guidance. She supposed she
still needed his approval, and, too, he understood the demands of international artistic fame better than most. Yet
the isolation demanded by his profession never bothered
him the way it often did Juliana. He was content to sit for
hours at the piano, alone with his work, day after day,
month after month, year after year. He had little sympathy
with his sole student's need to be with people on occasion.

He blew out his match and dropped it in an ashtray, exhaling a noxious cloud of smoke. "Juliana," he said, "we
need to talk."

Her heart pounded. *He's found out about J.J.!* But that
was impossible. Shuji would never have gotten through
dinner if he'd known she'd played Mose Allison at a SoHo
club that very afternoon. He'd have gone after her with a
steak knife. "About what?" she asked.

"What's happening to you."

"Me? I've just returned from a grueling European tour,
and Saturday night I'm doing my hundredth concert this
year at Lincoln Center. That's what's happening to me."
Shuji held the cigarette in the corner of his mouth, not in-

haling. They were at a tiny, bring-your-own wine Italian restaurant just off Broadway on the Upper West Side. It wasn't glitzy, and if any of their fellow diners recognized the two world-famous musicians, they left them alone. Juliana was drinking decaffeinated café au lait, hoping it would counteract the wine and food and jet lag so she could go home and run through the Beethoven concerto she would be performing in two days.

"And after the concert?" Shuji asked. "Then what?"

"I go to Vermont for a week or so on a well-deserved vacation, and then I come back and spend the next few months working and recording. I don't have another concert until spring. I'm cutting back some this year. You know all that, Shuji, so what are you trying to get at?"

"Don't go to Vermont," he said.

"What?"

"You heard me. Don't go."

"Shuji, I need rest. Damn it, I *deserve* a break!"

"You need work."

"I work all the time. I've been on the road for four months—"

"The real excitement of being a pianist is in the practice room, not on the concert stage. Juliana, you've been operating at a killing pace the past few years. I know that. And you know I support your cutting back from a hundred concerts a year. But I don't support your going to Vermont, at least not right away. You need to experience the excitement of the practice room again, and as soon as possible."

"Jesus Christ, Shuji, I'm only going to be gone a week!"

Shuji took a deep drag on his cigarette, held the smoke a moment, then exhaled. Juliana coughed and drank some of her café au lait, but he paid no attention. As usual, he was absorbed totally in his own thoughts. If we were married, she thought, we'd last two weeks.

"A pianist doesn't look forward to a vacation where there is no piano," he said.

You shit, she thought, but held back. She owned a small, antique Cape Cod house overlooking the Batten Kill River in southwestern Vermont; during the winter, she liked to keep a fire going in the center chimney fireplace. She would sit in front of the flames with an old quilt spread on her lap and read books, not thinking about music. It was true she didn't have a piano in Vermont. She didn't even have a stereo. What she had was silence.

"Shuji," she said carefully, controlling her impatience. "I am not you. I need this time-out, and I'm going to take it."

"It would be a mistake."

"Why all of a sudden would going to Vermont be a mistake? It's not as if I've never done it before."

"I was in Copenhagen, Juliana."

"Shit."

"Yes."

Copenhagen hadn't been one of her more memorable performances. In fact, it had been distinctly forgettable. But Shuji didn't comprehend things like bad nights, and Juliana knew better than to make excuses. "It was an inferior performance," she admitted, "but skipping Vermont isn't going to change that—and what the hell are you sneaking into my concerts for? Haven't you got anything better to do?"

"I was in Paris also."

"Well, then, you know Copenhagen was an aberration." She had received a standing ovation and rave notices in Paris—and had earned them.

But Shuji was shaking his head solemnly as he crushed his cigarette in the ashtray. "I'm not interested in what went on on the surface, I'm interested in what's going on *beneath* the surface." He always talked like that; it drove her nuts. "I heard something in Copenhagen and in Paris— on a 'bad' night and on a 'good' night, if you insist. It was an uneasiness, I believe, a hint of unpredictability. No one else would notice, of course, but soon they will, if you let it get away from you. Be aware of it. Control it. Find out what it is, Juliana, and use it to your advantage. The only place you can do that is in the practice room."

What he'd heard was J.J. Pepper creeping into her work, but that wasn't something Juliana wanted to discuss with Eric Shuji Shizumi. "Fine. I'll work on it after Vermont."

"You're in a funk, Juliana."

"I'm not."

His black eyes probed her face. "Are you afraid of burning out?"

"No."

"I was, when I was thirty. You don't remember. You were just a child and had no understanding of such things. But despite all the acclaim, the recordings, the bookings, I wondered if I'd still be around when I was thirty-five. Countless young pianists are just flash-in-the-pans, brilliant for a few years and then gone—*poof.* Sometimes it's their choice, sometimes not."

"I'm not going to go 'poof,' I'm going to go to Vermont."

"God knows the public's fickle, always searching for a new star, and our competition system thrusts pianists into the public light at an incredibly young age. The pressures of being a virtuoso are enormous. You're so exposed, so vulnerable. At thirty, the novelty's worn off. You've made a great deal of money, and you must decide if you want to be in this thing for the long haul or not."

"I've never considered *not* being a pianist."

"Haven't you?"

He gave her an unreadable half smile, aware that she was lying. Of course she had. Lately, more than ever. But she couldn't tell Shuji about the mornings she'd lain in bed wondering what her life would be like if she'd never taken up piano, if she never played again. What would she do?

What *could* she do? She couldn't tell him about her mounting exhaustion as the tour had worn on, about her fantasies of sticking a jazz improvisation into the middle of a Mozart sonata, about her tiresome fights with her manager, who wanted her to maintain a hundred-concert schedule and at the same time expand her repertoire and do more recordings. She couldn't tell Shuji about her boredom with the review, the constant travel, the fancy dinners, the men she met. She couldn't tell him about the growing monotony of it all and her fear that the monotony would follow her into the practice room, where it never had before. J.J. had counteracted some of the monotony, but she wouldn't be around forever—and Shuji couldn't know about J.J.

He was right. She was in a funk. But in twenty years, she'd never once told Eric Shuji Shizumi he was right. They argued and struggled and discussed, but she never gave in to him, never permitted herself to be intimidated by his legendary status. When that happened, she would lose her independence as an artist and, she thought, as a person.

"I'm not worried about being around when I'm thirty-five, and I'm not in any funk." She pushed aside her café au lait and sprang up, feeling tired and scared and so furious she couldn't see clearly. Why the hell couldn't Shuji just leave her alone! Why did he always have to push and press! "I hope to hell you're happy, Shuji. You've ruined Vermont for me."

"Good," he said.

"Bastard. Go to hell."

She stalked out, leaving him with the bill and a smug look on his handsome face.

From his shabby hotel room on Broadway, Hendrik de Geer put a call through to United States Senator Samuel Ryder. The Dutchman had been given the senator's

Georgetown number, and he wasn't surprised when Ryder picked up on the first ring. It was precisely nine o'clock, when Hendrik had said he would call.

"You have your answer?" Ryder asked.

The Dutchman heard the tension in the young senator's patrician tone, but he took no pleasure in it. "I will meet you at Lincoln Center on Saturday night." His English was excellent, only lightly accented; he spoke Dutch only when there was no alternative. It was the language of his past. "After the concert. You'll have a car?"

"Of course."

"Meet me there."

"All right. But take care the Stein woman doesn't see you."

Hendrik closed his eyes, just for a second, and felt the pain wash over him. The Stein woman...*Rachel.* But— "I need no instructions from you, Senator." His voice was cold. "Bloch knows none of this?"

"Do you think I'm a fool?"

"Yes. You tell people what they want to hear, Senator. I know. See to it you tell Bloch nothing, do you understand? Otherwise, my friend, we have no deal."

Two

Senator Samuel Ryder, Jr., edged into the narrow wooden booth of the crowded, smoke-filled Washington, D.C. diner. It was not the sort of place he frequented, ever, but he had chosen it for this meeting—a breakfast meeting not on any calendar known to his protective, thorough staff. His aides would have been horrified to see him give the chubby waitress a halfhearted smile as she slapped a sturdy mug of black coffee down in front of him.

"See a menu?" she asked.

The unappetizing menus were printed on cheap white paper and shoved between pieces of peeling plastic. "No, thank you," Ryder said, concealing his distaste as he looked for any sign of recognition in her bored eyes. There was none. "I'll just have coffee for now."

She shrugged and waddled off, moving her bulk with surprising ease. Ryder tried the coffee; it was hot and strong, although not of high quality. He didn't mind. During the past month he'd slept little. Coffee kept him going, as well as his sense of duty, of optimism. Things would work out; they had to.

Without a sound, Otis Raymond materialized in the opposite bench and slid into the corner with the ketchup and sugar packets and A1 sauce, as if he were the one afraid to be seen. Ryder, forty-one and single, tall, sandy-haired, square-jawed, and well-dressed, stuck out in the greasy diner. Army Specialist Fourth Class Otis Raymond—the Weasel, his buddies in Vietnam had called him—fit right in. He had to be forty, but he was even ganglier than Ryder remembered. Otis still looked like a teenager, a doped-up kid on the road to hell. He wasn't aging, he was yellowing. His bug-bitten skin, his sunken eyes, his teeth, his fingertips. Even his hair had a dead, yellowish cast.

Otis grinned. "Shit, man, it's been a long time. You done good since 'Nam, huh, Sam?" Fortunately, he seemed not to expect an answer. He rubbed his hands together. "I gotta have coffee. Fucking freezing up here. How the hell do you stand it?"

"You get used to it," Ryder said.

"Not me, man."

The chubby waitress appeared with a mug and a fresh pot of coffee. She poured Otis a cup, refilled Ryder's, and took out her order pad. Although Ryder gagged at the thought of what such a place might serve, he knew if he didn't eat, Otis wouldn't either, and the Weasel looked even more gaunt and hungry than Ryder remembered. He ordered ham and eggs. Otis said, "Make that two," and gave Ryder a manic grin. "Can't remember the last time I had a decent breakfast. You?"

"I usually play tennis early Friday mornings," Ryder said.

Otis laughed, snorting. "Tennis, shit. You wear them little white shorts?"

"They're considered de rigueur, yes."

"Fuck that."

The Weasel pulled out a crushed pack of Camels and tapped out a cigarette, taking three matches to light it. The matches were cheap and damp, and his hands were shaking. Ryder had a feeling they always shook. He dragged deeply on his cigarette, his fingers trembling noticeably. Raymond had always believed he and Ryder had some sort of special rapport because he'd saved Ryder's life in Vietnam, but of course that was absurd. Raymond had just been doing his job. Ryder didn't feel he owed Otis any special thanks. He appreciated the former helicopter door gunner's extraordinary skill with an M-60 machine gun, his principal weapon, which he'd treated with more care and concern than he had himself. But that came as no surprise: Otis Raymond had never planned on making it out of Southeast Asia. And in many ways, he hadn't.

Breakfast arrived, smelling of salt and grill grease, and the Weasel attacked his with the relish of the half-starved. The coffee and cigarette seemed to have calmed him, and his hands were steadier. He bit into the butter-slathered toast. "Bloch thinks you're up to something, Sam." Otis seemed to enjoy calling a U.S. senator by his first name. He swallowed the toast. "That's why he sent me up here. He doesn't give a shit what you do, so long as he gets his money. He's not worried about you giving away his operation, because he knows if you do, you'll end up swimming in shit, too."

"He's overextended," Ryder said coldly, wishing he could feel as confident as he sounded.

"Yeah, I know, but that don't matter. He's putting the screws to you so you can pull him out. Man, he's been doing this crap for years. You try and mess him up, you don't come out of it. He will—you won't."

Ryder said nothing. It rankled him that Bloch—Master Sergeant (ret.) Phillip Bloch—had sent Otis Raymond as his messenger. The Weasel, for the love of God. A drug-addicted loser giving him, a United States senator, advice!

"Don't bullshit Bloch, man. You got something going, level with him."

The acidic coffee burned in Ryder's stomach as his contempt for Raymond and Bloch and the underlife they represented again assaulted him. They'd been in Vietnam together—or, more accurately, at the same time. Weasel, Bloch, Ryder. And Stark. Mustn't forget Matthew Stark, although he'd tried. Of the four, only Ryder had successfully put their shared past behind him. He'd overcome all that had happened to him in Vietnam, all he'd done, all he'd seen, all he'd had done to him. He'd been a first lieutenant, a platoon leader, and Bloch had been his platoon sergeant. Stark had been a helicopter pilot, Otis Raymond his door gunner. They'd all survived their tours of duty.

Ryder understood tragedy as well as anyone—better than most, he felt. But why dwell on what you couldn't change? Why not move forward? He loathed men like Otis Raymond, still living the war, letting it destroy them, but at least Otis wasn't always whining and complaining the way so many were. Ryder had never had much in common with the men with whom he'd served, the men he'd led. Most were from the dregs of American society and had gone to Vietnam not because they believed in or understood the cause for which they were fighting, but because they had had no other real option. "I got into some trouble," Otis had explained once. "Judge told me, go to school, go to war, or go to jail." But Ryder came from an old, prestigious central Florida family and was himself the son of a U.S. senator; going to Vietnam for him had been an honor and, as his father's son, a duty.

"What more does Bloch want from me?" Ryder asked, hating the hoarseness in his voice. Normally his strong sense of self, which some called arrogance, could conceal his fear.

"Anything he can get, Sam."

He licked his lips, resisting the impulse to bite down. "What does he know?"

Otis shrugged. "He knows de Geer's in New York, that you two got something cooked up."

"Did de Geer tell him?"

"The sergeant's got snitches all over camp. He knows what's going on."

"He would," Ryder said, dispirited.

If he leveled with Bloch, the Dutchman would be furious and perhaps impossible to control. Technically, de Geer worked for Bloch, although as an independent his only loyalty was to himself. It was in his role as Bloch's messenger that Ryder had first met the Dutchman. De Geer turned the screws on Ryder on the sergeant's behalf—demanding more money, more favors, making those demands impossible to refuse. But now Ryder was the one turning the screws on the Dutchman.

Still, Ryder knew that if he didn't level with Bloch, the sergeant would keep digging until he found out what he wanted to know. Right now, Ryder didn't need that kind of interference. He needed to keep Bloch where he was, at least for the moment. "Can't you stall him?"

"Me?" Otis gave a croaking laugh that ended in a fit of coughing. He slurped some coffee and settled back, his bony frame almost disappearing against the tall wooden back of the booth. "Shit, Sam, you got a sense of humor, huh? I don't stall Bloch— Man, nobody stalls that fucker. I try, I'm a dead man."

"My God, what have I gotten myself into?"

Ryder hadn't intended for Otis to hear him, but the skinny army combat veteran nodded solemnly. "You know it, Sam, don't you? Let me help, okay? Trust me, I know Bloch. Man, I ain't going to let you go down."

My God, Ryder thought, am I so desperate I need Otis Raymond to protect me? "Thank you, Otis, but I can handle Bloch. Everything will work out."

"That's what you always say."

"It will. Trust *me.*"

"I gotta give Bloch something."

"Of course. I understand that. Explain to him that Hendrik de Geer and I are meeting at Lincoln Center tomorrow night to discuss a plan to get Bloch enough money to purchase the weaponry he needs and to get into his permanent camp—and out of my life for good. That's to his advantage as well as mine. Our current arrangement is too dangerous for us both."

Otis nodded at Ryder's plate, and Ryder shook his head and pushed it over. "I ain't had a good plate of eggs in I don't know when. You should see the crap the sergeant feeds us. Granola, for chrissake. So, what kind of plan?"

"I'd rather not say."

"Man, you gotta."

"Look—"

"You want Bloch at Lincoln Center, then you clamp up right now."

"That's the last thing I want!"

Otis dug into Ryder's cold eggs. "Then talk to me, Sam."

"I'm going after a diamond." Ryder measured his words carefully, trying to ignore the grinding pain in the pit of his stomach. He was so afraid. Dear God, he was afraid. But everything *would* work out. "It's the largest, most mysterious uncut diamond in the world."

"Huh?"

"And if I can get it—if—I intend to turn it over to one Master Sergeant Phillip Bloch."

Three

A young woman in a fresh white apron smiled across the counter in Catharina's Bake Shop at the tiny dark-haired woman. "May I help you?"

"Yes," Rachel Stein said, only vaguely aware that in this place, her faded Dutch accent seemed right. "I'm here to see Catharina Peperkamp—Fall, I mean." It was impossible to think of Catharina married, with a child. "Catharina Fall."

"And who should I tell her is here?"

"Tell her Rachel."

It would, she believed, be enough.

The waitress went back to the kitchen, and Rachel took a piece of broken butter cookie from a sample basket on the counter. For many years when she was young, she'd often been mistaken for a child, but now, with deep lines etched into her forehead and around her serious mouth and small, straight nose, people thought she was an old lady when she was only sixty-five. She'd gone from looking too young to looking too old. Her cab driver had offered to help her out of the taxi! She'd declined, of course, but thanked him lest he not offer his help the next time to someone who truly needed it. She supposed a face-lift would help, but although she could easily afford one, she refused even to investigate the procedure. In her opinion, people needed to see in her face, in its lines, what life had done to her. She believed that. But she kept herself well-groomed—her nails were always manicured, her hair perfectly styled—and she wore expensive, fashionable clothes. In that way, life had been good to her.

Within thirty seconds, Catharina Fall rushed out of the kitchen, wiping her hands on her apron, a panicked, uncertain look on her face. Rachel wished she could smile to reassure her. But she couldn't. A smile, now, would be a lie. Yet she wasn't surprised the impulse was there; everyone had always wanted to protect Catharina.

"My friend," Rachel said quietly, holding on to her emotions, "you look wonderful."

"Rachel." Catharina put her fist to her mouth and held back a sob. "I don't believe it's you."

She's going to throw me out, Rachel thought. She can't bear to see me. I'm a reminder. A shadow. As she is for me.

Instead Catharina burst from behind the counter and threw her arms around Rachel, crying, "My God, Rachel. Oh, Rachel," and Rachel found her own eyes filling with tears and her arms going around her strong, good friend. She'd missed her. Without realizing it, she'd missed her.

It had been more than forty years.

Catharina was sobbing openly, and the people around them were pretending not to notice. "I can't believe… I never thought I'd see you again." She stood back and brushed away her tears without embarrassment; flour stuck to her nose and she tried to laugh. "Oh, Rachel."

Rachel's throat was so tight it hurt. A sob would relieve the tension, but she blinked back her tears and refused to cry. She was a master at self-control. She hadn't expected Catharina to have this kind of impact on her. "My dear friend," she said, squeezing Catharina's hand, then releasing it. *I must be strong.* "It's so good to see you. I heard about your shop, and I thought, while I'm in New York I'll have to stop and see you."

Catharina had stopped crying and was shaking her head. "You know that's not true."

Rachel had to smile, and some of the tightness in her throat eased. "Achh, I never could fool you. It's always been that way between us, hasn't it? You always know when I'm not telling the truth. Even after all these years. But come, let's pretend for a little while."

"Rachel…"

There was fear in those deep green eyes. Rachel wished she hadn't seen it. "Please, Catharina."

"All right." Catharina nodded, but the fear didn't go away. "We'll have tea."

"Wonderful."

She pointed to a small table in the far corner. "There, go sit down. I'll bring a tray."

Rachel quickly took her friend's hand. "Don't be afraid, Catharina."

"I'll be all right. Now go sit down. I'll bring the tea."

"As you wish. I'll wait for you."

The big, open newsroom of the *Washington Gazette* was filled with the noise of bustling reporters, computers, typewriters, and telephones. Alice Feldon had been at her desk for two hours and had yet to sit down. She didn't mind. It was a sign things were hopping. What she did mind—what irritated the hell out of her—was that she couldn't find Matthew Stark. Again. She ignored the skinny, sorry-looking man who wanted to talk to Stark and scanned the newsroom. She had to squint her eyes because her glasses were on top of her head instead of on the bridge of her too-prominent nose. She was a large, lumpy-fleshed, big-boned woman, and she had no illusions about herself or the blue-collar tabloid she worked for. Last night, during a bout of insomnia, she'd painted her nails a shade of lavender she'd found on her daughter's shelf in the medicine cabinet.

"Where the hell's Stark?" she demanded of no one in particular.

A young reporter three desks away looked up nervously from his computer screen. A *Post* type if she'd ever seen one. His name was Aaron Ziegler, and he'd majored in journalism, which she considered a dumb thing for a reporter to have done. She'd hired him because he didn't show her any of the practice obituaries he'd done in class reporting. "He went for coffee," Ziegler said. "Promised he'd be back in five minutes."

"When was that, a half hour ago?" Alice growled and glared at the skittish guy as if it was his fault she was stuck with a lazy shit like Matthew Stark. She should have fired him four years ago when she'd come in as the *Gazette*'s metropolitan editor. He'd been occupying space for six months and hadn't done a damn thing that she could see. But he was a name, and the *Gazette* had precious few names. The boys upstairs had pressured her to give him a chance. She sighed at Ziegler. "Go find him, will you? Tell him he's got company."

Ziegler was already on his feet. "Any name?"

The skinny guy sniffled, shifting his weight from one foot to the other. "Just tell him the Weaze is here."

Alice wrinkled up her nose but didn't say a word. Ziegler hid his grin as he headed out of the newsroom. Like most everyone else at the *Gazette,* he was intimidated by Matthew Stark. Alice wasn't, although she couldn't understand why. Lazy or not, he was the scariest sonofabitch she'd ever known.

Catharina's hands shook as she poured tea from a white porcelain pot. She had prepared the tray of Darjeeling, lit-

tle sandwiches, round scones, two pots of jam, and a plate
of butter cookies herself. Rachel understood that her sudden appearance was a shock for Catharina. Forty years
ago they'd said goodbye in Amsterdam, and Catharina,
who stayed there a few more years, had cried and promised
she would stay in touch. Rachel hadn't shed a tear or made
a promise, because she had already cried a lifetime of tears
and no longer believed in promises.

"Don't be nervous," Rachel said kindly. She added sugar
to her tea. They were strangers, she and Catharina. And yet,
how could they ever be? "I haven't been to New York in
so long. There's no other city quite like it, is there?"

"No, there isn't," Catharina said. She added a drop of
cream to her tea but didn't touch it.

"But how are you, Catharina?"

"Fine. I'm fine."

"That's good." Rachel concealed her own awkwardness
as she tried some of the tea. "I can see why you opened a
bakeshop. You were always a wonderful cook, and you
took such pleasure in it. Nobody could make the meager
rations we had in the war tolerable the way you did—and
remember your beet stew?" Rachel laughed, not a happy,
carefree laugh, but still a laugh. "It was ghastly, but much
better than anything we'd had in weeks." She was suddenly
silent, observing Catharina's discomfiture with a small
sigh. Did her old friend never think about the war? Rachel
asked softly, "Adrian's a decent man?"

"Yes, wonderful." Catharina seemed relieved at the
switch in subject. "He's so kind and strong."

"He's a banker?"

"Yes, and he loves it."

"I'm glad. I've often wondered what would have happened to you if he hadn't come along when he did. Holland—" Rachel shrugged and thought perhaps it would be
best not to dig any deeper than was strictly necessary. "You

needed to get out of there. Wilhelmina would have suffocated you. Have you been back?"

"To Amsterdam, once, when Ann died. Johannes was inconsolable. I'd always hoped they'd die together." She quickly picked up a scone, absently coating it with raspberry jam. "And to Rotterdam seven years ago, when my daughter made her Dutch premiere in the church in which Adrian and I were married. He didn't come—he and Willie have never gotten along, and their fighting would have spoiled everything."

"Does she still think you'll come back?"

"Of course."

Rachel nodded, remembering the tough, solid woman who was Catharina's senior by a dozen years and had been Rachel's closest friend. Wilhelmina Peperkamp had held the Nazis in the strongest contempt from the very beginning, long before Austria, Czechoslovakia, Poland, certainly long before the German occupation of The Netherlands. Rachel had never met anyone more reliable. "Yes, I can believe that."

"Do you see her?"

With their five-year age difference, the friendship between Wilhelmina Peperkamp and Rachel Stein had been more a meeting of equals. Catharina had always been the baby. They'd all protected her—Wilhelmina, Johannes, Rachel, her brother Abraham. Everyone. They'd seemed to believe that if they could prevent the war from touching her, they could somehow preserve some of their own innocence. But the war had touched her. Nothing they could have done would have stopped that. It had robbed her of her youth, her girlhood. Rachel saw that now, understood, but she wondered if Catharina felt she'd failed them all.

"How can I see Willie?" Rachel said with a snort. "You know she doesn't travel, and I won't go back. She sends me cards at the holidays. She tells me about you, Juliana, her begonias."

"Do you write to her?" Catharina asked.

"No, but of course that doesn't stop Willie from doing what she feels is right. If it did…" She lifted her small shoulders in a noncommittal shrug. "I don't know. Maybe then I would write. Catharina." Rachel sighed, taking a tiny sandwich of smoked salmon. She wasn't hungry, but she knew she needed to eat. Five years of near starvation had developed in her a practical attitude toward food. "Do you have any idea why I'm here?"

"I can guess."

"I've seen him," Rachel said without further preamble. "I've seen Hendrik de Geer."

Catharina shut her eyes and held her breath, and Rachel thought her old friend was going to faint. "Catharina?"

She opened her eyes. "I'm all right," she said weakly. "I'm sorry."

"Please, don't."

"I'd convinced myself he was dead."

"Hendrik dead?" Rachel hooted. "He'll outlive us all. He's blessed that way, you know—or cursed. Remember the time he brought us the chocolate? We'd had nothing but sugar beets to eat for days and Hendrik showed up with chocolate. I thought I'd never tasted anything so wonderful. He was so proud of himself, and we were too thrilled even to think to ask him where he'd gotten it. But you know Hendrik. He's the kind who picks up the world each morning and gives it a good shake. For once, Catharina, I want it to go the other way around. I want the world to give Hendrik de Geer a good shake."

Catharina stared down at her tea, which had become cold, the cream filming on the top. She hadn't touched her scone. "Where did you see him?"

Rachel nibbled on a watercress sandwich. "On television, two weeks ago. It was fate, I think. Abraham and I have retired to Palm Beach." Fleetingly, she thought of the last thirty years, during which she and her brother had become two of the savviest, toughest Hollywood agents. It seemed so distant now. The past, Amsterdam, seemed so much closer. "I never liked Los Angeles, I don't know why. Anyway, now I have a whole new group of politicians to watch. I always watch politics, of course, since Hitler. One of our senators is Samuel Ryder—very handsome, charming, on the whole too conservative for me, but nothing I can't live with. One day I'm watching the local news, and a reporter catches Sam Ryder as his car pulls up to the curb and starts firing questions at him—you know how they will—about some controversial bill he's sponsoring, and sitting beside him is Hendrik de Geer. Hendrik! In a limousine with a United States senator."

The bell at the door tinkled, and Rachel looked around, pausing as two young women entered the shop, loaded down with shopping bags. Rolls of bright Christmas wrapping paper poked out of one bag.

"You're certain?" Catharina asked.

"Absolutely. After all these years, do you think he's changed? No, he looks just as he did in Amsterdam. I knew immediately it was he. My stomach told me, before my brain." She remembered how she'd run to the bathroom and vomited. That was something she would never admit to Catharina, for whom, she felt, she must remain especially strong. "I called Ryder's office at once and demanded to know why he was riding around with Hendrik de Geer, and, of course, they thought I was crazy. But I persisted, and finally they put the senator on."

"You told him—"

"I told him everything I could think of about Hendrik. Yes, that's exactly what I did. I talked and talked. Everything just poured out of me, because now I think the time has come. I told him Hendrik de Geer betrayed me and my family and the people who were hiding us to the Nazis, and that he was a Nazi collaborator and has never answered for what he did."

Catharina regarded her old friend with despair. "He's never even admitted he did anything wrong. Oh, Rachel, what's the point? You know what he is—"

"*That's* the point. I do know what he is!"

Rachel balled one tiny hand into a fist and thumped the table with her bony knuckles. Dishes rattled. Catharina jumped, looking startled and hurt.

Inhaling deeply, Rachel calmed herself and went on with quiet intensity. "He says Hendrik conned his way into seeing him to urge him to support an increase in defense spending but that he, Ryder, knows very little about him and had no way of getting in touch with him. I don't believe him, but no matter. He's agreed to investigate my allegations further if I can corroborate my story. I asked Abraham, but he thinks I'm crazy and that Ryder is only trying to pacify me and look good to a Jewish constituency. Maybe he's right." She laughed, remembering the shouting match she and her brother had had. But they had been fighting all their lives; they had good fights. "Abraham's content to believe Hendrik de Geer will meet his fate one day, if not until the moment of his death. Me, I believe Hendrik will even fast-talk God!"

Rachel grinned, but the light in her dark eyes faded as soon as it appeared. "I intend to make Hendrik answer for Amsterdam," she said, her gaze on the fair woman across the table, not easing up, not letting her off the hook. "You can help me, Catharina. *You* can corroborate my story."

"You can't make Hendrik answer for anything," Catharina said, tension strangling her words. "No one can. Rachel, he's a hard, hard man. Please don't do this. Don't go after him. Leave the past alone. Not for his sake, not for mine—for your sake, Rachel. You *know* what he is!"

Rachel filled her teacup once more, her hand steady. "I can't leave the past alone."

She could see the mix of anguish and determination in her friend's face and understood, because she had waged the same battle with herself and made her decision.

Catharina sighed softly. "Of course, how could I even ask you? It's just that I'm afraid for you, Rachel."

"I know." Rachel smiled and waved a hand, but she couldn't dismiss the pain in Catharina's beautiful eyes. She'd forgotten what it was to have someone—aside from Abraham of course—care about her. "The future holds nothing for me. It never did, even when I was twenty. I think only of the past. I can remember so clearly, as if it happened just this morning, how my father would sit me on his knee and tell me about diamonds, let me help him sort them. So boring! But there was such life in his eyes. Do you remember?"

Catharina nodded sadly. "Your father was one of the gentlest, wisest men I've ever known."

"He was younger than I am now when he died." Rachel drank some tea, replacing the cup on its saucer with a firmness that underlined her own resolve. "Don't be afraid for me, Catharina. I'm doing what I must do, what I want to do. I know exactly the kind of man I'm facing, and I don't care. If Hendrik wins, he wins. But at least I'll have tried. All I want is for him to understand what he did."

"He never will, Rachel," Catharina said.

"We'll see."

"Hendrik never intended for bad things to come of what he did, and when they did, he couldn't admit he was at fault. He couldn't accept the consequences of his own actions—he probably still can't. It's not in his nature. You're not going to change him. Hendrik de Geer will always be out for himself."

"Let's not argue," Rachel said. "I won't force you to help."

Catharina looked shocked. "No, that's not what I meant. Of course I'll talk to Senator Ryder, if that's what you want, but I'm pessimistic that anything will come of it. Even now, Hendrik probably already knows you're after him. He won't stick around. And Rachel, my God, you've suffered enough."

"We all have," she said, fire coming into her eyes. "But not Hendrik."

"I know, but…"

Rachel reached across the table and grabbed Catharina's strong hand, squeezing it tightly, aware of how small and frail her own hand was—but it was only bones, skin, muscle. Nothing that counted. The bond between them, what was unseen and immeasurable and timeless, was all that mattered. "You live on Park Avenue and have dried dough under your nails. Only you, Catharina. My friend, my dear, dear friend, I know how difficult this must be for you. But you don't have to see him. You—"

Catharina was looking at someone across the room. "Oh, dear heavens."

Rachel felt her heart pound. Hendrik—was it Hendrik? Had he found her? She whispered, "What's wrong?"

"Juliana. I forgot, I invited her to tea."

Resisting the impulse to draw a heavy sigh of relief, Rachel turned around and looked at the young woman grabbing a butter cookie and waving to her mother. Blond hair falling over her open black cashmere coat, dark green eyes sparkling, smile bright—a fascinating combination of strength and delicacy was this Juliana Fall. Full of piss and vinegar, Abraham would say. "So that's your Juliana? She's very beautiful, Catharina. You're fortunate."

"I know. Sometimes I wonder how I produced such a child. From the time she was a tiny girl, her whole life has been music. I don't understand. Adrian and I aren't musical, but with Juliana, there's never been anything else. Have you ever heard her perform?"

"Not in person, but I've listened to her on the radio

many times. And Senator Ryder has tickets for Lincoln Center tomorrow night. He suggests we meet there, after the concert, and—Catharina?"

She'd gone white. "Rachel, she doesn't know. Juliana. I haven't told her."

"About Amsterdam? *Nothing?*"

"I couldn't. Even Adrian..." Catharina shut her eyes briefly; Rachel watched her fight for self-control with a mother's willpower as her daughter made her way to the table. "Neither of them knows what happened. I know I'm overprotective, but I didn't want any of that to touch them. I just can't talk about Amsterdam."

"That's your right," Rachel said carefully. Having never married, she had never had to make such decisions. "I understand."

"You'll keep her out of this?"

Rachel smiled reassuringly, and although she didn't understand, perhaps didn't approve, she felt good about being able to comfort her friend. "Of course. There's no reason whatever for Juliana to be involved in this."

Matthew Stark was in the middle of an argument on shortstops with a couple of sports reporters when Ziegler found him in the *Gazette* cafeteria. At thirty-nine, Stark was a dark, solidly built, compact man with a face that might have been good-looking except for the shrapnel scars. His eyes were deep-set and a very dark brown; people told him that sometimes they seemed black. He had on jeans, a chambray shirt, and his heavy, handmade Minnesota Gokey boots.

"Sorry to bother you," Aaron said, "but Feldie's got a guy downstairs who wants to see you. He looks like somebody out of *Night of the Living Dead.* Calls himself the Weaze."

"Weasel? Hell, I thought he'd be dead by now."

Without rushing, Stark refilled his mug and walked back with Aaron, a curly-haired kid who wore tassel loafers and suits and didn't know a damn thing about baseball. Matthew knew he scared the hell out of Ziegler, but he didn't let that trouble him.

"Feldie was getting pretty impatient," Aaron said.

"Right."

When they returned to the newsroom, she had put her glasses, big black-framed things, on her nose. "Don't hurry, for Christ's sake," she said.

Stark didn't. He hadn't heard from Otis Raymond in a couple of years, but he'd had twenty years of his troubles and expected he'd have twenty more, if either of them lived that along. "Where's the Weaze?" he asked.

"I parked him over at your desk. He says he has a hot tip for you. Who is he?"

"Nobody who'll sell newspapers."

Otis Raymond sat restlessly on a wooden chair next to Stark's desk. Matthew just shook his head as he approached the thin, ugly figure and noticed the swollen bug bites along the back of the scrawny neck, the yellowed eyes and skin. He had on ragged jeans and an army issue jacket that didn't look warm enough for him. He was shivering. It seemed crazy now, but lots of guys owed SP-4 Otis Raymond their lives. He'd been good. Damn good.

"Weaze," Matthew said, coming up behind him. "So you're alive."

Weasel turned around on the chair, grinned, and rose unsteadily. His clothes hung on him, and he looked like hell. According to the book, he and Stark shouldn't have become friends. A warrant officer and a spec-four, a helicopter pilot and a gunner. They'd flown Hueys together, and they'd survived two tours. Not many in their positions had. It was as good a reason as any for a friendship.

"Matt—yeah, hell, I'm still kicking. Christ, I'm hitting forty, you believe it?"

Stark went around and sat down, and Weasel dropped back in his chair, eyeing the cluttered desk. "Figured you'd have an office."

"A piece of the wall is about the best you get in a newsroom."

"Yeah, I guess. I don't know much about this stuff. When'd you quit the *Post*?"

"Two years before the last time I saw you."

"Oh. Right. Shit, man, I can't remember nothing anymore."

"You never could. What's up?"

"I got trouble, Matt."

Stark waited for him to go on, but Weaze was gnawing his thin, yellow-purple lower lip, and he'd crossed one foot over the other. Except when he was behind his M-60, he always had an excess of useless, unfocused energy. Stark had often wondered where Otis Raymond would be today if he'd been able to channel that energy.

"You gonna help?" Weaze asked.

"Maybe. What kind of trouble are you in?"

"Not me this time. Ryder."

It wasn't a name Stark wanted or expected to hear, but he kept his face from showing it. "What's Ryder got to do with you?"

"I owe him. He tried to set me up after 'Nam, give me a hand, remember? I fucked up, made him look bad."

"He survived. The Sam Ryders of the world always do. You don't owe him a damn thing, Weaze. If anything, he owes you. Whatever trouble Ryder's got, let him handle it."

Weasel gave a honking snort, and Stark recalled that in the last ten years Otis always seemed to have a runny nose. "Shit, man, I thought I could count on you."

"You can. Ryder can't."

"He's in deep shit, Stark, and you know what a goddamn asshole he is, he'll never learn, and if we don't pull him out, he'll go down. Man, I mean it. This time he's in it."

"That's his problem."

"May be a story in it for you."

"Too much history between me and Sam Ryder, Weaze. No objectivity."

"Then a book, maybe."

Weasel somehow sounded both hopeful and smug, as if he'd struck the right note, the one that would make Matthew Stark do what his old buddy wanted him to do. "Forget it, Weaze," Matthew said. "That part of my life is over."

"Oh, come on—for old times' sake, then?" Otis Raymond laughed hoarsely, coughing. "'Member the good ol' days, huh, Matt?"

The good ol' days. Jesus. "You never change, Weaze. Go ahead, tell me what you've got. I'll listen."

Otis started chewing on the knuckle of his index finger, as if he'd gotten further than he'd expected and now didn't know what to say.

"I can't help," Matthew said, "if you don't level with me."

"Hey, I'm doing the best I can."

The Weaze had his own rhythms, and Stark knew better than to push. "What're you doing in D.C.?"

"How do you know I haven't been here all along?"

Weasel's look was filled with challenge, saying he was just as good as Matthew Stark and anybody who didn't believe it could go to hell. Getting a straight answer out of Otis Raymond had always been one big pain in the ass, Stark remembered. He managed a smile. "You wouldn't stay anywhere the temperature falls below freezing."

"Yeah, right." Weaze laughed, one of his high-pitched, slightly hysterical laughs that always gave people goose bumps. It ended in a fit of coughing and then an ugly grin. "Fuck winter. I been to see Sam, that's what I'm doing here. Had coffee together, me and Sam. Bought me breakfast. He's doing good, you know? Man, I wouldn't be surprised to see his ass in the White House. I'd vote for him. Yeah, shit, why not? No, forget it. I know you never liked him, but, you know, he means well."

"I know too many good men who are dead because of Golden Boy Sammy Ryder and his good intentions. So do you, Weaze. No point in you being one of them."

"Don't make no difference to me if I am."

Stark said nothing, knowing there was nothing he could say that would make any difference. He didn't give a damn what kind of mess U.S. Senator Samuel Ryder, Jr., had gotten himself into, but Otis Raymond, crop-picker at fourteen, Huey door gunner at nineteen, was another matter. He was a loner and a survivor, and he considered the greatest accomplishment of his life not getting killed in Vietnam—and coming between Sam Ryder and a rush of AK-47 bullets. Since then, he hadn't been able to slip quietly back into the daily routines of his old life. What Otis Raymond was and what he had been no longer mattered. The bond was there. Stark couldn't abandon him.

"Sam wouldn't like it if he knew I was here," Otis said. "You make him nervous, you know."

"Good."

Weasel laughed a little. "Christ, you two. He's got some plan, Ryder does, to get money to get himself out of the mess he's in. He wouldn't give me all the details, but it sounds nuts, really crazy, Matt. Says he's going after a diamond, goddamn biggest uncut diamond in the fucking world. You believe it? Jesus, what a stupid asshole."

Coming from Weasel, that was almost a compliment: it meant Ryder needed him.

"He's meeting a guy tomorrow night at some concert at Lincoln Center—a Dutchman. Name's Hendrik de Geer."

"Know him?"

Weasel shrugged his bony shoulders and pulled out his pack of cigarettes, tapping one out unconsciously and sticking it on his dried, cracked lower lip. "Sort of. He's nobody you can't handle, Matt. I thought maybe you could show up tomorrow night and look into this thing."

"Look into *what?*"

"The de Geer connection, what Sam's got cooking with this diamond thing."

"And begin where?"

"How the fuck do I know? You're the reporter."

"All right," Matthew said. Sometimes he forgot what a cocky little shit Otis Raymond could be. "What about you? You want to hang out at my place until we figure this thing out?"

Weasel shook his head, lighting his cigarette. "Naw, can't." He grinned, showing crooked, badly yellowed teeth. "I gotta be heading back."

"Where to?"

"Some place warmer, that's for damn sure."

"Weaze—"

"Buddy, don't ask me questions I can't answer. You do your thing, I'll do mine."

"He's not worth it," Stark said in a low voice.

"Man, who is? You gonna help or not?"

"Yeah. I'll see what I can do—for your sake, not for Sam Ryder's."

The Weaze sniffled and coughed, his breathing rapid and noisy, and he laughed, a hollow, wheezing sound that Stark found utterly desolate, the sound of a wasted life. "You do remember," he said in his raspy voice. "Man, I knew you would. I did good back in 'Nam, huh? I was okay there."

Matthew felt his mouth suddenly go dry. Behind his stoicism and quiet air of competence, he'd always felt helpless where Otis Raymond was concerned. "You were the best, buddy."

Dragging on his cigarette, Weasel headed out. He gave Feldie a grin that was almost a come-on, and Matthew had to laugh. He could hear his buddy's out-of-tune whistle as he disappeared down the corridor. The stupid shit thought he'd won. That Matt Stark was on the story and all was well.

Stark stood up, feeling the sorrow and anger he always felt after he saw Otis Raymond, but he kept the mask in place, the one that said he was always in control, always at a distance. He picked up his coffee and went over to Feldie's desk. She'd finally sat down, but he'd been aware of her looks in his direction—suspicious looks tinged with concern. Feldie was a stickler for facts—give people the facts, she said, and let them arrive at their own truths—and a damn fine editor, but she also cared. Trying to reform him gave her something to do besides going after facts and pleasing the big guns upstairs. But she'd never admit as much, and although Matthew admired her for it, what the hell. He'd had his fifteen minutes of fame. He still led a pretty good life, and as much as Feldie carped, he did get his assignments in, more or less on time. Maybe a few years ago he'd had the drive and ambition to do more—to make a difference. But that was a few years ago.

Feldie pulled off her glasses and snapped them closed. "Well, what did he have to say?"

"Nothing."

"You two yakked it up enough."

"Catching up."

"On what? I want facts, Stark."

"You don't get facts from Otis Raymond."

"You're not going to tell me," she said. There was resignation in her tone, and maybe a little respect.

Stark smiled. "Nothing to tell."

"Christ, Stark, you drive me fucking crazy."

"Without me around, who'd give you ulcers? I'm going up for some fresh coffee, you want anything?"

"No, jackass, I want you to tell me what that conversation was all about!"

Mug in hand, Stark started across the newsroom but, as if remembering something, turned back around. "Hey, Feldie, you want to do me a favor?"

"No. Sit your ass back down and tell me what that sorry-looking bastard wanted. He said he had something for you—"

"I'll be taking the shuttle to New York tonight," Matthew said, cutting her off. "Probably spend the weekend. I'd like to take in tomorrow night's concert at Lincoln Center, on the paper."

She frowned, opening up her glasses with both hands. "Why?"

"Something to do while I'm in town. I figure the paper can afford to spring me a ticket."

"You're checking out something this Weaze character said, aren't you? He gave you a hot tip."

"I just like music."

"Then who's playing?"

"Has to be someone good." He grinned. "It's Lincoln Center, right?"

"Stark, damn you."

But he ducked out for his coffee, leaving Alice Feldon sputtering.

Juliana immediately sensed her mother's tension when she came to the table, but Catharina smiled tenderly and introduced her friend. Rachel Stein rose, also smiling. "Ahh, Juliana, I'm so happy to meet you at last. You could only be a Peperkamp."

"You know my mother's family?" Juliana was surprised: she had never met anyone who did. She knew Aunt Willie and Uncle Johannes, of course, but none of their friends, none of the people who'd known her mother when she had lived in The Netherlands. "You're Dutch, aren't you? I detect an accent."

"We knew Rachel in Amsterdam," Catharina supplied quickly.

"Yes, and I'm sorry I can't stay," Rachel said. "A pleasure meeting you, Juliana."

"Likewise. You're sure you can't stay another minute? I'd love to talk."

But Rachel hurried out, and Catharina swept away the remains of their tray and had a fresh one brought over. "It's so good to see you, Juliana. I missed you. Now," she said, filling two porcelain cups with hot tea, "tell me about your tour. Was it successful?"

"Yes, but, Mother—"

"A friend of mine heard you in Vienna. She said you were magnificent."

Juliana sighed. She wasn't going to hear about Rachel Stein. She considered asking but knew it would do no good. Only on rare occasions would her mother discuss her life in The Netherlands, and then in the most general terms. Even her father remained relatively ignorant of that phase of his wife's life. Catharina Peperkamp Fall had survived five years of Nazi occupation when she was little more than a girl, and she'd left her homeland not on the best of terms with her family, especially Aunt Willie, who was, to say the least, difficult. She hadn't seen her older brother and sister since the concert in Delftshaven seven years ago, and neither Wilhelmina nor Johannes would travel to the United States. But no matter how deep her own curiosity, Juliana hated to pry into a past her mother obviously didn't want to discuss. In any case, she knew better. Catharina would only tell her daughter precisely what she wanted her to know, no more.

Already, simply by changing the subject she was exerting her will. If Juliana pressed for information on Rachel Stein, her mother would only get upset—and still would not talk about Rachel and how they'd known each other in Amsterdam and what she was doing in New York. You don't need to know these things, her mother would say; they are of no consequence. You shouldn't worry. You should be happy. They were the refrains, well-meaning but maddening, of Juliana's childhood. She'd learned not to argue and, eventually, to keep quiet about her own problems, because they would always cause her mother more grief than they did herself. As a result, Catharina Fall had no idea her daughter was playing jazz incognito in a SoHo nightclub, no idea Shuji thought she was in a funk, no idea she both dreaded and looked forward to her long-awaited performance at Lincoln Center tomorrow night, her final concert of the year. Juliana wouldn't tell her. Her mother would worry that something wasn't quite perfect in her daughter's world. And Juliana didn't want her mother to worry.

"Tell me everything," Catharina said.

Juliana did. At least everything her mother would want to hear.

When Stark returned to his desk an hour later, Alice Feldon had left a note on his keyboard. "I want a story out of this. You can pick up your ticket at Lincoln Center before the concert. By the way, Juliana Fall will be performing the Beethoven Piano Concerto No. 1 in C Major, Opus 15, with the New York Philharmonic. That's Beethoven as in Ludwig van."

Matthew grimaced. "Sounds like a yawner."

Four

Master Sergeant (ret.) Phillip Bloch settled back in the oak swivel chair and watched a fat cockroach scurry across the pine floor of the rustic fishing camp he was using as his temporary headquarters. A rich man's idea of country living. There was natural pine paneling on all the walls, a big fieldstone fireplace, lots of dark, sturdy furniture. He had a little fire going now, just to take the edge off, and the place glowed. It was a hell of a lot nicer than anything Bloch had ever known. But you couldn't keep out the cockroaches. They crawled over a fancy hand-braided rug just as easily as over some old rag. Didn't make no never-mind to them. Sometimes Bloch liked to catch the cockroaches, especially the fat ones, and squeeze them between his fingers. It was something to do to pass time. He'd hung around in enough of the cesspools of the world to have learned to amuse himself.

He pressed one knee up against the rolltop desk, a giant hunk of furniture, probably worth four thousand dollars. It was pushed up against a paneled wall, just beyond a double window with a view of the lake and a stand of tall, gangly yellow pine. Bloch was a tall, muscular man in his early fifties, gray-haired, square-jawed, a maniac about fitness and nutrition. His men called him a nuts-and-seeds freak. That was all right with him; he could kill ninety-nine percent of them with his bare hands. He made sure they knew it.

Right now he was listening to Sam Ryder whine to him from his office on Capitol Hill. *United States Senator* Ryder. Twenty years ago in Vietnam, Bloch had known Ryder would go far, and he'd cultivated his relationship with his platoon leader. Kept his eyes open. Listened. Ryder had a unique gift for making people think they were hearing what they wanted to hear when what he was telling them was damn near nothing. But Sammy Ryder did aim to please. At first Bloch had thought the handsome young lieutenant from central Florida and Georgetown knew exactly how he was wagging folks' tails, but after a couple of months on patrol, the sergeant realized Ryder wasn't talking in circles on purpose. It was just the way the poor dope thought. He *believed* what he was saying; he *believed* he was being forthright. He was absolutely, A-plus, fucking sincere.

"Don't ever send Otis Raymond to me again," Ryder said, but his words came out more as a plea than an order. He knew where he stood with Phillip Bloch. Never mind who had outranked whom; they'd straightened all that out twenty years ago. "If you have something to say to me, then say it yourself. I think that would be a more appropriate method of operation."

"Okay, Sam. Fair enough."

"Good."

Bloch chuckled to himself: the stupid fuck thought he'd gotten his way. He kept his eyes on the cockroach, still moving slowly, and said congenially, "I like the idea of this diamond, Lieutenant."

"I'm glad you do," Ryder replied, obviously relieved. It was a crazy idea, that was for sure, but Bloch liked crazy ideas. No risk, no gain.

"I think you're right—it could solve your problems and mine. So I wouldn't screw up this opportunity if I were you, Lieutenant."

"I have no intention of screwing up anything. Give me some time, Sergeant. I have no proof this diamond even exists, much less where it is. And—for the record—I'm a United States senator."

Ryder knew who had the upper hand, but that didn't stop him from using that cold, superior tone Bloch had always hated. It emphasized the class gulf between them. Ryder had everything: money, looks, power, reputation. But in Phil Bloch's opinion, that didn't change a damn thing. Maybe in other people's eyes it did, but not in his. If Ryder had a reason to act superior, maybe Bloch wouldn't have minded so much. But as far as he was concerned, Samuel Ryder, Jr., didn't amount to a pile of cold shit.

"Yeah, you're a senator all right," the sergeant said, "for the time being."

"What's that supposed to mean?"

The superior tone had vanished, and the awe and dread that had always been there underneath surfaced. Now that's the real Sammy Ryder, Bloch thought. No backbone. It made him easier to manipulate than he liked to think. Bloch had gotten to be a master sergeant—had stayed alive—because he knew how to read people. He'd been a career military man, but from the beginning he'd planned for this day. Now that he was retired, he was finally able to set up a military camp the way he thought one ought to be set up. He'd already begun training and dispatching mercenaries. Ryder knew about that. But the good senator didn't know about the arms dealing. During his army years, Bloch had managed to pull together a small, illegal arsenal of weapons and ammunition, which he was now using as his nest egg. If Sammy found out about that part of his business, he'd start screaming about scruples and the law and all that bullshit, mostly because he'd be scared shitless he'd get caught. Bloch didn't want to have to listen to any more whining. The arsenal was only the beginning. He had bigger and better plans for the future. And he'd get there, no question about that. He just had to watch for opportunities, know how to capitalize on them—and know just when to turn the screws on "friends" in high places.

"Just stating the facts," Bloch said, scratching the back of his neck. Damned bugs. He'd never get used to them. "You ain't going to be a senator forever, Sam. Thinking about the White House one of these days, aren't you? Be interesting, won't it, having an ol' skeleton like me rattling around in one of your closets. Better deal with me straight now, don't you think?"

"I'm doing the best I can!"

"That's what I like to hear. So tell me." Bloch leaned back as the cockroach veered suddenly and started plodding across the huge, round braided rug toward the rolltop desk. "Is the Stein woman still on your ass?"

There was a shocked, horrified silence on the other end. No ragged breathing, no cry of outrage or despair, and no—thank God—whining. Bloch waited patiently, his eyes on the cockroach. It had slowed up, as if it knew where it was heading, but it didn't change course, incapable, apparently, of doing anything now but move ahead.

"You know about her?"

"Sure, Sam."

"But how? I never mentioned anything to you—or to Raymond. Was it de Geer? I can't believe—"

"Hell, no, it wasn't that damned Dutchman. I ain't heard shit out of him since he left for New York. He's an independent sonofabitch. I hope to hell this whole thing's not riding on him. No, Sam, I heard about the Stein woman and her little visit to you from some people I have in Washington who let me know what's going on. She spotted de Geer, recognized him, wants his ass for some crap that went on forty years ago. She's been making a pain in the ass of herself. It got back to me."

"You've got spies in my office?" Ryder's voice squeaked with fear and indignation. "Damn it, Sergeant, I won't stand for this! It's bad enough you're holed up in my fishing camp like a pack of rats, jeopardizing me and everything I and my family stand for, bad enough you send de Geer to me in the first place as your 'intermediary' to squeeze me dry when all I've ever done is cooperate with you, do everything in my power to accommodate you, but spies I will *not* tolerate!"

"Catch your breath and save the speech, Sammy. Way I see it, you don't have much say-so about what I do or what I don't do. Answer the question. Is she or isn't she still on your ass?"

Ryder was silent, and Bloch had no trouble envisioning Mr. Golden Boy weighing all his options. He always took his sweet time. Even in combat, no one could rush Sam Ryder when he had to make up his mind. So long as he saved his own butt, he didn't worry about any other consequences of his stalling.

Finally, he said cautiously, "She thinks I'm going to help her. I don't know what she'll do when she finds out I have no intention of doing so. If I turn in de Geer—well, it's unthinkable. At the moment all she can do is make accusations. She has no proof of a direct connection between me and de Geer. However, if she goes to the press with this, and they decide to investigate, anything could happen. They could even end up on your doorstep, Sergeant." Ryder hesitated. "I'm not sure it's wise to say where you are— for your sake."

"Oh, hell, Sammy, don't deny me my fun. Wouldn't it be a sight?" Bloch snorted. "A bunch of reporters' coffins all lined up, ready to go in the ground, for messing with old Phil Bloch. Look, I want you to let me worry about Rachel Stein."

"She's not your problem, Sergeant. *Don't* get involved. Let me handle things on this end."

"Sure, sure. I'll just keep working my ass off down here and hoping you don't fuck up. Biggest uncut diamond in the world, you say? Shit-fire, sure, I'll let you handle it." Bloch dropped the mock-amiable tone as he sat forward. "Listen, you goddamn asshole, don't you tell me what the fuck to do. You're the one who got his stupid butt in a sling, not me. If you weren't such a stupid fuckup to begin with, you wouldn't have to worry about guys like me."

Ryder didn't say a word.

"Got that, *Senator?*"

"I should hang up," Ryder said stiffly.

"Yeah, but you won't. Not until you tell me what you're doing to get hold of the diamond."

"Sergeant, one day—"

"One day you're going to see me in hell, but that's about all, Lieutenant. Talk."

"You leave me no choice."

"That's the whole idea, Sammy."

When Ryder finished, Bloch hung up and leaned back, thinking. He had a few men he could trust. They might not be ready to die for him yet, but they'd do a job or two. He called them in.

The cockroach had made it to the foot of his chair. Bloch sighed at the inevitability of it all. You wait, you're patient, you act when the situation demands, and everything just works out.

He bent down, picked up the cockroach, and squeezed.

Five

❧⌘❧

Rachel Stein arrived at Lincoln Center early and waited in the lobby, staring outside at the dusting of snow on the plaza and the glittering holiday lights. She hadn't seen snow in years. It brought back the past, and she remembered prowling the streets of Amsterdam with her brothers and sisters and cousins, all gone now, all dead. She'd felt so safe there, before the war. Jewish refugees from Germany and the east had begun to flood in, but they'd all told themselves persecution couldn't happen here, not in Amsterdam. Sometimes if she let her mind drift, she could hear the laughter of all those she'd loved and see their smiles, so bright, so innocent, and the other sounds and images wouldn't invade, the cries, the prayers, the skeletons. Abraham said he'd blocked out everything. He never cast his mind back prior to the moment he'd planted his two worn shoes on American soil, ready to work hard, making a success of himself. He couldn't even speak Dutch anymore; he'd forgotten it completely. He said he wanted other people to remember, but not himself.

Rachel might have envied him, if she believed him.

As she stared outside, she watched a fat snowflake float slowly to the ground, as if coming from nowhere, and she imagined herself dead, her body lying in a field, its fluids seeping into the soil, mingling with the water there and then condensing into the air, into clouds, becoming snowflakes. She imagined her friends, her family, all making up parts of a snowflake, together once more. A pleasant warmth spread through her.

All these thoughts of dying! Well, why not? She wasn't afraid. Not since she was eighteen had she been afraid of death. You live, you die. Everyone did.

"Well, good evening, Miss Stein."

She turned at the sound of Senator Ryder's voice and had to smile at his infectious charm. "Don't you look dashing tonight, Senator," she said in her soft, hoarse voice. "So handsome!"

He laughed. "Thank you. And you look lovely, as always."

He was lying, of course. Her simple black dress made her look thinner, even older. Not that she cared. It was a good dress. Forty years ago a slice of bread had seemed such a luxury. Now she had so much: a big house, a housekeeper, a gardener, a grand wardrobe. When she died, her nephews would get rid of the help and sell everything else and invest the profits. They didn't need anything she had. I must change my will, she thought suddenly. Although she wasn't a religious woman, she decided she would contact a rabbi when she returned to Palm Beach and ask him to suggest appropriate charities. Her nephews might be annoyed with her, but the "sacrifice" would be good for them, perhaps encourage them to be more generous in life than she'd been, thinking she never had time for it.

Politely taking her arm, Senator Ryder escorted her down the wide aisle to the orchestra seats. She noticed the looks they received from other well-to-do concert-goers who, of course, recognized the handsome senator. She could just imagine what they were thinking. He was single, divorced from a pretty, shy woman who, it was said, couldn't tolerate the scrutiny of a public life, although what other kind of life she'd expected to have with a member of the Ryder family, Rachel didn't know. She'd left him shortly after his election to the Senate. No children had been involved. Now Ryder escorted a variety of women, always elegant and always beautiful, to different functions, but Rachel supposed he was never seen with someone like herself, tiny and wrinkled and unwilling to smile just for the sake of smiling.

"I'm glad you came," the senator said as they took their aisle seats.

"I am, too."

It was warm in the hall, and Rachel felt tired. Since tea with Catharina, she'd had her doubts about tonight. Perhaps it had been wrong to involve her old friend, wrong to put her in the position of having to avoid her own daughter's questions. If she'd had a child, Rachel wondered, would she feel the same need to protect her from the past? She felt her spine stiffening. *I would kill Hendrik de Geer before I let him touch a child of mine!* Or of a friend? Although Juliana Fall wasn't her daughter, Rachel felt a keen responsibility toward her, and she'd promised Catharina. You're not like Hendrik, she told herself. *If you make a promise, you must do everything in your power to keep it.*

Ryder gave her one of his heart-melting smiles. "I assume Mrs. Fall is here?"

"Yes."

"Wonderful. I look forward to meeting her."

The lights dimmed, and Rachel could feel the senator's strong shoulder brush up against her. Such an honest face, such a handsome man. She didn't trust him.

Matthew slouched down in the soft seat, deciding he looked absorbed in the concert rather than bored, but not caring either way. Leave it to Feldie to get him a ticket down in the front with the tuxedos and designer gowns. He hadn't worn a tuxedo in his life and didn't intend to start now, but, still, Feldie would have no grounds to gripe. His outfit—deep berry wool jacket, dark gray wool polo shirt, and dark gray wool pants—had cost him more than the *Gazette* paid him in a week. She wouldn't, however, be happy about his shoes. He had on his Gokeys.

Sam Ryder was a half-dozen rows down to Stark's right, but Matthew had taken no pleasure in having instantly spotted the senator among the sold-out crowd. He wasn't with a Dutchman. He was with a small old woman Matthew didn't recognize. He and Sam Ryder lived in the same town and once upon a time, at least for a while, had operated in the same social circles. But the junior senator from Florida had always preferred to think that Matthew Stark no longer existed. It was just as well.

Says he's going after a diamond, goddamn biggest uncut diamond in the fucking world. You believe it?

Weasel talk. Still, this was U.S. Senator Samuel Ryder with whom they were dealing, and, yeah, Stark thought, I believe it.

Ah, Weaze, my friend, he thought as the Schubert symphony wore on. What have you gotten me into this time?

Juliana shoved her black leather satchel into an out-of-the-way corner of her dressing room and tried to put its contents out of her mind. A 1936 black crepe dress, rose-colored stockings and matching T-strap shoes, a multicolored sequined turban, a Portuguese shawl that used to hang over Grandmother Fall's piano in her proper Philadelphia home, and a bag of bright makeup. All of it was pure J.J. Pepper. Juliana knew she was taking a chance, but there had been a cancellation and Len had offered her the Club Aquarian stage at eleven. She'd never played for the late-night crowd. How could she refuse? "Oh, Len, I can't, I'm doing Lincoln Center tonight." God. She'd told him she'd be thrilled.

But it meant leaving directly from Lincoln Center and making a risky, mad dash down to SoHo.

She had to be crazy.

She'd planned carefully. She'd change into the black dress backstage after the concert and put on her black boots and black cashmere coat. In the cab, she'd pull the turban on over her blond hair so she wouldn't have to tint it pink or purple or whatever, and drape Grandmother Fall's shawl over her coat, to make it look more J.J. Len would recognize cashmere when he saw it, but she'd have to take her chances. Finally, she'd slip into J.J.'s rose-colored shoes and gob on some makeup. She'd already have the stockings on; nobody would see those under the boots.

It was all, she thought, a matter of timing and guts.

But first she had a Beethoven concerto to perform. She breathed deeply, shut her eyes, and focused her energy, and for once the prospect of a memory lapse held no terror for her whatsoever. Forgetting a passage in front of a sold-out Lincoln Center audience, the New York Philharmonic Orchestra, and one of the world's great conductors, she thought, was the least of her troubles.

"You've lit your candle at both ends," she said to herself, "and if you don't watch it, your ass is going to get burned."

Holding his emotions rigidly in check, Ryder survived the first half of the concert. He had cultivated a taste for classical music, but he'd been relieved to see he wouldn't have to sit through any difficult modern compositions. Even so, he found himself twitching with impatience. He wanted tonight over and done with—another tactical objective achieved.

During the intermission, he resisted looking around for

de Geer, uncertain the Dutchman would actually be inside the concert hall. He smiled only briefly at Rachel Stein, trying to discourage conversation. He realized they had nothing more to say until they met with Catharina Fall, a meeting he was confident wouldn't last long. He was playing a dangerous game, manipulating Rachel Stein, Phil Bloch, Hendrik de Geer. But what choice did he have? Everything would work out.

"Have you seen Juliana Fall perform?" the old woman at his side asked.

Catharina Fall's daughter. Her appearance tonight had provided him with a convenient way of getting everyone together with the least possible risk. The women wouldn't have to see de Geer; the Dutchman could see them, from the lobby, from inside the concert hall, or from outside. It made no difference to Ryder. He was quite confident de Geer wouldn't want to risk a face-to-face confrontation with either woman. It was all so easy. Providential.

"No," he replied. "I haven't had the opportunity, although I understand she's very good."

"Phenomenal, I've been told. So we must pay attention."

How could he listen to a piano concerto when all he wanted to do was to move on to the next objective? But he knew he had to wait until the end of the concert. He clenched his teeth and said nothing as the pianist strode out onto the stage.

Then he couldn't have spoken if he'd wanted to.

Juliana Fall. My God, he thought, how have I missed her?

She was a vision. Everything about her was beautiful, elegant, heart-stopping. She was draped in flowing ice blue, her only jewelry a simple sapphire pendant, and her hair, the lightest of blonds, bounced on her shoulders. Her skin was translucent. When she smiled at the audience, it was as if something big and hard slammed into his chest, and he couldn't get enough air. He forgot about the old woman at his side, about the diamond, about the predicament he was in, about Hendrik de Geer and Phillip Boch and all the sordidness he had to face. Now he couldn't stop staring. Nothing mattered except the woman on stage.

"She's lovely, isn't she?" Rachel Stein said, irritatingly matter-of-fact.

Ryder gave a curt nod. His jaw ached. He took a quick, sustaining breath. Never had he been so affected by a woman.

The crowd settled down as Juliana Fall sat at the piano, and the concerto began. Sam Ryder never took his eyes from her. He studied how her long fingers danced on the keyboard, how her expressive face changed with the music, how she used her entire body to bring forth the incredible sounds from her instrument. Her concentration seemed unshakable. It was as if no one else was there, just her and the orchestra. There was a wildness, a sense of daring to her performance that Ryder hadn't expected. She seemed always on the verge of going over the edge, of making a mistake that would leave her audience gasping and horrified.

What would it be like to have her concentrate like that on him? To have that wildness unleashed in bed? Ryder felt the stirring of an erection and shifted, hoping Stein wouldn't notice, and then he realized he'd been biting down hard on a knuckle. He pulled his hand from his mouth, and immediately his fingers formed a tight fist. He shoved his hand into his lap.

He wasn't aware that the concerto had ended until the people around him were jumping to their feet, roaring and clapping, and suddenly he remembered where he was and what he was supposed to be doing. He rose unsteadily, grasping the back of the seat in front of him.

Hendrik de Geer had found the concert interminable and was glad it was over. He was not a man who endured immobility well—nor United States senators who played games with him. The Dutchman took some small pleasure in observing Sam Ryder's reaction to Juliana Fall. She was very attractive, but there was something remote and untouchable about her. Yet she had that zany streak that made her paint her hair pink and dress up in strange clothes, nothing like the dress she wore tonight. Hendrik felt a strange protectiveness toward her. He wouldn't want a man like Ryder to get too close to this unpredictable young woman, this child of Catharina.

Inside him, an alarm went off, and Hendrik reminded himself that he was a practical man. He never permitted himself to let sentiment motivate his actions or force him to make mistakes, although, of course, he understood how well sentiment could motivate others and force *them* to make mistakes.

Once more he looked across the seats, down from his on the left, and saw Rachel Stein. It would be dangerous, he knew, to let the past influence his judgment of her and the situation. He had never anticipated seeing her again. Hers was a name he had learned not to remember, even in his nightmares. His unconscious couldn't tolerate the thought of her, of her family, of what he, with all his good intentions, had let happen to them. Yet tonight there she was, so small and self-righteous—and so old. He remembered what a pretty mite she'd been. He used to love to bring her gifts, to see the light in those dark, intense eyes. Now she hated him. There was no forgiveness in her heart; she believed she was the only one ever to have suffered. Such arrogance, Hendrik thought.

Seeing her again, he'd almost lost control of himself. But what would that have accomplished? Senator Ryder had invited Rachel Stein to Lincoln Center tonight for a reason, and Hendrik, too, for a reason. Instead of falling apart, the Dutchman decided to wait and see what those reasons were. He had a fair idea already, but he had to know for certain.

He didn't join the standing ovation. Ryder would be furious if Hendrik let himself be seen, but he didn't care. He left the concert hall, moving quickly up the aisle, his eyes focused straight ahead. Catharina would be here tonight. If she saw him, she would say nothing. Hendrik could almost feel her shock, her hatred as he thought of her. His breathing became rapid, and he felt a stitch in his side, but he didn't slacken his pace.

Trust me, my Catharina.

But of course she never would.

Ryder's reaction to Juliana Fall had been more visceral than to anyone he'd ever met in his life, but sensing Rachel Stein watching him, he tried to control it.

"Juliana's quite a performer," the old woman said quietly.

"Yes, amazing." Ryder coughed as he fought to recover his composure, hoping this impossible woman didn't notice how little he had left. "She's an amazing talent."

On stage, Juliana Fall took her bows alone, with the conductor, with the entire orchestra. Her smile was dazzling. Her shining hair flopped carelessly down the front of her shoulders as she gave her final bow. Ryder could almost feel its softness on his fingers.

"You must understand something, Senator Ryder," Rachel said.

"Please—not now. In a moment."

She ignored him. "Hendrik de Geer is the kind of man who would destroy Juliana Fall if he felt he had to to save himself."

Ryder swung around. "No!"

"You heard me," she said calmly.

Ryder swallowed, fighting himself. The manipulative little witch! But he couldn't lose control, not now. Juliana Fall was an unexpected twist; he'd expected to find her as distasteful as her mother's friend. Ryder was furious. This wasn't at all what he'd planned! Rachel Stein was the one to have been caught off balance.

"Once I was young and beautiful and talented, as was Juliana's mother," Rachel said wistfully, "but Hendrik de Geer robbed us of that, he and his Nazi friends."

I don't care! Ryder thought wildly. He had to finish it now and regain the momentum. People were streaming into the aisle. "I'm very sorry about your past, Miss Stein, and I'm sympathetic to your suffering." He paused, feeling his sense of control seeping back into him. Yes, he thought, I can handle this. "I wish I could help you bring this de Geer to justice, but I'm afraid there's nothing I can do. I know a good deal less about him than you do yourself and have been unable to learn more. If you wish to bring charges against him for his actions in Amsterdam during Word War II, I can only encourage you, although I must warn you that you're unlikely to get very far. Greater criminals than he have gone free. In any case, I have to tell you that what you choose to do from this point is your responsibility."

Rachel Stein made no response. She simply nodded dully, as if she'd withdrawn into herself, as if she were sorry she'd ever believed in him or anyone else. Ryder brushed off the stirrings of pity. The woman's maudlin, he told himself, and there *is* nothing I can do.

He added, "I only met de Geer that one time." He sighed, lifting his shoulders in a helpless, innocent shrug. "As I told you, I had no idea of his Nazi past."

"Then there's no point in our meeting with Catharina going forward," Rachel said tightly.

"I'd like to explain my position to her—"

"Why waste your time? In fact, why did you even bother with tonight if you knew you could do nothing? A telephone call would have been sufficient."

"I felt the need to tell you in person, face-to-face. And

I didn't give up trying to get information on de Geer until right before the concert."

Her dark, intense eyes shot up at him. "I don't believe you, Senator. I should have known from the beginning that you would do nothing to help me. Hendrik de Geer is responsible for the deaths of twelve people, but they were not Florida voters, were they? Well, I am not ready to give in, not yet. You say you met Hendrik only that one time? All right. I will find out if you speak the truth. I will find out if there's any connection between you and Hendrik de Geer." She narrowed her eyes, her anger and determination palpable. *"I will find out."*

Still fuming, she marched past him.

Sam Ryder watched the tiny, shattered woman disappear into the crowd drifting toward the lobby, but he didn't dare relax. She would leave and accept that her threats were empty, but, nevertheless, Ryder no longer felt that telling Bloch about her had been such an act of weakness. Surely, though, she was intelligent enough to recognize her defeat. There'd be no more calls, no more visits, no more letters. He was sorry not to meet Catharina Fall, in case she would have been able to provide more leverage for him against de Geer, but at least he'd gotten rid of Rachel Stein. One tactical objective achieved. Now on to the next. The Dutchman would be waiting outside in Ryder's car.

But Juliana Fall…

Ryder admitted he didn't want to involve her in his difficulties, but he didn't see that he'd have to. She was a pianist. Beautiful, unforgettable. He would just have to leave her out of it and concentrate on making de Geer do his bidding.

Yet, as he walked stiffly out into the aisle, he looked longingly back toward the stage. It seemed so empty. She was back there, somewhere, accepting congratulations, flowers.

De Geer can wait, he thought. You're a United States senator. Use your influence.

He threw his coat over his arm and headed backstage.

Adrian Fall took his wife's arm as she stumbled into the aisle. He was a tall, fair-skinned man with handsome, angular features, and she loved him dearly. He had come into her life just when she'd begun to believe she would never be able to love and trust anyone again, and he'd taken her away from Amsterdam, from her past, from her memories. He understood that these were things she couldn't talk about. He never pressed her, just allowed her to be what she was. Together they'd spoiled and adored Juliana, building a new life, their own life. He was a quiet, dear, understanding man, but right now she wished he'd just stayed home tonight. He knew nothing of Rachel Stein, nothing of Hendrik de Geer. How could she explain to him?

"Catharina," he said, worried, "what is it? Are you all right?"

She gulped for air, not seeing him. She was white, shaking all over. "Yes, fine, I just…" There wasn't enough air! *I'm going to faint.* "A headache."

"You're hyperventilating. I think I'd better get you home."

Home, she thought vaguely, trying to stop gulping for air now that Adrian had told her what was wrong. There was too much oxygen in her bloodstream already. Ah, Adrian, always so steady, so right. Her mother used to say the best cure for hyperventilation was a bag over the head. *Oh, Mamma!* Her mother would be strong now. She wouldn't simply go home. She wouldn't be tempted to lock herself in her rooms high above Park Avenue and never come out.

Catharina stretched herself and put a shaky hand to her mouth. My God, she thought, I've seen him, too. Hendrik! She had sensed he would be here tonight. He had walked right past her, and she'd only caught a glimpse of him. It was enough. His face was seared in her memory.

She touched Adrian's hand, letting his warmth anchor her in the present. She had to warn Rachel that Hendrik was here. That much she had to do, no matter her shock and fear. "I'm supposed to meet a friend," she told her husband softly.

Adrian shook his head firmly, the stolid, practical banker. "You're in no condition to meet anyone."

Catharina looked down the aisle toward the seats where Rachel had sat with her senator. Rachel was gone already, and Senator Ryder—

"No!"

He was making his way backstage! Had Rachel misled her? Had she decided to involve Juliana after all? With a mad lunge, Catharina shot out into the aisle, but Adrian grabbed her by the waist, and she crumpled against him.

"Darling," he said gently, "let me take you home."

She was so grateful for her husband, for his goodness, but now she struggled against him, telling herself this time she had to fight, she had to go to her daughter and protect her from this. "Juliana—"

"She'll understand, Catharina. You don't have to congratulate her after every performance. She knows she has your undying support. Look, I'll call her in the morning. Besides, Shuji's here tonight." Adrian gave her a small smile, maintaining a sense of false cheer, but there was no answering twinkle in his wife's eyes. He was terrified. "They'll have to have their postperformance fight. You wouldn't want to interrupt."

"You don't understand…"

"I think I do. You're not yourself tonight. Catharina, you can't do everything. You can't be all things to all people. You're overtired. We'll go up to Connecticut for a few days if you want." They had an old farmhouse they were restoring themselves in Litchfield County. "The air will do you good."

Catharina found herself unable to argue, and she nodded meekly, feeling foolish, a child again, the silly, innocent girl whom everyone had tried to protect. She went with Adrian into the lobby but still looked around madly for Rachel. What was happening? *Rachel, my God, where are you?* Was their meeting off? If not, what would she tell Adrian? If so, what would she do next? Go home and pretend none of this had ever happened?

But Rachel was gone, and Adrian, his arm tight around his wife, led Catharina toward the exit. When they were outside in the cold December night, she looked back toward the bright lights of the performing arts center and felt herself strangling with indecision.

Adrian opened a cab door, and she climbed inside.

Sam Ryder had gotten waylaid by an elderly gentleman and his fur-coated wife, and Stark was able to beat him backstage, where he knew Sam would be headed just as soon as he got rid of the old couple. Matthew had seen the senator's reaction to Juliana Fall. He had to admit she'd nearly knocked him out of his seat when she'd walked on stage, but he could keep his perspective. An ex–chopper pilot, ex-author, ex-famous reporter and an internationally known concert pianist just weren't going to make it. Fantasyland. Besides, she was probably just your basic airhead-artistic type who would say, "Matthew Stark?" Which, he realized, more and more people were doing these days.

Sam Ryder, however, didn't think like that. He'd never met a woman who didn't want anything to do with him, and he assumed none existed. Maybe Matthew was wrong, and Juliana Fall would drop dead for him. But he didn't think so.

He flashed his press credentials and approached her dressing room, ducking aside, within earshot but out of sight. He grinned to himself: hot-shot reporter that you are, snooping on a piano player. A good-looking Asian guy stalked past him and went in to see Ms. Pianist herself.

"Shuji—Jesus Christ, scare the shit out of me, why don't you!"

Matthew felt the corners of his mouth twitch. *Shit?* Well, he thought, maybe Ryder hadn't met any Dutchman and Weaze had sent him on a wild goose chase, but it seemed poor old Sammy Ryder just might need Stark's help after all—to rescue him from one Juliana Fall.

Juliana guiltily shoved the black crepe dress behind her and manufactured a welcoming smile for Shuji. "Sorry," she said, "but you startled me. How are you?"

Banalities, she thought. Shuji hated them, and he frowned at her because, of course, she should have known better. She had not asked the obvious questions. What did you think of my performance tonight, Shuji? Did I sound like I'm in a funk? She wasn't sure she wanted to hear the answers, even if she had time, which she decidedly did not.

"Interesting performance," Shuji said.

From long experience, Juliana realized that could mean anything. She dropped her dress, ever so casually, on a chair. Crumpled up, it looked like a normal black dress. A few months old instead of fifty years. Something Juliana Fall might wear to a postconcert dinner.

"You were on tonight," Shuji continued, folding his arms across his chest. He was dressed entirely in black, as was his custom, and looked as fit and energetic as ever. His only vice was an occasional cigarette. "But still I heard something. I'm not sure I liked it, but I'm not sure either, that what I heard is without possibilities. I've been thinking, Juliana, and—"

"Look, Shuji," Juliana interrupted, a perilous act in and of itself, trying not to show she was in a tearing hurry, "whatever it is, I'll listen for it, all right? But right now I'm tired."

If possible, his frown deepened. "You don't want to discuss this?"

"No."

"All right." He spoke tightly, gazing at her through narrowed eyes, and she knew it decidedly was not all right. "Are you still planning to go to Vermont?"

"For a few days, yes. I need some time out."

"I thought we'd agreed you wouldn't go."

Oh, shit, she thought, will you just *leave?*

Shuji walked around, pacing angrily, and picked up her sequined turban, which she'd forgotten completely. "What the hell's this?"

"A turban."

"What for?"

"I don't know. It's not mine. Someone must have left it here." She huffed in frustration. "Damn it, Shuji, a few days in Vermont isn't a vacation. The way I've been going, it's hardly even a break. Don't ruin it for me, okay? Look, I don't want to argue with you, and anyway now's not a good time to talk. I'm in a hurry. I forgot you were coming, and I made plans."

There, she'd said it. Shuji spun around toward her, his narrowed eyes flashing angrily. "You forgot I was coming?"

She almost smiled—she'd known that would get him off the track. "I've been rattled lately—which is one reason I could use a break."

"I take time from my own busy schedule to attend this concert, and you *forgot* I was coming? You ungrateful little witch!" He slammed the palms of his hands together with a restrained fury she found reassuring. Eric Shuji Shizumi was always easier to deal with when he was roaringly pissed. "How the hell have I put up with you all these years!"

"Just be glad you never married me," Juliana said lightly, attempting to diffuse his anger.

Shuji just glared at her.

A gentle rap on the door interrupted them, and Shuji hissed impatiently but quickly recovered his poise as a tall, boyishly handsome man poked his head in and said, "Excuse me—"

Juliana held back a groan. "Yes, what is it?"

"Be nice," Shuji warned under his breath. "Wouldn't want your public to think you're a snot."

She resisted making a face at him. He gave her a wry, nasty grin and, without another word, stormed out. *Damn him,* Juliana thought, *damn him, damn him, why couldn't he just leave her alone?*

"I'm sorry to disturb you, Miss Fall," the man in the doorway said. He gave her a dashing smile that was unexpectedly sincere. "I'm Samuel Ryder."

He paused, obviously expecting that she would recognize his name. She didn't. She did, however, notice his eyes, a dreamy baby blue, a child's eyes in a man's face. They were oddly appealing—and somehow disturbing, perhaps because the rest of him seemed so polished and sophisticated. She said automatically, "Pleased to meet you."

"I wanted to congratulate you on your performance this evening." He came into the dressing room, at once bold and tentative. "This was my first opportunity to hear you, and I assure you, it won't be my last. You were mesmerizing."

She hadn't heard that line in a while but silently chastised herself for being so cynical. Maybe he meant it. "Thank you," she said politely. "It's very nice of you to take the time to tell me so personally." *Now will you leave so I can become someone else?*

He didn't seem to know what to say next. On purpose,

she'd left him no natural opening. He caught himself twisting his fingers together and suddenly shoved them into the
pockets of his elegant evening overcoat. It was unbuttoned
and underneath was a stylish black tuxedo over an obviously trim body. Juliana could almost hear her friends telling her not to be so damn critical—a rich, handsome,
interested man was a rich, handsome, interested man.

She felt a touch of sympathy for him. He looked so lost,
so lonely. Had she had that effect on him, her music? The
Beethoven was a powerful piece. Yet she knew if Samuel
Ryder was attracted to her, even just for tonight, it had little to do with her performance or who she really was. Experience had taught her that. Like others before him,
Samuel Ryder was taken with his own fantasies about who
she was and what she could mean to him. He was capti-
vated by his own image of her. He knew nothing substan-
tive about her temperament, her family, her intense,
volatile, nonromantic relationship with Shuji. He knew
nothing about J.J. Pepper.

She suspected Samuel Ryder wouldn't approve of J.J.

But there was something so sweet and melancholy about
the way he looked at her that she couldn't be angry with
him for his assumptions, nor could she denigrate how he
felt. He was good-looking enough that she wondered if she
was being too nasty in wanting to get rid of him. Even
Shuji, who rarely noticed such things, had once com-
mented that she was entirely too picky about men. Maybe
he had a point. But Len's baby grand at the Club Aquarian
was waiting. Should she invite Ryder along? *No, don't be
an ass!* J.J. was her secret.

She smiled and watched his eyes melt. "It was nice
meeting you, Mister Ryder, but if you'll—"

Another man appeared in the doorway. He was dark-
haired and dark-eyed, with a hard, scarred face that Juliana found both compelling and a little frightening. His

clothes were expensive but casual—and sexy. The face, the attire, the tough, compact body all seemed to go with the deep sardonic voice. "Hey, Sam, thought that was you." He walked in, uninvited, and nodded at Juliana. "Ms. Fall."

I will never get out of here, she thought.

But Ryder's reaction interested her. He had stiffened visibly and paled. "Stark—Matthew," he said, managing a smile as he put out his hand. There was no friendship in the gesture. Whoever Matthew Stark was, Sam Ryder didn't want any part of him. "It's been a long time."

"I guess it has," Stark said, shaking hands briefly. "I caught the concert and spotted you. Thought I'd say hello."

That's bullshit, Juliana thought unexpectedly. Matthew Stark had anticipated the effect he would have on Sam Ryder. But that, she reminded herself, was hardly her problem. "If you gentlemen don't mind—"

Matthew turned and grinned at her look of controlled frustration. "Come on, Sam, we're in the lady's way. I'll buy you a drink."

"I'm sorry—bad night." Regaining his composure, Ryder turned to Juliana, his baby-blue eyes shining with embarrassment and anger. "I apologize for the intrusion."

Juliana bit back a laugh when she realized he meant Stark, not himself. "It's all right," she said, not caring whom he meant, just so long as they both got out of her way.

"Miss Fall, I was wondering—" Ryder stopped himself, red-faced, and glared at Stark, who just smiled back, staying put. Ryder turned back to Juliana, obviously controlling his anger. "It's been a pleasure."

He brushed past Stark, who was leaning against the open door, looking relaxed and distant. Juliana felt bad for Ryder and realized Stark's presence had prevented him from asking her to dinner, which, she supposed, was just as well. She hoped Stark would take the hint and move along, too. But he didn't. To hell with him, she thought, whipping up the turban and tossing it back into her bag with her rose-colored shoes. He could stay if he wanted. *She* was leaving.

"Nice turban," he said. "Didn't peg you for the sequins type."

She gave him an ice-cold look. "Excuse me, won't you?"

Stark made no move to get out of her way. "Take it easy," he said, his own equanimity in stark contrast to her almost compulsive energy. "I'm on my way, okay?"

She almost told him *good, go.* Instead she remembered her position and Shuji's lectures on how to treat her public, although somehow she didn't think this solid, hard man fit into that category. Had he pulled an Aunt Wilhelmina and snored through the Beethoven? Why was he here?

"I take it you don't know much about Sam Ryder," Stark said.

She picked up her black crepe and considered just starting to undress right in front of him, but her eyes fell on his, dark and remote, and she reconsidered. "No, we just met tonight. Now—"

"You called him Mister."

"So?"

"He's a senator. I guess you didn't know that."

"A *senator*— Oh, shit."

"A U.S. senator," Stark said, adding, "That's U.S. as in United States."

She rolled her tongue inside her cheek. Stark's eyes, she noticed, seemed black, but she couldn't be sure. "I'm not amused."

"I didn't think you would be."

"And who are you?"

"Ah-ha. The name *Matthew Stark* doesn't jingle any bells behind those cool green eyes. My, how the mighty have fallen. You and my editor ought to get together."

Should she have heard of him? Probably not, she decided. He was just trying to annoy her—and succeeding remarkably well. "Mr. Stark, I'm running late."

"As I said, I'm on my way. Just one more thing." He placed one hand high on the doorjamb and looked at her. She could feel the sweat on the stray wisps around her hairline, dripping slowly between her breasts, matting her dress to her. She was hot and madder than hell but trying not to let him know it—and, at the same time, she felt herself daring him. Egging him on. He grinned at her. "If I were you, toots, I'd tell this Shuji character to stick it and head for Vermont." He straightened up. "Night."

Her back stiffening, Juliana gave him a steely look. His eyes seemed to change from black to a dark, dark brown, warmth coming into them, excitement. Toots, she thought, almost dispassionately. She couldn't remember ever being called toots.

Stark was already out the door. Juliana shook out her black dress, putting all her pent-up irritation into the effort. Toots, for God's sake. As for Vermont and Shuji—

How had *Stark* known about Vermont?

She leaped out the door after him. "You bastard, you eavesdropped on me and Shuji!"

Matthew Stark turned around and grinned. "That's right. Bumped into him on his way out. Told him I thought you deserved a break, too. Lucky I read my program notes or I wouldn't have known who he was."

"You've never heard of Shuji?"

"Not until tonight. Last music I listened to was by George Thorogood and the Destroyers."

It was something to seize on, and Juliana laughed, returning to her dressing room and shutting the door.

Matthew got the hell out of there—fast, before he did something he'd really regret. Like tell Juliana Fall she had the sexiest damn laugh he'd heard in ages. The lady was an artsy-fartsy type and damned cool, but he'd seen the impatience all over her stiff, trim little body. What was she in such a big hurry over? A man? No, he doubted she'd get into such a state over something as simple as a lover, romance, anything like that. Most men would be happy to wait for her, and he suspected she knew it. Ryder sure as hell would. Hell, I might, too, Stark thought, remembering how sweat had made the thin silk of her dress cling to her breasts, outlining their shape. Forget love and romance. Maybe a night of romping, good sex would put her in a hurry.

Shame on you, Matt, the lady probably doesn't do stuff like that.

Not, he thought, seeing those deep, dark gorgeous eyes of hers once more, that she wouldn't be damn good at it.

He wondered what he was going to tell Feldie.

The hell with it, he thought, why start worrying about that kind of thing at this late date? He went for a beer and thought some more about Juliana Fall's laugh.

Six

Hendrik de Geer was smoking a cigar in the backseat of Ryder's chauffeured car, waiting on Broadway, when the tall senator slid in next to him breathing hard and obviously agitated. "Put that thing out," he said sharply, snatching a silk handkerchief from his pocket. He didn't bother to shake the folds from it before he wiped his brow. "I hate cigars."

The Dutchman shrugged impassively and put out his cigar, which he would finish later, in privacy. Ryder balled up his handkerchief and shoved it into the pocket of his overcoat, and Hendrik wondered, with some amusement, just how badly the pretty pianist Juliana Fall had treated him. With the skill of the practiced politician, Ryder composed himself. "You were at the concert? Did you enjoy it?"

"Yes, and no, I did not. Did you?"

"Yes—yes, of course. It was a fine performance." Only the distant, pained look in Ryder's eyes betrayed his lingering passion for the blond pianist. "Juliana Fall's a remarkable musician, don't you agree?"

"Music doesn't interest me."

Ryder gave Hendrik a thin, patrician smile, but the Dutchman took no offense. He was what he was, and long ago he'd stopped trying to change. Ryder said mildly, "Let's get to the point, shall we? I assume you saw who I was with tonight."

"Rachel Stein," Hendrik said without expression.

Ryder looked straight ahead in the dark, chilly car, as if avoiding the Dutchman's eyes could dissociate him from what he was saying. "She wants your head."

"She deserves it. However, I'm not a masochist."

"Neither am I."

"Of course not. Rachel Stein wants my head, and you'll give it to her because otherwise she'll talk—and someone may look deeper into the possible connections between us. I shouldn't think that's something you or Sergeant Bloch would want."

"Very perceptive of you, de Geer," Ryder said bitterly. "She can do me incredible damage, and with no justification, I might add."

Hendrik smiled, truly amused. "Ahh, yes, you're the innocent in all this."

Ryder made no argument, didn't even hear the light sarcasm in de Geer's voice. God, how he hated this! He had planned for this moment for days, since Rachel Stein had first given him the details of de Geer's betrayal of her family and the Peperkamps, and now that it was here, he could barely concentrate. He was still seeing Juliana Fall's eyes, dark and beautiful against the pale hair. She must have thought him a fool. "You're such a silly ass, Sam," his wife had said when she'd left him. Other women didn't agree—he didn't agree—but the sting of her words had stayed with him. His wife had been one woman he could never impress. *That's the kind you always go for, isn't it, pal?* But no, Juliana Fall wouldn't be like that. If only Stark—*damn him!* What was he doing there tonight?

"But you have terms," the Dutchman said calmly.

With almost physical force, the senator shoved from his

mind the image of smug, arrogant Matthew Stark. *Steelman,* the men had called him, always with respect. They could count on Stark. He was reliable. Straight up. Nerveless. Ryder had wanted a nickname like Steelman, not Golden Boy. But that was all in the past. Who was the U.S. senator, and who was the has-been writer? Their meeting backstage was an unfortunate coincidence, that was all. That was all he would permit it to be.

"Yes," he said, finally, "I have terms. You can solve my problems at the same time you solve your own."

Ryder turned, observing the Dutchman's ill-fitting suit, his unstyled hair, and blunt, callused hands. How had such a man come to have so much power over him? But no longer, Ryder thought. At last, no more. "I know about Amsterdam. Rachel Stein told me everything when she came to me after she saw us in the car together on the six o'clock news. That was a bad piece of luck, but I warned you about meeting me in person. But perhaps things will work out for the best, hmm? After Rachel and I talked, I did some investigating on my own and found out even more. You're here tonight, de Geer, because you know you caused the deaths of twelve people and Rachel Stein would like nothing better than to see you brought to justice for what you did. You're here because you know I know. You could disappear. I'm no fool, I know you could. But you have a good thing going with Bloch, and you're getting old. It wouldn't be easy to start over again, especially when there's no need. You have only to get me what I want, and I'll forget everything I know about you."

Hendrik had learned not to dismiss so easily this man with the innocent eyes. "We've discussed this before. I'm here, am I not? Tell me what it is you want."

"The diamond."

The Dutchman made no sound.

"You know what I'm talking about. I know you do.

The Stein woman doesn't believe it exists or she'd never have mentioned it when she came to me to complain about you. She has no idea of my interest in the stone—but I'm convinced it *does* exist. What's more, you're going to get it for me."

"I know of many diamonds, Senator—"

"Don't, de Geer. Don't waste my time."

Hendrik regarded the young senator without emotion. "I have to be sure. This diamond's name?"

Ryder's eyes went cold. "The Minstrel's Rough."

Otis Raymond shifted back and forth on his feet as he stood on the hand-braided rug next to the big oak rolltop desk. Behind him, a fire roared in the stone fireplace, but, as always, Raymond seemed cold. A fine specimen of the U.S. Army, Bloch thought. Shit. It never ceased to amaze him that SP-4 Raymond had survived Vietnam, and as a door gunner no less. Had to be dumb luck.

"Good evening, Raymond."

"Sergeant."

Bloch leaned back in the swivel chair. "I just got a call from Sam. He said Stark showed up at Lincoln Center tonight. You wouldn't know anything about that, would you?"

"Matt Stark? No, Sergeant. I ain't seen him in a couple years."

"You didn't stop in to see him while you were in Washington?"

"No. Uh-uh. I was there on your time. I just did what I was supposed to do."

"Of course. Then why was Stark in New York?"

"I don't know. Ask him."

"I might, Raymond. I just might."

Otis sniffled, unable to stand still. "Anything else?"

"No, you're dismissed."

A short while later, Bloch received another call. "It's done," his man in New York said.

"An accident?" Bloch asked.

"Of course."

"Satisfactory." He watched the bright flames, enjoying the smell of the burning birchwood. "Very satisfactory."

Seven

Matthew arrived in the newsroom early Monday morning, too damn early, and drank two cups of coffee even before Feldie showed up. He wasn't doing any work. He just sat at his desk, staring at the Plexiglas partition above it where he'd hung the poster of the movie that had been based on his book, *LZ*. They'd kept the title. The movie had won lots of awards—so had the book—and now was available on tape for VCR; the book was required reading in college courses on the Vietnam War. He used to have some of the reviews stuck up on the partition next to the poster, but he'd pulled them down about a year ago. No reason. Just tired of looking at them, he supposed. A few months ago, *Time* had done a piece on whatever happened to Matthew Stark, the helicopter pilot who'd been awarded a Distinguished Flying Cross and survived two tours in the central highlands, only to return to Vietnam one more time as a freelance journalist, publishing articles with *The New Yorker, Atlantic Monthly, Harper's.* When he finally came home he wrote his book and joined the *Washington Post.* He was the tarnished hero, the Vietnam vet people could dare to like.

Then he got sick of it all or ran out of things to say—something. He'd quit caring about what had brought on the change of heart. He'd resigned from the *Post,* done nothing for a while, then, still with a reputation left, showed up at the *Gazette* to do a tabloid's version of investigative reporting.

He sipped some coffee and admitted he felt better. Nothing like a newsroom to help him forget a long Sunday of nightmares that had haunted him, awake and asleep. He called them nightmares, although they weren't. They were memories.

"Asshole!"

Alice Feldon stomped over to his desk, the front page of the *New York Times* crushed in one hand, her glasses down on the end of her big nose. "Goddamn you," she said. "I stick my neck out for you, I call in a few chips to get you a ticket to a sold-out concert at Lincoln Center, I *trust* you, you son of a bitch, and how the hell do you repay me?"

"Relax, Feldie. It was a dead end, all right? No story."

"Bullshit." She flung the *Times* at him. "There, read. A woman slipped and fell outside Lincoln Center after the concert Saturday night. Died. Her body wasn't discovered until yesterday afternoon."

"Great story, Feldie. I'll get right on it."

"I don't need your sarcasm. The woman's name was Rachel Stein. Mean anything to you?"

"No."

"She was with one Senator Samuel Ryder at the concert—your old pal."

Matthew rubbed his forehead. "Jesus Christ."

The story started on the lower half of the front page. Rachel Stein had been a prominent Hollywood agent; she had recently retired to Palm Beach. A quote from Ryder's office said she had become a prominent supporter of the senator's and he was deeply grieved by her death.

"This guy Weasel—he a friend of Ryder's, too? Is that why you were at Lincoln Center, because Ryder was there?

They say Stein's death was accidental. You have any other ideas?"

Stark let Feldie rant. The world's largest uncut diamond, Ryder's troubles, Weasel's dumb urge to help him. Now this.

"Look, Stark, goddamnit, I don't feel sorry for you. You could quit this job and still make more money on royalties and interest than I do putting in a sixty-hour week. I could *fire* you, you'd make out fine, which is probably the biggest reason I don't." She pushed her glasses up on top of her head. "People used to say you gave a damn."

No one talked to him like that except Alice Feldon. No one else dared. Matthew liked it that he didn't scare her. "Maybe I never did."

"I don't believe that." Her voice had softened, and she let out a heavy sigh. "Was this Otis Raymond character in Vietnam with you and Ryder?"

"Weaze is a burned-out Vietnam vet. Country's bored with them, Feldie. About all I get from him is bullshit. If there's a story in this, you'll get it. I promise."

"All right, Stark. You're a journalist. Follow up."

Muttering that she ought to give up on the lazy shit, Alice stalked back to her desk. Matthew drank some more coffee and read the piece on Rachel Stein's death. She could easily have slipped. He remembered how tiny she was, how wrinkled and old-looking, even if the article said she was only sixty-five. She wasn't used to snow and ice. So maybe she slipped and maybe she didn't—did it make any difference? He went back to the beginning and reread the piece.

And there it was. Rachel Stein had emigrated from Amsterdam in 1945, having spent the last months of the war in a Nazi concentration camp. She was a Dutch Jew.

A *Dutch* Jew.

And the man Ryder was supposed to have met, Hendrik de Geer, was also Dutch.

Stark looked up at the *LZ* poster, not seeing it. Something else was stirring around in his head, but he couldn't pin it down. He pulled out the program he'd saved from the concert, just in case Feldie wanted proof he'd attended, just in case he felt like cutting out the picture of Juliana Fall and sticking it on his partition.

He flipped to Ms. Pianist's bio. There was the usual garbage. First and only student of Eric Shuji Shizumi, who didn't want her to go to Vermont. Attended Juilliard, which stood to reason. Career launched after winning various prestigious piano competitions, including the Levenritt at Carnegie Hall, which Stark was glad he hadn't had to sit through. The bio neglected to mention she was beautiful. He remembered the way her dress had clung to her. Hell, yes, she was beautiful. He skipped the stuff about her technique and conception of the Beethoven concerto and dropped down to the last personal items. She lived in New York, where she'd been born and raised, the daughter of Wall Street banker Adrian Fall and Catharina Peperkamp Fall, owner of Catharina's Bake Shop on upper Madison Avenue—and a Dutch immigrant.

And what a handy coincidence that was. Feldie was right: he was a journalist. As such, he didn't believe in coincidences.

A year ago, before J.J. Pepper, Juliana had bought an aquarium and put it up behind her concert grand piano, near the French doors that separated her dining room and huge living room overlooking Central Park. She'd filled the aquarium with water and added goldfish, six of them. Their names were Figaro, Cosima (after Wagner's wife), Puccini, Carmen, Bartók, and the Duke (after Duke Ellington; to Shuji he was Ludwig). They didn't talk, and they weren't much to look at, weren't, in fact, any company at all, but they were something alive to have around during her long hours of isolation. She could turn around in her chair at the piano—she practiced far too many hours for her back to tolerate a bench—and have a nice chat with them, as she was doing now. They fit her itinerant lifestyle more easily than would a dog or cat. It was easy to get people to feed fish while she was away, but she had a feeling if they ever forgot, they'd just flush the bodies down the toilet and buy new ones for her. Would she ever know?

Shuji had won. She'd decided to postpone Vermont. Saturday night at the Club Aquarian had gone too well, been too much fun. She needed to work. She had to get J.J. Pepper out of her system. There was no time for decent practice on the road, and she needed to get back into it. If she did at least eight hours a day at the piano for the next two weeks, she'd be back in shape—like a runner. The real work of being a pianist, Shuji had said. He had a point, although she was still so irritated with him for ruining Vermont for her that she wasn't about to tell him so. Once she'd established her schedule, she could spare a few days in Vermont without compromising her progress. Without guilt.

But she couldn't just leap back into her old routines. Yesterday, after a meager three hours of practice, she'd ended up trotting off to the Metropolitan Museum of Art to see the Christmas tree.

Today she'd done a little better. She'd climbed out of bed at eight, just an hour later than she'd meant to, and had done ten minutes of stretching, although twenty would have been better. She should have gone jogging in the park if it was warm enough or jumped on her stationary bike. She'd jumped into the tub. Her "healthy breakfast" was two of her mother's famous butter cookies and a pot of tea. A proper schedule would put her at her Steinway by nine, there to stay for eight to ten hours, with occasional breaks and time out for lunch and dinner. Today's schedule had put her at her piano at eleven with lots of breaks.

It was just three o'clock, and so far she'd had four fish-talk breaks. But she refused to be hard on herself. All she needed were a couple of days. She'd be back to her old self, as demanding and absorbed in her work as ever.

"What do you say, Duke, back to the Chopin?"

Duke wiggled and darted away. Chopin had little effect on him. She was working on the Piano Concerto No. 1 in E minor, a bitch of a piece, which she happened to love. It wasn't the music that had her talking to fish. It was something else—the isolation, she supposed.

The doorman called up, startling her, and informed her that a Matthew Stark was downstairs in the lobby and wanted to see her, was that all right?

"Damn," she said, surprising both herself and the doorman. She remembered Matthew Stark vividly—the sardonic laugh, the dark, changeable eyes. She couldn't imagine what he wanted with her. She didn't even know why he'd been in her dressing room Saturday night. Just to say hello to Sam Ryder? To her? She doubted he'd been even momentarily tempted to ask her to dinner. He'd called her *toots*. What was he doing downstairs? She didn't need the distraction right now, but what the hell. "Send him up."

For no reason that made any sense to her, she considered her appearance: black sweatpants, oversized sweatshirt with the bust of Beethoven silk-screened on the front, scrunchy black socks, sneakers. She wasn't wearing makeup, and her hair was up in a ponytail.

At least it isn't pink, she thought as the doorbell rang.

She went into the large foyer and opened the door only as wide as her chain-lock would permit because she was a New Yorker and didn't trust anyone. But the man she peeked out at was definitely the one who'd made her feel like such a ding-a-ling the other night. He had on a black leather jacket, a black sweater, jeans, and heavy leather boots. No hat, no gloves. Somehow she wouldn't expect any. Snow had melted into his dark hair, but his scarred face didn't even look cold. She hadn't realized it was snowing. Maybe the Chopin was going better than she'd thought it was.

Stark gave her a lazy, unselfconscious grin. "A ponytail? How un-world-famous of you."

No one had ever been that irreverent to her. Absolutely no one. "Don't you think you should wait until I let you in before you turn on the sarcasm?"

"It never occurred to me."

She believed him. "What do you want?"

"Five minutes. I'd like to ask you a couple questions."

"About what?"

"A few things. I'm a reporter."

"I only have your word on that."

"The way I've been going lately, that might be the best you'll get. But here." He fished out his wallet and handed a press card through the opening. "Check me out."

Juliana managed to take the card without touching his fingers. As she glanced at it, she could feel his dark eyes on her. "You're with the *Washington Gazette?*"

"Uh-huh."

He sounded amused, and she recalled she was supposed to have heard of him. Well, bullshit. "No wonder I didn't recognize your name." She gave him a haughty look and one of her cool, distant smiles, both of which she figured he deserved. "I don't read the *Gazette.*"

"Nice try, sweetheart, but nobody knows me from the *Gazette.*"

She felt her cheeks redden with anger and embarrassment—and, she thought desperately, awareness. He was still standing out in the damn hall, and already she was noticing little things. The lopsided grin, the muscular thighs, the thick, jagged scar on his right hand. It probably wasn't from anything as simple as slicing cucumbers.

"Forget it," she said. "I've never heard of you, and I don't care if I haven't."

"You going to check me out or leave me standing out here all afternoon?"

She shut the door and considered just going back to her work. He would hear the Chopin and get the message. But she went to the phone in the living room. Curiosity, she supposed. She tapped out the number for the *Gazette* printed on his card. The switchboard routed her call to Alice Feldon, who verified that Matthew Stark worked for her. "If you want to call it work," she added, half under her breath.

"Would you mind describing him?"

"Why?"

"He's outside my door, and I'm not sure I want to let him in."

"I see. I guess I can understand that. Who are you?"

"My name's Juliana Fall. I—"

"Stark's pianist. I'll be damned."

Stark's pianist. My God. What was going on here?

"He's about five-eleven, dark, scarred face, wears a black leather jacket and Gokey boots, and—"

"That's him. Thank you."

"Wait—put him on, will you?"

"I'll have him call you," she said, and hung up.

She unlatched the chain lock and let Stark open the door himself. "You've been confirmed."

"Sounds ominous."

He walked into the living room. Juliana followed. It was a huge room that overlooked Central Park, now a Currier and Ives Christmas card under the light covering of snow. She saw him eyeing the place, as if he didn't expect the dust on the windowsills, the marble fireplace, the piano, the hodgepodge of expensive furniture, the books, magazines, photographs, clippings, letters, awards, and junk

stacked everywhere. For the first time since her return from
Paris, she noticed it herself. And the two big Persian carpets needed vacuuming.

"Goldfish, huh?" he said, walking over to the tank and
taking a look. Then he glanced back at her. "Nice place you
have here. No cleaning lady?"

"I've been away for a while and haven't taken the time
to clean up and— Well, I do have someone come in to
clean, but she hasn't been in yet. She doesn't come on a
regular basis. It's hard to concentrate with the vacuum running and someone flitting around with a dustcloth. To be
honest, a little dust doesn't bother me."

"I'll bet."

She felt his eyes on her and was aware her ponytail was
coming loose and she probably looked a little vague. She
usually did this time of the day, after hours of practice. It
took a while for her to pull herself out of her heightened
state of concentration.

"What do you do when you throw parties?" he went on.
"Just shove all the stuff under the couch and turn the lights
down low so nobody'll notice the dust?"

She ignored his dry tone. "I don't throw parties."

"You just attend them."

"As a matter of fact, yes."

"La-di-da."

Her elastic band was at the end of her ponytail. She
pulled it out, letting her hair flop down, and noticed his
eyes widen slightly. She wouldn't have noticed at all if she
hadn't been looking. So, she thought, he's paying attention.
A reporter's eye for detail, she supposed. Nothing more
than that.

"Mr. Stark," she said coolly, "did you want to ask me
something or did you just want to insult me?"

He looked at her, a touch of the warm, dark brown coming into his black-seeming eyes. "I'm sorry." There was an

abruptness to his words, and she suspected they were ones he didn't say very often. "It's obvious from the looks of this place, and of you, that you work hard at what you do. I didn't expect that."

"You thought I just woke up one morning and knew how to play the piano?"

He grinned. "Something like that."

"Well, I didn't." She decided to leave it at that. "What do you want to ask me?"

"I'm half working on a story," he said, walking over to the dusty Steinway. A dozen or so nubby pencils were scattered on the floor under the piano and her chair. He picked one up. It was two inches long. "Some life still in it, I guess."

"I do all my markings in pencil. I don't take time to re-sharpen my pencils when I'm working, so I start with about a dozen and throw them on the floor when they get dull. I hate dull pencils."

"Nothing worse."

Despite his wry tone, he was as fascinated as he was amused, Juliana could tell. "When I run out, I gather them up and sharpen all of them at once. It saves time. Look, I can't dress up what I do or how I do it. If my methods, this place, shatter your image of what a concert pianist ought to be like, then so be it. How can you be half working on something?"

"In the immortal words of Alice Feldon, by being a lazy shit." He started to put the stubby pencil on the piano rack but stopped himself and dropped it back on the floor. "Wouldn't want to get mixed up. Aren't the Dutch supposed to be tidy?"

Juliana frowned at him. "How do you know I'm Dutch?"

"Research," he said.

"What kind of research? I thought you weren't a music reporter. If this is a formal interview—"

"It isn't. Relax, okay?" He looked at her, his eyes dropping to Beethoven glowering on her front. She felt like an idiot. "Mind if we go sit down?"

She sighed. "As you wish."

He sat on the couch, amidst several musty books on Chopin and Mozart, while she lifted a huge stack of newspapers and magazines and letters off a wingback chair. "Four months of mail—and I forgot to stop the paper before I left." Only, she thought, because she'd just started having it delivered. She'd wondered if reading the morning paper would help her feel more in touch with the world. Or maybe it was just one more thing to do in the morning before practicing. "I haven't gone through it yet."

"So I see. Need a hand?"

"No."

She said it too quickly. She knew it, and she could see, so did he. She didn't want him getting too close. He was so different from the men she knew. Sitting down, she gave him a quick, sweeping look, taking in the scarred face, the strong dark hands, the boots that looked as if they'd been worn a long time and would be worn even longer. Shuji, she thought, wouldn't like him.

"Go ahead and ask your questions," she said.

Stark crossed a foot over his knee and held it by the ankle. He looked totally at ease, and suddenly Juliana wondered what would get this man worked up. What would make him angry? What would make him laugh?

"I was at Lincoln Center Saturday night to see a Dutchman, Hendrik de Geer," Stark said. "Do you know him?"

Juliana laughed incredulously. "Is there any particular reason I should?" she asked, hearing her own sarcasm.

Stark didn't react. "Sam Ryder didn't mention him?"

"No, should he have?"

"I don't know, I'm fishing. De Geer and Ryder were supposed to have gotten together at the concert."

"Is your half story about Senator Ryder?"

"Maybe."

She looked at him thoughtfully, her lips pulled in slightly in concentration. "You don't like him, do you?"

"I don't like many people. You've never heard the name Hendrik de Geer?"

"Not that I can recall."

"I guess that might not be saying much. You'd never heard of Sam Ryder, either."

Juliana sat up very straight, stiff and insulted. "Are you always this hostile to people you interview, Mr. Stark?"

"Call me Matthew, all right?" He gave something that passed for a smile. "How come you didn't go to Vermont?"

"I've been on tour since September, and I have some pieces I want to add to my repertoire. Vermont's not going anywhere."

"I guess not. You put in long hours?"

"Right now I am, eight a day minimum. To get back in shape."

"Then you're following Shuji's advice."

"He's often right about this sort of thing."

"That piss you off?"

She couldn't resist a grin and madly wondered what this intense, remote man would think of J.J. Pepper. "Sometimes. But tell me more about this Hendrik de Geer. Is it just because he's Dutch that you thought I might have known him?"

"Frankly, yes. I always check out a coincidence. And there's nothing more I can tell you about him. What about your mother, think she might know him?"

"My *mother?*"

"Sure. She's Dutch, too."

Juliana stared at him, unable to believe he was serious, but nothing in his gentle-tough face, in the unreadable dark eyes and earthy grin, suggested he was—or wasn't. "My

mother left The Netherlands more than thirty years ago,"
she told him, "before I was born. She has a sister in Rotterdam, but they don't get along, and a brother in Antwerp
whom she rarely sees. No Hendrik de Geers, I'm afraid.
Not that I know of." Which, she thought, remembering tea
with Rachel Stein, wasn't saying a hell of a lot.

"Okay. Sam Ryder attended the concert with an older
woman, very tiny, dark, well-dressed. You wouldn't know
her, would you?"

Juliana tried not to react, tried to keep her face as unreadable as his. Rachel Stein—it had to be! But she shook
her head automatically, her instincts telling her to deny she
knew anyone of that description. She should talk to her
mother before bandying about Rachel Stein's name and
their relationship to a reporter. They were both Dutch, like
this Hendrik de Geer. But what did any of them have to do
with Senator Ryder—or with each other, for that matter?

"No," she said, shaking her head for added emphasis,
"I don't think so."

"Know anything about diamonds?"

Juliana felt herself go numb. "Diamonds? No, how
would I? I'm a pianist."

"Then you don't know anything about the world's largest uncut diamond?"

Oh, Jesus. Could he mean the Minstrel's Rough? No,
impossible. Juliana resisted the impulse to jump up and
pace. Matthew Stark didn't even know about the Peperkamp diamond tradition. How could he know about the
Minstrel?

Her mother, Rachel Stein, the Dutchman Hendrik de
Geer, Senator Ryder—was this the connection among
them? The mysterious, legendary Minstrel's Rough? When
cut, it would be worth millions.

No, don't be silly, she told herself, annoyed. She'd never
really believed her uncle's tale. What he'd handed her

seven years ago was simply a rock with an interesting story behind it. If a diamond, one of only moderate value.

But what if?

Her heart thudded and her hands had gone clammy, but she called on her training and years of experience as a performer to maintain an outward air of self-control. Matthew Stark hadn't lifted his perceptive eyes from her. She could feel them probing as he waited for her to give herself away. Well, she thought, I won't.

"I told you," she said calmly, "I don't know anything about diamonds. I don't even like them."

Stark climbed slowly to his feet, his black eyes never leaving her. He walked over and fingered the diamonds in her ears, first the left, then the right. They were simple posts that she wore nearly every day, just so she wouldn't have to fool with picking out earrings. Stark's touch was very light, but not quite delicate. "What about these?"

"They're different."

"Why?"

"They're blue diamonds. Colored diamonds are the rage now. Once they were considered practically worthless."

"I thought you didn't know anything about diamonds."

She smiled haughtily. "Obviously I know about the ones I wear."

The particular two in her ears had been cut by her great-grandfather Peperkamp, who'd been around during the wild early days when the South African diamond mines were discovered and the De Beers empire founded. But she didn't think she should tell Matthew Stark that.

He pulled back, and she looked up at him, carefully controlling her breathing like she did when she had the pre-concert jitters and didn't want anyone to know. She was more aware of Matthew Stark, his earthiness and obvious maleness, than she felt she ought to be. "Any more questions?" she asked coolly.

"Juliana." He spoke her name without anger, but his gaze was dark and distant, and she knew there would be no middle ground between them. "I'll let it go for now, but lies don't work with me. Remember that."

"I'm not—"

"Just remember."

He walked past her to the foyer, and she was surprised at how softly the door closed behind him. For a minute she didn't move. She took a huge gulp of air and flopped back in the chair, exhaling at the ceiling. "Jesus Christ," she muttered. "*Jesus.* Next time—well, the hell there'll be a next time!"

But something told her there would be. Whatever was between her and Matthew Stark felt very unfinished. And he was the kind of man who finished things. He was also the kind of man, she thought uncomfortably, who would push and dig and ask questions until he learned that the world's largest and most mysterious uncut diamond was the Minstrel's Rough…that the Peperkamps had been in the diamond business for four hundred years…that she was the last of the Peperkamps—and hadn't given him straight answers to his questions. He'd put all the pieces together.

He'd figure out she had the Minstrel.

Which, of course, she did.

Could someone else put those same pieces together and arrive at the same conclusion? Was someone else after the Minstrel?

Who?

She catapulted herself—not to the piano to escape this time—but to J.J.'s room, J.J.'s closet. She had to get out. She had to be someone else for a while, to be with people, to sort this mess out.

Her eyes fell on a midcalf black wool skirt with a slit up the back and a low-cut red silk blouse that had been very, very daring fifty years ago. She immediately saw it dressed up with lots of rhinestones, black-seamed stockings, red shoes…and lavender-tinted hair.

She pushed the Washington reporter's dark gaze from her mind and got started.

Juliana Fall was a liar, and she didn't know Rachel Stein was dead. She was also one very attractive woman, and as he hung around the glittering Beresford lobby, Matthew thought more about her vibrant eyes than her skirting of the truth. He'd expected the Juliana Fall he'd met Saturday night to live in a building like the Beresford. The one he'd met this afternoon could have lived anywhere, the Beresford or some hole in the Bronx. The dust, the clutter, the sassy ponytail had surprised him. They didn't fit his stereotype of the world-class pianist. Hell, he thought, she was probably up there sharpening her pencils or playing some piece written while Napoleon was trouncing Europe.

Napoleon, she'd say, who's he?

Maybe he wasn't being fair. Whatever she knew or didn't know, it was plain enough to Matthew that Ms. Pianist wasn't in any funk, as her eminent teacher had suggested.

The lady was just flat-out bored.

For the first time in years, Stark felt like having a cigarette. He'd quit smoking after Vietnam, figuring he had a full quota of poisons in his system, but right now he just didn't give a damn. The tough, cynical, scarred, smart, heroic, tarnished Matthew Stark. He'd had his picture on the covers of *Time* and *Newsweek;* he'd appeared on network television and PBS specials. He was supposed to know more than your average Joe Six-Pack. Be more.

What a lot of bullshit that was. He was trying to coax information out of a gorgeous space cadet of a piano player whose big excitement for the day probably was feeding her goldfish. Who the hell wouldn't be bored banging on a piano all day in that great, fancy, lonely apartment? Concerts added a little interest, he supposed, but she couldn't give one every day, and they, too, had to get old after a while. Things like that generally did. Preserving a reputation was damn tedious. Making one was the fun part.

The uniformed doorman came over and asked if he could help. Matthew said no thanks. The doorman then politely suggested he be on his way. Matthew shrugged and didn't argue. The guy had his job to do.

He went and stood outside, across the street at the bus stop in front of the Museum of Natural History. He didn't know what he was waiting for, but his instincts told him—damn reliable instincts they'd been, too, once—that he'd just given Juliana Fall something to nibble on besides some piece written by a guy in a white wig.

His description of Rachel Stein and Weaze's nutso talk about the world's largest uncut diamond had clicked with her—and she'd lied about both. Matthew wanted to know why, and he wanted to know what she was going to do about it. If anything. She might just sit upstairs talking to her goldfish and playing the piano and forget he'd even been there.

But he remembered the scared, interested, comprehending look in those deep dark green eyes, and he didn't think she would. His questions had chased away the vagueness and boredom he'd seen in her eyes when she'd pulled the door open for him. Ahh, he thought, nothing like an adventure to kick up the spirit.

He'd give her an hour.

Word was getting around that J.J. Pepper was back. Between four and six, when she liked to play, the Club Aquarian would start to fill up, and people wouldn't just eat and gab. They'd listen, which Len Wetherall could appreciate. J.J. was good—and a hell of a sight to watch, looser than she had been in the spring and summer. New Zealand or wherever the hell she'd been had done her some good. Or coming back had.

Len settled back against the bar, sipping a cup of black coffee and having a look at the postcards she'd just handed him. He figured she got them from some New Zealand tourist office in town. They weren't made out, of course; no postmark, nothing like that. Merrie, his wife, had said quit worrying about damn New Zealand and focus on the hair—it was lavender today—if he wanted to know what game J.J. Pepper was playing. But he wasn't sure he did. It could just ruin everything. Not so much for him, maybe, but for her.

She was at the baby grand, warming up with a couple of slow and easy tunes. It was early, not crowded, but that wouldn't last. Right now, she looked as if she'd been made for the place. Her low-cut blouse was the same shade of red as the single rose on each table, the only touch of color in the gray and black decor. Nearly everyone had a clear view of her on the round platform stage, carpeted in gray, just eight inches off the floor. It stood between the dining room on one side and the high-tech bar on the other, and behind it were semiprivate seating areas, with low black lacquer tables and gray suede half-circle sofas. From every corner, you could hear J.J. Pepper's rich, ringing sounds— and see that damned lavender hair.

Fifteen minutes after J.J. had gotten started, a dark-haired man came in alone and asked who the lady at the piano was. He just gave a curt nod when he was told. Len didn't like that. The guy had a serious, cut-the-bullshit face, and he didn't take off his black leather jacket when he slid onto a stool at the far end of the bar. He ordered a beer and turned around so he could see the stage.

Len didn't like that, either.

J.J. was into her piece—she never called them tunes—

and hadn't spotted him. She'd moved into some hotter stuff, was really getting into it. Her lavender hair was coming out of its pins, and a big lock flopped down her forehead. She was grinning and biting her lip, and for a second Len held his breath, thinking she was going to let out a hoot.

The guy down at the other end of the bar just sipped on his beer and watched, tight-lipped.

Al, the bartender, started to whoop and slap the bar, his version of clapping, and Len turned back to see what the excitement was all about.

"Holy shit," he breathed.

He couldn't believe it. J.J. had kicked off her red shoes and every now and then she'd slam out some high notes with her right foot.

"Babe's getting the moves down," Al said. "What'd we ever do around here without her?"

Len grinned. "Damned if I know."

When she finished, J.J. bounced up off the bench, smiling and sweating like the world had just been lifted off her shoulders, her blouse and skirt askew. She straightened them up, not very well, and stuck stray hairs back up in their pins as she trotted up to the bar. Al had her usual Saratoga water with a twist of lime waiting. Len didn't touch the stuff himself. Regular water was fine with him.

She drank down half the glass and wiped her mouth with a cocktail napkin, her eyes glittering. "It's good to be back."

"No Club Aquarian in New Zealand, huh?"

She was beaming. "Nope."

Len slid the postcards across the bar to her. "No slides of you up on a mountain?"

"It's hard to take pictures of yourself."

She turned her back to the bar and looked around, checking out what there was of an early crowd. When her eyes fell on the guy sitting alone, her smile vanished and her cheeks went white, the too-red blush she used suddenly looking false and garish, not so fun anymore.

"Something wrong, babe?" Len asked, cool.

She shook her head and put her cold glass to each of her cheeks, the condensation on the glass running the pancake makeup. But some of her natural color returned. Her lavender-tinted hair looked as stiff as she did. She said tightly, "It's nothing I can't handle myself."

Still in her silk-stockinged feet, she took her mineral water down to the end of the bar and jumped onto the stool next to the dude in the black leather jacket. He was a tough-looking bastard, and Len didn't especially want to mess with him, but he would if he had to. At night he had a bouncer, but during the day he was his own bouncer. He was damn good at it.

All he needed was a reason.

Matthew held back a grin as Juliana turned to him and blinked her sparkling gold eyelids at him, pursed her very red, very kissable lips, and said, her liquid voice frozen into pointy icicles, "You followed me."

"That's right, I did." He motioned for another beer. She was still breathing hard from having pelted out those high notes with her feet. She had her toes curled around the bottom rung of the stool; they were the kind of toes he could too easily imagine trailing up his calves in the middle of the night. He wasn't sure he liked the effect that Juliana Fall—or whoever she was—was having on him. "Hard to lose that purple hair in a crowd."

"How dare you," she said, so pissed off she was gritting her teeth.

"'How dare you' is what cool, sophisticated, world-famous concert pianists say. Hot little jazz pianists who play with their feet say, 'Fuck you.'"

"Of all the sneaky, *arrogant*—" She sucked in a breath and let it out. "Damn you."

Matthew grinned. "That's better. I like the gold eyelids, by the way. They set off the purple hair. Very regal looking."

He sipped his fresh beer, watching her breathe in through her nose. He'd have been embarrassed as hell getting caught with purple hair, but she seemed more furious than anything else, which was okay with him. He liked it that she was willing to take him on. He scared the shit out of most people. He'd spotted her strutting out of the Beresford with that crazy hair and had recognized her immediately—he'd been paying more attention to that cute little shape of hers than he'd realized. At first he thought she'd seen him from her living-room window and had donned her silly disguise to get past him, but her arrival at the Club Aquarian squelched that theory. The purple hair and old clothes and raccoon coat, and, Jesus, the red vinyl boots were for real.

He gave her a long look, trying not to appear too entertained. If he pissed her off too much, he might not get anything out of her at all. Her blouse was low-cut for Juliana Fall, but on J.J. Pepper it looked just right—crooked, a peek of one pale breast and white, lace-trimmed bra showing. Very sexy and very disconcerting.

"I take it I've stumbled on a little secret of yours," he said.

She didn't say a word. Ahh, what a clever bastard you are, Stark thought sarcastically. Won't Feldie be impressed with this major discovery. And, shit, he couldn't wait to tell Weasel. Wouldn't he be proud of what his buddy Matt had turned up?

"From what I gather," he went on, "Len Wetherall doesn't know about Juliana Fall. He assumes you're really J.J. Pepper."

"I am really J.J. Pepper."

"Yeah, but he doesn't know about Juliana Fall. Right?"

"Shhh!"

"My, my, Shuji?"

Her eyes shut, then opened, and she shook her head. "He doesn't know."

"Ah-ha."

This time the eyes narrowed, deep and vivid and fierce. "Don't make fun of me."

"This is a hell of a story, you know. 'Internationally acclaimed concert pianist dyes hair purple and bangs out jazz in SoHo nightclub with silk-stockinged toes.' Wow."

"It's not dye, it's mousse."

"Mousse, then."

"And the feet—I've never done that before."

"All the better. Feldie'd love it."

Feldie would bounce his ass off the paper if he turned in a story like that.

Juliana gripped her glass, and for a second he thought she was going to throw her water at him. Instead she set the glass down hard. He could see her fighting to maintain her composure. He admired the struggle, admired her control. He knew he was giving her a hard time. But, he thought, remembering her fight with Shuji, her ego was strong enough to handle anything he dished out. And if she slipped, even just a little, she might tell him something he could use. Not about J.J. Pepper. If dressing up weird and playing jazz alleviated her boredom, gave her something to worry about besides the morning reviews, that was fine with him. Maybe it was her version of living life on the edge. He wanted to know her connection, however tenuous, to Sam Ryder, to the tiny, tragically dead Rachel Stein, to the Dutchman Hendrik de Geer, to the diamond one or all or none were after.

"Are you going to do the story?" she asked tightly, but the fierceness was still there.

Hell, yes, he thought, that would drive in the last nail on the coffin lid of my reputation. "Maybe."

"You're lying. You're just trying to make me talk about

something I've already told you I know nothing about. You're trying to blackmail me, aren't you?"

"I think of it as a deal."

"Bullshit," she said.

Down the bar, Len Wetherall slid to his feet, as graceful and big as Stark remembered him from when he was with the Knicks. Getting slam-dunked by a six-foot-nine, two-hundred-forty-pound ex–basketball superstar not known for his even temper was not Matthew's idea of a graceful exit. He tried to look a bit less menacing to Juliana, not that his menacing looks were having any discernible effect.

"Look," he said, "I'm not interested in hurting you. A buddy of mine is in some trouble. To help him, I need your cooperation."

"Or you'll do the story—or just give it to someone else on the *Gazette* who'd do it?"

She gave him an I-dare-you-fucker look, but this time she was the one bluffing. He had her scared. She didn't want her secret to get out.

He sighed. "No, I won't do the story, and I won't give it to anyone who would. I've never been one for blackmail. And I frankly don't care if you can play piano with one hand and one foot tied behind your back. My editor doesn't care, my readers don't care, and probably ninety-nine percent of the people in the world don't care. Ninety-nine percent of the people in your world may care, but they don't read the *Washington Gazette*."

Her mouth drew in in a straight line, and she looked away. This time he didn't care if she felt bad. If she couldn't stand the truth, then she'd better get the hell out while she was still young enough to do something else with her life.

"Talk to me, Juliana," he said.

The softness of his voice surprised him, and her, he would have guessed, but before he could find out for certain, a giant hand clamped down on his shoulder and lifted him up off the stool. Matthew looked up into the deep brown eyes of Len Wetherall. It wasn't only Wetherall's size his colleagues had respected, but also his tenacity and his intelligence—not to mention his temper.

"The lady doesn't want to talk," the former basketball superstar said, his tone misleadingly mild.

Juliana sipped her water and didn't bother even glancing around. Matthew considered hinting he'd tell Wetherall what she'd been up to at Lincoln Center on Saturday night if she didn't help him out, but he doubted that would do any good. First, he'd just told her he'd been bluffing. Second, if he did tell, Wetherall would just toss them both. Third, no matter what he did, he assumed he was out the door anyway.

"You finish your beer?" Wetherall asked.

"All set. I'll need the check—"

"It's on the house."

"Thanks, but I pay my way."

Matthew pulled out his wallet and dropped a ten on the bar. Len let go, and Stark tried to give Juliana a look that told her what he thought of her chickenshit attitude, but she wouldn't meet his eye. He gave up and headed for the door.

On his way out, he glanced back and saw that Juliana had swung around on her bar stool and was watching him leave. He expected a look of apology for getting him thrown out, even an indication that she appreciated his not telling her boss how she'd wowed the Lincoln Center crowd on Saturday night without once banging out any notes with her feet and now was willing to talk.

But all she gave him was a cocky little smirk. Even with Len Wetherall hovering over her. Matthew was hard-pressed not to march back in there and haul her ass off the stool.

The little pissant was enjoying herself.

Juliana's feeling of victory didn't last. Len leaned back

against the bar next to her and said idly, "Dude called you Juliana."

"Yes, I know."

"Is one of the *J*s in J.J. short for Juliana?"

"No. J.J.'s not short for anything."

"Right."

She'd finished her water and was anxious to get back to the piano. It would feel good to drop back into another world. Sometimes it felt as if she *were* parachuting into a new world, just floating, seeing everything around her, never really landing. Other times it felt as if she were free-falling and wouldn't be able to get her chute open in time, that even if she did, it would be too late. She'd tried a few times to explain this feeling to Shuji, but he couldn't understand it. His approach was much more matter-of-fact and controlled. He said he never left this world and neither did she, so quit talking nonsense. Maybe that was one reason she liked jazz. It required precision and technique, but not that same level of predictable control.

"Thank you for intervening," she said. She hated lying to Len. He'd offered her friendship, trust—his stage, for God's sake. And what had she given him in return? A purple-haired pianist he couldn't understand. A potential bombshell.

"Anytime. But that's one mean-looking gentleman, J.J. I'd prefer not to have to mess with him again, myself."

"I couldn't agree with you more."

She left it at that, unsure herself exactly what she meant. She didn't know what to make of Matthew Stark. Undeniably he had a menacing look about him—the scars contributed, certainly—but she didn't think he was in fact mean or dangerous. Or was she just being naive? He was sarcastic, yes, but he had a smile that intrigued her, and even if he'd been less than sympathetic toward her dual identities, he hadn't given her away.

"You want to talk?" Len asked gently.

Reluctantly, she shook her head. But that, too, was a lie. She did want to talk. About who she was, about who Matthew Stark was, what he wanted. About the Minstrel's Rough. She remembered the soft, heavily accented words of her uncle as she'd prepared for the second half of her concert in the little Delftshaven church.

"The existence of the Minstrel has never been confirmed. It's best that way, Juliana. It's a very, very valuable stone. Once cut, it would be worth many millions of dollars for its size and beauty alone. But its mystery, its status as a diamond legend, adds to that value. People will do terrible things for such riches. I know."

She hadn't thought then to ask him how he'd known. It was all a joke to her—an adventure. How many concert pianists had crazy uncles passing them uncut diamonds backstage? But now she wondered if she should get in touch with her uncle and tell him about Matthew Stark, ask him about Rachel Stein, Hendrik de Geer. Uncle Johannes might talk where her mother clearly wouldn't.

"Len, does the name Matthew Stark mean anything to you?"

"LZ," Len said, without hesitation.

She looked up at him, blank.

"Hell, babe, where you been?" Len laughed. "You telling me you've never heard of *LZ?* Don't you ever go to the movies?"

"Rarely," she said. It was the truth. *"LZ's* a movie?"

"Yeah, and a book—author's Matt Stark. Book came out six or seven years ago, the movie a year or two later. It got best picture and best director, as I recall. The book was a bestseller."

"What's it about?"

"Jesus, I don't believe you. It's about Vietnam chopper

pilots. *LZ* stands for landing zone." He looked at her. "You know, where helicopters land."

She hadn't known. "I see."

Unfortunately, now she did see. She'd made a fool of herself. Stark must think she was a hopeless dingbat. How could she explain? When his book had been a bestseller and his movie a hit, she hadn't had time to read books or go to movies. She had played piano. She had studied music history, music theory, music composition. Her friends were musicians and her enemies were musicians. Her world was music, and it consumed her. Lately, that had begun to change. She had the *New York Times* delivered, even if she didn't always read it, and she was trying harder to keep track of what was going on in the world. But she had some catching up to do. She still had to find out who the Matthew Starks were. If he'd written LZ recently, she might have recognized his name. But seven years ago? Not a chance.

"That the guy I just tossed?" Len asked. "Matt Stark?" He laughed. "Well, I'll be damned, don't you pick 'em. Go on and get your butt back to the piano, babe. Play."

She nodded, thanking him, and did.

Eight

United States Senator Samuel Ryder, Jr., was backpedaling as fast as he could.

Plausible deniability. That was what was required now.

He stared into the flames of the fire he'd built in the cozy study of his Georgetown town house and tried to think of ways he could distance himself from Phillip Bloch and Hendrik de Geer.

"Jesus," one of his aides had said, handing him a copy of the Monday morning paper, "can you believe your luck? Talk about your providential accidents. You get to look like a nice guy on the front page of the *Times* and get her off your back at the same time. This lady was a no-win situation."

Yes, indeed. What luck.

Which one had done it, he wondered. Bloch? De Geer? Each had so much to lose. Each was capable of giving a tiny old woman a little shove. Or having someone else do it.

Each had learned of her threat from him.

It's not your fault! Rachel Stein had known the risks before she came to him.

Her death might have been accidental. Indeed, as his aide had said, providential.

He wished he'd hear from de Geer. There'd been nothing since their meeting outside Lincoln Center, *while Rachel Stein was dying—or before? After, perhaps? Could he kill a woman and then smoke a cigar?* The man was a lowlife. He could do anything. But if he came up with the Minstrel, then—at last—Sam Ryder could put an end to his relationship with Phillip Bloch, be free of him once and for all.

And if not?

Plausible deniability. That was what would be needed. It wasn't his fault. He didn't know. *I didn't do anything!* Yes, those were the words he needed to be able to say, with credibility. Just in case.

His telephone rang. He tried to ignore it, but the damn ringing persisted. He was alone in the house, mercifully so. Cursing, he snatched up the receiver. "Yes?"

"Lieutenant."

Bloch. "What is it? I asked you not to call here—"

"Cut the bullshit, Sam. How're you coming with the diamond?"

Ryder stiffened, remembering the Dutchman's warning reiterated in the car on Saturday. De Geer would cooperate, he said, on one condition: Ryder was not to mention the Minstrel, Rachel Stein, or the Peperkamps to Bloch. "If you do," he'd said, "I will kill you."

"Sergeant," Ryder said carefully, "I've made careful plans, and I cannot have you interfering. You could ruin everything. Please, just let me handle things on my end. Look—look, I'm taking a chance, all right? Guessing. This stone might not even exist, and if I can't come up with it, I don't want you to blame me. I've told you as much as I have out of courtesy." *And if de Geer finds out…* He refused to consider the possibilities. He was a U.S. senator. De Geer couldn't touch him.

"Bullshit, Lieutenant," Bloch said, laughing at him. "You told me because you knew if you didn't I'd come up there and wring your fucking neck. But did I say I wanted to interfere? Just want to ask you a couple of questions, that's all. Tell me some more about Stein's connection to de Geer."

"What more is there to tell? He betrayed her family and the people who were hiding her."

"Those're the ones I'm interested in. You say Stein told you de Geer pretended to be helping them while they were in hiding, bribing the Germans with diamonds. Where'd he get the diamonds?"

"From a stash the Peperkamps had, I believe. They were careful to keep diamonds that would be used for war purposes out of Nazi hands and offered them only to Germans who wanted them for their personal use, and—" A cold shiver ran up his spine and he stopped, hearing the dead silence on the other end of the receiver.

"What's that name again, Sammy? Peperkamp?"

Damn. Oh, damn it to hell, Ryder thought. Well, it wasn't his fault. Bloch had manipulated him into talking, into dropping the name Peperkamp. In any case, there was nothing the sergeant could do with this knowledge. So what if he knew their name?

"Don't tell de Geer I told you," he said.

"Sure, Sammy. No problem. You think they've got this diamond?"

Ryder said nothing, wishing only that he could be warm and safe and away, far away, from the fear that had gripped him since Phillip Bloch had called three months ago and said he was setting up a temporary camp at Ryder's isolated fishing camp in northwest Florida. There had been nothing Ryder could do about it then or now. Bloch would do as he pleased. The only way to get rid of him—*my only chance!*—was through the Minstrel. It would provide Bloch the means to get a permanent camp, out of Ryder's life. But first he had to get the Minstrel, and to do that, he had to deal with Hendrik de Geer.

"It's about all that makes sense," Bloch said.

Of course it was. The Minstrel's Rough had to be in Peperkamp hands—if it existed. Rachel Stein decidedly did not believe it did. "It's said Hendrik used the Minstrel as collateral to help us," she'd told him in her desperate attempt to get the senator's backing to go after the Dutchman. "But that's nonsense. Where would he get his hands on such a stone? The Minstrel's a myth. Hendrik de Geer has always been out for himself, and he'd promise anyone anything to save himself."

In his own desperation, Ryder had seized on the Minstrel and decided it *had* to exist. It had to. And that the Dutchman could get it for him—could be *made* to get it for him. It was a gamble—an insane gamble, perhaps. But it had to work.

If only he knew where de Geer was now.

"I will come with the stone," the Dutchman had said. "Wait. Do nothing and talk to no one. Otherwise you will answer to me."

The cold shiver had developed into a cold sweat, and Ryder leaned in toward the fire. Who frightened him more? Bloch? De Geer? Lowlifes! His only chance was to play them off against each other.

"I want their names, Lieutenant," Bloch said. "I want to know who they are, where they live, everything."

"I can't!"

"In case you fuck up, Sammy, I want to be able to go after the stone myself. So talk."

"My God." Ryder breathed deeply, sweat pouring down his back even though he was so cold. "Will you promise not to interfere—damn it, Sergeant, will you give me a chance?"

"Sure, Sammy."

Bloch might have just laughed in his face; it would have been no less convincing than this empty promise. But what choice did Ryder have? He knew when he was beaten. If he didn't talk, Bloch would come to Washington. And then what would Ryder do?

"All right," he said stiffly, trying not to sound defeated. "According to Miss Stein, there are four Peperkamps. Johannes Peperkamp, a diamond cutter in Antwerp, is in my opinion the most likely candidate to have or know where to find the Minstrel."

"Johannes Peperkamp, diamond cutter, Antwerp. Sounds good. Go on."

"But he's the main one—"

"And if he doesn't know diddly? Then what? You said there were four. I want the other names."

Ryder shut his eyes, tasting the salt of his sweat on his upper lip. The fire crackled at his feet. "There's a Wilhelmina Peperkamp. She resides in Rotterdam and is a retired civil servant of modest means. I don't believe—"

"That's two. Next."

"She has a sister, Catharina Fall, who lives in New York and runs a bakery. She apparently was willing to corroborate Miss Stein's accusations against de Geer, but now with her—umm—death…" His voice trailed off. *Why* had he brought that up?

"Handy, wasn't it? A loose end we don't have to worry about."

Sinking deeper into the couch, Ryder recalled how Master Sergeant Bloch had never been able to tolerate anything he deemed a loose end. In combat, that compulsion had saved lives. But this was civilian life. Ryder bit down hard on his lower lip, nearly drawing blood, but he told himself it made no sense for Bloch to have killed Rachel Stein or to have had her killed. *It was an accident. You saw how old and frail she was.*

Until now, *frail* had not been a word he had associated with the tough, cynical, and somehow warm-hearted old Hollywood agent.

"That's three then," Bloch said. "Who's number four?"

Ryder didn't move. He opened his eyes, and in the red-orange flames he saw the pale silken hair of Juliana Fall, the dark green eyes, the curve of her breasts. Bloch wouldn't dare touch her. She was too famous, too beautiful. "A young woman," he said hoarsely. "She couldn't possibly know anything about any of this. She's not—"

"For chrissake, her *name*."

"No!"

"Goddamnit, then, I'll find out myself."

"Don't—no, don't. Fall." He put a shaking hand to his mouth, as if somehow it might catch the words as they came out and keep them from Bloch. "Her name is Juliana Fall. She's Catharina Fall's daughter."

"Lives in New York, too?"

"Yes," Ryder hissed.

"Then that's all four."

He could hear Bloch's yawn. "Sergeant, I've been more than fair to you. At least tell me what you plan to do—"

"Sammy, Sammy. I'm going to make sure you don't screw up. Isn't that what I always do?"

Nine

Hendrik de Geer walked along Schupstraat, one of the main streets of Antwerp's busy, highly congested and very wary diamond district. The buildings were mostly unremarkable, but inside were some of the greatest diamond minds and some of the most sophisticated communications and security systems in the world.

The Dutchman knew enough about the code that operated here not to be lulled into a false sense of security. He moved slowly but with apparent purpose, not wanting to attract attention to himself. It was a gray day, cold and damp on the North Sea, and the streets were crowded with diamontaires. Hendrik noticed neither the weather nor his own sense of ambivalence as he walked past a group of men in the distinctive garb of the Hasidim. Many of Belgium's Jews worked in the diamond business. As moneylenders, cutters, and polishers and as a persecuted people, they had dealt with diamonds for centuries. Cutting was one of the few crafts they had been permitted to practice, and as moneylenders they were often asked to exchange diamonds for gold and silver. When forced to flee their homes, they could take the easily portable gems with them, knowing diamonds were valued virtually anywhere and would help them to reestablish themselves. The Holocaust had decimated the twentieth-century diamond industry in Amsterdam and Antwerp, but, although Amsterdam never fully recovered its prewar status, Antwerp had regained its place as the diamond capital of the world. Here again could be found the most highly skilled cleavers, the ones who knew what to do with difficult roughs.

Among them was Johannes Peperkamp, a Gentile, an old man but still a legend in the business. He had knowledge, and he had instinct. No matter what problems a rough presented, he could cut it successfully, and few remembered the rare times the hands of Johannes Peperkamp—or any Peperkamp—had reduced a valuable rough to splinters.

But Johannes was in his seventies now. Age, computers, and lasers were cutting into his business, and Hendrik wasn't surprised to find that his old friend's shop was located in one of Schupstraat's lesser buildings. Security wasn't as tight as it would have been in other buildings, and Hendrik, speaking in Dutch to the Flemish security guard, was quickly permitted to go upstairs. As he mounted the two dingy flights and approached a door with a frosted-glass window, Hendrik felt no change in himself. His heart wasn't pounding. He wasn't sweating. He was doing what had to be done. That was all.

He zipped his jacket halfway. Until now, he hadn't noticed the cold. He sighed at his weakness and pushed open the door.

Johannes Peperkamp was sitting at his ancient desk eating his lunch—bread and cheese and a cup of hot tea. His eyes looked glazed, and he chewed slowly. He hadn't heard Hendrik enter.

Closing the door behind him, Hendrik took a moment to stare. He remembered Johannes as a vibrant and healthy man, gentle in his way, intelligent, already one of the world's premier diamond cleavers. He'd had little choice in the matter. When you were a Peperkamp male, you were expected to be in diamonds. At least in Amsterdam you were for the last four hundred years. After WW II Johannes had taken his business to Antwerp. Now he was the last of the Peperkamp males; Juliana Fall was the only member of the next generation. The Peperkamp diamond tradition would die with her uncle.

So many years gone since he'd last looked into those blue eyes, Hendrik thought, weighing the passage of time. They'd both survived to grow old. It seemed so inconsequential now, more than forty years later. If they'd died during the war, would they have missed so much? He didn't think so. And they'd have died as friends.

Although Hendrik knew not to judge the power and success of anyone involved in diamonds by his surroundings, it seemed Johannes's day had passed. How many diamontaires even knew Johannes Peperkamp was still alive, still working? His shop was small and pathetic. Hendrik remembered the large roughs, the people flowing in and out, the feel of life and success, back in Amsterdam. This place was little more than a small, shabby room. It contained all the paraphernalia of his trade—the lights, wedges, hammers, mallets, saws, loupes, and roughs. A yellowed photograph of Johannes with Harry Winston, which had appeared in *Life* magazine, hung on the wall. The years hadn't worn well on Johannes. Time and technology—computers, lasers—were making him obsolete.

The old cutter swallowed a bite of his bread and cheese and wiped his long fingers with a paper napkin as he started to glance up. "Yes? I'm not expecting—" He spoke in Dutch, but his mouth snapped shut and his piercing eyes fastened on his fellow Dutchman. "Hendrik de Geer."

There was no wonder in the old man's tone, no surprise,

not even any hate. Already he'd reduced Hendrik to a non-entity. At most, a bug crawling across his floor. Hendrik had forgotten how arrogant and unshakable Johannes could be—how he'd looked down his big nose at Hendrik. The de Geers weren't diamond people. Hendrik had grown up on the fringes of that world, not in its midst as Johannes had.

"So you remember me," Hendrik said, although there had been no question in his mind that Johannes would. "I'm honored."

"Don't be." The old cutter set down his sandwich. "None of the memories are good ones."

"Then perhaps your mind isn't as sharp as it once was. We used to skate the canals of Holland together in the winter, before the war, and race bicycles in the summer. Remember, Johannes?" Hendrik was surprised by the sadness in his voice. "Those were fine days, ones not to forget."

Johannes shrugged. In all the years he had known him, Hendrik had never seen Johannes Peperkamp show fear. He would today, unless he was a fool. That was some consolation, Hendrik decided, for this miserable predicament. As much as they'd been friends, a part of him had always wanted to make Johannes sweat.

But for now, the old man continued to chew his lunch, and not even his fingers shook. It was as if he believed there was nothing left Hendrik de Geer could do to him.

"Do you know why I'm here, Johannes?"

He sipped his tea, swallowing. "I'm sure you'll tell me."

There was that tone of cool superiority once more, and moving deeper into the shop, Hendrik recalled fewer moments of friendship and more those of indignation. He'd never been good enough for the Peperkamps. When he was a boy, his mother had tried to tell him that that was all in his head, but he knew better.

Catharina...

Yes, she was different. The others had expected him to

fail, and yet they'd put their trust in him—and he'd done what he'd had to do. As he was now.

He said without drama, "I must have the diamond, Johannes."

The old cutter gestured to his shop. "As you see, I have many diamonds—not so big, perhaps, as in the past, but some fine stones. Take what you want. It makes no difference to me."

"These diamonds don't interest me."

"They don't interest me, either, but they're all I have. I'm an old man, Hendrik. Not very many people bring me the big diamonds anymore." He held up his large, bony hands. "They don't trust these." Then he pointed to his eyes. "Or these."

Johannes spoke without self-pity and shrugged as he resumed drinking his tea. Hendrik moved closer, but the old man looked at him without interest. If he hadn't known Johannes Peperkamp better, Hendrik might have panicked, thinking he'd come to the wrong place.

He took the teacup from the old man and set it down. Nothing in Johannes's expression indicated fear or anger— or even curiosity. *I am nothing, am I, old man?* Hendrik thought, but he refused to let his frustration show. "You know what I want, Johannes."

"To be honest, no, I don't."

"Yes, you do, damn you!"

The old cutter sighed patiently. "Why don't you just tell me, Hendrik?"

"The diamond," Hendrik said. "The Minstrel's Rough."

Johannes laughed derisively and sucked something from his teeth, as if he had nothing better to do. "Don't be ridiculous, Hendrik. I no longer have the Minstrel."

"I don't believe you."

"As you wish."

"Even if you don't have it, you know where it is," Hendrik said, fighting to regain the upper hand. Damn Johannes Peperkamp and his smugness! "You'll get it for me."

"Why would I do that?" With the stubborn self-righteousness that had always infuriated Hendrik, Johannes looked into the younger Dutchman's eyes. "Only once in my seventy-three years have I ever been indiscreet. Never again, Hendrik. Never. It doesn't matter what I know or what I don't know—I will not cooperate with you." He picked up his tea, pursed his thin lips, and took a sip. Peering over the rim of the cup, he said, "You must kill me first."

"Then I wouldn't get what I want, would I?"

Hendrik spoke in a mild tone, pleased with how unperturbed he sounded, and he slowly spun Johannes's swivel chair around. Holding its wooden arms, Hendrik leaned over and searched the beady blue eyes. There was superiority there, all right, and hatred. He'd expected that. But there was also anguish. Sadness. *That* Hendrik hadn't expected. Had Johannes hoped he'd changed? Shaken, Hendrik almost turned away.

"Exactly so," Johannes said. "You wouldn't get what you want. Kill me if you must. It makes no difference. I will not give you the stone."

"You have family, Johannes. What if their lives were in danger?"

"My wife is dead."

Ann. Intelligent, beautiful. She'd been a Jew married to a Gentile, but she'd survived the war—only just. Hendrik had put her out of his mind for forty years. Once more he shoved aside the thought of her, and as he did so, he straightened up.

"Your sisters are still alive." He tried to sound cold and determined, as Senator Ryder had in the car on Saturday night, but he felt the uncertainty churning deep inside him, just as he knew the handsome Ryder had. They were not so different, the foolish senator and himself. They hid their fears behind an air of competence. Would Johannes see through his one-time friend? Hendrik warned himself he was thinking dangerously and went on steadily, "Wilhelmina lives in Rotterdam, and Catharina is in New York. Juliana, your niece, has an apartment on Central Park West. I know where they are, Johannes. I can find them."

Now, he thought. Now the fear would come. Hendrik waited, but the old diamond cutter merely wiped his mouth with his napkin and climbed slowly to his feet.

"Catharina you would never harm, and Wilhelmina would cheerfully welcome the opportunity to slit your cowardly throat."

He sounded slightly amused at the thought, but Hendrik couldn't contradict him—they both knew Willie Peperkamp. If her older brother-cooperated with Hendrik de Geer to protect her, she would only be annoyed.

"And Juliana's too famous," Johannes went on. "There'd be so much publicity if you touched her. Too risky. However—" The old man took his jacket from a peg on the wall next to his desk and shrugged his bony frame into it. "However, it's been a long, long time, Hendrik. You could have come for the Minstrel anytime, but you didn't. That means there are others involved. Someone else has guessed you've seen the Minstrel and is twisting that arm of yours that twists so easily. To whom did you promise the stone this time? Never mind, it makes no difference." Johannes gestured politely toward the door. "Shall we go?"

Catharina's Bake Shop had closed for the evening. In its gleaming kitchen, its proprietor rolled out pastry at an island counter. She patted the dough carefully, lovingly with the strong, broad hands, their cuticles and lines caked with flour and drying dough, the nails blunt and tough.

Juliana watched silently from the kitchen door. She'd

come straight from the Club Aquarian and had used her key to enter the quiet, darkened shop. It was silly to be thinking about her mother's hands, but she couldn't stop herself. They were so unlike her own. Juliana had long, slender fingers, and although she kept her nails cut short, they were always manicured. Twice a day she massaged a European cream into them. They were strong hands. To be a pianist, they had to be. But suddenly she envied her mother's wide palms and thick fingers. If Juliana had been born with Peperkamp hands, everything might have been different.

"Hello, Mother."

Catharina didn't look up. "Yes."

She hissed the yes, clipping it off. Usually she just said, "Yaa," drawing out a long, broad *a*. She pounded the dough, her usual care and gentleness abruptly gone.

"Mother, is something wrong?"

"Nothing that concerns you."

"Mother, talk to me—please. Look, a reporter's been asking me about your friend Rachel Stein. I know she was with Senator Ryder on Saturday at Lincoln Center. Ryder was also supposed to meet with a Dutchman by the name of Hendrik de Geer. Have you ever heard of him?"

Catharina sprinkled flour on the wooden rolling pin and slammed it down on the dough. She had yet to glance up, to see her daughter in her lavender hair and raccoon coat. She was the rock of Juliana's existence, her stability, the one thing she could count on in her frenzied life not to change, and something was desperately wrong. More than a visit from a friend she hadn't seen in a long time, more than a daughter asking too many questions. Juliana had never seen her mother so withdrawn and uncommunicative.

"Mother?"

"You should be in Vermont, Juliana. You need rest."

"I wish you'd talk to me. Look, don't I have a right to know what's going on?"

Still not looking up, Catharina banged the rolling pin on the counter.

"Mother, what is it?"

"Rachel," she said at last. "She's dead."

"Oh, my God—I'm so sorry. What happened?"

Still Catharina didn't look up, still she continued to work. "She fell outside Lincoln Center and hit her head and died. It was in the papers this morning." The words came out machine-gun style, but more heavily accented than was usual for her. "The police say it was an accident. That Rachel slipped on the snow and ice."

Juliana worked at controlling her breathing, a relaxation technique she often used before a performance. "How awful," she said. But something inside her told her not to believe it. Did Stark know? Had the bastard been playing games with her?

With the top of a bent wrist, Catharina brushed wisps of white-blond hair off her pale, sweaty forehead. A bit of flour stuck in her eyebrow. The tight anger seemed to disappear all at once, and Juliana watched the pain and grief descend, filling the soft eyes with tears and drawing out the lines in the attractive face. Her lower lip began to tremble, and then her hands. She quickly began to smooth the flattened, ruined dough with her fingers.

"Go to Vermont," she said. Finally, she looked at Juliana but didn't even see the hair or the coat. "Please."

"Mother, what aren't you telling me? I wish you'd be honest—"

"I am being honest!" Her head shot up, and more curls fell into her face, but the tears hadn't spilled out from her eyes. They shone in the dim light. "I've lost a good friend, Juliana. I don't want to burden you with my sadness."

"That's bullshit, Mother," Juliana said quietly.

Catharina picked up the rolling pin.

"You just want to get rid of me. You don't want me in town. Why not? Is it because of what happened to Rachel?"

"Don't be silly." Catharina tried to smile, but there was too much fatigue and sadness—and terror—in her face. "Rachel's death was a tragic accident." Her voice cracked. "She was a childhood friend, Juliana, *my* friend. I know I'm not being myself, but—her death has nothing to do with you."

"Why did she come to New York?"

Catharina sighed. "To see me."

"And Senator Ryder?"

"I know nothing about that. Rachel knew many powerful people, including senators. Now she's dead. Whatever business she had with Senator Ryder is none of our affair. Take your vacation, Juliana. You look tired."

"You hadn't seen Rachel Stein in a long time, and she shows up in New York just like that?"

"It's easy to lose track of people as you get older."

"Mother—"

Catharina abandoned her ruined dough. "That's the end of it, Juliana. It's finished. Did you see I made chicken pies today?" She brushed back a fallen curl. "Something new. Take one with you to Vermont."

"Mother, damn it."

But under the best of circumstances Catharina Fall was closemouthed—discreet, she called it. At the moment, however, Juliana wasn't sure she had much room to criticize. She had never told her mother about Uncle Johannes's visit backstage seven years ago, about his gift—if one wanted to call it that—of the Minstrel's Rough. Her mother knew the Minstrel existed, knew the four-hundred-year-old tradition. All the Peperkamps did. But Uncle Johannes had advised her not to mention the Minstrel to her mother, and she never had.

My God, where will this end?

"What about Father? Does he know any of this?"

A dumb question, she thought. Catharina Peperkamp Fall told her husband as little as she did her daughter—unless he'd been feigning innocence all these years.

"Know any of what?" Catharina countered. "There's nothing to know."

"Well," Juliana said in a falsely cheerful voice, "I suppose the Dutch don't have their reputation for stubbornness without foundation."

"Go to Vermont," her mother said. "And wash your hair first."

Of course she wouldn't ask why it was lavender to begin with. Juliana said goodnight. On her way out, she didn't take a chicken pie.

Ten

Matthew took the shuttle back to Washington and headed straight to the *Gazette*. It wasn't the first time he'd shown up in a newsroom after hours, but his colleagues on the *Gazette* didn't know that. He ignored their curious looks and went over to Aaron Ziegler's desk.

"Burning the midnight oil, Ziegler?"

The young reporter looked up at Stark and nodded, his expression betraying a mix of eagerness and nervousness. "I've got your information. I didn't tell Feldie, but she knows I'm doing some research for you."

"She around?"

"No."

"Good. Give me what you've got."

"I haven't written anything up yet."

"That's okay. Just spit it out."

Ziegler, his rep tie loosened, consulted a steno book on his neat desk. Stark remained standing. He didn't know what to do to make the kid less nervous, so he didn't do anything.

"The world's largest uncut diamond naturally varies from time to time because it doesn't stay uncut for very long—unless you're talking about the Minstrel's Rough." He glanced up, his eyes questioning Matthew.

Stark said, "I don't know if I am or not. Give me what you've got."

"Well, it sounds pretty far-fetched."

"Don't worry about that. If it's not what I'm looking for, I'll just keep digging."

"All right. Supposedly 'the world's largest and most mysterious uncut diamond' is the Minstrel's Rough."

"Supposedly?"

"That's just it—no one's ever been able to verify the thing even exists. It's been *rumored* to exist for the last four or five hundred years, and there have been a number of unconfirmed sightings of it. Nothing can be substantiated, but I gather it's not supposed to be. Part of the legend—the mystery—is that the Minstrel can never be proven to exist. That way no matter how big the current biggest uncut diamond is, people will always wonder if there's one bigger."

"The Minstrel."

"Right."

"Sounds like a lot of bullshit, Ziegler."

"I know. But the mystery surrounding the Minstrel adds to its symbolism. Supposedly it's in the hands of caretakers who'll never cut it, in remembrance of those who have suffered persecution and hatred. In other words, it's a reminder that no story is more important than human life. Which brings me to the Minstrel's 'alleged' potential as a cut and polished stone. Not only is it huge, but it's an ice white."

"What's that?"

"The highest grade of diamond, as close to pure and colorless as possible. If the Minstrel does exist and ever is found and cut, it could be worth millions. Over the centuries there've been countless sightings and loads of attempts to track it down, but still no Minstrel. But the material I've read treats it strictly as legend."

Matthew's thoughts were already racing. Just who the

hell was Sam Ryder planning to buy off with those millions? Because Sam, of course, was enough of a dumbass to go after a mythical diamond. The Weaze was right about that, no doubt. "Shit," he muttered, then sighed. "Okay, Ziegler, thanks. Anything on the other business?"

"That was considerably easier," Aaron said, looking more relaxed, if not at ease. "Rachel Stein came from Amsterdam. She was a member of an old diamond-cutting family that was wiped out during the Holocaust. She and her brother Abraham were the only survivors. Pretty grim stuff. I have a lot on her life in the U.S., but you were just interested in the Dutch connection, right? There wasn't much. They were hidden by a Dutch family through much of the war but were discovered in its last months and deported to the death camps. As I said, there wasn't a lot of detail. As for Juliana Fall—there was a nice, fat folder on her in the library."

"I'll bet," Stark said.

"As you said, the Dutch connection comes from her mother, whose maiden name was Peperkamp. She grew up in Amsterdam. There was a file on her—a review of her bakeshop. I went ahead and checked under Peperkamp. You're not going to believe this, but there's a diamond cutter named Johannes Peperkamp."

Here a Peperkamp, there a Peperkamp. "Go on."

"There wasn't much recent stuff. He started out in Amsterdam and moved to Antwerp after World War II, and he's cut a number of famous large diamonds, including the Breath of Angels, which is now in the Smithsonian. He's the last of the Peperkamp cutters, who apparently got into the business in the sixteenth century when they provided safe haven for Jewish diamond merchants fleeing the Inquisition in Antwerp and Lisbon, which until that time were the principal diamond cities."

"Any relation to Catharina or Juliana Fall?"

"None mentioned, but that's not surprising. Juliana would have been just a kid when most of the material in the folder was published."

"Any mention of Hendrik de Geer?"

"No. I couldn't find anything on him."

"Any connection between this Johannes Peperkamp or Juliana and Catharina Fall and Rachel Stein?"

"None that I could find."

"Okay. Thanks, Aaron. I appreciate it."

Ziegler beamed. "Should I keep stalling Feldie?"

"By all means."

Matthew went for coffee, pure rotgut but hot, and sat in the cafeteria for an hour talking sports with a couple of reporters. The Caps were playing the Bruins at home and losing in the third period. He wondered if Juliana Fall had ever been to a hockey game. They could go together, and she could get up on the organ and play the national anthem. Hell, that'd kill her reputation faster than getting caught as J.J. Pepper. Did she even know what the inside of a hockey arena looked like? He doubted it. Had she ever eaten a hotdog from a concession stand? Had she ever eaten a hotdog at all? Probably called them frankfurters.

He pulled himself up short, got a refill, and headed back downstairs.

His telephone was ringing. He picked it up. "What?"

"Oh. You are there."

He recognized the liquid voice instantly and dropped into his chair. "Shall I call you Juliana or J.J.?"

"Usually I'm called Miss Fall—or Ms. Fall."

"Still mad, huh?"

"That's irrelevant. Why didn't you tell me Rachel Stein was dead?"

"Because you would have said, 'Rachel who?' I described her to you, if you'll recall, and you said you didn't know her. I didn't think there was any point in telling you she was dead."

"You were trying to trap me," Juliana said. "Besides, you didn't believe me anyway."

"No, I didn't."

"I might have told you more if you'd been honest with me."

He felt himself grinning. "And I might have told you more if you'd been honest with me. Want to talk now?"

"There's nothing to say."

"Then why did you call?"

"I only met Rachel Stein once, but I—well, I want to know more about this story you're half working on."

"Why?"

He heard her take a breath, controlling herself; he irritated the hell out of her. "Curiosity, I guess," she said stiffly.

"More interesting than painting your hair purple and dressing up in nutty clothes to play jazz? You're bored, Juliana Fall, and I've got better things to do than to unbore you." Then again…he thought, but left it at that.

"Do you know why Rachel Stein was with Senator Ryder on Saturday?" she asked, her voice cool now, distant and very calculating.

"No, do you?"

"Of course not. You and Senator Ryder know each other, don't you? Why were you at the concert?"

"I like music," Stark said. The woman was holding back on him, which was one thing. But holding back and expecting him to talk was another, and it pissed him off. "Let me ask you something, Ms. Fall. Are you any relation to a diamond cutter by the name of Johannes Peperkamp?"

Not a sound came out of her. Matthew leaned back, listening. Finally she said, even more cool, even more distant and calculating, "Why do you ask?"

"Curiosity, I guess," he said, mimicking her.

He'd pushed her too far. She called him a bastard and hung up. He'd memorized her phone number when he went to her apartment, and he reached for the phone to call her back. But he stopped himself. What the hell was he doing? Juliana Fall had no business getting mixed up in anything that involved Otis Raymond and Sam Ryder. She was a pianist, for God's sake. Let her get her kicks out of keeping Shuji from finding out about J.J. Pepper and Len Wetherall from finding out about Juliana Fall.

He put on his coat and went home.

Wilhelmina Peperkamp scrubbed a batch of clay pots in her tiny kitchen, oblivious to the bright morning winter sun screaming through her window. Her apartment was on the first floor of a restored seventeenth-century building in Delftshaven, where she had lived for the last forty years. Literally Delft's harbor, it was the quietest, most picturesque section of Rotterdam and virtually the only one that had escaped the 1940 German bombings. The rebuilt Rotterdam was pleasant enough—likeable, efficient, and convenient. But it was the cobblestone streets and centuries-old buildings of Delftshaven Wilhelmina had grown to love.

She was elbow-deep in water and had just begun to have some success with the stubborn mildew on one of her pots when her telephone began ringing. She considered not answering, but she received so few calls she changed her mind. Grumbling to herself, she put down her stiff wire brush and wiped her hands on her apron as she picked up the phone. "Yes?"

"Willie…"

She recognized the soft, unhappy voice at once. "Catharina, what's wrong?"

"I'm sorry, Willie, I don't mean to sound so upset—"

"Never mind," Wilhelmina responded abruptly. She had

spoken in Dutch, Catharina in English, automatically, as
if it never occurred to her to speak in her native language.
Ordinarily Wilhelmina would have remarked on her sister's
thorough Americanization. This time she didn't. Catharina
rarely called, least of all when something was bothering
her, and Wilhelmina opted to speak in her own excellent
English. "What is it, Catharina?"

"It's Rachel—Rachel Stein. She's dead, Willie. It was
in the papers here."

Rachel. Even after all these years, Wilhelmina thought,
I can still see her lively, tiny face and the expressive eyes
that had had no effect whatever on an officer of the Green
Police. They were bastards, all of them. Nazis, *Dutch*
Nazis. So filled with hate. That one had kicked Rachel like
a dog and dragged her away—and Wilhelmina, too. But
that was of no consequence; she'd failed to protect Rachel,
and the Nazis had taken her away.

Now she was dead.

Wilhelmina reached for a cotton towel and dried her
dripping forearms, cradling the phone between her shoulder and chin. She looked down at her hands, red and rough
with work and age. They had never been pretty hands; she
had never been a pretty woman. But her plainness hadn't
bothered her; she had other qualities.

"Willie?"

"I'm here."

Her eyes remained tearless. She hadn't cried in many,
many years, although she had lost many friends. It was the
worst part of growing old. Slowly, she sat at her small
table where already a half-dozen of her clay pots were
lined up, scrubbed and empty.

"I'm sorry to have told you so abruptly," Catharina said.
"I know it's shocking."

"How did she die?"

"She fell on the ice—an accident, they say."

Wilhelmina was instantly alert. "You have doubts?"

"I don't know. I—I don't know what to think."

"Tell me everything, Catharina."

Haltingly, Catharina related the events since Rachel's appearance at the bakeshop for tea, requesting corroboration of her story to Senator Ryder. Although she was alone, Wilhelmina refrained from showing any visible reaction to what she was hearing. Not since the winter of 1944—*Hongerwinter,* the Winter of Hunger—had she and Catharina discussed Hendrik de Geer or even spoken his name. There was no need. He was a man neither would ever forget. Wilhelmina had tried.

"I'm probably overreacting," Catharina said. "But I don't know. It's late here. I haven't been able to sleep. Juliana came by the shop earlier, and she's asking so many questions. She—she's asked me about Hendrik. I wouldn't talk to her, I… Willie, how can I tell her? This doesn't concern her! It can't touch her—I won't let it!"

"You've never told her about Amsterdam?" Wilhelmina tried to keep the condemnation out of her tone, but it was there; she could hear it herself. And of course Catharina would be listening for it.

"No, I did not. Don't interfere, Willie. What I do or don't tell my daughter is between us."

"You were the one who called me," Wilhelmina pointed out, her sister's agitation all that kept her tone mild.

"I know! I thought… I don't know now what I thought, just that you have a right to know about Rachel, I suppose. Maybe I thought you could help." Catharina paused and gave a small, bitter laugh. "I always do, don't I? Nothing's changed. Oh, Willie, I'm not blaming you. God knows I haven't changed, either. When something goes wrong, who do I call? My big sister. I *want* you to be strong, Willie, I expect it, just as you expect me always to crumple and do as you say."

"It's all right," Wilhelmina said, feeling tired. Catharina had Adrian, Juliana her piano, Johannes his diamonds. What did she have? Her pots of flowers. Well, she wouldn't feel sorry for herself. Her flowers were enough.

"I'm probably being silly," Catharina said, breathing deeply, nervously, and Wilhelmina felt her younger sister's uncertainty, her dread of censure. Too many times she'd had big sister Willie tell her she was being foolish. "When I saw Hendrik at Lincoln Center, at first I thought it must be my imagination."

"Have you ever imagined seeing him before?"

"No, of course not."

Wilhelmina had.

"It was so strange seeing him again," Catharina went on, calmer now. "He's the same."

Wilhelmina snorted. "Did you think he'd be any different?"

"I suppose not. I—I can't believe he had anything to do with Rachel's death. It must have been an accident."

"Perhaps."

"I'm not afraid, Willie, I wouldn't want you to think that—not for myself, anyway."

"For Juliana?"

"Yes."

Wilhelmina had to smile at her sister's eternal naiveté. "Catharina, please. Hendrick would never hurt Juliana."

"You sound so sure."

"I am. Don't you see? Juliana's your daughter. Hendrik could no more hurt her than he could you."

Catharina cried out in surprise and disbelief. "But he did hurt me!"

"Not in any way he would understand. In the mind of Hendrik de Geer, he saved you. That's all he knows."

"Willie…"

Her hands were trembling, but she blamed age rather than emotion. "Call me if there's anything more."

"What should I do about Juliana?"

"If I were you, I would tell her everything."

"No."

"But, of course, I'm not you. Just—how do you say it? Lay low, I believe. Do nothing. Juliana will stop asking questions soon enough. Now that Rachel is dead and any threat against him eliminated, Hendrik will simply disappear. He must be very good at that by now."

"You really think he will?"

"Why wouldn't he?"

"Because he was at Lincoln Center on Saturday. If he was going to disappear, wouldn't he have done it then?"

Not if he came to kill Rachel he wouldn't, Wilhelmina thought. But Hendrik had never been one to do his own killing. Catharina had a point—one, of course, Wilhelmina had already considered.

"Unless you want to go after Hendrik yourself, Catharina, there's nothing else you can do but pretend you never saw him on Saturday."

"How—how could I go after him myself?"

"That's something you must answer for yourself. I cannot."

"I have to go, before I wake Adrian."

"You've not told him what's been happening?"

"Of course not. Goodbye, Willie."

Wilhelmina was appalled, but she said goodbye and hung up. She made herself some café au lait, ignoring the sinkful of flowerpots. Hendrik de Geer. She'd hoped he was dead, although she'd never believed it. She took her coffee into the living room and sat on her chair by the window, watching her narrow, picturesque street. She missed the pots of begonias that had stood on her windowsill. They'd all become diseased and died. Perhaps it was an omen.

"No matter," she said aloud, accustomed to talking to herself after so many years of living alone. "They were old enough to die."

Johannes Peperkamp stood on the deck of the old cargo ship and looked out at the busy Amsterdam harbor. It was still early, very cool, and the ship was an old one that smelled of bad fish and rancid oil. He remembered how he'd dreamed of being a sailor when he was a boy, and home sick for days with influenza. While he was recovering, his father had sat with him and filled his head with another dream, the legend of the Minstrel's Rough. The Minstrel had made the Peperkamp diamond tradition real for Johannes, something that was exciting and mysterious. For a long time now, that excitement and mystery had been absent. Diamonds were work. They provided a living. That was all.

He had been looking out at the city since dawn, watching it slowly rise out of the darkness into the new day. Not since Ann's death had he been back to Amsterdam. For both of them, it had been a city of painful memories. But she'd wanted her ashes brought to the *Jodenhoek,* the old Jewish quarter, and he'd acceded to her wish. During the sixteenth century, thousands of Jews had fled to Amsterdam for its tolerance and religious freedom. With them, they'd brought diamonds and their knowledge of the gems. They were predominantly Sephardic Jews escaping persecution in Lisbon and Antwerp, and their diamond money had helped finance the Dutch East India Company. With it, Amsterdam could establish its own route to India and become the main European port of entry for diamonds. The Netherlands' golden age followed, and it became for a time the major seafaring nation of the world.

In 1940, Nazi Germany invaded, violating Dutch neutrality, imposing and encouraging intolerance and hatred.

After four hundred Jewish men were rounded up, beaten and deported in early 1941, the Dutch responded with a general strike. The furious *Reichskommissar,* Dr. Arthur Seyss-Inquart, the Viennese attorney who'd engineered the *Anschluss* of Austria with the German Third Reich, crushed quickly and brutally crushed the strike. Resistance moved underground. Before the Allies liberated all of The Netherlands in the spring of 1945, seventy-five percent of its Jewish population—one hundred thousand people—had been killed.

Ann had been one who lived. A part of her, at least.

The old cutter's eyes filled with unbidden tears. How happy they'd been before the war! And even after, when they'd still had each other. Now he felt so tired. The brisk morning air didn't penetrate his fatigue as a kaleidoscope of images from the past spun around him. Perhaps Wilhelmina was right—he should have killed Hendrik de Geer when he'd had the opportunity, before, in Amsterdam. But he'd been unable to believe Hendrik had actually betrayed them. Wilhelmina had accused her brother of being overly sentimental. Perhaps she was right about that, too. Hendrik had been his friend.

Hendrik, Hendrik…damn you, why?

Blinking back the tears, Johannes pictured his niece, so young, so beautiful, so talented. He'd seen Juliana just twice, for brief visits, since Delftshaven seven years ago. Neither had mentioned the Minstrel's Rough.

I should never have given it to her, he thought, ashamed. At the time, he'd felt himself growing old, felt keenly the recent loss of his wife, the knowledge that there was no one to carry on the Minstrel tradition. He'd decided it was his duty to pass the legendary rough on to Juliana, to let her choose the course of its future. A cowardly way out, perhaps. Forty years ago, Catharina had begged him to toss it into the sea. From the moment she first saw the diamond, she'd hated it. She always would. The tradition meant nothing to her. It had been soiled by Amsterdam. By Hendrik de Geer's betrayal.

Perhaps he should have listened to her as well.

He became aware he was no longer alone on the deck, but he neither looked around nor changed position. Hendrik left him alone much of the time, because, after all, Johannes was an old man and what could he do? He'd considered throwing himself overboard into the icy waters of the canal but realized his suicide would accomplish nothing. Hendrik would only find another way to get hold of the Minstrel. He would go to his sisters…eventually to Juliana. No, the best Johannes could hope for was to buy time for the others—to give them a chance to find out he was missing, to figure out what was happening, and to take precautions. For once, he appreciated the careful, suspicious mind of the older of his two sisters. Wilhelmina would guess what was going on. She would act.

So he would wait, he thought, and looked up into the cold face of Hendrik de Geer.

"You look tired, Johannes," the younger Dutchman said.

The old diamond cutter shrugged. "I'm old. I get tired."

"I know you, Johannes, perhaps even better than you know yourself." Hendrik pulled his watch cap down over his ears. Despite the sharp wind, Johannes wore neither hat nor gloves. "You haven't given up. You're still trying to think of a way out of this."

Johannes turned back to the water, saying nothing. What was there to say? Hendrik did know him.

"There is no way." The younger Dutchman's tone was curiously quiet. "We're caught between two opposing sides, as we were before."

"As you were, Hendrik," Johannes replied, aware his one-time friend was referring to the war, when the Dutch had tried to remain neutral in the face of German aggression, as they had successfully in the first World War. "I was against the Nazis from the beginning. I was never noncommittal. You, Hendrik—you have always been just for yourself."

"Perhaps you're right." There was no self-condemnation in his tone, only acceptance—resignation. "But that doesn't change anything. You know that getting the Minstrel won't be enough. You'll have to cut it as well, and you're thinking, ah-ha, this is my chance. I can make the wrong cut, use too much pressure, whatever is necessary to render the Minstrel worthless. And you think that will be the end of it. But it won't be, Johannes. As you said, I'm not doing this on my own. Me, I would kill you for the trouble, maybe, and move on, cut my losses. You know that's my way. But the men I work for aren't like me. They believe in vengeance, and they don't like loose ends."

Johannes sniffed. "That's not my concern."

"It is, Johannes. Think of your sisters. Think of your niece."

Johannes turned to the man he had once called his most trusted friend, and he felt a tug of emotion, in spite of everything. What had happened to turn Hendrik into this? He had aged, his skin weathering, marred by the brown spots of age, lines cutting deep into his face, muscles sagging, although not as much as in other men of seventy. But in Hendrik de Geer, always so strong and agile and fierce in Johannes's memory, the signs of advancing years were a particular shock—a reminder of how long ago Amsterdam had been, of how young Hendrik had been. Johannes thought suddenly: had they all asked too much of him? But no. There was no excuse. Much more had been asked of even younger men.

"And what about you, Hendrik?" Johannes said. "Have you thought of them?"

"Yes. You called my bluff in Antwerp, Johannes. You know I'd never hurt them. If I were as ruthless as the men

I've worked for during the past forty years, none of you would be around for me to worry about. I'd have the Minstrel myself instead of being forced to get it for someone else. But I've never bothered with it. I do think about your sisters and your niece—and of you, too, my friend."

"And as usual you believe everything will work out because you want it to. You're an optimist, and you're selfish. You'll do whatever you have to do to save your own skin."

The cold, blue eyes of the younger Dutchman held Johannes's a moment, and they might have shown doubt, could have, but Hendrik turned away, his expression grim. "Johannes, understand me—I had no choice."

"No, Hendrik, you made your choice."

"I wasn't the one who told you about the Minstrel. I've kept the secret since Amsterdam. Achh, never mind. Just get me the stone, Johannes. Cut it for me. Let me handle the rest. If you cooperate, nothing will happen to Wilhelmina, Catharina, or Juliana. I promise you."

"I believed your promises once." The older Dutchman turned away, refusing to look at Hendrik. "Never again."

"It's Catharina I worry about, more than Willie or Juliana," Hendrick said quietly, staring, as Johannes did, out at the city of their birth. Like Venice, low-lying Amsterdam was built on pilings. As boys, they'd played together on the canals that drain the city. "Juliana is a pianist, in the public eye, which should help protect her, and Willie's as tough as anyone I've ever encountered. She can take care of herself. But Catharina's not a survivor. You were a fool, Johannes, to have given her the diamond in Amsterdam."

"It was her choice."

"But she was a child! She didn't understand."

"Don't underestimate her," Johannes said, but he could hear the sudden despair in his voice. The unbearable sadness. He would never see his sister again. He knew it.

For a long time, neither man spoke.

"In most things, it's true, I take care of myself first," Hendrik said at length. "I've always been that way."

"Not always, Hendrik."

"Yes, Johannes, always. When we were boys, you took no notice—and it never mattered then. What harm could I do? Little Hendrik with the bright blue eyes and curly blond hair. I was harmless. But during the war, you finally saw what I am. I know you don't trust me—God knows I've given you enough reason not to—but in this you must." He pulled the old cutter's arm and made the Dutchman look at him. "Do you understand, Johannes? *You must.* I repeat. If you do as I say, if we act quickly, nothing will happen to your sisters or to your niece."

"You promise?" There was no hope in Johannes's voice, only sarcasm and resignation. Hendrik de Geer would never change.

"You *must* get me the Minstrel."

"Why don't you tell your people I threw it into the sea?"

"Because they wouldn't take my word for it. The Minstrel presents too important an opportunity for them to pass up without being positive that it's lost. Johannes, if you know anything, know now that I'm telling you the truth."

Johannes lifted his bony shoulders in an impassive shrug, feeling the wind slice through his jacket, his shirt, his very soul. He couldn't remember ever feeling so cold. "It's there," he said, looking out at the city skyline. "In Amsterdam. We have only to go to my safe-deposit box and get it. I told you."

"I hope so," Hendrik said.

For a moment, Johannes could sense the weariness in him and suddenly wondered if he might be wrong after all. Perhaps Hendrik, too, was tired of the sparring, the memories, the grief, the hatred. Was it too much to forgive? But, no, Johannes thought, I mustn't be sentimental; I mustn't imbue Hendrik with my own values and morals. Hendrik de Geer would never tire of the games he played with people's lives for his own advantage. He would never tire of believing in himself, believing he could involve his friends in his schemes, put them into danger, and everything would work out because he wanted it to.

"Trust me, my friend," the aging mercenary, the one-time friend, said softly, leaving the deck as silently as he'd come.

Johannes welcomed being alone. He continued to stare at the water and looked out toward the west, toward the sea, thinking about its seeming infinity, and in that he found comfort.

Hendrik de Geer drank straight from the bottle of good Dutch gin—*jenever*—in his dirty cabin. He liked to drink alone, preferred it. He'd never really been a lush: too dangerous, given his lifestyle. There were lost days, of course, but generally speaking, in drinking, as in everything else, he was a man of supreme self-control. He knew exactly how much he could consume without endangering himself.

Yet now he wanted to finish off the bottle, and perhaps another. He wanted oblivion.

How could I have let this happen?

Boyhood friend, lifelong foe, premier diamond cleaver, old man. Whatever he had been and whatever he was, Johannes Peperkamp no longer had the Minstrel's Rough.

It wasn't in Amsterdam. This trip was an act of desperation—a ruse. The Minstrel was not here. There was no safe-deposit box.

Hendrik moaned aloud. "What am I to do?"

Run…

It was his first impulse. Always his first impulse.

He gulped the gin and rose from his chair, stumbling as he made his way to his bunk. His eyes brimmed with hot, worthless tears, blinding his vision but not the images that burned in his head.

Catharina tearing at his sleeve, screaming, "No, no, no!"…the unearthly emptiness of the house…the smug looks of the Green Police when Hendrik had confronted them.

Images. Memories. But what was done was done. That the Steins and the Peperkamps had been captured by the Nazis wasn't his fault. He had been cheated—lied to!

And yet he hated himself, now more than ever before, with desperation and anger, without hope. The cool detachment of recent years was gone. He knew he couldn't change. Johannes was right. As always, Hendrik thought he could handle everything. Make everyone happy. Get the stone, get Ryder off the hook with Bloch, maintain his own position with Bloch, keep the Peperkamps out of it. He'd never considered the possibility that Johannes wouldn't have the Minstrel's Rough.

Hendrik swore fiercely but broke off when a young deckhand rushed into the cabin. "It's the old man—something's wrong."

The Dutchman threw down the gin and moved quickly, but when he got to the deck, Johannes Peperkamp was lying on his back, ashen and unconscious. The sharp, cold wind gusted, but the old man made no attempt to get out of it.

"My God!" Hendrik felt a faint pulse in Johannes's neck and tore open the old cutter's jacket and shirt. "My friend, don't die now. It won't help either of us."

He pounded on Johannes's chest and screamed to the deckhand, a red-faced boy, and together they administered cardiopulmonary resuscitation, Hendrik continuing to scream orders.

"It's no use," the deckhand cried, tired and repulsed. He'd never touched a dying man before.

"Keep going!"

"I'm cold—"

"Damn you, there's still a pulse!"

The boy sat back on his knees, frightened. They'd picked up Hendrik in Antwerp—he was an old friend of the captain's—and the boy had steered clear of him. "He's not going to make it."

Hendrik gave the boy a fierce look and said in a low, deadly voice, "Keep going or I'll kill you. I can do it."

"You're crazy," the deckhand said, but he kept going.

It was dawn, and a pinkish light glowed over Central Park. Juliana sat at her piano. It was quiet in her apartment; there was no music on the rack. She rolled up the sleeves of her flannel nightgown and shut her eyes.

Behind her, the aquarium bubbled. She could hear herself breathe.

She had tried to call Uncle Johannes in Antwerp. He wasn't at his shop or his apartment. She didn't know where else he could be.

She had resisted the temptation to call her mother at the bakeshop. She would be there, baking cookies. *Speculaas.* Dutch spice cookies. For Christmas.

Juliana's fingers found the keyboard. They brushed the cool ivory.

She played.

Something, nothing. She didn't know what. Her fingers were her only cues. They knew the right keys, the right phrasing. Her mind wasn't involved. It didn't matter, not here, not alone. Everything blended together. Scales, arpeggios. Beethoven, Schoenberg. Eubie Blake, Duke Ellington. Music poured out of her, uncontrolled, and filled the room.

The sound ended the silence and the bad thoughts.

When you have bad thoughts, her mother used to say when Juliana was small and woke up crying from her nightmares, you should try to think of something else.

Something happy. Imagine yourself at a picnic in the country with your father and me. Picking wildflowers. Playing in the stream.

Think happy thoughts.

Repress.

It was always easier to do at the piano.

She played until she hurt, and when she stopped, tears and sweat poured down her face and her back and between her legs, and her muscles ached, and she didn't know how long she'd been at it. Hours? Minutes?

The first bright light of morning shone over Central Park. She went over to the couch and sat where Matthew Stark had sat and watched the street below fill with people. She would remain upstairs, alone, playing piano and talking to her fish.

Thinking happy thoughts.

Eleven

"Stark—shit, man, I was hoping you wouldn't be in." Weasel's voice was low and nervous over the telephone. "Thought maybe you'd be a step ahead of me, you know?"

Matthew held the phone with one hand, his forehead with the other. He'd drunk a few too many beers last night during the last period of the hockey game, trying to figure out what the hell to do about his promise to Weasel. What did he have to work with? A gorgeous flake of a piano player. A diamond that maybe existed, and then again maybe didn't. A screwup of a United States senator that only some warped sense of obligation to Weasel kept Matthew from going to see and ask some questions. A Dutchman who might already have exited the scene. A dead Hollywood agent. A couple of Peperkamps.

And Weasel himself. A half-dead former door gunner who'd been able to hit eighty-four targets with ninety-six bullets but still didn't know that the Sam Ryders of the world didn't need his help.

What he had to work with, Stark had decided, was zip. But some ingrained, persistent item in his code of honor had flipped on, and he knew he couldn't walk away and just let events take their course. He'd tried to call Juliana

Fall late, after the hockey game, to say he was sorry for needling her and charm her into telling him whatever it was she wasn't telling him. He'd gotten her goddamn message machine, the golden voice saying she couldn't come to the phone right now. Drinking his final beer, he'd wondered what she was doing, who she was with tonight. He'd conjured up an image of her, pale blond hair flowing over her raccoon coat, a delicious mix of J.J. Pepper, jazz pianist, and Juliana Fall, concert pianist. A mix that didn't exist. She was one or the other, not both, maybe not either.

He hadn't left a message.

Now he was back at the *Gazette,* avoiding Feldie and wondering if maybe the best way to keep Otis Raymond alive was to do nothing. Tell the little jackass to crawl back into his hole and stay there. To live, damn it.

"You know I'm never a step ahead of you," Matthew said now, aware Weasel would love that. "What's up?"

"You make any progress on the diamond?"

"No."

"Shit, Stark, maybe you have lost it."

Matthew took no offense. "Whoever said I had anything to lose?"

"I do, buddy," Otis Raymond replied, confidence creeping back into his voice. One thing he knew: he could count on Matt Stark. Hadn't they survived as a scout pilot and scout gunner, part of a "pink team," when so damn few did? "Hey—I ain't got time for bullshit. Got a pencil? Jot this one down. Johannes Peperkamp, diamond cutter, Antwerp. I don't have the spelling."

"I don't need it," Matthew said, swearing to himself. "Where'd you hear that name?"

"Things starting to hang together, huh, Stark?"

"No, things are not starting to hang together, goddamnit." His head was pounding; from now on, he'd limit himself to two beers. "Where the hell are you getting your information? Damn it, Weaze, level with me. I can't get a handle on this business if you don't give me everything you've got. Who's behind all this, who—"

"I can't talk, man." Weasel's voice dropped even lower. "Folks know I've given you this much, I'm dead."

Matthew sat very still. He'd stopped breathing. His headache had vanished. His thinking was clear and ice-cold. Otis Raymond never exaggerated the danger he was in. Never. Vietnam had taught him that. If Weaze said over his CVC that there were a half-dozen NVA regulars firing up at him, then there were a half-dozen NVA regulars firing up at him. Not three. Not ten. Six.

Stark felt something clamp down in his gut. "Get out," he said, his voice like stone. "Don't get yourself killed over Ryder. Wherever you are, Weaze, get the fuck out. Come to Washington. I'll put you up."

"I don't know if I can get out."

"Do it."

"Man, if I can…"

"Do it, goddamn you."

"Jeez, Stark, I—" Weasel stopped, and the nervousness turned to panic as he went on rapidly, "Shit, oh *shit,* I got a guy bird-dogging me!"

Matthew jumped to his feet, but he didn't lose control. He couldn't. It was a self-indulgence that wasn't going to do Otis Raymond a damn bit of good. "Weasel, where are you? I'll come for you myself."

The line went dead, and Stark lost his control because now nothing that he did mattered.

"Goddamnit, Weaze!"

The only answer was the patient hum of the dial tone.

Stark's teeth were ground together so tightly his jaw ached, but he took a breath, sucking in his emotions with the stale air of the overheated newsroom. Weasel was going to let himself go down because of Sam Ryder, and there wasn't a damn thing Stark could do about it—except keep plugging away at all the fucking crazy leads. The Minstrel's Rough, more damned Peperkamps. *I told you, I don't know anything about diamonds...*

Bullshit, toots.

Slowly he became aware of Alice Feldon at his side. He had no idea how long she'd been standing there. "Are you all right?" she asked, more curious than worried. He understood—no one had better rein on himself than Matthew Stark.

He nodded and cradled the receiver.

"This buddy of yours is in trouble," she said.

"Nothing he thinks he can't handle."

"What do you think?"

He looked at her without expression, but the despair was eating away at him. "Life expectancy zero."

"What does that mean?"

"It's what the grunts used to say about door gunners."

"Weasel?"

"Yeah. He was a door gunner, and he lived. He was twenty-one years old when he left Vietnam. You might say the rest of his life has been anticlimactic." Matthew pulled his leather jacket off the back of his chair. His arms and legs were rigid; he moved without grace. "If the Weaze calls again, find out where he is. Don't let him hang up until you do."

"I'll try."

He looked at her, the black eyes remote. "Don't try, Feldie. Do it."

Anybody else would have nodded her head and kept her damn mouth shut, but that wasn't the kind of smart Feldie was. She put out a hand and touched Stark's elbow. "Hey, there, slow down."

He took a breath. "I'm sorry."

His voice was tight and sandpapery, and none of the tension went out of him, but Feldie nodded, satisfied. "At least now you don't look like you're going to go off and kill somebody."

He tried to smile. "Who, me?"

"Yeah, now what aren't you telling me?"

"Feldie, Weasel's got to get out of there. Make him understand that."

"I'll try, okay? But what—"

"When I've got anything that makes sense, we'll talk."

"All right, fine. Look, I've got a guy on hold. The call came through on my line. You want to take it?"

"Who is it?" He was thinking of Juliana.

"Some guy. Wouldn't give his name."

Ryder? Stark headed over to Feldie's desk and picked up the phone; she hung in there right beside him, glasses on the end of her nose. He scowled at her. "You mind?"

"Hell, yes," she said, and remained rooted to her spot.

He ignored her and punched the button on the phone. "Yeah?"

"You always did have a winning way with people, *sir.*"

The voice on the other end was deep and precise, the sarcasm just hinted at, all of it disturbingly familiar. Matthew sat down, tense and alert.

"Lucky your competence made up for your personality."

"Who is this?"

"You don't remember?"

There was a short, spasmodic laugh, and then Stark did remember. He didn't move; he didn't breathe. He sat very still and listened, hoping he was wrong, knowing he wasn't.

"And here I've been thinking I was the basis for the villain in that book of yours," the voice went on. "I read it, you know. I forget what cesspool I was sitting in at the time but sure did get some chuckles out of that one. At least you didn't whine. Christ, I get sick of all the whining."

Matthew reached for a pencil and a scrap of paper, just

to have something to grip, to keep him anchored in the present. His mind—his very soul—had begun to drift back.

In heavy black letters, oblivious to Alice Feldon, he wrote: Bloch.

Sergeant Phillip Bloch. He'd been a platoon sergeant in Vietnam, a hard-bitten, ritualistic man on nobody's side but his own. He'd saved people, and he'd killed people. It didn't matter to him which or who.

"I'd heard you were dead, Sergeant."

"Did you have a party?'

"No. I didn't do a damn thing."

The laugh came again, a laugh of nightmares and ghosts. "You're a cold bastard, *sir,* but that's okay. Wouldn't have made it out of 'Nam two times as a chopper pilot if you weren't. I kinda was counting on you not making it out, you know, but you and me—we're a lot alike. We know how to survive."

Matthew made no comment. There was no need. Bloch knew what Stark thought of him.

"How's the newspaper business?" Bloch asked, his tone deceptively jovial.

"I do my job."

He glanced at Feldie, who didn't even roll her eyes.

"Working on a big story?"

"You didn't call to chitchat."

"That's right, buddy." The jovial tone disappeared. "I'm calling to warn your ass off a story. Whatever you got, drop it. You hear? That way, nobody gets hurt. Our paths just ain't meant to cross, you know? Shit happens every time. So you just bow out now, and we'll go our separate ways."

Stark pressed the pencil hard into the paper. The point snapped. He kept pressing. So Bloch was in it. From the moment Matthew had first seen Otis Raymond's thin, yellowing, bug-bitten body in the *Gazette* newsroom, he'd guessed, deep down in a place inside him he didn't like to go, that Phil Bloch's name would come into it, sooner or later.

Bloch went on smoothly, "You know what story I'm talking about."

"No," Stark said, although he knew lying would be pointless. Yet he had to try. For Weasel's sake, maybe even for Ryder's—and maybe even for his own, although he didn't care to think so. He preferred to think he could handle Phillip Bloch. If necessary, beat him.

"Then let me refresh your memory—Otis Raymond."

The pencil snapped in half, the sharpened end skidding across the desk onto the floor. Behind him, Feldie jumped, startled. But Matthew remained very still. He had no room in which to maneuver. Right now Bloch was in control. He knew what was going on; Matthew didn't.

He had to listen. Play the sergeant's game. Buy time.

"Ya'll used to call him Weasel," Bloch said. "That help?"

Matthew set the eraser end of the pencil down on the pad; his hands were rock steady. "I haven't seen the Weaze in ages. He checks in every so often and lets me know he's alive."

"He check in last week? He drop in, Stark?"

Bloch's tone was smug, knowing. If he'd been within reach, Stark would have strangled him. But that, too, was Phillip Bloch: he always managed to stay just out of reach.

"Why should I tell you, Bloch?"

"I know about the calls, *sir*." The sarcasm wasn't as subtle now. "You can quit protecting him. The sonofabitch tipped you off. Now I gotta deal with you, and no use pretending I don't, that right?"

Matthew maintained rigid control. "Ninety-nine percent of the time Weaze talks bullshit. I know that."

"Forget it, Stark. I know, you hear me?" There was that curt, terrible laugh again. "I fucking *know*. Whatever Raymond told you, you ain't treating it like bullshit. I suggest you start doing so, right now."

"Let me talk to Weasel," Matthew said stonily.

"I don't give warnings twice. Remember that."

Bloch hung up.

Stark slammed down the receiver, but there was no satisfaction in that, so, lunging to his feet, he picked up the whole damn phone and hurled it to the floor. Fellow reporters glanced up, saw it was Matthew Stark, and resumed working, looking nervous.

Feldie simply said, "Jesus Christ."

Without a word, Matthew picked the phone up off the floor and set it back on the desk. It wasn't broken. Given the often volatile nature of reporters, newsrooms were generally equipped with sturdy telephones.

"You want to tell me what that was all about?" Feldie asked.

"No."

"I'm your editor—"

"I know what you are, Feldie, and I respect that." He looked at her, trying to get some warmth back into him. "But the answer's still no."

She sighed, hesitating as she pushed her glasses up on top of her head, but finally she nodded. "Okay—for now. You play this the way you have to. I'll cut you some slack."

"Thanks. Look, I need a favor."

"Jesus, I don't believe you. What?"

"A ticket to Antwerp."

"What do you think this is, the fucking *Post?*"

"I'll be at Kennedy Airport tonight. I'm heading for New York right now." He gave her a strained smile as he slung his jacket over one shoulder. "Want me to say thanks again?"

"Twice in one morning? I don't think I could stand it. Get out of here, Stark. Bring me back a story."

* * *

Hendrik de Geer vomited once more into the sharp, cold wind. He made no sound as his guts twisted in agony. There was nothing left anymore to come up. He had filled the harbor with his *jenever* and his bile. Dutch gin, now just another of his enemies. When he was younger, he could stay drunk for days when he chose to, and there was never any vomiting or pain. Oblivion had come more easily then. Once he'd thought it was because he had less to forget, but now he knew that to be untrue. Another lie he'd told himself. It was because he'd had more years ahead of him, and he'd fancied that he'd have plenty of time to make up for the bad he'd done. When he'd envisioned himself as an old man, he assumed he would look back at his youth and see himself as well-intentioned but, at times, in over his head. Outmatched. But the good he'd done would outweigh the bad. He'd been convinced of that.

No longer. Now he had few years ahead, many behind. There was little time left to make up for the bad. He had no delusions. They were gone, with the laughter of his friends, with their trust. Perhaps he'd meant well then, as now. Perhaps not. What difference did it make? Only consequences mattered.

There was no more gin.

He collapsed on the deck and slept, in the wind.

It was late afternoon before Matthew caught up with Juliana Fall. He'd taken the shuttle into LaGuardia, then hustled a cab straight to the Upper West Side. The doorman at the Beresford said she wasn't in. Had he seen a woman in a raccoon coat and red vinyl boots leave? Yes, he had, but that wasn't Juliana Fall.

No, it wasn't. It was J.J. Pepper.

She was sitting at the baby grand in the Club Aquarian, playing Mose Allison, her hair tinted pink, her emerald velvet dress something out of an old Greta Garbo movie. The long bell sleeves were trimmed in mink. She had her shoes on, and her red lips were pursed in concentration.

Stark walked past Len Wetherall at the bar and right up onto the stage. Juliana didn't look up. She seemed unaware of his approach, of anything but what she was doing. The dim light caught the gleam of perspiration on her forehead and upper lip, and he could see the hair matted at the nape of her neck, where it was still more blond than pink. The effect was outrageously sexy. But Matthew told himself he couldn't care.

She finished her tune and took a breath, ready to begin the next, but Stark tapped her on the shoulder. She jumped and nearly fell off the bench. He felt himself going for her, but she caught her balance before he could help and looked around, dazed.

As she focused on him, the clouds disappeared from her dark eyes. She brushed away the glistening drops of sweat on her upper lip and didn't smile. "Stark—what do you want?"

"If I'm going to get tossed," he said in a grinding, tight voice, still hearing Weasel's panicked cry, "I want to make it worthwhile."

Her hand dropped to the middle of her gaudy rhinestone necklace, but she looked more excited than nervous. Not so glazed, not at all bored. She gave him a half smile that made his heart race. "What're you going to do," she said in that liquid voice, "torture me for information?"

Jesus, he thought. "Don't tempt me."

She lifted her round shoulders in a little shrug and picked up a glass of water off the piano, took a sip, deliberate and unintimidated, and set the glass back down. Pink-haired, purple-haired or pale blond, Matthew thought, the woman was breathtaking—and irritating as hell. He had to rock her.

He stared down at her, a hard, ugly stare that had no discernible effect on her. She just blinked at him.

"The name Peperkamp keeps turning up," he told her. "Catharina Peperkamp Fall, J.J. Pepper—got that from Peperkamp, didn't you? Now I'm on my way to Antwerp to check out another goddamn Peperkamp. Johannes Peperkamp. I'll wager anything you want that he's related to you. And you know what else? He's a diamond cutter. Imagine. Think he knows something about the world's largest uncut diamond?"

He watched her swallow and turn white under the appleblossom cheeks. The regal calm had vanished, but he had to admire her control. She didn't try to get away, and she didn't yell for Len Wetherall. She said, "Johannes Peperkamp is my uncle."

"Lo and behold, the lady does know something."

"He's an old man." One pale, slender hand reached back and gripped the keyboard, as if anchoring her in a world she knew and wanted to believe in. "Leave him alone."

"I'm not going to leave anybody alone, including you, sweet cheeks. An old buddy just may get killed because you think this is a goddamn game, like painting your hair pink and wearing funny clothes. Well, darling, it's not a game."

Juliana was shaking all over now, white-faced, angry, humiliated. Stark fought the impulse to lift her into his arms. He wanted to kiss her, to make the shaking stop. But he didn't relent. He wasn't going to let Weasel go down because some bored piano player wouldn't talk; she was, however, hanging in there better than most people did when he got going.

"Tell me more about your uncle," he said.

"No."

Straight up and to the point. He liked that.

"You're crazy," she said.

"Just wild. Diamond cutters, bakers, piano players,

chickenshit politicians." His voice was low and deep and dark, and he knew he had her scared. She'd have been a damn fool if she weren't. "You all can have a party when you get my buddy killed."

Juliana breathed in sharply but said nothing.

"Where's your uncle live in Antwerp?"

"I won't tell you."

"That's okay. I'm a reporter. I'll find out."

"Stop it!" She balled her hands into tight fists, looking as if she were going to hit him. "Damn you, you have no right to—"

"I have every right to help a friend in trouble, and if I have to make you feel bad to do it, tough shit, lady. What do you know about the Minstrel's Rough?"

"Stop!"

"Hell, no, I'm not going to stop."

"Oh, yes, you are, bub."

The voice behind Stark was bass-pitched and menacing. Matthew hadn't forgotten about Len Wetherall. He just didn't give a damn. He didn't turn around but looked straight into the wide, terrified, curious, pissed-off eyes of Juliana Fall, gorgeous eyes, and he had to stop his heart from melting and his brain from telling him to lay off her. But then he heard Bloch's laugh and one of Weasel's pathetic sniffles, and he felt himself hardening, drawing up his resolve inside himself, accepting the need to do what had to be done.

"If the Weaze ends up on a board because you wouldn't talk, darling, count on seeing me again." Without giving her a chance to answer, he turned around and looked up at Len Wetherall. "I wouldn't fuck with me if I were you."

He walked out. No one said a word, no one laid a hand on him. No one did a damn thing but let him go.

One piece flowed into the next. Juliana didn't care; she had to play. Wanted to. Len had said, "Dude's in a bad mood," and she'd only nodded, unable to speak. He'd asked her what she was doing messing around with Matt Stark; he'd said himself he wouldn't want to mess with a guy in a mood like that, with a face like that. When she still didn't talk, he told her to get a drink and calm down, then play. She couldn't drink, she couldn't calm down.

But she could play. Had to.

As she played she thought not about the music but about the old man backstage in the little Delftshaven church seven years ago with his crumpled paper bag holding the Minstrel's Rough, which she hadn't known what to do with and so didn't do anything with it except take it home with her, and her mother's trembling hands and the quick dark eyes of Rachel Stein and the dreamy baby blue eyes of Samuel Ryder and Matthew Stark who, yes, was a mean-looking sonofabitch. But the hell with that. To hell with *him.* She wasn't afraid.

Something touched her shoulder, and she screamed, leaping up, disoriented.

Len caught her around the middle before she could collapse. "It's okay, babe," he said tenderly, taking her weight. "I think you'd better head on home."

"Why—what—" She looked up at him as he lifted her off the bench and stood her up, like a limp doll. "What was I playing?"

"You don't know?"

She shook her head, still holding on to him. Her heart was beating rapidly; she felt dazed and unsteady.

"You started out with jazz," Len said, "but then you went into some kind of hairy-assed shit."

Chopin. She remembered a nocturne. The Nocturne in B Major, Opus 62, No. 1. She'd been playing it for years. But she remembered some Liszt, too, and some Bach and Bartók. Not whole pieces, but phrases here and there.

She remembered hearing them, not playing them.

"Oh, hell," she said.

"You played that stuff from memory."

"I know I—" She licked her lips, but her tongue was as dry as her mouth. "I think I'll go home."

Len got her raccoon coat and helped her on with it. She was dripping with sweat, and her big eyes were still glazed. He'd seen it happen before, that daze, when musicians were totally absorbed in what they were doing, and it took a while before they came to. He'd experienced that level of concentration himself on the court. He'd be unaware of the crowd, and even afterward, when he watched a tape of a play, he'd know exactly what he'd done, why he'd done it, how, but he wouldn't be able to remember how it had all come together at that precise moment. He'd just done it. It was organic, a part of him.

Just as what had poured out of J.J.—as he'd stood at the bar in stunned silence and folks around him just held their breath—had to be a part of her.

"Watch out you don't freeze, babe," he told her.

"I will. Thank you."

He put her in a cab himself. Insisted on it. The lady was on the edge, he thought, and in trouble.

It was dark and cold on upper Madison Avenue but crowded, the restaurants filling up. Catharina's Bake Shop was closed. Even Catharina herself had gone home. Juliana considered heading down to Park Avenue, to her parents' apartment, and battling it out with her mother. Maybe even her father would get in on it and demand that his wife be more forthcoming, although that had never happened in the past. There was no man in the world more understanding and loving than Adrian Fall. But his sympathy to his wife's feelings, his acceptance that there were things about her past he would never know, had contributed to a conspiracy of silence—and Juliana's frustration. How could a father argue with a mother's desire for their child to be happy?

A couple passed her on the street, dragging a Christmas tree behind them. They were laughing together and singing "Deck the Halls," and for no reason at all, Juliana thought of Matthew Stark. He was a difficult man, to say the least. Remote, confident, unpredictable. He didn't exactly tiptoe around her. *Myself, I wouldn't want to mess with him,* Len had said. Yes, she could understand that. The changeable nature of his eyes, the scars on his hands and face, and the dark, gravelly voice suggested a certain toughness—but also, in her opinion, an intriguing vulnerability.

Suddenly she imagined herself dragging a Christmas tree along Madison Avenue with him, maybe even singing, and it was strange that the image didn't seem wrong, impossible, absurd.

You're in trouble, she thought, and hailed another cab.

Twelve

Wilhelmina watered the spider plants and strawberry geraniums in her kitchen window. She hadn't slept well, and when the telephone rang, she found herself reluctant to answer it. Who did she want to talk to? No one. But whoever it was would only call back. Resigned, she put down her watering can and picked up the receiver.

In flat-accented Flemish, a man identified himself as Martin Dekker of Antwerp. Wilhelmina sniffed. She had little use for Belgians. "What can I do for you?" she asked, pinching off a dried leaf from her spider plant.

"You have a brother, Johannes Peperkamp?"

"Yes."

"I'm his landlord."

He's dead, Wilhelmina thought, with no particular feeling that she could describe. My brother is dead.

"I don't want to frighten you unnecessarily," Dekker went on quickly, "but Mr. Peperkamp hasn't been to his apartment since the day before yesterday. A man was just here looking for him—a diamond dealer. He says your brother hasn't been to his shop, either, and he owes him several diamonds. That's not like Mr. Peperkamp, as I'm sure you know. I was wondering if you might know where he is."

Wilhelmina crumpled the leaf in one hand. "I haven't seen Johannes in more than five years," she said. Actually, not that she thought about it, she realized it was probably longer. She shrugged. "He's a grown man. Maybe he has a girlfriend."

"I don't think that's likely."

Neither did Wilhelmina. Far more likely that her brother had been wandering around and fallen off a pier. He'd always loved the ocean. Johannes was getting old, and he'd lived alone since the death of his wife, to whom he'd been devoted, ten years earlier. Poor Ann. She'd been so kind and lovely—everything Wilhelmina wasn't.

A note of exasperation crept into Martin Dekker's voice. "Miss Peperkamp, if you're not concerned—"

"I didn't say that." Wilhelmina was used to people taking offense at her. Although she wasn't a cruel or uncaring woman, she lacked subtlety and had long ago quit pretending to have any. She was a direct woman, and that was that. "Have you checked his apartment? He isn't dead in his bed, is he?"

The Belgian was taken aback by her bluntness. "I checked. He isn't there."

"Humph. He hasn't missed a day of work in years, I'm sure."

"That's what I was thinking."

She sighed, and once more she found herself fighting images of Hendrik de Geer. She'd been fighting them for forty years. Did Johannes's disappearance have anything to do with Hendrik's presence at Lincoln's Center, Rachel's death, this business with Senator Ryder? Achh, she thought, annoyed, and threw the crumpled leaf into the trash.

"Well, perhaps I should come to Antwerp and see what my brother's about."

The landlord agreed and hung up, much cheered to have

the matter resting on someone else's shoulders. It's so often that way, Wilhelmina thought, and so often the shoulders are mine.

Juliana walked down the quiet, narrow streets of Delftshaven, trying to let the crisp air dispel the all-too-familiar numbness and disorientation of jet lag. She had decided to follow Matthew Stark to Antwerp, but via Rotterdam and Aunt Willie. She didn't know her way around Antwerp, didn't speak the language, and didn't have the slightest idea how to get to Uncle Johannes's apartment—all, certainly, handicaps shared by Matthew. But she preferred to be one step ahead of him, not shoulder to shoulder and definitely not two or three behind. She wanted to get to Uncle Johannes *before* he did.

She'd headed straight from her mother's bakeshop to the airport and had gotten a flight to Schiphol Airport, arriving early that morning. It was a simple matter to get a taxi to Delftshaven, where she'd decided to walk a couple of blocks to clear her head before knocking on her aunt's door. She'd slept some on the plane, having done what she could about her pink hair in its stainless-steel bathroom. If anyone had recognized her, her reputation would have been shot to hell, but, as Matthew Stark could tell her, odds were she wouldn't be.

She put him out of her mind as she rang her aunt's doorbell. Wilhelmina Peperkamp wasn't the most lovable person, but Juliana sensed she was utterly reliable.

The old Dutchwoman answered her door in a shapeless wool dress, heavy socks, and sturdy shoes. Her hair was cut short in no particular style, and she wore no cosmetics.

"Juliana?" Her blue eyes crinkled as she squinted at her niece standing on the front stoop. "That's you, isn't it? What's happened to your hair?"

Juliana dragged her fingers through her hair, stiff with

mousse and sticking out in odd places after the long flight, but she didn't bother to indulge Aunt Willie with an explanation. Wilhelmina was stubborn, sour, difficult, and critical. Nothing ever pleased her. Without any effort, she could make people feel frivolous and silly. She would never understand J.J. Pepper. Suddenly Juliana had her doubts about having come. Aunt Willie could easily tell her she was being ridiculous and send her home.

"Yes, it's me," Juliana said, and let it go at that. What the hell, she thought. She was here.

"Come in, then," Wilhelmina replied without surprise, and opened the door, eyeing her niece's green velvet dress and the smudged eye makeup. "I had a dress like that when I was younger. But I think it suits you better."

A compliment? Juliana didn't know what to make of that, remembering how her aunt had snored through her Dutch premiere seven years ago and afterward had admitted as much.

"Of course," Aunt Willie went on, "that was fifty years ago or more. But I suppose if we old women hadn't turned in our clothes to the secondhand shops when we were younger, what would crazy young people have to wear today?"

Juliana surprised herself by laughing. "I was waiting for the other shoe to fall."

"Pardon?"

"Never mind."

According to her mother and Juliana's own limited experience with her aunt, Wilhelmina Peperkamp seldom gave a compliment without some kind of stab. It seemed she didn't want a person to think she was actually being nice—or maybe she just worried about giving anyone a swelled head. Juliana supposed it was just as well that the world's second largest ocean separated the Falls and Aunt Willie, although the distance hadn't prevented her from criticizing her younger sister. She'd expressed in no uncertain terms her irritation with Catharina for not teaching her daughter Dutch. That Juliana had had little interest in learning Dutch—something she regretted later, but not at age eight—didn't faze Aunt Willie.

"You don't seem surprised to see me," Juliana said.

"Surprise is for the young."

Aunt Willie's apartment was small and tidy, consisting of a living room, a kitchen, and a bedroom. The furniture was old but well kept, and there were plants in most of the windows. Juliana followed her stocky old aunt, so familiar and yet a stranger, into the little kitchen.

"I'm packing cheese sandwiches," Wilhelmina said, going to the counter. She sliced some thin pieces of cheese off a wedge of aged Gouda.

Juliana sat at the table, covered with a faded but still serviceable white cloth, and fingered one of a line of scrubbed clay pots. They were old but immaculate.

"Are you going somewhere?" she asked.

"Antwerp."

"But that's where I'm—" Catching herself, Juliana didn't finish.

Wihelmina nibbled on a slice of cheese. "That's where you're what? Juliana, I don't like playing games. I prefer directness."

Avoiding an answer, Juliana took a slice of cheese when her aunt offered it on the end of her knife. She wasn't fond of aged Gouda; it was too strong, too much like eating mold. But it gave her a moment to think: if she told Aunt Willie everything straight off, she might in turn not tell her niece a damn thing. She was, after all, her mother's older sister.

"Why are you going to Antwerp?" she asked casually. "You told me you haven't been to New York to visit because you hate to travel."

"Antwerp isn't as far as New York." Wilhelmina carefully wrapped the cheese back up and returned it to the refrigerator. "But it's true, I don't care to travel. Once a year I visit friends in Aalsmeer, and they take me to the flower festivals and feed me too much because they pity me."

Juliana couldn't hide her surprise. "Why would they pity you?"

Wilhelmina laughed. "Because I'm old and alone. Always when I return home, one of my plants is wilted or dead. Do you have plants?"

"No. Goldfish."

"Fish? Do you eat them?"

"Of course not. They're pets."

"Sentimental Americans," Wilhelmina muttered, and resumed her lunch-making. She got a half-dozen cookies from a tin and fixed a thermos of hot tea.

Juliana watched, fascinated. "Isn't Antwerp just a couple of hours from Rotterdam by train?"

"About ninety minutes." She screwed the top down on the thermos. "Since the war, I always carry food with me. Once you've known hunger…" She waved a hand, not completing the thought. "Does your mother know you're here?"

"No," Juliana said guiltily. "I came sort of on the spur of the moment."

"You should call her and tell her where you are."

"She won't like it."

"Of course not, she's your mother."

Juliana looked up at her old aunt and winced suddenly at her own rudeness. It had only just occurred to her that she should have offered to help pack lunch. But Aunt Willie always seemed so self-sufficient. "Have you talked to Mother recently?"

"Yes. She called to tell me about Rachel Stein."

"Did she also tell you—"

"Our conversation was a private one, Juliana. Now go call her. You may use my phone, but be quick about it. Calls are expensive."

With Aunt Willie looking on, Juliana dialed her parents' Park Avenue home. As expected, she got the housekeeper, who promised to relay to Catharina and Adrian Fall that their daughter was out of town and had called to say hello.

"You didn't tell her where you were," Wilhelmina pointed out when Juliana hung up.

"I'm thirty years old. Aunt Willie, aren't you even curious as to why I'm here?"

She swept the lunch into a paper bag. "You'll tell me soon enough. Come, let's go to Antwerp."

"But how do you know I'm going—"

"Juliana, I'm not a fool." The old Dutchwoman put on her wool coat and tucked the lunch bag under her arm. Juliana followed her out of the apartment, putting her own coat back on. "I like the raccoon," Wilhelmina said. "I'm used to you in your cashmere and silk."

"You've only seen me a few times."

"So?"

Juliana gave up.

Naturally Aunt Willie didn't drive. They took the underground tram to Central Station, where trains to Antwerp were frequent and on time. Juliana had always enjoyed her trips to The Netherlands. A crowded nation with one of the highest standards of living in the world, it depended on a modern, well-run system of mass transportation. Even Aunt Willie had no complaints. They found a seat on the train, and she insisted Juliana go in first so she could sit by the window for the view.

"It's good that you're here," Aunt Willie said. "We can see about your uncle together."

Juliana was instantly alert—even, given the events of the last few days, afraid. "What do you mean? What's wrong?"

"Sit down and don't fall to pieces on me."

Stiff and insulted, Juliana sat down, but her heart was pounding painfully. She thought about the unanswered phone calls to Uncle Johannes. If Matthew Stark could get his name and be on his way to Antwerp, so could others.

But how? Who? *Why?*

Crazily, she thought of Shuji. Would he say she was in a full-fledged funk?

"Good," Aunt Willie said, satisfied. "I was afraid you were going to do something silly like faint. I've always considered playing the piano a frivolous career, but perhaps your training has prepared you better for life than I'd anticipated."

"What about Uncle Johannes?" Juliana asked.

Wilhelmina nodded and said stoically, "Johannes is missing."

Someone at the exclusive *Diamantclub* at 62 Pelikaanstraat gave Matthew the address of Johannes Peperkamp's shop and pointed him in the direction of Schupstraat. As he walked down the busy, gray streets of the diamond district, he appreciated the chilly breeze and the bright sun, both of which helped him to chase off the fatigue that gnawed at his eyes and muscles. He hadn't slept on the flight over. He couldn't relax in the air unless he was doing the flying, but even if he'd been at his town house in Georgetown, he doubted he'd have slept.

He wasn't thrilled with himself for the way he'd treated Juliana. She was a musician, and she had different priorities. Whatever happened to the Weaze, it wasn't her fault, even if she was holding back information—which, goddamnit, he knew she was. But Weaze could have gotten out the day he'd shown up in Washington. He could have let Sam Ryder sink in his own shit (as Otis Raymond had so effectively put it), instead of risking himself to try and pull Ryder out. Stark sometimes forgot Otis had a mind of his own. He was a trained, experienced combat soldier who knew how to assess danger. Matthew was no longer his helicopter pilot; he no longer had to feel responsible for SP-4 Otis Raymond.

But he did.

Damn it, he thought, you just don't want anything to happen to the little jackass.

In the dreary, gray building on Schupstraat, a thickset, middle-aged security guard told Matthew in heavily accented English that he was very, very sorry, but he had bad news to relate about Johannes Peperkamp.

Stark automatically clicked into his distanced-journalist/distanced-soldier mode. He'd never met Johannes Peperkamp. *He's Juliana's uncle.* So what. You're just the fact collector.

He asked in a steady voice, "What do you mean?"

"I'm sorry to have to tell you," the guard said, "but Mr. Peperkamp has died. We got the news just a few minutes ago." He pronounced just *shoost*. Thumping his broad chest, he continued, "Bad heart. He was an old man, you know. He died in Amsterdam." Stark pushed away the image of Juliana's gooped-up beautiful eyes, shining with concern for her uncle and with determination to protect him from a relentless American reporter. He had to stay focused on his job. "When?"

"We don't know how long he's dead. A day or two, no more."

Matthew held his frustration in check: had he come to the wrong fucking city? He asked neutrally, "When did he go to Amsterdam?"

"Day before yesterday. He leaves in the afternoon with another man, but they don't say when they will be back. I don't know if they went to Amsterdam together."

"Did you see the man?"

"Yes."

"Can you describe him for me?"

The guard regarded Matthew with sudden suspicion. "Why?"

"I'm a friend of the Peperkamp family," Matthew said quickly. "I know his niece, Juliana Fall."

"Ahh, the pianist. Yes, the man with Mr. Peperkamp was perhaps sixty-five or seventy, fair. He spoke Dutch, I remember. I don't recall any name."

"Hendrik de Geer?"

"It's possible. As I say, I don't recall."

It had to be, Stark thought. The elusive Dutchman...and another link to the Peperkamps. "Do you know if Mr. Peperkamp was working on or aware of any information on an uncut diamond called the Minstrel's Rough?"

The guard smiled, indulging the ignorant American. "The Minstrel does not exist, in my opinion. It's a myth." The smile turned supercilious. "No one here treats it seriously."

I'll bet the hell they would, Stark thought, if someone had the fast track on it. Then, guiltily, he remembered Juliana's fierce protectiveness toward her uncle. Here he'd been screaming at her about his buddy ending up dead, and her uncle was the one being zipped up in a body bag.

"Has anyone told the family?" he asked.

"I don't know."

After some persuasion, Matthew was able to get the old diamond cutter's home address, but he had little hope of finding anything useful there. Still, he thought, he might as well finish the job and have a look. Anything to delay his having to look into the pale, beautiful face of Juliana Fall and see what happened to it after she found out the fun was over, her adventure over before it got started, her uncle dead.

Aunt Willie insisted that Juliana eat. "You're too skinny," she said. Exhausted as she was from her mad dash out of New York—it was always so much harder to fly west to east than east to west—Juliana had to admit the cheese sandwich and hot tea tasted good. They helped fill that dead, empty spot inside her that kept reminding her she was in Europe chasing after a reporter who undoubtedly wouldn't take kindly to being chased. What would Matthew Stark do if he found out she had the Minstrel's Rough? What would any of them do? Her mother and Aunt Willie didn't know. She'd kept her promise to her uncle that she wouldn't tell them.

Aunt Willie seemed to have no dead, empty spot to hold her back. She ate her lunch calmly, without comment, but held on to the cookies. Juliana decided she must be waiting for an emergency. An earthquake or a nuclear attack. Wilhelmina Peperkamp's natural competence had a way of making the people around her—and even her own sister across an ocean—feel inadequate. But Juliana dealt on a regular basis with some of the most ambitious and competitive people in the world, and she was more fascinated by her aunt's manner than intimidated.

"Now," Aunt Willie said when they'd finished lunch, "you must tell me everything about why you are here."

"Why me first?"

Aunt Willie picked crumbs off her skirt. "Don't you trust me?"

"Of course I trust you. It's not that."

"Then what? Juliana, I'm not like your mother. You're her daughter, and she doesn't talk because she feels she must protect you." Wilhelmina put her little collection of crumbs on her tongue. "You're not my daughter, and even if you were, I don't think people can be protected from the past."

Juliana agreed, having long been frustrated with her mother's reticence, but she said, "You won't get very far with me by criticizing my mother."

"I don't criticize, I just tell the truth." She looked past Juliana, out the window. "Talk if you want to."

"I do want to, Aunt Willie, but why do you have to make everything so difficult? Oh, never mind. Look, I'll tell you right now I don't know very much and what I do know has me confused."

"One thing at a time," her aunt said.

Sighing, Juliana began with meeting Rachel Stein over tea with her mother and proceeded from there, neglecting only to mention her knowledge of what the Minstrel was, where it was, and all its mystery and legend. Aunt Willie listened without interruption, and when Juliana had finished the old Dutchwoman leaned back against her seat and closed her eyes. For the first time, Juliana noticed how lined and dried her aunt's fair skin was.

"It doesn't look very good for Johannes, I'm afraid," Aunt Willie said. "Did this Matthew Stark tell you how he'd gotten his name?"

"No," Juliana replied, feeling a pang of fear for her uncle, whom she recalled with affection as a gentle, cultured man. She'd get rid of the Minstrel now, immediately, if it meant helping him—or anyone. But he'd warned her, seven years ago, against such temptations. He'd told her to hold her knowledge of the Minstrel close and never, never to act without knowing precisely what the risks were. Don't look only at the consequences of not acting, he'd said. Look, too, at the consequences of acting. With whom would you be dealing? What would those people do if they knew you had the stone—if they got it? Is saving one life worth the loss of many others?

They were sound questions. At the time, she'd thought them melodramatic.

"Aunt Willie, do you know anything about what's going on? Do you know this Hendrik de Geer, what his role might be?"

Wilhelmina opened her eyes, her expression grim. "I can't say for certain what this is all about, but as for Hendrik de Geer—yes, I know him. He's a devil."

"In what way? How do you know him? Does Mother—"

"Yes, your mother knows him. And Rachel did, too. We all did, Juliana. He was our friend, before the war, during."

"But you just said—"

"I know what I said. Hendrik betrayed our friendship, and until I talk to your mother, I will tell you no more about him. But you must be careful of him, Juliana."

"You know you're not being fair," she said simply.

Wilhelmina shrugged, unconcerned with fairness.

"What about Rachel Stein? How did you know her?"

"Ah, Rachel." Wilhelmina's eyes softened, and she sighed. Juliana sensed her sadness—and anger. "It's not right what Rachel suffered. There's no excuse. None. She was a good woman, Juliana, a dear, funny, sad friend, and perhaps one of the most intelligent people I've ever known. You should have seen her before the war. Oh, did she have the devil in her eye! She and her brother stayed with me during the occupation. They were Jews, so we had to be extremely cautious."

"You hid them?"

Aunt Willie nodded solemnly, without pleasure or pride.

"But I had no idea! Mother never said anything about it."

"Why should she? Many people hid Jews, but not enough. Tens of thousands were murdered. Rounded up like cattle, deported, starved, tortured, shot, gassed. My actions saved two people. Two very dear, very important people to me, but still only two."

"Nevertheless—"

"Nevertheless nothing. I have no reason to brag."

Juliana tried to imagine her aunt forty years younger, Rachel Stein, her mother, what they must have gone through as young women. Younger than she herself was now. Would she have had the courage to hide Jews from the Nazis? She would like to think so. But she hoped she'd never know such a thing. It was something, she thought, that should never be tested.

"The Steins must be very grateful to you, Aunt Willie," she said.

"In some ways, yes, of course, but it's difficult," Wilhelmina said, matter-of-fact. "They were made into victims, Juliana, persecuted simply because they were Jews, and simply because I was not a Jew, I was put into a position of power over them—along with your mother, your uncle, your grandparents. We could help them or we could destroy them."

"But you chose to help."

"Chose? I'm not so sure. For me, there was never any question of what I had to do. It's like getting up in the morning. You just wake up. You don't expect anybody to thank you for doing it."

Juliana nodded, furious with her mother for never having breathed a word of any of this. What did she think she was protecting her daughter from? But she put that aside for now. "Do you think Rachel Stein and her brother would ever have wanted the chance to repay you?"

Aunt Willie looked at her, truly mystified. "For what? They owe me nothing. They never did. I failed them in too many other ways."

"I don't understand."

"I hope you never will, Juliana. None of us had much control over our fates, but they least of all. Rachel and her family weren't the only ones we helped—there were strikers, too, and men between the ages of eighteen and fifty who were being rounded up for the labor camps. The *onderduikers,* we called them."

"What does that mean?"

"The hidden people. *Onderduik* means to dive under. In Holland we have no wide forests or caves, very little countryside. To conceal people we had to put them in our houses, in our attics and cellars, often right under the noses of the Germans. But the Steins were with us the longest. For almost five years we lived in close proximity to each other, always fearful of discovery, rarely having enough food, enough heat. Sometimes we would get on each other's nerves. It's only natural. That kind of situation can breed resentment as well as gratitude." She breathed heavily. "But I'm talking too much. Your mother will be annoyed with me."

For a moment, Juliana was silent. She was proud of her aunt, amazed by what she'd done, amazed at her courage, but concluded that saying so would only irritate her. Instead she asked, "Was Mother living with you at the time?"

"Your mother's story is for her to tell."

"But Rachel Stein came to New York to see her."

"Yes, she did."

"Aunt Willie, you know as well as I do that Mother isn't going to tell me a damn thing."

Wilhelmina sniffed. "Watch your language."

"I have a *right* to know."

"Do you?"

"All right." Juliana sighed, knowing she was defeated. She didn't want to waste time with pointless arguing. "The paper said Rachel Stein came to the United States after World War Two. Why?"

"She and Abraham chose not to stay—they couldn't. Their community, their family and friends were all gone, and the country itself was decimated. We had just suffered a terrible famine. The Netherlands wasn't fully liberated until the spring of 1945, almost a year after France and Belgium. The Allies had tried to take Arnhem in the fall of 1944. The plan—Operation Market Garden, it was called—was to create a corridor up through the southeast part of the country into Germany and take control of the three major rivers, isolating the Germany forces occupying Holland. Then the

Allies would make the final push into Germany. If it had worked, it would have shortened the war considerably."

"But it didn't work," Juliana said, more or less guessing. Her knowledge of World War II military history was limited.

"No," Wilhelmina said heavily, "it didn't work. The Germans responded by tightening their grip on The Netherlands. Food shipments to the cities in the west were cut off, there was virtually no oil or coal, transportation was nearly impossible to obtain. It's said we had less than five hundred calories a day on which to survive—and there were the *onderduikers* to feed, as well. Your mother was the only person I knew who could make fodder beets and tulip bulbs palatable. It was a terrible, bitter winter. *Hongerwinter,* we call it. The Winter of Hunger."

Juliana said nothing. What was there to say? Her mother had never mentioned such suffering. Never.

"In any case," Aunt Willie went on, "there was nothing left in their country for Rachel and Abraham. They chose to emigrate to the United States, and we drifted apart. It happens." Wilhelmina was silent for a moment, lost in the past, but she recovered herself and dipped into her paper bag for the cookies, six of them, wrapped in waxed paper. "Here, have a cookie. By the way, have you noticed we're being followed?"

Juliana turned sharply from the window, but her aunt grabbed her arm, stopping her from looking around. Nodding that she was back under control, Juliana whispered dubiously, "Are you sure?"

"Of course," Wilhelmina said without arrogance and let go of Juliana's arm. "I lived under German occupation for five years. I know when I'm being followed—and I don't like it. The Nazis did too much of it during the war. Now I have no tolerance even for the neighborhood children tagging along behind me."

Under different circumstances, Juliana might have considered her aunt hopelessly paranoid. But not now. Not after Matthew Stark's wild, unnerving visit to the Club Aquarian and her own mad flight to Rotterdam.

Her voice deceptively calm, she asked, "What does he look like?"

"A Nazi." The old Dutchwoman's mouth was a straight, uncompromising line.

"Aunt Willie, for God's sake."

"He followed us onto the train. He's very blond—"

"So am I. So are *you*. That doesn't make us Nazis."

Wilhelmina ignored her niece. "His hair is cut short, and he's neatly dressed. Too neatly, in my opinion. A young man shouldn't be too tidy. I know you think I'm narrow-minded, but that's my way." She shrugged, lifting her heavy, square shoulders. "The war's been over a long time now, but I will never forget—or forgive."

Juliana didn't comment on her aunt's views. "What do you think we should do about this guy?"

"For the moment, nothing."

"And just let the sonofabitch follow us?"

Aunt Willie smiled. "I like your spirit, Juliana. But don't worry—we'll get rid of this Nazi in Antwerp."

When they arrived at the train station in Antwerp, Aunt Willie moved quickly through the crowd, assuming her niece would keep up. She did.

"The Nazi doesn't know we've spotted him," her old aunt said. "Ha! Such arrogance. But it makes our task much simpler."

She took Juliana firmly by the elbow, and together they leaped into a bus, leaving their tail behind.

Wilhelmina was beaming. "Well, that was easy."

"Jesus, Aunt Willie," Juliana said, but she was impressed, although not at all relieved to have confirmed that Aunt Willie was right: the man had been following them.

Thirteen

Otis Raymond ducked into the fishing shack and collapsed onto his bunk, lying on his back on the stinking mattress. With the back of one skinny hand, he wiped some of the dirt and sweat off his face. He was sweating and shivering at the same time. It wasn't as cold as Washington, but colder than he was used to. All the campaigns he'd been involved in had taken place in warm climates. He liked the heat, had gotten to where he couldn't stand the cold. He'd told the guys, "Gimme mosquitoes, dysentery, malaria—just keep your friggin' snow."

He could almost feel his bones rattling inside him. He kept getting thinner, must have picked up a worm or something, and he couldn't keep up with the younger guys, even some of the older ones, the fitness freaks. Christ, he was what, forty? Never thought he'd live even this long.

With a squeaky chuckle, wheezing, he sat up. "You call this living?"

His head wasn't right, either. Too much booze, too much dope, even though Bloch was pretty strict about that stuff. God wasn't as straight as the sergeant. But Otis found ways around rules and regulations; he always had. He had a bottle stashed now. Wouldn't make much difference, though, if he drank it or not. No matter what he did lately, he kept thinking about the old days and the guys he'd saved—but mostly about the ones who'd died. He'd hated having guys go on his ship. He remembered how the poor dumb fucks, the unlucky bastards, would scream for their mothers and girlfriends and wives, or how they'd yell, "fuckin' shit," or just scream and scream without any words at all, and he could still see the blood and guts and bones and smell the dead and dying stink of them. They'd have to dip the chopper in water, him and Stark, to clean out the blood and guts.

He'd seen men die since Vietnam, but it wasn't the same. Maybe because he was older, maybe because they weren't the first, maybe because he just didn't give a shit anymore—it just wasn't the same. He didn't give a flying fuck if he died himself. When he'd first gone to Vietnam, he didn't figure on living at all. Didn't know what to do with himself when he did make it out. Go back home and pick tomatoes?

He still didn't give a damn whether or not he died. Christ, if he did, would he be risking his scrawny neck to help Ryder and get information to Stark?

"Shit," he muttered, getting out his bottle. "Ryder's an asshole—Stark, too. What the hell they want me to do? Screw 'em."

He drank from the bottle and lay back in his bunk. The mattress was full of bugs. He woke up every morning with bites all over him. Fuck it. He didn't care.

"Hey, Stark, buddy." Tears welled up in his eyes. "Man, I'm counting on you."

Matt'd get Ryder's ass out of the fire, but Otis had quit believing that was the main reason he'd gotten Stark involved. Yeah, he wanted to help Sam, why not? But more than that, he wanted Stark to take out Bloch. He might be the only one who could do it. If he stayed on the story, he'd end up at the camp.

Someone had to do something about Bloch. Goddamn wild animal, the sergeant was. Always had been. Otis didn't know why the hell he'd signed up with the fucker, except he didn't have shit else to do and Bloch was offering good money. Stark'd known right from the start what the sergeant was, told Otis, too, but he'd ignored him, just like he'd ignored his daddy who kept telling him he could come on home, he could stay with him and Mamma, find a regular job, eat good. Jeez, when was the last time he'd seen his old man? Five, six years? Probably dead by now.

He drank some more, the warm booze dribbling down the sides of his mouth and onto the mattress, maybe killing off a few bugs. Bloch slept in the main house, living it up, the bastard.

If Matt could see him now. Otis sniffled, imagining his old buddy's black eyes on him, telling him like no words could what a stupid asshole he was for taking orders from Bloch. For not telling him in the first place Bloch was involved. What the hell. Matthew Stark was on the story now, thanks to Otis Raymond. They'd all be thanking him soon. Yeah. The Weaze'd be responsible for saving Ryder's stupid ass and seeing Bloch go down.

Good ol' Weaze.

Nobody had ever expected him to do shit. He remembered how surprised everybody was when he got noticed for his marksmanship at North Fort. Fucking wowed them, he had. Ended up a door gunner because of it. "We can use you, buddy," they'd said.

He grinned and closed his eyes. They burned from lack of sleep, too much bad living, and too many goddamn memories. But shit. It'd all be worth it. Stark'd say to him, "Hey, good going, Weaze," the way he had before, back in 'Nam, when Otis hadn't been brave so much as plain doped-up crazy. This time he was being brave. He knew the risks, knew what he was doing. Yeah, after this, he'd haul out his medals. Brag a little.

The door to the shack creaked open, and Bloch and two of his bodyguards walked in, just like they'd been out fishing all day. Bloch was even cleaned and pressed. Beside him, Otis had always felt like a dirty, slimy worm. It was the one thing the sergeant liked about him, called it proper respect.

Otis wiped the dribbled whiskey off his mouth. He didn't care if Bloch saw the bottle. He squinted at the sergeant and the guards from the gloom of his corner and wished they'd shut the fucking door. They were letting in the cold air.

"Raymond," Bloch said.

Out of habit, Otis climbed to his feet. The rules of soldiering were all that made sense to him anymore, maybe all that ever had. He sucked in what was left of his stomach. "Sergeant?"

"You've been out of camp, Raymond." Bloch's voice was steady, his tone without condemnation or doubt. "You went into town without permission."

No use denying it, so Otis just stared straight ahead. He couldn't figure out why, but he wasn't seeing anything. Just blankness, not even dark. Nothing. It was weird.

Bloch shifted his position on the dirty floor. "You made a telephone call while you were there. Do you want to tell me about it?"

"Do I need to, Sergeant?"

"No," he said softly, almost sadly, but Otis knew better. Bloch didn't have feelings. "I don't suppose you do, Raymond. The call was to Washington, D.C. You talked to Matthew Stark, didn't you?"

Otis didn't move, didn't speak. No point in bluffing. Bloch already knew who he'd called and what he'd said. Bloch knew everything. Otis wasn't surprised, he wasn't impressed, he wasn't even scared. That was just Bloch. One thing: Stark'd handle him. Otis wished he'd have a chance to warn Stark that Bloch was onto him, but what the hell. Matt was good.

"Raymond?"

Otis idly scratched an insect bite on his forearm, and suddenly he smiled. His mind wasn't going after all. Shit. The uncontrollable visions, awake or asleep—they weren't the mindless wanderings of a fucking lunatic.

They were the dreams of a dead man.

Yeah, he thought. Bloch can't kill me. I'm already dead.

Fourteen

Juliana and Wilhelmina got off the bus near a small tenement building just outside the diamond district. As they
walked up the front steps, Wilhelmina scowled at the dead
geraniums sticking up out of the window boxes. There was
no excuse for such laziness. She rang the doorbell, and a
round, bald-headed man came to the door and let them in,
introducing himself as Martin Dekker. He was younger
than she'd expected, perhaps in his late forties. But these
days most people seemed so young. They didn't remember the war, the bombings, the starvation, the treachery of
the Nazis and their collaborators. And if people like herself didn't tell the young, refused to talk, how could they
know? What assurance could there be that it all wouldn't
happen again?

She introduced herself and Juliana, speaking Dutch.
She didn't bother to translate, assuming Juliana could follow along well enough.

"I'm so glad you came," the Belgian said cheerfully,
leading them upstairs as he jingled a huge ring of keys.
"There's still been no word from your brother."

"Have you called the police?"

Dekker shook his head. "I thought I should wait for you."

And let me go through the trouble, Wilhelmina thought irritably. People always seem to sense her ability to make difficult decisions. She didn't like to any more than they did and wasn't, in her opinion, more competent to do so, but she wasn't one to leave the dirty work to someone else. It was peculiar how people wanted her to be decisive and then were uncomfortable with her because she was.

"It's not like Mr. Peperkamp to disappear like this," Dekker went on. "He's always been such a good tenant. Now he's late with his rent, and—" he made an exaggerated sigh of despair "—and nothing from him. Not a word."

Wilhelmina hoped he didn't expect her to pay her brother's rent. She only wanted to find him, not settle his debts. Not getting the desired response, the landlord unlocked the door to Johannes's apartment and excused himself, thumping quietly back downstairs.

"He doesn't speak English?" Juliana asked.

"I don't know," Wilhelmina said. "I didn't ask."

They went into the two-room apartment. A fat, half-smoked cigar lay cold in a brass ashtray, and the sleeve of one of Juliana's recordings stood in front of the elaborate, outdated stereo system. She was smiling, and her hair was longer. Johannes owned all her recordings. Wilhelmina didn't own any, but sometimes she heard them on the radio.

"For so long I've thought of Johannes as the muscular, stubborn boy he was before the war," she said, half to herself, except that she spoke in English. "He won so many speed skating races on the canals. I would watch, all bundled up, drinking hot cocoa with my friends."

Juliana asked softly, "Did you learn to skate yourself?"

"Mmm, yes, but I've forgotten long since." There had been too many years when she'd had to devote so much of her energy just to survival and then to putting aside the past and going on. Not forgetting, of course—simply going on.

For the first time in her life, Wilhelmina felt sorry for

her older brother. Johannes Peperkamp, the famous diamond cleaver. The cutter with the incomparable eye.

Now he lived in dreariness.

Ignoring Juliana's look of concern, she went into the galley kitchen, little more than a converted closet off the sitting room, and automatically put on a kettle for tea. The kitchen was clean enough, but there were no begonias in the windows. She could feel the loneliness that had crept into her brother's life. There was none of the cheerfulness and sparkling cleanliness in this place that there had been in his big apartment with Ann.

She inspected the refrigerator. Four kinds of cheeses and half an eel were neatly wrapped and there was a tin of butter cookies, but the milk had soured and a basket of mussels was beginning to smell. Even during his days of fame and greater fortune, Johannes hadn't been an extravagant man. He was naturally frugal and spent little money on himself. What he was saving it for Wilhelmina didn't know, and yet she did the same. And neither was one to waste food. There had been too many days in their lives without it.

"It doesn't feel right here, does it?" Juliana asked, standing behind her aunt.

Without speaking, Wilhelmina shook her head and turned off the heat under the kettle. She no longer wanted tea. Together, she and Juliana went into the bedroom, but there was nothing there either, nothing to say, nothing to find. The double bed was neatly made, and on the bureau were two photographs, one of Ann, laughing, just a touch of the familiar sadness behind her eyes, and one of their wedding day before the war. Wilhelmina could remember more clearly than she could remember anything that had happened last week how she and Rachel had wished that one day they would have a marriage like Johannes and Ann had. What dreamers they'd been.

Now there were no more dreams, only memories.

"Let's go," she said.

"Aunt Willie…"

"I'm fine. We'll bring Mr. Dekker the eel. That will have to satisfy him."

But downstairs in the entryway, a dark figure was trying to communicate with the Belgian landlord in bad French. Juliana let out a small cry and jumped backward, but too late.

The black-brown eyes turned to her. "Shit," he said.

She stared back at him, insolent and unapologetic. "Fancy meeting you here, Mr. Stark."

"Jesus Christ, why the hell couldn't you stay out of this?"

So this was the American reporter, Wilhelmina thought, observing him with interest. He was rather tough-looking, with dark, distant eyes, but there was something in the scarred face she found compelling. Nothing obvious or boastful—just there. Competence, knowledge, pain. If she had to guess, she would say this was a man who understood that objectivity wasn't so easy to maintain. In her mind, that was good. She believed objectivity was wrong.

She glanced at Juliana, whose expression was one of distaste mixed with acceptance—and, she thought, excitement. How interesting. Juliana often seemed so vague and bored with the real things of life, at least from what Wilhelmina could tell from her limited experience with her niece.

Matthew Stark sighed heavily, dread clouding his eyes, and Wilhelmina felt her heart skid. This was not a man given easily to emotion. Something was wrong.

"I gather you two don't know." He paused, his mouth straight and hard, but not uncaring. "Johannes Peperkamp was found dead of a heart attack earlier today in Amsterdam. He'd left his shop with a Dutchman whom I have reason to believe was named Hendrik de Geer. I'm sorry."

Amsterdam, Wilhelmina thought. Of course, Amsterdam. *Hendrik…*

She closed her eyes, hardly noticing how they burned, and her mind filled with images, old pictures, living now only inside her. She saw her brother as a young man, tall and laughing as he swept beautiful Ann onto the ice.

"Aunt Willie, are you all right?"

Juliana's soft voice, filled with grief and shock, broke into her memories, and Wilhelmina took the last step down into the entryway, level with Matthew Stark. Juliana followed unsteadily. Catharina had spoiled her daughter, Wilhelmina thought. Juliana knew so little of the world. She had money and sophistication, fine clothes, a magnificent education, and an incomparable talent, but she'd never experienced cold or hunger or even death, as common as it was. Now Johannes was dead. And Rachel. Juliana's white, frozen face seemed inconsequential. Wilhelmina found it difficult to feel sympathy toward someone who'd never really suffered.

And it was sad—wrong—that her niece had never really known her own uncle. But that wasn't Juliana's fault. None of this was her fault, and Wilhelmina regretted her silent criticism. Juliana was good and kind, and Wilhelmina was proud of her. She was her niece, the last of the Peperkamps.

Oh, my God.

But Wilhelmina shook off this thought. It strained her imagination to think Johannes would have turned over the Minstrel's Rough and four hundred years of Peperkamp tradition to their pianist niece. Even at her best, Juliana wouldn't be likely to take the Minstrel tradition seriously. Not since Amsterdam had any of the Peperkamp siblings mentioned the stone. Surely Johannes had tossed it into the sea. And yet, how could he?

Dear God, Wilhelmina thought with a sharp, sudden, terrible sense of loss. My brother is dead. Gone.

"I'm all right," she said finally, because she had to, for

herself if no one else. "Johannes lived a long life. He was a good man."

"I know," Juliana said.

Wilhelmina looked at Matthew Stark, his expression unreadable as he watched Juliana. Yet she could feel the tension in him, telling him to stay where he stood when what he wanted to do was to go to Juliana. Ahh, no, she thought, he's half in love with her already.

The dark eyes lifted to the old Dutchwoman. "You're Juliana's aunt—Willie, is it?"

"Wilhelmina," she said, her voice clear and strong. There was nothing now to do but go on. Find Hendrik. Stop him. She would mourn her brother forever, but in private. Meanwhile, it seemed there was work to be done. *Hendrik—what treachery are you up to this time?* "My name is Wilhelmina Peperkamp."

"Another Peperkamp. Johannes and Catharina's sister?"

"Yes. I live in Rotterdam."

"Do you know why your brother was in Amsterdam?"

"To pick up diamonds." The lie came without effort; she had no reason to trust this American, no reason to tell him anything. "I'm feeding his cat."

"You came all the way from Rotterdam to feed a cat? Okay, if that's the way you want it. Don't tell me a damn thing if you don't want to. I'll find out what I need to on my own. Just go back home, both of you. Get the hell out of this mess."

"We'll keep your advice in mind, Mr. Stark," Wilhelmina said impatiently. She hated to be told what to do. "But right now you've brought us sad news, and I think you should go."

"All right. Do you know anything about Hendrik de Geer?"

"*Goeden dag,* Mr. Stark."

"That means?"

"Goodbye."

Stark turned his hard gaze to Juliana. "You want me to leave?"

Juliana stared at him a moment, and Wilhelmina could see the doubt in her niece's eye. My heavens, she thought, Juliana wants to tell him no! Achh, what was this?

But Juliana nodded stoically. "Yes, I think you'd better."

Without a word, Matthew spun around and left. Wilhelmina stood beside Juliana and watched him pound down the steep front stairs. "A difficult man," she said.

"I know, but I'm not sure it's wise to let him go off on his own like this, Aunt Willie. He knows things he hasn't told us."

"And we know things we haven't told him, don't we?"

"Yes, but—" Juliana's jaw set hard. "I don't know about you, Aunt Willie, but I have no intention of just going home and forgetting about this—and no Vermont, either, damn it."

"Vermont? What's in Vermont?"

"Safety. Innocence. It's where Mother wants me to go."

"Bah. Some things you cannot escape. Shall we go?"

"Where? I'd like to follow Stark back to the United States—"

"So would I."

"But you don't have a passport."

"I do. I planned one day to go to New York to see your mother, but I changed my mind."

"Why?"

"She was the one who left."

"I should have guessed. You have your passport with you?"

"Yes. When I decided to go to Antwerp this morning, I thought I might have to go to New York, to see your mother." Hendrik, she thought, Hendrik… Had it finally come to this? She felt so tired suddenly, so old. "Come, we'll have to take care we're not followed."

She gave the eel to the landlord, who had been standing by unobtrusively, and explained she would be back later to settle her brother's affairs.

"What happened?" Martin Dekker asked, apparently not having followed the English exchange. "Where's your brother?"

She looked at the Belgian and said, her voice quiet and steady, "He's dead, Mr. Dekker. Johannes is gone."

Fifteen

U.S. Senator Samuel Ryder, Jr., adopted a carefully constructed expression of pensiveness and control as he looked across his walnut desk to the wine-colored leather chair where Hendrik de Geer sat, a rumpled, ashen-faced, spent, tired old man, reeking of sweat and gin. Ryder felt no sympathy. His aides had volunteered to call security—had pleaded with him to let them call—but the senator had refused. He'd insisted de Geer be ushered into his office, into the quiet, formal surroundings of a United States senator.

The room was unchanged from the days when it had been occupied by Samuel Ryder, Sr., the longtime senior senator from Florida. When elected, Sam had brought out all the furnishings that had been in storage—the desk, the carpets, the chairs, the mementos. Everything. There was only one addition: a portrait. It had been painted shortly before the senior Ryder's death, an ominous picture of a man remembered for his soft baby blue eyes and deadly incisiveness, and it hung above the desk, behind his son, where Sam, Jr., wouldn't have to look at it all the time.

"Are you absolutely positive that Johannes Peperkamp didn't have the stone?" Ryder asked, concealing the panic brought on by the Dutchman's succinct, unemotional testimony about the events over the past few days in Amsterdam. "He *must* have!"

"That's what I thought, as well," the Dutchman replied calmly.

Did you kill him? Ryder's mind burned with the question, but he didn't ask it, instead convincing himself that the operational details of de Geer's activities weren't his concern. He licked his lips, rubbing one finger into the polished walnut of the edge of his desk. He refused to meet the Dutchman's impassive, penetrating gaze, as if that would dissociate him even more from the events he'd put into motion.

"Then who has it?" Ryder asked.

"No one. The Minstrel is lost—if it ever existed."

Ryder slapped his slate blotter. "It has to exist, and it can't be lost!"

"Why, because you don't wish it?"

"Damn it, man, do you know what this means?"

The Dutchman leaned back deeper into the chair, looking as if he might fall asleep—or fall down dead—at any moment. He had disengaged himself. "It means you must devise another plan to get Bloch his money," he said. "You're a clever man, Senator Ryder. You'll think of something. With Rachel Stein's death, you no longer have any hold over me. Even if I did know where to locate the Minstrel, I would no longer feel compelled to get it for you. If I'd known about her death before I left for Antwerp, I'd never have gone."

"I don't believe she was ever your sole motive for going along with me. It was a factor, to be sure, but the Peperkamps were your friends—"

"That was many, many years ago. Now, I'm afraid, they would all be delighted to hear of my death. You know what Rachel Stein said about me. It's all true."

"Did you kill her?" Ryder asked suddenly in a low,

hoarse voice, regretting his words almost immediately. He couldn't believe he was articulating such an accusation! Why couldn't he be as cool and imperturbable as de Geer—as Matthew Stark had always been? Steelman. The chopper pilot the men all wanted to ride with. His skill, his uncompromising sense of duty, his steady nerves, his reliability were all highly regarded by the men he transported, dusted off, and aided in combat. Ryder himself had never commanded such respect. It was something he'd learned to live with.

The Dutchman withdrew a cigar and a small pocketknife, shaking his head in feigned despair. "The man you must think I am, to kill an old woman, to throw her down on the ice." He sighed, deftly cutting off the end of the cigar, pocketing the knife, and putting the cigar in his mouth. "I was sitting in your car when Rachel died. I had no interest in killing Rachel Stein. I've done enough to her."

Ryder rubbed his forehead with all eight fingers, his thumbs planted firmly under his cheekbones as if holding his head together. "Then it must have been an accident after all."

Hendrik de Geer laughed a cold, unpleasant laugh, the unlit cigar sticking on his lip. "You're a fool, Senator Ryder—a blind, dangerous fool. You don't believe that any more than I do. You told Sergeant Bloch about Rachel, didn't you? He can arrange to have old women pushed down as easily as he can blackmail a United States senator."

"He's not blackmailing me," Ryder said sharply. "I'm helping him establish himself as a self-sustaining force for freedom—"

"Oh, spare me, Senator. I've been in this world a long, long time. You need not make your excuses to me. How much did you tell Bloch?"

Ryder didn't answer at once. He folded his hands on his

blotter and sat very still controlling his anger and distaste for the Dutchman. At the moment, it was more important to think clearly. He had to debate with himself what to tell Hendrik de Geer and what to handle himself. How would the Dutchman react to a full account of Ryder's conversations with Bloch?

But de Geer was impatient—and, as always, entirely too perceptive. "You told him everything, didn't you?"

"I didn't—"

"Don't lie to me!" The Dutchman didn't raise his voice, but the intensity of his words deepened the piercing blue of his eyes and brought him forward in his chair, the unflappable impassiveness shattered. "You told Bloch what you know about the Minstrel."

"I had to—don't you see? Look, de Geer, you know Bloch. He wants the diamond. You must get it for him, don't you understand? If you don't...for God's sake, man, if you don't he'll go after it himself. Do you want that to happen?"

"That's not my problem," the Dutchman said, rising, his disgust underlining his words.

Ryder fought the urge to jump up and plead his case, and he felt the familiar gnawing of indecision, the aching emptiness of simply not knowing what to do. "I can't control Bloch—he'll go to the Peperkamp women, he'll try each one until he's positive none has the diamond or until he gets it. Or he'll expect me to do this, despite my valid unwillingness to be involved on that end. You can't let this happen! De Geer—for God's sake, help me!"

Hendrik de Geer lit his cigar with a match, puffed, shook out the match, and dropped it on the senator's desk, where its smoking melted through layers of wax. The room filled with the smoke of the cigar. Without pleasure, the Dutchman looked at Ryder and smiled. "I'll help myself."

* * *

Alice Feldon wasn't relieved to see Matthew Stark wander into the *Gazette* newsroom. She was standing at her desk as usual, glasses on top of her head, her nails painted something called African Violet. Stark couldn't have spent more than a few hours in Antwerp. She'd just come from fighting the money boys upstairs about his bebopping around, spending the paper's money with no discernible progress on *any* kind of story, large, medium, or small.

"You're the ones who've been telling me to give the man a chance," she'd said. So go suck an egg, she'd felt like adding.

Yes, they'd replied, but did she know how much it cost to fly to Belgium?

Stark moved past her desk, his black leather jacket unzipped. Underneath was a black denim shirt and, for a change, heavy charcoal cords. And those damn boots, of course. Alice tried to imagine him in tassel loafers and couldn't. The man was informal to the point of insolence. But she knew he gave such matters little or no thought. People could take him or leave him. He didn't give a damn which.

"I thought you were in Antwerp," she said.

"I was."

"And?"

The black-brown eyes were leveled at her. "And now I'm back."

"Jackass," she said, unintimidated. "I want a progress report on my desk in an hour. You can't be trusted, Stark."

"Zeigler in?"

"Forget it. He's not doing any more errands for you. I haven't got the staff to waste on a story that's going nowhere fast. You prove you're nursing something important, I'll give you all the help you need. Get me some facts, damn it. Until then, you're on your own."

"Never mind," Stark said, as if he didn't hear her. He was

looking around the big, open newsroom. "I see him. Love your nails, Feldie. Make you look like a real dragon lady."

She shoved her chair in under her desk, just missing her fingers. "Stark, goddamn you, I'm serious!"

He gave her one of his slow, disarming grins. "You're always serious, Feldie. Loosen up."

"You don't come up with a story this time, you lazy ass is out of here. I mean it, goddamnit."

"That's not much of a threat," he said.

He sauntered over to the massive copy machine, where Aaron Ziegler was feeding in paper and looking bored out of his mind. Rookie reporter or not, he had on a dark suit, rep tie, white shirt, and shiny Weejuns. Alice thought he had to have a trust fund or something. God only knew he couldn't afford clothes like that on what the *Gazette* paid him. Dread and excitement came into his face when he saw Stark, but five minutes with Alice earlier that day had reminded him which side his bread was buttered on, so to speak. He glanced up at her.

She nodded. Oh, why the hell not? Somebody else could feed the copy machine.

In her sturdy shoes and worn coat, with her single carry-on bag held firmly under her arm, Aunt Willie looked a bit like a bag lady after they'd cleared customs at Kennedy Airport. "Where do we get the bus?" she asked.

"We can take a cab," Juliana said, leading the way.

"A cab? Why, isn't there a bus?"

"A cab's easier. Come on."

Wilhelmina made no comment, but Juliana could feel her aunt's disapproval. Americans were extravagant and wasteful. Why should her niece spend the money on a taxi when she could use public transportation? Material success meant nothing to Aunt Willie, and neither did the inconvenience of taking a bus or a train. Juliana wondered what her aunt would have to say about the expensive sportscar she had sitting in a garage. She seldom used it, except to escape to Vermont on occasion.

Vermont. Shuji. Now that her uncle was dead, the dilemmas she'd faced only a few days ago seemed trivial.

"When I'm gone," Uncle Johannes said in his gentle way, *"the Minstrel is yours to do with as you must. No one can tell you what is right, what is wrong. That is for you to decide. Do you understand, Juliana?"*

She hadn't. The largest uncut diamond in the world, the mystery surrounding it, the legend, the myth, the tradition. It was all so much mumbo jumbo to her. Her throat tightened as she remembered the quiet, intelligent man with the soft, proud look in his eyes as he'd come backstage seven years ago in Delftshaven. She'd felt an instant bond with him—as if she could do anything, be anything, and he still would be there for her. You're the last of the Peperkamps, he'd told her. Until then, she had never thought about it. The Peperkamps had been strangers to her.

She'd stuck the Minstrel's Rough away and tried to forget about it. And, as he'd requested, she'd never mentioned it to her mother or her aunt.

Now she wasn't sure what to do. Over and over again on the flight to New York, she'd considered telling Aunt Willie she had it, asking her advice. But she'd resisted. Were people dying because of the Minstrel? Would telling Aunt Willie about it endanger her?

Am I in danger?

Although this was her first trip to the United States, Wilhelmina seemed unimpressed and asked no questions about the sights as they drove into Manhattan. Juliana didn't bother to point out any landmarks.

Wilhelmina was leaning back against the torn seat, frowning thoughtfully. "Do you think your reporter has gone back to Washington?"

"I don't know. It's possible, I suppose. He might try Mother."

"He'll get nothing out of her," Wilhelmina said with assurance.

"I suspect you're right. I certainly never have."

"Well, we'll just have to locate him and find out what he's up to. You can do that, Juliana. I'll see to Catharina."

"Me? Aunt Willie, Matthew Stark isn't going to stand for me hanging around."

"So?"

"So I'm not about to follow him around like a puppy dog with my tail wagging!"

"Achh, so much pride. I don't understand this about puppy dogs and tails."

"Never mind. I just think you and I could accomplish more if we stay together."

"You do, do you? And just what information do we have that we can act upon?"

"You and Mother know who Hendrik de Geer is. You could tell me."

Aunt Willie snorted in disgust. "And what would that accomplish? Would it tell us where he is? No, it would not. Would it tell us what this Senator Ryder is up to? No, it would not. Would it tell us if Rachel's and Johannes's deaths were acts of God? No, it would not. Would it—?"

"Okay, Aunt Willie, you've made your point. But I still think Mother should tell me what happened in Amsterdam."

"So do I, but it's not my place to make her."

"Aunt Willie—"

"Are you sure this driver knows what he's doing? I hate cars. I don't want to come all this way and then die on a highway in New York City."

Juliana sighed and tried again. "Aunt Willie—"

"If I do," she persisted, "just have me cremated. Don't

bother with the expense of having my body shipped back to Holland."

"You're impossible."

"Yes, I know. But I'm honest."

"To a fault," Juliana said.

His head pounding with fatigue and frustration, Matthew indulged himself in a fresh round of self-reproach for having mentioned to Juliana that he was on his way to Antwerp. Dangling such information in front of her was the equivalent of handing her a free ticket and driving her to the airport. How could he not have realized that she just might follow him?

But he had to admit he'd felt a certain satisfaction in running into her at her uncle's apartment. It meant she wasn't so self-involved that she didn't give a damn about an old diamond cutter who just happened to be a relative. It meant she was tough and tenacious enough to risk at least trying to find out what was going on.

It meant the prospect of bumping into him in Antwerp hadn't bothered her one bit.

Now, though, the adventure was over. Her uncle was dead—*two* people were dead. That was too much of a co-incidence for Stark. Rachel Stein and Johannes Peperkamp had something to do with Otis Raymond and his problems. With Sam Ryder and Phil Bloch. Whatever was going on, Matthew couldn't justify bringing Juliana Fall and her stout, cranky old aunt further into it. No more encouragement, no more questions.

Do whatever you goddamn well please, ladies, just leave me alone and stay the hell out of this mess.

But Juliana knows something about the Minstrel's Rough, he thought; you know damn well she does. Probably the aunt does, too. You should ignore *feelings*, goddamnit, and go after the facts.

He shook his head, adamant. He could see the dark, beautiful eyes of Juliana Fall widen and fill with unspilled tears when he'd told her about her uncle. She was a piano player, for God's sake. Let her entertain herself with J.J. Pepper. He couldn't control what she did, perhaps, but he could control what he did.

And what he was going to do was leave her the hell alone.

Aaron Ziegler thrust a sheet torn off the wire in front of him. "I found the Peperkamp obit," he said proudly. "It was just a couple of lines, a repeat mostly of the information in the folder I already gave you. He died of a heart attack in Amsterdam. He was part of a dying breed of highly skilled cleavers who eschewed lasers and computers in doing their work. His wife was Ann Visser, whose father was in the House of Asscher in Amsterdam before World War Two. The Nazis murdered him in Auschwitz. She died ten years ago."

"Thanks," Stark said. "I appreciate it."

"Sure."

"Want to do me another favor?"

Aaron shifted from one tassel loafer to the other. "Okay."

"See what you can find out about a retired army sergeant by the name of Phillip Bloch." He handed Ziegler a scrap of paper he'd scrawled names on during the flight from Belgium. "You can try the guys listed here. They might be able to help."

"Is there anything specific you're after?"

"Yeah. I want to know where he is."

Juliana's apartment building was an outrage, of course, but Wilhelmina resisted comment as her niece led her past the uniformed doorman into the marble lobby, then to the brass elevator with its smiling elevator man. Juliana explained that Central Park West attracted numerous performing artists and she felt comfortable there, she could be herself. Wilhelmina wondered, how could you be anyone else? To her, the place felt like a museum or a queen's palace.

And the apartment itself! So many locks, so many rooms! Juliana told her aunt she could choose whichever bedroom she wanted, except for the "blue" one and the "rose" one.

"I use the blue," Juliana said.

"And what about the rose?"

"My friend J.J. stays there when she's in town. She's left a lot of her stuff in the closet."

"Oh."

Wilhelmina investigated. In and out, in and out. She counted closets, bathrooms, bureaus, fireplaces, paintings, vases. She found some comfort in seeing the film of dust on virtually everything. Perhaps Juliana's material possessions didn't mean too much to her.

She settled on a tidy, sparsely furnished room in the back. It was the smallest. Juliana had taken a shower while Wilhelmina looked around, and she grinned from the doorway, her hair up in a big white towel. "This is the former maid's room, Aunt Willie," she said.

"Is it? How charming."

"Did you want to see Mother this afternoon?"

"Yes, of course."

"She isn't going to talk to you in front of me, you know."

"Then you can always leave. Now hurry up and get dressed."

In less time than Wilhelmina thought her niece would have been capable of, Juliana joined her in the living room, wearing a pretty multistriped mohair coat and a black mohair scarf tied over her hair, which was still slightly damp. She had a leather satchel hooked over one shoulder.

"We can get the bus across the street and take it over to Fifth Avenue," Juliana said, "then walk over to Madison—unless you'd rather take a cab."

"The bus is fine," Wilhelmina said, buttoning her coat. She nodded to the satchel. "What's in there?"

Juliana grinned. "Bus tokens."

But when they climbed onto the bus, Juliana slipped two tokens from her coat pocket. Wilhelmina sniffed. Better to be told something was none of her business than to be lied to. However, she said nothing, more interested in the man standing on the corner just down from the bus stop, leaning against a nude tree on the wide sidewalk. He was a solid, pleasant-looking man, perhaps in his midthirties, with a fleshy face. He wore a trench coat and a tweed cap. Wilhelmina had spotted him watching them as they'd crossed the streets from the Beresford.

Now, as they got onto the bus, he flagged a cab. He would know the bus route, possibly even guess where they were heading. Not that it mattered. She didn't think he'd have any difficulty at all following the bus and getting out at the same stop they did.

"Aunt Willie, is something wrong?"

Juliana had responded well to the Nazi who'd followed them in Rotterdam; Wilhelmina had been impressed with her niece's display of nerve and competence. And she'd seemed to take no real pride in what she'd done, which was good. Wilhelmina believed one should act in accordance with one's own tolerance for risk, not to impress or shock anyone else. In her experience, that was when trouble started. Better to deal with an admitted coward than an unadmitted coward. She loathed bravado.

Nevertheless, being followed in Europe was quite different than having one's own home watched. Wilhelmina shook her head. "No, nothing."

"You saw him, too, didn't you? The man in the Burberry, right?"

"Yes."

Juliana smiled, her eyes shining. "It sounds like an Agatha Christie novel, doesn't it? *The Man in the Burberry Coat.*"

"Juliana—"

"It's all right, Aunt Willie." Her expression was grim but also surprisingly determined; she would deal with what was happening and not fall to pieces. "We'll handle him."

Of that, of course, Wilhelmina had no doubt.

Sergeant Phillip Bloch stormed into the fishing lodge and kicked the chair out from under his desk, putting all his pent-up rage into that one motion. He didn't sit down. His body was rigid with tension; he felt as if he could break himself into pieces, like chopping wood.

That idiot Ryder, he thought. *That goddamn, fucking idiot!*

Bloch tried to calm himself. This level of stress wasn't good for his health; he had to take things in stride. Ryder wasn't going to turn smart overnight. He'd just let Hendrik de Geer go off as he pleased, and now Johannes Peperkamp was dead, and Ryder didn't know where the Dutchman or the diamond was.

Jesus!

Ryder, who didn't know shit about people, had said de Geer was a drunk and had just gone off on his own. He'd disappeared. Bloch didn't believe it. De Geer had his own reasons for not killing Ryder and being done with the stupid asshole. Whatever those reasons were, Bloch didn't trust them, and he was going to make damn sure he didn't have that stinking Dutchman flying back in his face.

"Christ," he said aloud, his teeth gritted, "do I have to do *everything* myself?"

It was so fucking simple. With the old man dead, all you do is go to the Peperkamp women. Wilhelmina Peperkamp, Catharina Fall, Juliana Fall. You take them one by one, nothing fancy. You point out that their brother or uncle would have made arrangements to pass along the

Minstrel's Rough to one of them. You point out that means one of them has it. You let them know that you want it. They argue, you grab them by the throat and say, "Get me the Minstrel or else." One of them does, and bingo.

You don't act wishy-washy. You have to *believe* that one of them has the stone.

Once you get it, you have it cut, polished, and evaluated, and you go about snipping off any loose ends still hanging in your face. Rachel Stein-type loose ends. No big deal. Just the things that have to be done to achieve the larger objective. Means to an end. Like stuff he'd had to do in Vietnam.

Then you cash in on the world's largest and most mysterious uncut diamond—now cut—and you say hello to the big time.

To do anything, you couldn't rely on fucking incompetents.

"I don't have the maneuverability you do," Ryder had whined.

Christ.

"You have to understand, Matthew Stark is nosing around. You know what he thinks of me."

Same thing I do, Sammy.

Bloch grunted, calmer. Yeah, Ryder had a point about Stark. Neither of them could afford to have that sonofabitch climbing up their backs, trying to bring them down. Guess it was time he and Steelman—Christ, he hated all those dumbass nicknames—came to terms.

He sat down at the desk and picked up the phone.

Juliana found her mother sitting disconsolate in a quiet corner of the bakeshop kitchen, a pot of tea in front of her. Aunt Willie had broken the news about their brother's death and retreated to the shop, for coffee and something to eat, she'd said. Juliana knew better; her aunt wanted her sister and niece to have a chance to talk.

"Just don't mention our gentleman in the trench coat," Aunt Willie had whispered.

Juliana knew better. He'd stayed behind the bus until they got off and was waiting across the street from the bakeshop when they arrived. Juliana had both horrified and delighted her aunt by waving to him.

"Shouldn't we call the police?" she'd asked.

"Why? Because there's a man smoking a cigarette on Madison Avenue?"

"He followed us."

"That's true. But even if we could prove it, what would he tell the police? 'I'm a fan of Juliana Fall's. She's so pretty.'" She lifted a broad palm in dismissal.

They'd decided to let him stand outside in the cold.

Catharina bit her lip, and tears streamed down her pale cheeks when she saw her daughter. "Thank God— Oh, thank God. I've been so worried!"

She took Juliana's hand, squeezing it hard, as if to make sure she was really there, and Juliana sat down, her frustration with her mother gone. She felt so guilty. Her mother's only brother was dead. Juliana hadn't known her uncle well, although she'd loved him, and she didn't have any siblings or any cousins on the Peperkamp side of the family. But she was close to her Fall cousins and would hate to lose any of them. She knew so little of death.

"I'm sorry, Mother—for worrying you, for Uncle Johannes. For everything."

Catharina nodded, accepting the apology as readily as she always did, believing in her daughter, trusting her. Juliana could only wonder what her mother would do when she learned she'd had the Minstrel's Rough for the last seven years.

She won't find out, Juliana vowed silently. I won't tell her. I'll figure a way out of this so she won't have to know.

"It's all right," Catharina said at last.

"Mother, I…"

But Juliana found herself unable to go on. She couldn't press her mother for answers now, not with her grief and shock so raw. And did she really have the right to demand to know what had happened to her mother long before she was born? What about her mother's right not to tell her daughter certain things about her own life? If I have a child, Juliana thought, would I want her to know everything I've done? Aren't there feelings, events, decisions that I will want to remain private?

"I want you to know how sorry I am about Uncle Johannes," she said. "I know you didn't see much of him in recent years, but I also know that didn't make any difference to how you felt about him. In your own way, you're a close family. I think I see that now."

Catharina caught her lower lip and released Juliana's hand so she could brush away her tears. "What are you going to do?"

"I don't know," Juliana said truthfully.

"Aren't you working on the Chopin concerto?"

Juliana smiled, rising, and gave her mother a quick hug. "You're just as impossible as Aunt Willie, just not in the same way. But I do love you, Mum."

"And I love you, too," she whispered. Then she sat up straight, inhaling, determined. "Send Aunt Willie in here."

"Well, Steelman."

Matthew recognized the voice instantly and sank back against his chair. "Bloch."

"You don't take to warnings, do you?"

"You tell me."

"My man saw you in Antwerp."

Damn it, Stark thought, how stupid could he have been? He'd never even considered that Bloch would have someone watching Johannes Peperkamp's shop, his house.

And Juliana?

Damn it to hell. If Bloch had had a man at the Peperkamp house, he'd seen her and the old aunt. How much did the bastard know?

Bloch went on, pleased with himself, "You were picked up at the old man's house not long after Juliana Fall and Wilhelmina Peperkamp got there. They're a real Mutt and Jeff, aren't they? I hear Fall's quite the looker. What do you think?"

"I think I should have blown your fucking ass to bits when I had the chance."

"That's what you get for playing by the rules. But that's history. I'm concerned with right now. Want me to give you a rundown of what I know?"

"No."

"I know you were at Lincoln Center the same night as Ryder and the Stein woman, and I know you've been to New York to see Juliana Fall and to Antwerp looking for her uncle. And you know why you've been to those places, *sir?* Because your old buddy Specialist Otis Raymond has been snitching to his hero Matthew Stark."

"Let me talk to Weasel," Stark said stonily.

"He's unavailable."

"What the hell does that mean?"

"I trusted him, you know, tried to give him a hand. But that's the way it goes sometimes."

Stark felt everything inside him turn cold. "If you touch Otis, I'm coming after you, Bloch. I don't care where the hell you're hiding, I'll find you."

"Stay out of this," Bloch said, adding with heavy sarcasm, "Steelman."

"Bloch—"

The sergeant hung up.

Hey, Steelman, we just landed our asses in some serious shit...sir.

That was Otis Raymond. Matthew raked one hand through his hair and tried to regain his sense of balance, of distance. The Weaze had never played by the book or worried about making it out of Vietnam. There was no future for him, not much past, just the present. He'd treated his M-60, standard equipment for a door gunner, with more care than most of the people he knew. But he'd cried like a two-year-old when a low ceiling prevented them from pulling out a stranded platoon and they'd had to go in later, too late, for the casualties. He'd laughed hysterically when he shoved grunts out of the chopper eight or ten feet above the ground, yelling, "Playtime, fellas!" He'd been proud of his medals, of the lives he'd saved; he never said much about the lives he'd taken. Just that one time.

You just do what you gotta do. I figure, my time's up, it's up, and they must figure the same. You know? Shit, I guess you don't. I'm the one does the shooting, huh?

He was right, at least for a time. Toward the end of his first tour, Stark had switched from slicks to gunships, AH-1G Cobras. Snakes, they were nicknamed. He'd wanted a chance to shoot back for a change. It hadn't made him feel any better. By then, nothing did. The snakes didn't need door gunners, and he and Otis Raymond were finally split up. It didn't last. He'd transferred to light observation helicopters, the scouts, and once more Weasel was his gunner. Crazy, stupid, ugly, brave, cocky SP-4 Otis Raymond. He figured one day someone was going to make a movie out of him. The best damn gunner in Vietnam, he'd said of himself more than once. He might have been right. He'd lived, hadn't he? And somebody had made that movie. But Otis had never read or seen *LZ,* and Matthew had never gotten around to telling his old buddy that the nutty, heroic loner of a door gunner in both the book and the movie was modeled after SP-4 Otis Raymond.

Matthew felt empty and so goddamn alone.

Sixteen

~∞~∞~

Catharina's Bake Shop was warm and crowded, and Wilhelmina had enjoyed just sitting quietly for a moment, experiencing her sister's life. It seemed a satisfactory one, but she wished Johannes were there. They could have tea and cookies and get to know each other again. But that was not to be.

Juliana emerged from the kitchen looking shaken, but she managed a quick smile at her aunt. "Your turn. I've got to go out, but here's the key to my apartment. I'll meet you back there."

"Where are you going?"

"SoHo. I won't be gone long."

"And what of our man in the trench coat?"

"He won't follow me, Aunt Willie." This time her smile was genuine, lighting up her dark eyes. "You can count on that."

Wilhelmina wasn't so certain and found Juliana's confidence unsettling, but she made no argument. If the man outside meant them harm, he would have done something by now or at least been less obvious. He seemed to be keeping an eye on them. But why? On whose orders?

Sighing, she nodded. "Just be careful." And she, too,

managed a smile. "Don't leave me having to explain to your mother!"

Juliana laughed and went to the counter to order something to eat, and Wilhelmina retreated to the back, where she found her sister seated at a small table in the storeroom. Even dressed as she was in simple pants and a pullover, with her softly graying hair piled on top of her head, Catharina looked elegant. In the same outfit, Wilhelmina thought, I would look dumpy. It was one of the many differences between them.

She'd fixed a pot of tea and had a plate of *speculaas* and bread and cheese in front of her, untouched. "Willie," she said, her voice cracking, and she went on in Dutch, "I hate to say it, but I'm so glad you're here. I mean…"

Wilhelmina laughed, taking no offense. "I know what you mean, Catharina."

"Johannes…" Her voice trailed off, her eyes once more filling with tears.

"Yes. We'll miss him, won't we?"

"I'd begun to think he'd never die. Willie, what's happened to us? I remember when I was a little girl I could never imagine being away from my family. I wanted to live with Mother and Father forever—and you and Johannes. I thought you'd always be close by."

"You were the one who left," Wilhelmina pointed out, but without condemnation; it was a fact. She filled two simple white mugs with tea.

"I know, but I never thought we'd drift so far apart. I—"

Catharina cut herself off and began pulling distractedly at her hair, upsetting several pins, so that part of a braid came loose. Wilhelmina remembered how blond her little sister's hair had been as a girl, how she used to braid it for her so carefully and tenderly, not wanting to pull. Catharina's hands trembled, but she shoved them quickly into her lap.

"You're so strong, Willie," she went on, trying to smile. "I—I can't lie to myself, you know. I can't pretend I'm not relieved you're here. All these years…" She inhaled deeply. "And I still depend on you."

"There's nothing wrong with that, Catharina."

"But who do you depend on?"

"Myself. But that's only because that's all I have."

"What about me?"

Wilhelmina sighed, feeling awkward; she didn't like to discuss these things. "You're my sister. It's enough that you don't hate me."

Catharina held back a sob and shook her head, as if she couldn't believe her sister's words. "Oh, Willie, how could I ever hate you?"

"Sometimes, Catharina," she replied quietly, "I wonder how you could ever not. But enough of this nonsense. We must talk, don't you agree?"

Quickly and succinctly, in Dutch, they filled each other in on the events of the past few days, but Wilhelmina found herself facing more questions than answers.

"So Hendrik hasn't changed," she said at length. "He's out for himself and always will be. After all this time, he's finally going after the Minstrel."

Catharina nodded, neither agreeing nor disagreeing. "But Willie, is it possible Johannes went with Hendrik voluntarily?"

"No." Wilhelmina put a small chunk of cheese on a slice of the dark bread; it was just what she needed after the exhausting trip. "Johannes would never give Hendrik the Minstrel. Hendrik had to have coerced him somehow— he had to have some kind of leverage. Us, I would think. Hendrik would know Johannes would rather die than to give him, of all people, the Minstrel. So threatening Johannes with his own death would do no good. Even threatening him with my death alone wouldn't make Johannes go for the Minstrel—he would know better than to engage in any ridiculous protective sentiments toward me. Hendrik knows this."

"Johannes cared about you."

Wilhelmina waved a hand impatiently. "I know that, but he cared for me in a different way than he cared for you. Catharina, you've always been the favorite—Mother's, Father's, Johannes's, Hendrik's, mine. And Johannes may not know Juliana very well, but she's your daughter and she's all that represents the future of the Peperkamps. If he were threatened not with his own life, not with mine, but with the lives of you and Juliana, he would tell Hendrik anything. *Do* anything. Next to all of us, the Minstrel's Rough and four hundred years of tradition mean nothing."

"But you said yourself Hendrik wouldn't hurt me!"

"Of course he wouldn't." With a satisfied sigh, Wilhelmina swallowed the last of the bread and cheese. She added sugar to her tea and took a sip. "But the more I think about it, the less inclined I am to believe Hendrik is acting alone. Perhaps someone is threatening him.

"Who? Not Senator Ryder?"

"Who knows? It's all very complicated, I'm sure."

Catharina shuddered. "Willie, please, don't tell me this."

"What do you want to do, pretend nothing has happened?"

"I want to leave well enough alone."

Wilhelmina studied her sister for a moment. "And do you believe we can, Catharina?"

She waited for an answer while her younger sister sat rigidly in the chair, her eyes glazed and unfocused. She hadn't touched any of the food or her tea. Wilhelmina dunked a spice cookie and ate it in two bites.

"Of course you're right," Catharina said tightly, more hair falling out of its pins, and she added almost inaudibly, "We can't."

"I wish that we could. Believe me, I do. Have you been followed?"

Catharina's round soft eyes grew even larger as she took in her sister's words. "You, too?"

"Yes—and Juliana."

"Juliana!" Catharina jumped up, her face ghastly white. "No, Willie. She can't be involved!"

"Why, because you don't wish her to be?"

"That's cruel."

"We must look at the facts and not let our judgment be influenced by wishful thinking."

"Juliana has no place in this," Catharina said sternly, returning to her chair.

"We might not have that choice."

"She's *my* daughter, Willie."

"Yes, and she's also an adult. She must make her own decisions and deal with their consequences. Catharina, she's thirty years old."

Catharina broke a cookie in half, then into quarters, then into crumbs. "You don't have a daughter, how could you understand?"

"Achh, I understand more than you think. Because of who she is—her career in music, her growing up here with all this wealth—Juliana knows little of the world. You can't stop her from finding out what it is."

"You think I've spoiled her."

"Life has spoiled her. She's been very lucky, Catharina, to have you and Adrian, to have so much." Wilhelmina smiled, trying to take the edge off her words. "Except for not teaching her Dutch and, perhaps, being so close-mouthed about the past, you haven't done anything I wouldn't have done in your position. You don't want what we suffered in Amsterdam to touch her. I understand that. We didn't want the war to touch you, but it did. That wasn't our fault or yours. It was just something that happened."

"Willie—"

"Catharina, talk to her."

"I don't think I can." She brushed the cookie crumbs off her trembling fingers. "Willie, I don't want to lose her."

"I know."

"Do you?"

"I believe I do. More than thirty years ago I watched a ship sail with my only sister aboard. She'd married an American, the man she loved, and I was happy because she was so happy. But I'd lost her. There was no going back, no making up for what was done. Never in my life have I felt so alone as at that moment." She looked into her sister's soft green eyes. "You see, I do understand how you feel."

Catharina looked stricken. "You never told me you didn't want me to go. Willie—"

"I did want you to go. You deserved your life with Adrian."

"But if you'd told me you cared..."

"What? It would have changed anything? Never mind, Catharina, you know I despise these emotional discussions. Let us consider our options, shall we? It seems to me the best thing for us to do now is locate the Minstrel—if for no other reason than to keep Hendrik from getting it." She looked at her sister and asked matter-of-factly, "Do you have it?"

"No, of course not!" Catharina was indignant. "I'd have thrown it into the ocean, you know that—and so did Johannes. I hate that stone. If you ask me, it died with Johannes. There's no one to carry on the tradition."

"What?" Wilhelmina asked sharply, suddenly acutely alert. "Catharina, what did you say? There's no one to carry on the tradition?"

Catharina was frightened by her sister's wild look. "That's right, there isn't. Why wouldn't Johannes just turn the Minstrel over to someone else in the business and let another diamond family take over as caretaker? Just because the Peperkamps have had it for so long doesn't mean— Willie?"

Wilhelmina was shaking her head, more pale and shaky than she'd been in a long, long time—since she'd heard the boots of the *Gestapo* Green Police outside her window. She said woodenly, "Another family wouldn't be the Peperkamps."

"Well, of course not, but…" Catharina grabbed her chest and gulped for air as she realized what her sister was getting at. "Juliana—*no!* She can't have it! She'd have told me!"

"Would she?"

"Yes!"

Catharina quickly cleaned up the table, her hands shaking violently, knocking a cup to the floor. It broke, but she paid no attention, gathering up the tray and fleeing from the little storeroom into the kitchen. She threw everything into the giant sink and began sobbing uncontrollably, shutting out what was happening, shutting out the truth.

Her daughter had the Minstrel's Rough. Catharina knew it.

"I'm staying with Juliana," Wilhelmina said quietly behind her. "I'll look in her apartment for the stone and let you know what I find. Johannes must have given it to her during one of the few times he saw her—perhaps even in Delftshaven, when we were all together. And right under our noses, too. He wouldn't have told you because you wouldn't have approved and because I would have felt it my obligation to tell you."

"Why?" she asked hoarsely.

"Because you're her mother."

Catharina said nothing, not looking around as her sister left.

For seven years Juliana could have had the Minstrel. Seven *years!* And without ever once hinting to her own mother, confiding in her! What else did Juliana know? What had Johannes told her that she'd been waiting to hear from her mother all this time?

"Juliana, Juliana," she whispered, "why don't you talk to me?"

But she knew. Because you don't let her. She protects you, too, like everyone else does.

A brisk wind had kicked up. Juliana pulled her glittery shawl more tightly about her and headed around the corner to the Club Aquarian, running hard into a wind tunnel. She'd turned into J.J. Pepper in the bakeshop restroom. The giant shawl had disguised the mohair coat, and she'd tucked her blond hair under a black, rhinestone-studded turban. Her red vinyl boots, gobs of makeup, two handfuls of rhinestones around her neck and on her wrists, and the black twenties shift she'd worn under the coat, guessing she wouldn't have to take it off for her mother, had completed her bit of subterfuge.

She'd left the man in the Burberry coat making a half-hearted attempt to pretend to be interested in a gallery window as he smoked a cigarette. Halfway to the club, she'd realized that now Aunt Willie would have to deal with him alone and had felt a passing guilt. But her stalwart old aunt had outwitted Nazi occupiers for five years; she could handle someone following her on the streets of New York.

Instinctively protective of her fingers, she shoved her hands deep into her coat pockets; she'd forgotten gloves. The brisk air revived her, pushing back the bone-deep fatigue and the thought of Matthew Stark's dark eyes searching hers in the stairwell of her uncle's tenement. Had he guessed yet that she had the Minstrel's Rough? What would he do when he did?

A group of corporate types had the entrance to the Club Aquarian blocked, anxious for their after-work drinks—

maybe even to hear J.J. Pepper perform. They all looked
so normal. She wondered if that was what she was missing in her life: normality. Sometimes she dreamed about
living a nine-to-five life, what it would be like to put on
dress-for-success clothes in the morning and rush out to a
corporate job with a properly stodgy briefcase tucked
under one arm, to be in an office with people all around
her. After work she could dress up and go to a concert if
she wanted to and sit in the balcony, anonymous. She
would have a life she could count on, routines.

The long, daily hours alone at the piano were her only
constants. She could wear whatever she felt like, and there
was no clock to punch, no one to tell her what to do—except Shuji. But she didn't have to listen to him or to anyone else. And there was seldom anyone around to see her
sweat, concentrate, hurt.

She thought of Matthew Stark again—his remoteness, his
wry sense of humor, his strong sense of self. He didn't give
a damn what *The New Yorker* or *Vogue* or anyone else said
about her. Toots, he'd called her. Sweet cheeks. It was a
change from the most beautiful concert pianist in the world.

She wondered where he was. What he was doing. If he was
thinking about her as much as she was thinking about him.

Len was at the bar, and he didn't mention her lapse into
classical the other evening. "Another time we'll talk," he
said. "You've got a crowd waiting."

Nodding gratefully, she kicked off the vinyl boots and
slipped on J.J.'s gold T-strap shoes from her satchel, then
went straight to the piano. There was a crowd—an appre-
ciative one. She didn't think she could do much for them.
She was too tired, too preoccupied. She wanted to know
what Aunt Willie and her mother were saying to each other.
She wanted to know who was after the Minstrel. And why.
What she was supposed to do about it. How Senator Ryder
was involved. What Uncle Johannes had been doing in

Amsterdam. Who Hendrik de Geer was. How Matthew's buddy was doing.

She wanted answers, and all she had were questions.

That wasn't true. She had one big answer: she knew where the Minstrel was.

She began with a few Eubie Blake pieces, slipped in some Cole Porter, and then was moving. Lost. Transported. She focused on the music, on her playing. She stayed with it. Controlled it instead of letting it control her. Then lost the need to control or be controlled and played only to play. She could feel the motivation, if not define it; feel the need. For the first time in months, she had something real to communicate. Mood, feeling, loss, confusion, terror. It was all there at her fingertips.

When she finished, she bounced up, filled with energy, sweating, exhausted. She grinned at Al, who had her Saratoga water waiting. Len was there at the bar, clapping with the rest of the crowd. It felt good. She'd moved them, but more important, she'd moved herself.

"See those walls?" Len said. "They're shaking, babe. I knew they would be when you put it all together. You're letting loose, not holding on so tight. I like it. Now what're—" He stopped and narrowed his eyes, watching her go white as she stared down the bar, mouth open, her entire body stiff. "Shit, not again. Stark?"

She gave a little shake of her head, unable to talk. She felt as if she were going to crack and crumble, like one of those cartoon characters, Sylvester the Cat or Wile E. Coyote when they'd slammed into a brick wall.

"Somebody I need to toss?" Len asked darkly.

"No." It came out as a breath. "Please, no."

"Okay, babe. You just tell me."

"I will," she mumbled.

She glided away, her feet not making a sound on the floor, and slid against the bar next to Eric Shuji Shizumi.

* * *

Matthew double-parked on the narrow tree-lined street in front of Senator Samuel Ryder's town house. Cars could just squeak by his. If they couldn't, the hell with them. They could back up and go another way. He wasn't going to be long. Although they lived within the same half-dozen blocks, he and Ryder never seemed to bump into each other. For a while they had, at least on occasion, but that was back when Stark worked for the *Washington Post* and was still being invited to some of the more desirable Washington parties. The ones where you didn't wear Gokey boots and drink beer and talk baseball. He'd still go to those parties when he didn't have anything better to do, like read the latest books panned by the *New York Times Book Review* or catch a game, and he'd provide the touch of cynicism and distance people expected from him. In drawing rooms filled with antiques and sterling silver and men and women who used poll results to tell them what was going on "out there," he was a reminder of how different they all were. The chosen people. They'd all read *LZ,* of course— or pretended they had. "It's so realistic," they'd tell him, as if they knew.

That was another thing about Juliana Fall, he thought suddenly: no damn pretending. If she didn't know who the hell you were, you got that blank look and that was that. Of course, with her pale beauty and international reputation, she'd get along just fine with the Washington crowd. Artists weren't supposed to keep up with current events. They could be forgiven their airheadedness.

He bounded up the curving front steps and gave the garnet-red door two firm whacks. Ryder's was a high-style Federal with black shutters, a Palladian window, pilasters, shiny brass fittings, and a delicate wrought-iron rail. An unadorned pine cone wreath hung in the middle of the door, put there, undoubtedly, by a conscientious housekeeper.

The appearance of taste and perfection was important to the Golden Boy. Stark thought of his own town house. It needed renovating. Badly.

Ryder answered the door himself, in neatly pleated trousers and a casual sweater that made him look even more the rich, handsome, perfect young senator. They'd be begging him to run for president before long. Matthew wasn't fooled—or impressed. He knew what Sam Ryder was, and he wouldn't be getting his vote come election day.

Stark took no pleasure when Ryder went pale at seeing him on his doorstep. "What do you want?"

"We need to talk."

"I can't, I haven't the time—I'm going out."

"It'll just take a minute."

Matthew pushed past him into the foyer, elegantly simple with its cream walls and Queen Anne furnishings. Such perfection. Ryder left the door open, and a chilly breeze floated into the warm house.

"I don't want you here," the senator said, his tone an unconvincing mix of arrogance and fright. "Get out before I—"

"Before you what? You're not going to do anything, Ryder. You couldn't risk it, not with Phil Bloch on your ass."

The baby blue eyes widened, and Stark could feel his former platoon leader's tension. But then Ryder gave a small supercilious laugh, as if he'd found relief in Stark's words, as if to say, oh, so that was what all this was about. Just Phil Bloch.

"Bloch? I hate to disappoint you, Matthew, but I haven't heard that name in years. I can't believe you two are still at it. What's he up to these days?"

Stark's gaze was relentless. "You tell me."

"Look, Matthew, honestly, I don't have time to talk. I'm due at a dinner in half an hour—"

"I don't care if you're due at the White House."

Matthew spoke in a level, deadly voice. "I want to know what you're in with Bloch for, what you're doing about it. And I want to know where he is."

As he straightened up, Ryder made the mistake of looking into Stark's black-brown eyes, and Matthew watched the air go out of him. "I— Damn it, I don't know what you're talking about!"

Matthew clenched and unclenched his scarred fists. He wanted to choke the bastard—not that it'd do any good. Some people you could count on never to change. "Weasel's been snitching to me," he said. "The dumb bastard thinks he's helping you. Bloch knows what's been going on. I want to get to him before he gets to the Weaze."

"That's not my problem."

"You owe him."

"I don't. He was just doing his job."

"And you weren't."

"Look, I didn't ask for his help."

"I know. Weasel still thinks you're worth more than he is. I don't, Ryder. If Otis Raymond gets himself killed because he was trying to help you, I won't forgive and I won't forget. And I won't keep my mouth shut. Not this time. Count on it."

"If he gets himself killed, it'll be because he trusted you!"

"Talk, Ryder."

Matthew could see the sweat pouring down the senator's face; he took no pleasure in it. "Otis Raymond is a drug addict and a loser," Ryder said. "Whatever he told you about me I'll deny. You have no proof, and you'll get none."

"Where you're concerned," Stark said, "I don't need proof."

Ryder licked his lips. "Don't threaten me, damn you!"

"Tell me about the Minstrel's Rough, Sam."

"I—I don't know what you're talking about."

"Okay, then let me give you an idea of what I know.

Rachel Stein, the woman you were with the other night at Lincoln Center, said something that made you decide you could get your hands on the Minstrel, give it to Bloch, and solve all your problems. The Dutchman, de Geer, is your connection to the diamond. He went to Johannes Peperkamp in Antwerp, who took him to Amsterdam to get the stone—only it was a wild-goose chase, wasn't it?" Matthew had no sympathy for Ryder's white, stricken face, graying slightly around the mouth as he realized how much the former helicopter pilot already knew. Stark kept his voice steady, unemotional. "You're not going to collapse, Ryder, so don't pretend you are. The old man didn't have the stone, did he?"

"Matthew…" Ryder's voice was little more than a pathetic whisper. "Matthew, you don't know what you're talking about."

"Did he, goddamn you?"

Shit, Stark thought. Shit, damn, *hell.* The old man didn't have the stone. Did that mean one of the Peperkamp women did? Is that what Ryder thought—de Geer, Bloch? With Phil Bloch, thinking something was made it so. Matthew focused again on Ryder, barely able to control the impulse to back the senator up against the wall and make him talk. But he'd never operated that way, and he wasn't going to start now.

"If anything happens to the Weaze or to the Peperkamps, Sam, I'm coming after you." He didn't raise his voice. "I don't care what shitpile you're hiding under. I'll keep digging until I find you."

"You're a has-been, Stark." But Ryder's voice squeaked, undermining his words. "You're grasping. You want a story so badly you'll listen to nonsense. I don't know what Otis Raymond told you, and I don't care. I'm not involved. I'm not afraid of you, Matthew. Now get out."

With the knuckles of one hand, Ryder brushed at the drops of sweat on his upper lip. Stark knew he had him scared, but not scared enough to talk—or at least not scared enough of him. Ryder had Phillip Bloch to worry about; the sergeant didn't have any of Stark's scruples getting in his way.

"I should have tossed your stupid butt out of my ship in Vietnam after the stunt you pulled then."

"Get out, Matthew," Ryder said hoarsely. "Damn you, get out!"

Stark's dark eyes never wavered. "Make sure I don't get a second chance at you, Sam. I might not resist."

Shuji's mouth was a grim, thin line, and his black eyes were two tiny pits of fury. He looked just as she'd envisioned he would at this moment—as if he was going to go after someone with one of his authentic short swords— namely, his sole student, one Juliana Fall, aka J.J. Pepper.

"Hello, Shuji," Juliana said, surprised at how relaxed she sounded.

He looked at her. "A turban," he said. "For Christ's sake, a rhinestone-studded turban."

"Usually I leave my hair down."

"And no one recognizes you?"

"No, because it's never blond. It's pink or lavender. Sometimes blue."

"Goddamnit," Shuji said.

"How did you find out?"

"I have friends who frequent SoHo clubs *and* Lincoln Center and Carnegie Hall. One thought he recognized you, but he believed he had to be seeing things. I... My God, you look ridiculous."

Juliana tried to smile. "I know. Fun, isn't it?"

"It is not fun, Juliana."

"It is for me. Why are you here?"

"I had to know if this black rumor were true." He drank some of his martini, too much. "My God. Jazz, pop, blues."

"Don't be so damned sanctimonious. I happen to like jazz, pop, and blues."

He sighed. "Do you have any idea what this will do to your reputation?"

"I've only been in this business since I was eleven years old. Since I'm so damned dumb, why don't you tell me?"

"Juliana—"

"I *know* what I'm doing, damn it. I don't care what this does to my precious reputation. That's right, I *don't* care. I enjoy playing the Aquarian, and if people don't like it, well then to hell with them. Being J.J. Pepper gets me out of myself, out from under the pressures of being Juliana Fall all the time. It's important to me, Shuji. And if I'm in a funk, this is helping me, not hurting. I need an outlet. And musically, playing here is enriching me, not ruining me."

Shuji was unimpressed. "Your work in the practice room should be your outlet."

"My work is my work. I don't want to give that up—I can't. But I need this, too."

"Let me hear the Chopin," he said, tight-lipped.

"Now?"

"Yes, why not?" He nodded to the baby grand. "There's a piano."

"I'm J.J. Pepper here."

"Play the Chopin, Juliana, or I walk out of here."

His gaze was hard and direct. Shuji wasn't one to pussyfoot around, and she knew he meant what he said. "And then what?"

"And then I'll remember fondly the eleven-year-old girl who begged me to teach her, not the thirty-year-old ingrate who has turned her back on me and everything we've worked for together for almost twenty years." His tone was scathing, filled with bitterness, edged with sadness. "You've been J.J. Pepper for eight months. Eight months, damn you, and not a word."

"I wanted to tell you."

"You didn't."

She stiffened. "You're right—I knew what a jackass you'd be about it."

"The Chopin," he said.

She got up and walked over to Len. "That's Eric Shuji Shizumi at the end of the bar," she said, whipping off the turban. Her blond hair tumbled onto her shoulders. "I've lied to you, Len. My real name's Juliana Fall. I'm a concert pianist."

Len folded his arms on his chest. "Names aren't what's important here. It's who you are, babe, what you want to do, that counts."

"I don't know the answer to that."

"Well, until you do, it's okay by me if you want to keep up with your J.J. Pepper act. Just no hairy-assed stuff, okay?" He grinned at her. "Unless you want to do brunch."

She managed a smile. "That would really kill Shuji. May I play now?"

"Piano's yours, Juliana Fall, muddy bass and all."

She glanced over at Shuji. He was still working on his martini, not smiling, not understanding, wrapped up in his own hurt and anger. A pang of horror sliced through her as she tried to imagine going on without him. What would she do?

She sat at the piano and played the first chord of Chopin.

But she couldn't continue. She couldn't betray Len, her Club Aquarian audience—J.J. Pepper's audience. She couldn't betray herself. And, finally, she couldn't betray Shuji. Playing the Chopin now, here, would be a lie. He wouldn't see it that way, of course, but she couldn't help that. She switched to a short Duke Ellington piece she thought everyone might like, even Shuji.

But when she finished and turned around, he was gone. In his place at the bar there was only a half-drunk martini.

Seventeen

Hendrik de Geer blew on his frozen fingers as he stood at the edge of Central Park opposite the Beresford. It would be a bitterly cold night. He longed for a bottle of gin, but he had forsworn drink. Sentiment and drink would make him careless. He couldn't permit that to happen. It was clear to him, now that the coward Ryder had told Bloch everything, that the sergeant would have to find out for himself if the Minstrel was lost. He would never settle for anyone else's word; the possibilities for the stone were too tremendous. Hendrik well understood that kind of thinking.

It left him with two choices. One, he could walk away. Two, he could act.

But first, before he made up his mind, he must gather information. He had already discovered that Catharina was being watched. Now he was at the Beresford, and he could see one of Bloch's men standing out at the bus stop in front of the Museum of Natural History, stamping his feet in the cold.

So the daughter was being watched, too. Bloch was taking no chances—he never did—but he was not yet prepared to make his move. The sergeant was a hard, unyielding man with no apparent weakness. He was just starting out in this business, but already he had a solid reputation. He paid well and on time. That was what had drawn Hendrik to his employ. Profit and survival. They had been his chief interests for many years, and if Phillip Bloch wished to make them possible, then Hendrik would work for him.

Several well-dressed men and women, in tuxedos and furs, came out of the Beresford, followed by a stout old woman in an unremarkable wool coat, a scarf tied peasant-style around her head, and ankle boots.

Across the street, Bloch's man threw down his cigarette.

Hendrik squinted as the woman came into the glare of the street lamp, and he saw the plain, square face.

Wilhelmina!

He almost laughed aloud. Of course she would be here! Even given the underworld in which he'd operated for forty years, Wilhelmina Peperkamp remained the most suspicious person he had ever encountered. Ah, Willie. He could see she'd already spotted Bloch's man. Once Hendrik had been attracted to her bluntness and competence and had found her plainness comforting, even appealing. She was so reliable. For a while, that had been enough.

She went across West Eighty-first, walking at a good clip, and Bloch's man started after her. Hendrik stayed where he was. He wasn't worried. Willie had outwitted the Nazis for five years. She would have outwitted them until the end, had she not trusted Hendrik de Geer.

In a few minutes, Bloch's man returned, looking dismayed and frustrated. This time Hendrik did laugh aloud. The man wasn't necessarily incompetent; he simply didn't know the kind of woman with whom he was dealing.

As he reached for a cigar, two men darted out of the dark, cold shadows of the park and came up on either side of the Dutchman. They flashed knives. Hendrik grunted, disgusted. Damned New York! He had no patience now for a mugging. Both men looked very fit, older than he'd have expected. Without a doubt, they thought they were fierce.

"Your wallet, old man," one said.

Hendrik shrugged, thinking he must be getting old. He should have heard them coming, anticipated this. But now he was at a disadvantage, and he wished not to attract attention. His fingers cold and stiff, he removed his wallet from his trouser pocket and handed it to the man who'd made the demand. The second man kept his knife pointed while his comrade inspected the wallet.

"What are you doing?" Hendrik asked, suspicious. "'Take the thing and go—"

Wait, he thought. If they were ordinary muggers, they would have taken the thing and gone. They would already have disappeared into the park with their booty. There was no need to check for identification.

They wanted to make sure who he was.

Before they obeyed Master Sergeant Phillip Bloch's orders and killed him.

"Bastard," Hendrik said without emotion.

"Huh?"

Their puzzled looks quickly changed to surprise, then pain and horror as Hendrik slammed his hand sideways into the throat of the man with his wallet. The second man sliced toward him with his knife, but the Dutchman was ready and dodged, the knife grazing his coat. While the other man choked and sputtered, Hendrik pushed his comrade down, moving fast, with an agility that amazed even him. His opponent had no chance to grab on to him.

He fled, running out into the middle of Central Park West. Cars screeched, horns blared.

Not until he was on the other side of the street in front of the Beresford did Hendrik look back. The two men had scurried away. In front of the museum, Bloch's other man had disappeared. Hendrik grunted to himself without satisfaction.

Twenty years ago he would have killed them all.

Aunt Willie had found nothing to her liking in her niece's kitchen and had gone out looking for something to eat. Juliana had taken no offense. Instead, with her aunt gone, she sat at the piano. She didn't expect to be able to practice. There were too many distractions. Yet she did, with an absorption that had eluded her for months. With her uncle dead, her mother not talking, her aunt outside in the dark, her building being watched, with Matthew Stark and his black-brown eyes and leather coat tugging at her emotions, she began to make progress on the Chopin. The real world hadn't thrown her off. It had become not something to escape, but something to express.

So simple.

If only Shuji would understand. But he never would. She remembered when she was eleven and she and her parents had gone to his magnificent Upper East Side house, and she'd thought him the handsomest, most incredible man she'd ever seen. She owned all his recordings, would listen to them late into the night, when her parents thought she was asleep. His ability had made her cry with rage and jealousy and amazement at all he could do and all she couldn't, at least not yet. But when Shuji had taken her alone into his studio, her first words were not to tell him how wonderful he was but to tell him she'd worn white for their introduction because he always wore black.

More than anything else, he'd told her many years later, it was that comment that had prompted him to take her on as his student. He knew he was a strong personality. He had no interest in molding another pianist into a mini-Shuji. He had wanted, encouraged, *demanded* her development as an independent artist.

Now he couldn't understand why she needed to color her hair pink and play jazz in a SoHo nightclub. He wanted her to be independent so long as she didn't break any of his sacred rules.

"The bastard," she muttered, still playing, "the goddamn *bastard.*"

She ignored the tears burning in her eyes and the fatigue gnawing at her muscles and the hollowness inside her, the cold, raw fear that had nothing to do with diamonds and coincidental deaths and men following her.

Shuji was gone. My God, she thought, what am I going to do?

Matthew drank a beer and watched part of a basketball game just to calm down, but neither helped. Weasel, Bloch—where the hell were they? He went for another beer, a Sam Adams, and took two sips as he sat down at the telephone in what passed these days for his study, of which the most notable items were his television and stereo system. His typewriter was covered and had about twelve issues of *Sports Illustrated* stacked on top of it. The bottom one, he noted, went back eight months. He didn't own a computer. Working on one at the newsroom was enough. He didn't like all those goddamn lights blinking at him.

He held the receiver in his hand and told himself not to do it.

He did it anyway. He had the number memorized, had already started to dial it twice this evening.

There were four rings, and then her voice came over the message machine. "I'm unavailable at the moment, but if you leave your name, number, and a brief message..."

"Juliana, if you're there, pick up the damn phone. If not—"

The machine cut off. "Matthew." She sounded vague, spaced. "What is it?"

The rigidity of his muscles began to ease as he listened to her. She had a beautiful voice. It made him able to en-vision her eyes, vivid and filled with energy. He began to imagine his mouth on hers. You're slipping fast, buddy, he thought, and drank more beer.

"Were you practicing?" he asked.

"Mmm, yes, I think so."

"You *think* so?"

"I sort of lost track. That hasn't happened to me in a while. I don't think about where I am, what I'm doing, I just get totally absorbed. Then when I stop, it takes me a while…" She paused to take a breath, as if she'd been run-ning. "A while to come back from wherever I've been, I guess. I was working on—what was it?" She sounded drugged. "I mean, I know what I was. It was the Chopin. It's just not easy to articulate my thoughts after concentrat-ing so hard. You should see what I'm like after I've been at it for seven or eight hours at a stretch."

"Dizzier that you are right now?"

"Oh, much."

Hard to imagine. But suddenly Matthew wanted to know what motivated this gorgeous, eccentric woman. What drove her to do what she did? What kept her at it? She had so goddamn much energy. She'd just returned from Antwerp, for the love of God. He could barely con-centrate on a basketball game, never mind Chopin. He re-membered how she'd been sweating after her Lincoln Center performance and yet still had been able to settle down. Did the woman ever just chill out?

In Vermont, he remembered. No piano there.

"I'm glad I'm not your neighbor," he said, hearing the humor in his tone.

She laughed, that cool, sexy laugh with just a hint of nuttiness. "The Beresford has very solid walls—that's one reason I live here. Aunt Willie doesn't like it. Wouldn't, I mean. But you were saying?"

"Juliana, this thing with the Minstrel, your uncle, Rachel Stein—it's damn serious."

"I know that." Clipped, pissed. Back on earth.

"I don't mean to sound patronizing, but it's more serious than it was even yesterday. Listen to me, Juliana. I want you to stay in your apartment as much as possible, and I want you to play piano and stay the hell out this mess."

"Is it Otis Raymond? Has something happened to him?"

He appreciated the note of worry and concern in her voice. "Not that I know of."

"Then what?"

Phil Bloch knows your name, knows you were in Antwerp, knows you could have the stone. Never mind whether you do or you don't. Never mind what you know and what you haven't told me. Just get the hell out, sweetheart.

But he said only, "New information. I'll explain another time. Watch yourself."

"Matthew—"

"Do it, Juliana. Trust me on this, all right? God help me. I know what I'm talking about."

For a few seconds she was silent. Then, "You know who's behind all this, don't you?"

She sounded breathless and excited and scared, and Stark knew if he gave her more, she'd be back on his doorstep, in deeper trouble than ever. He could almost see the brightness of those ice-cool emerald eyes. Christ, he had to find Bloch! But what good would that do? Coming down on Bloch's head might only further endanger Weasel. Goddamn Ryder…

"I can't talk," he said. "Just watch yourself."

"Won't talk, you mean." She was cool again, one tenacious lady. "You're in Washington, aren't you?"

"Take care of yourself. Why not take a trip to Vermont?"

She hung up on him.

Catharina sat at her bedroom window and looked down at the Christmas lights on Park Avenue. Tears streamed down her face, but she made no attempt to brush them away. Her thoughts had drifted back more than forty years, to the last Christmas with her mother and father in Amsterdam. She was just a teenager but had taken charge of the household. She'd planned for the holiday for weeks, scrounging up ingredients to make *speculaas* and *appelbeignets,* and Hendrik had brought rum and cocoa. What a feast they'd had! Johannes had managed to come, so tall and stoic, and Ann, so sweet and sad. Johannes had been marked for deportation to the Nazi labor camps and was in hiding, himself an *onderduiker,* and Ann, as the Jewish partner in a mixed marriage, was to report for sterilization procedures. She had refused and was in hiding, too. Her family—her parents and younger sisters—had been deported the previous year and there had been no official word on where they were. The rumors were too dreadful to believe.

But that Christmas they'd ignored so much, laughing and carrying on, and afterward Catharina had sent goodies back with Wilhelmina for Rachel and Abraham. In a rare display of affection and pride, her mother had hugged both her daughters and told them they were fine young women. Hendrik had said he agreed, and when no one was looking, he'd kissed Catharina on the cheek. How she'd blushed! For hours after, her face burned. He was twenty-five and a hero in the Underground Resistance; everyone adored him.

Now, finally, she brushed away her tears, wishing her

mother could be here with her. Catharina was nearing sixty herself. She was older than her mother had lived to be. And yet she wanted that stern, loving guidance, that soft lap, that strong shoulder on which to cry.

"You mustn't blame yourself, dear Catharina…"

"Oh, Mamma," she cried aloud, paralyzed with fear and indecision. Ever since her talk with Wilhelmina, she'd hidden herself away, looking for answers out the window, in the winter sky and the gray buildings and the Christmas trimmings. There were none. "If only you were here, Mamma, to tell me what to do!"

Drying her tears, she turned away from the window. She had a vision of her tiny daughter in pigtails and dirty sneakers, climbing up onto the piano bench, and she wanted to transport herself back in time and take that child in her arms and hold her, just hold her.

You must be strong, Catharina, she could hear her mother say. *You must be strong.*

She went into the library, where Adrian was sitting up late with a book. "Adrian," she said, maintaining a deliberate air of nonchalance. Her stomach was tight, aching, hollow. "Adrian—has Juliana ever come to you about opening a safe-deposit box?"

He looked at her, his handsome face filled with tenderness as he studied her. He had to see how upset she was. But he hadn't pressed her about the terrible tension that had gripped her since their daughter's last Lincoln Center performance. It wasn't that he didn't care or that he didn't want to know. Many times in the past he'd told her he wanted to know everything about her—everything she cared to tell him. But he'd also explained that he understood she was an intensely private woman, respected that, and had come to accept that there was a part of her he could never know. He blamed her family, the war. She'd been so young—old enough to remember, young enough not really to understand.

"Is she interested in getting one?" he asked, still watching her.

Catharina lifted her shoulders, her neck muscles crunching with the movement because they were so tense. Her carefree existence had spoiled her. She had her husband, her child, food, shelter, clothing. For so long she'd wanted for nothing.

"She has so many valuables," she said lamely. "I was just wondering. Perhaps it's something she should look into."

Adrian sighed, and she could see the resignation in his eyes: he wasn't going to get an explanation tonight, either. "I'll talk to her about it, if you'd like."

"Please."

"Are you going to bed?" he asked.

It was another way of asking if she thought she'd sleep tonight; she hadn't since Rachel's visit. Adrian had tried to comfort her, but even after they made love she would lie awake, staring at the ceiling.

"In a little while," she said, hearing the love in her voice, a love that went deeper than words—that could ignore half truths. But her mind was racing. *If Juliana has the Minstrel, what will she do? What will I do?*

Yes, Mamma, I know, she thought; I must be strong.

Juliana had been unable to return to her trancelike state after Matthew's call and had abandoned the piano. She was staring at the magnificent skyline, debating once more whether to tell anyone about the Minstrel's Rough, when Aunt Willie stormed in, muttering in Dutch.

"Are you all right?" Juliana asked, climbing up from the couch.

"Of course. I was followed, but no matter. Do you have any binoculars?"

"Yes, as a matter of fact. I usually keep them at my house in Vermont, for bird watching, but I can't identify many birds, just the usual sparrows and—"

Aunt Willie hissed impatiently. "Will you get them?"

"Why?"

"Achh!"

"All right, all right."

She dug them out of a drawer in the library and returned to the living room, where Aunt Willie was peering down at Central Park West, her face pressed up against the window. "I know I saw him," she said.

Juliana handed her the binoculars. "Who?"

"Hendrik de Geer." Wilhelmina looked through the binoculars only briefly, handing them back in disgust. "As I thought, he's gone."

"He was out there? But why—"

"He has his reasons, I'm sure. He always does."

"Aunt Willie, I'd like to know more about him. He betrayed you and Mother during the war, but how? What exactly did he do? Why's he here now? Damn it, if he's hanging around outside my window—"

"I'm tired," Wilhelmina said, yawning. "I'm going to bed. I suggest you do, too. You'll want an early start for Washington in the morning."

Juliana groaned, but she didn't say a word. Dealing with Matthew Stark couldn't be any worse than dealing with Wilhelmina Peperkamp.

After Stark's intrusion, Ryder forced himself to calm down. Sweat matted his shirt to his back and lined his face and armpits. He felt himself shaking as the old indecisiveness returned. *My God, does Stark know everything?* Ryder's breathing was rapid and light, but slowly, with practiced self-denial, he pulled himself together and headed upstairs, where he showered off the sweat and the stink of his fear. Stark's visit, he tried to tell himself, meant nothing.

He felt better when he put on his flannel robe and went down to his study. He got out a bottle of Scotch and sat in front of his marble fireplace. Drinking and watching the fire die, his mind drifted back twenty years. *Had it been that long?* Every moment of that horrible, tragic day seemed so vivid to him, still so very real. When he swallowed, he could taste the same sourness he'd tasted when he'd first realized the Huey he'd permitted to fly into a hot LZ was going down.

He remembered thinking that he didn't have to worry: Matt Stark was the pilot. Steelman had one month left on his harrowing year-long tour and had been awarded the Distinguished Flying Cross. The grunts felt secure when he was flying their slick.

This mission should have been easy and safe: the resupply of a platoon—First Lieutenant Samuel Ryder's platoon—in a cold LZ. What could happen? But the landing zone had turned hot and no one had told Stark until it was too late—and they were shot down.

"No one's fault," Ryder mumbled aloud in the silent study. "It was war. Anything could have happened."

Although he was the officer in charge, Ryder had been too dazed and terrified at first by what was going on to notice even that the Huey was receiving ground fire. The slick went down.

There was nothing even Matthew Stark could do.

Ryder remembered screams—heard them still in his nightmares. Too late, he'd rushed toward the downed slick…and he still could feel the icy grip of Otis Raymond as the door gunner had pushed him aside so a lieutenant wouldn't get torn to bits by AK-47 bullets.

The survivors were picked up by a search and rescue team and taken back to base camp. As a platoon leader, Ryder had faced the Viet Cong and the NVA, but he'd never been so afraid for his life as at the moment when he'd had to face Matt Stark. But the Steelman, his young, knowing face showing no emotion, had only looked at Ryder with those black eyes and not said a word.

With commanding officers buzzing around him demanding to know what the *hell* had happened out there, Stark hadn't made excuses or assigned blame to anyone other than himself. He accepted responsibility for his ship and its passengers. *He* had been in the pilot's seat, no one else.

"We got shot at," he said. "There's a war going on out there, you know."

The event, however, had scarred him as much as anyone, and as far as Ryder was concerned, Stark's actions proved it. He didn't go home a month later, but extended and got himself transferred—to Cobras for a while and then to a scout helicopter—the Hughes OH-6A Cayuse or Loach. He was assigned to a hunter-killer or "pink" team, with its primitive, effective strategy. The Loach—the hunter—would go in and draw fire to locate the enemy. Then the killer—the new Bell AH-1G Cobra or "snake"—would come in with guns blazing. The work, especially for the hunters, was dangerous; scout losses were huge. But they didn't carry passengers, and CW-2 Matthew Stark and SP-4 Otis Raymond, who'd stayed with his hero Steelman, had survived.

Sam Ryder, back home in Florida, had hoped they wouldn't.

Now, pouring himself another glass of Scotch, he put them out of his mind, his ability to repress well developed. He had to forget Steelman and Weasel; he had to make himself unavailable to Phillip Bloch. Regardless of what Matthew knew or didn't know, he had no proof—nothing he could print. And he'd have to be very, very careful before he printed anything about Sam Ryder; there was history between them. Stark wouldn't want to be accused of mounting a witch hunt.

Nothing had to happen. All Ryder needed was for Bloch to get hold of the Minstrel's Rough. Then, at last, he'd be satisfied and get out of Ryder's life.

Bloch had to get hold of the Minstrel.

But what will he do to get it? You gave him the names of the Peperkamps. He can find them. He can find Juliana.

"Juliana."

Her name came out as a breath. Why couldn't he stop thinking about her? She couldn't be involved with this mess; she could have nothing to do with the Minstrel. Bloch had no reason to go after her.

Unless he has reason to believe she has the stone. He won't be satisfied until he's positive she doesn't. Until he knows none of the Peperkamp women has the Minstrel, including Juliana.

Ryder inhaled deeply, then slowly swallowed a mouthful of Scotch. He had to hope Bloch would go to the mother and the aunt first and one of them would lead him to the Minstrel.

Besides, what Bloch did or didn't do was not Sam Ryder's responsibility.

He poured himself another glass of Scotch and took it to bed.

Eighteen

❧❧❧

Catharina set her plastic bucket down hard on the sidewalk in front of her bakeshop. Hot soapy water splashed out onto her sneakers, but she paid no attention. It was early, just after dawn, and cold. She dropped her scrub brush into the bucket and knelt down, her heavy corduroy pants worn at the knee from this very ritual. Every other morning she scrubbed the sidewalk from the door of her shop out to the curb. It was an old Dutch custom. Adrian and Juliana teased her about having the cleanest patch of sidewalk in New York. Twice she'd almost been arrested for her odd activity. Yet Catharina was convinced a clean sidewalk helped business. And even if there was no financial gain to be made from her efforts, New York was never so quiet as it was in early morning. She could think then. Dream. Remember.

But this morning she worked quickly because it was cold and furiously because she was trying so desperately not to think, not to dream, not to remember. Rachel... Senator Ryder... Juliana... Wilhelmina... *Johannes*. My God, what was happening to her world?

Again...

Despite the cold and the ungodly hour, the man was out

there, across the street, watching, not caring that she knew he was there. He was young, dark, and fine-featured, not very tall, and he wore clothes that didn't make him stand out in the upper-income neighborhood. This morning's outfit was a pair of heavy corduroy pants and a lambskin jacket. Nevertheless he looked tired and uncomfortable, and she'd thought, madly, of walking over to him and inviting him inside for coffee. But she remembered how young and innocent so many of the Nazis, Dutch as well as German, had looked, and she stopped herself.

Behind her, she heard a soft, distinctive laugh, and she paused, thinking she must have imagined it. It was a laugh of dreams and memories and a girlhood so short, so long ago, that every moment of it was etched in her mind, that much sharper, that much more bittersweet.

Hendrik...

Then the laugh came again, and Catharina tossed the brush into her bucket and rolled back onto her heels. She started to tuck a stray white-blond hair behind her ear but remembered her heavy rubber gloves, her hands warm inside them. Her nose felt cold and red. But as she looked up into the warm blue eyes of Hendrik de Geer, the years fell away. She saw none of his deep wrinkles, none of the scars the years had left, saw only the dashing, brave young man he had once been, at least to her.

"Aren't you ever afraid?" she'd asked him.

"Only for you, sweet Catharina," he'd told her, and she'd believed him.

"You're amazingly clean," he said now in English, "even for a Dutchwoman."

"It's my mother's influence." Her voice was hoarse and unnatural from the tension and an overwhelming sadness, not for the past that had been, but for the past that might have been. She spoke, too, in English. It helped to anchor her in the present. "Mother was always so busy with the

Underground Resistance, you remember? I was the youngest, and so I kept house. I wasn't very good at it, but Mother was an exacting woman and I learned quickly. If she found a loose button on a shirt, she would tear off all the other buttons, too, and I would have to sew them all back on."

Hendrik laughed again, and this time she could see how his eyes crinkled up at the corners. "She always reminded me of Wilhelmina."

Wilhelmina and their mother. Yes, they were alike, tough-minded and cynical, unwilling to give anyone the benefit of the doubt but, in their own way, loving. Realists, they called themselves. Perhaps it was so. They had guessed what Hendrik was long before anyone else.

Catharina started to her feet, the spell broken. Hendrik de Geer had never been dashing or brave, and her girlhood was long lost. She stumbled because she was stiff from kneeling and not so young anymore, and because Hendrik was there and hadn't been in such a long, long time. From the moment she'd spotted him at Lincoln Center, she'd guessed he would come, eventually. Perhaps she'd even wished it.

He grabbed her arm and helped her up, and she stood close to him as the wind gusted down the wide empty avenue. She felt lightheaded and for no reason at all thought of the cinnamon rolls she'd planned to make that morning, an old, comfortable recipe, and wondered if she'd ever get to them.

"What are you doing here?" she asked softly.

He smiled, his hand lingering on her arm. Through her old, heavy fisherman's sweater, she could feel the imprint of his thick fingers. He'd always been so solid. So strong. Even now, almost seventy, wearing his watch cap and old peacoat, he looked so very handsome and reliable. If only she didn't know better.

He said, "I wanted to see you."

"Yes." She looked away, at nothing. "Rachel…"

"I'm sorry she's gone."

"You knew she was after you."

He nodded, although she'd needed no confirmation. "Rachel wanted vengeance, Catharina."

"No, Hendrik." She pulled away from him, and his hand fell awkwardly to his side. "She wanted justice."

He looked pained. "I did what I had to do in Amsterdam, to save you—"

"To save yourself! I won't live with that guilt, Hendrik." But she did, every day.

"They were difficult times, Catharina," he said as if to a child. "The past is done."

"The past isn't over, not for any of us. It never will be, Hendrik." Her eyes were fierce and unforgiving. "Did you kill Rachel?"

"No!" He seemed so appalled, as if he'd never contemplated such a wrong. "No, Catharina. I couldn't."

"Not even to save yourself?" she asked with contempt, but then fatigue crept in—and sorrow. "Oh, Hendrik, just go away. Disappear as you did before."

He was shaking his head. "I've already tried. It's what my mind tells me I should do, but my heart tells me otherwise. Catharina, the people I'm involved with have found out about the Minstrel's Rough. They want it, and they'll stop at nothing to get it. Believe me, my dear, I know these men." He paused, his eyes as soft as they could ever be in a man who'd lived such a cold, hard life. "Let me take you away until I can satisfy them that the Minstrel doesn't exist."

Catharina blinked rapidly, over and over, but the tears flowed anyway, whipped from her eyes by the wind. She tried to brush them away but remembered the gloves and peeled them off, letting them drop onto the sidewalk. Her hands were shaking uncontrollably. My God, she thought, will they never stop? It seemed they'd been shaking since Rachel had walked into her bakeshop after forty years.

The Minstrel's Rough…damn that horrible stone!

"No," she said at last, in a choked whisper. "You're not going to save me and let others suffer. I won't let you!"

"I can save everyone."

She scoffed, sobbing. "As you did in Amsterdam?"

"Catharina, listen to me. Nothing will happen to you or your daughter—or to Wilhelmina. I promise you."

"And Johannes? You took him to Amsterdam, didn't you? You tried to make him give you that damned diamond. Hendrik, Hendrik, you never change."

"His heart was no good. There was nothing I could do." He took her hands and held them tightly, and she was surprised his were so warm. "You don't believe me."

"Hendrik, please." Her voice caught, and she was angry with herself for her tears, for thinking, hoping, he'd changed—for wanting to believe they both could pretend Amsterdam had never happened. "I can never believe you again."

He looked wounded, and yet at the same time not surprised, almost welcoming the blow. Then the earnestness, the frustrating, endearing, appalling optimism, the unshakable belief in himself, took over. "I can stop this, Catharina. If you tell me where the Minstrel is—"

"No!" She pounded him once on the chest with her fist. "Damn you, Hendrik, no! Even if I knew I'd never tell you. The Minstrel died with Johannes. Now go—for the love of God, Hendrik go."

"Catharina…"

She shook her head and resisted the impulse to run. Willie wouldn't; their mother wouldn't. And she had to protect Juliana. Catharina made herself look at him, into the eyes that had never told anything that was true. "Understand me, Hendrik—leave my daughter out of whatever trouble you're in this time. If you touch Juliana—if *any-one* connected with you touches her—there's nowhere you can go, nowhere you can hide that I won't find you. If you should die before I do, you'll see me in hell."

Hendrik swallowed and licked his chapped lips, and he whispered, "Don't hate me, sweet Catharina."

"I don't, Hendrik," she said, so tired. "I never did."

She pushed past him, knocking over the bucket as she ran inside and shut the door hard behind her, clicking shut the deadbolt lock. The sound echoed in the quiet shop.

Hendrik de Geer stood in the dirty water, and he looked without expression toward the shop. Catharina warned herself that he was the same thoughtless, selfish coward he had been in Amsterdam. How could she feel any pity for him after what he'd done? *Nothing* had changed. Not Hendrik, not herself, not their past.

She watched him through the window. He bent over, righting the bucket, and picked up one of her rubber gloves. He pressed it to his lips. Catharina bit back a cry as he walked over and hung the glove on the doorknob.

He said nothing, and then he walked off slowly down Madison Avenue, alone.

Juliana had changed into J.J. Pepper to keep herself from being followed to LaGuardia Airport and then changed back into herself in the *Gazette* ladies' room, leaving J.J.'s clothes in a paper bag under the sink. Then she proceeded to the newsroom. She was dressed in a chocolate wool gabardine suit with a Hermès scarf at her neck and her hair pulled back. She thought she looked distinctive, if not brass tacks. A reporter pointed out Matthew's desk, which was as yet unoccupied. She went over and sat on the straight-backed chair next to it, glancing at the notes and papers on his desk. She saw the obituaries on Rachel Stein and her uncle and felt her expression turn grim.

A tall woman with dark horn-rimmed glasses came over and asked if she could help her. Juliana introduced herself. "I'm Alice Feldon," the editor said, eyeing her. "So you're Stark's piano player."

Juliana winced. "When's he due in?"

"Your guess is as good as mine."

"It's very important I see him. I—I have new information for him. I'm sure he'll want to know."

"Don't count on it." She picked up a scrap of paper and a pencil, jotted down something, and handed both back to Juliana. "That's his home number and his address. You decide what you want to do."

Alice Feldon marched back to her desk, and Juliana picked up the phone but stopped herself from dialing. If Matthew answered, what would she tell him? *I was just wondering when you were coming in to your office.* He'd ask why; she'd tell him because she was there waiting for him. He'd tell her, "Then wait, goddamnit."

She tucked the scrawled address in her pocket and called for a cab.

With one of his men posted on the street, Phillip Bloch grinned at his former platoon leader from the front stoop of the elegant town house. "Morning, Sam."

"Bloch—*what are you doing here?*" Ryder went pale. "I thought we had an understanding that you would never come to Washington. For God's sake, get inside quickly."

"Calm down, Sam." Bloch entered the quiet foyer. He had a plastic container of fresh fruit salad in one hand, and with a plastic fork, he stuck a piece of cantaloupe into his mouth. At one time he'd smoked cigarettes incessantly. Now he received his oral gratification from various fruits and seeds. Sometimes he felt like a goddamn squirrel. He went on pleasantly, "I love D.C. Christ, I could buy a whole case of melons for what I pay for one stinking salad here."

Ryder bristled. "We can talk in the study, but I hardly think we should prolong this meeting, Sergeant."

"That's okay by me."

Bloch followed the senator into the study at the back of the house, passing an elegant dining room done in Queen Anne. The sergeant knew it was Queen Anne because for years his mother had kept a picture of a dining set—an Ethan Allen reproduction—taped on the refrigerator. It was what she wanted some day for her dining room, which was pretty much a wreck. Nobody in their household could afford it or even gave two shits whether or not she ever got it. Losers, his mother had called them; you're all a bunch of losers. She was an old lady now, but she probably still had that goddamn picture on her refrigerator.

The study didn't remind Bloch of anything he'd ever known, except maybe a whorehouse or two. Oriental carpet on the hardwood floor, cherry from the looks of it, leather club chairs and sofa, brass lamps, masculine ornaments, paintings of horses. A framed picture of Sammy as a decorated first lieutenant in the U.S. Army stood on an antique secretary, but about the only thing he'd done that entitled him to be decorated, in Bloch's estimation, was not getting any more people killed than he had. The frame, the sergeant noted, was silver, probably sterling.

"Fancy, fancy," he said, looking around the room. "About what I expected."

"Let's get on with this."

Ryder gestured nervously to the leather chairs, and they both sat. Bloch finished his fruit salad.

"Two things," Bloch said, still amiable. His men were feeding him nice, timely reports. He felt in control. "First, one of my men spotted Hendrik de Geer outside Catharina

Fall's bakery this morning. He ain't out of this. We tried to take him out last night, but—"

"For God's sake, don't tell me anything!"

"What, the place bugged or something? Sammy, Sammy, relax. Anyway, I figure de Geer's trying to get the diamond on his own. Not good. Second, as you well know, Matt Stark ain't lying down on this one. My man says he was here—"

"What?"

"Listen, Lieutenant, I've got to keep my finger on things."

"You've had me *watched?*"

"Don't be such a wimp. Yeah, I've had you watched— for your own protection as well as mine. Will you quit interrupting? I'll assume for now you didn't tell Stark anything, but if he keeps digging around, you won't need me to ruin you—he'll be glad to do the job."

"De Geer's a drunk, and Stark doesn't have a thing he can use. Just ignore them both. Sergeant, I think it's time you accepted reality. Tthe Minstrel's Rough was a good idea, but it didn't pan out. Let it go."

"Sammy, Sammy," Bloch said, shaking his head with feigned disappointment. "You give up too easily. We ain't even *started* to look for this stone yet."

"Not *we,* Sergeant." Ryder leaned forward, looking more terrified than determined. "I'm no longer involved. I told you, I can't be."

"I know, you're a United States senator. Bully, bully. Well, look, I just figured I'd be nice and let you know what's on my mind, okay? You get this diamond before I get it myself or you give me something else I can use to pin it down, we're square. I got commitments, you know, creditors barking up my ass. You don't want me sitting down in Florida forever, do you? Well, help me out." He grinned, setting his plastic container and fork on a butler's table. "But if you can't, I guess you might have my bones rattling around in your closet for a long, long time."

"Sergeant, you're not being fair." Ryder was close to hyperventilating. "If it wasn't for me, you wouldn't even know about the Minstrel. And as I told you, there's absolutely no guarantee it even exists. It's not worth the risk to you or to me—"

"I want the stone," Bloch said. "And I'll get it, with your help, Lieutenant, or without."

Ryder was panting, obviously horrified by what the sergeant proposed. Bloch watched the former platoon leader try to figure a way out, to distance himself from the very events he'd put into motion so that later on he could deny any involvement on his part. He'd seen that look a thousand times over the years.

"I can't help you," the senator said.

"Sure you can." Bloch rose, feeling full and confident. "You're the Golden Boy, Sammy. You can do anything."

Matthew's Federal town house, simple but elegant, was a surprise, until Juliana remembered *LZ*. It was easy to forget that the dark, cynical reporter had produced a bestselling novel, and she made a mental note to stop at a bookstore as soon as she could and buy a copy. After all, he'd been to one of her concerts. *Because of Samuel Ryder,* she reminded herself, *not because of you.*

She slowed as she came to the front stoop. There was no front yard, and the steps ended on the brick sidewalk. The street was tree-lined and narrow, very picturesque and European; Juliana thought Aunt Willie might actually approve. Over breakfast that morning she'd complained about her niece's German coffee maker, and Juliana had lectured her about West German democracy, the wrongness of collective guilt, the countless wonderful Germans she'd met over the years. Aunt Willie had merely grunted and said, "What do you know of the world?"

What indeed. She'd had no comeback.

As she mounted the steps, two men came up behind her, and she stiffened, turning and looking madly for a place to run. There was none, except inside. But the polished wood door was shut tightly. She paused on the second step and felt the breath go out of her. One of the men was dark-skinned and stocky, powerful, young; the other was curly-haired and very thin, also young. They wore heavy sweaters rather than coats, and no hats or gloves.

"Excuse me," Juliana said, "I must have the wrong address—"

"What's your name?" the darker one asked.

"J.J."

"J.J. what?"

"Pepper." She wished Len were here, or even Shuji with one of his short swords. "But I must be going."

"You looking for Matt Stark?"

"Who?"

"I'll bet he's the type who goes for a hot number like you."

"I haven't the faintest idea—"

She stopped, and the darker one smiled. But he wasn't the one who'd pulled out the gun. The curly-haired one had. Juliana didn't know anything about guns except that she didn't want one aimed at her.

"We want you to give Matt a message."

The darker one was still talking. She focused on him so she wouldn't have to look at the gun. "Okay," she said, and hated how small her voice sounded.

He bent down close to her face, and she could feel the heat of his breath and see the tiny red veins in his eyes. "Tell him to back off," he said, each word distinct. "Tell him Phil Bloch says so."

She nodded. "All right."

"Say it back to me."

Years and years of solfeggio and memorizing countless pieces had left her with an acute ear. "'Tell him to back off... Tell him Phil Bloch says so.'"

"Good."

She waited for them to leave, but they lingered, watching her as she debated whether to bolt past them or to scramble into the house. She didn't have a key, didn't know if the door was locked, didn't know if Matthew were there. Had he already left for the *Gazette?*

The darker one raised his left arm.

"No—"

But it came crashing down, swiping her across the side of the head. The blow sent her sprawling backward against the steps and crashing into the wrought-iron rail. She yelled as pain exploded in her shoulder and started to grab it, but he snatched her wrist and twisted it behind her back. She ignored the shooting pain in her shoulder and he tightened his grip. *Don't break my wrist...dear God, don't let him do it!*

"Just want him to know the sergeant's serious."

He released her.

She collapsed on the steps without making a sound and didn't even attempt to look back. She didn't want to know anything more about them; she didn't care where they were going or what they were doing.

My wrist...

You jackass, never mind your damned wrist! The sons of bitches didn't kill you, did they?

But she cradled her wrist in her other hand, focusing all her terror on it, and examined the bruise. There was no serious damage. She shut her eyes, shaking all over. The pain in her shoulder was already beginning to subside. You're all right, she told herself; you're all right.

Matthew? Had they hurt him?

Behind her, the front door opened. She whirled around,

terrified, but saw instantly it was Stark. He rushed down the steps and scooped her up, and she was glad for the warmth and solidness of him.

"It's all right, Juliana," he said.

"All right? *All right?*" She pushed him away and noted he was in perfect health, looking tough and competent but not at all pleased to see her. "Goddamnit, it is not all right!"

His black eyes narrowed, taking in her hard breathing and frightened, angry look. "Good, you're not hurt."

"In the great, grand scheme of things, no, I am not. No thanks to you, I'm sure. What did you do, watch through the window?"

"Pretty much."

"Thanks a lot." Then she noticed his gun, a big ugly thing. "You had a *gun?* Jesus Christ, why the hell did you wait? Were you waiting for them to blow my head off?"

"I didn't want to start firing when there was no need."

"No need—"

"You could have gotten hit in the cross fire."

"Oh."

"Do you want to go inside?"

Feeling calmer, she said, "If you don't mind."

He led the way. They went back to his kitchen, a cheerful, cluttered room with white cabinets and white tab curtains hanging in a window that overlooked a terrace. A couple of dead plants sat outside on the cold bricks. Aunt Willie would have had a fit. A battered pine table stood in front of the window, piled with copies of various newspapers—the *Post,* the *Times,* the *Christian Science Monitor*—and the most recent issue of *Motor Trend.* There were dirty dishes in the sink and two empty Sam Adams beer bottles on the counter.

"Need ice?" Stark asked.

She shook her head, which hurt, but not as much as it might have. "Did you know those men?"

"Not personally."

"They asked me to give you a message from Phil Bloch. He's a sergeant, I think they said. Did you know him in Vietnam?"

Matthew got two beers out of the refrigerator, opened them both, and handed her one. He took a gulp of his and sat down as he swallowed it. "Yes."

"You know, I've lived in New York all my life, and I've never been mugged, robbed, assaulted, or even seriously threatened."

"That's because you're a rich girl," he said.

"Well-off. I know rich girls."

"Have some beer, Juliana."

"I don't usually—" She sighed, cutting herself off, and tried the beer. She knew Sam Adams was supposed to be high-quality beer, but it still tasted like beer to her. "You're very calm, you know. I just got assaulted on your doorstep, and you're not even upset."

"That's because I figure these guys did me a favor."

"How?"

His expression didn't change. "Maybe they knocked some sense into that dizzy brain of yours."

She took a breath and held it, pursing her lips together.

"Not used to being called names, are you?" Stark laughed, not pleasantly. "The only child, the rich girl, the talented pianist. Everything's gone smoothly for you your entire life. You've never had to get dirt under your nails or suffer a whole hell of a lot or listen to people call you things you don't want to be called."

"Listen, you arrogant, inconsiderate shit," she said, her voice low and controlled, "you don't know anything about me, and until you do I suggest you keep your remarks to yourself. I was just backhanded up your front steps because of you."

"Is that right?"

"Yes, damn it, that's right!"

"And I invited you here, did I? I knew you were coming, did I? I knew there might be trouble and so did you, and that's why you played it smart like I told you and stayed the hell in New York like you were supposed to. Lady, let's not talk about arrogance, and let's not talk about being inconsiderate."

She thought she took his outburst well. She didn't cower, she didn't run, she didn't avert her eyes from his black stare. She just sat there and took it and even considered letting him have it right back. But she didn't. Her shoulder and her wrist hurt, and besides, he had a point.

Instead she drank some more beer. "I found out about *LZ,* you know. Len told me. I've never read it, obviously, or seen the movie."

"What's that got to do with anything?"

She ignored him. "When the book came out, and even the movie, I didn't have time to pay much attention to goings-on outside the world of music. I still don't. I have so much work, so many commitments, so much I want to do, and so much everyone else wants me to do. I'll never even come close to being the kind of pianist I want to be. I'm not saying I'm proud of being such a ding-a-ling, and I'm not saying that's how all musicians should or do operate, just that *I've* had to be single-minded about what I do."

"Juliana," Stark said, "what the hell does that have to do with any of this mess? Two people are dead, and you just—"

She shot him an irritated look. "I know two people are dead, damn you, and you don't understand. Maybe you can't. Maybe it doesn't matter to you. I haven't been single-minded about what I do just to make a name, to get to where I am today. I've just always been absolutely, compulsively driven to play piano. I don't know why, I've never known. Ever since I can remember, I've *had* to play.

I never imagined myself doing anything else. My status today is a result of that compulsion, not the reason for it. But I'm losing that need—no, maybe that's not the right word. The basis for it is changing. I need to be a part of the world."

She looked at Matthew, but he didn't say anything. She felt pale and weak and annoyingly vulnerable. Why was she trying to explain? "Never mind," she said. "I know Rachel Stein and Uncle Johannes are dead, and I know what happened out there just now, but I can't back out."

Stark settled back in his chair, one foot up on his knee, his eyes never leaving her. "You're not going to bird-dog me so you can get excited about playing piano again."

"That's not what I meant!" She felt her face heat up. "I am not doing this because I'm bored. I'm doing it because I have to. I have no choice. Ten years ago maybe I wouldn't have bothered. You and all the other jerks involved with this mess could have done as you damned well pleased. I'd have been fine. But now I can't *not* act. I can't run away. It's not so I'll be a better pianist." She sat back, angry with herself. She'd stopped trying to explain herself to people years ago. If they understood her, okay. If not, to hell with them. Why was it different with Matthew Stark? "Anyway, I'm here."

"For about five minutes."

"Look—"

"Sweetheart, your butt's back in New York as soon as I can get it on a plane out of here."

She clamped her mouth shut. "I knew I shouldn't have tried to explain."

His expression softened, but not much. "I'm glad you tried," he said. "It's just that it doesn't make any difference. Look, if it's any consolation, I understand a lot more about where you're coming from than I'd like to let on. I know what it's like to be single-minded about work. I was about

mine at one time—and like you say, not because I wanted
to be rich and famous, but because I needed to get down
on paper things that I needed to say. And I know what it's
like to get to the top and have the pressures of being there—
the expectations, the goddamn effort involved—interfere
with the work itself."

"Is that why you're at the *Gazette?*" she asked quietly.

He grinned. "I didn't have a J.J. Pepper to slide into."
He finished off his beer in one long swallow, set the empty
bottle on the table, and rose. "Tell you what, you be smart
and don't put up a fuss about going back to New York, I'll
tell you about Master Sergeant Phillip Bloch on the way
to the airport."

She had to ask. "If I'm not smart and do put up a fuss?"

"Darling," he said, leaning very close, close enough
that she could feel the warmth of his breath on her mouth
and smell the beer, "do you really want to know?"

Sweet Catharina...

Hendrik de Geer stumbled into the Upper East Side bar
and slid onto the stool as he ordered a double shot of gin.
He ignored the looks he received from the well-dressed
clientele. What did they know? The gin wasn't Dutch, but
it would do. Anything would.

I'd forgotten how sweet.

He filled his glass, drank down the needed liquid. How
much would it take before oblivion overtook him? One
bottle—two?

Breathe, Johannes...goddamn you, breathe!

They'd brought his body to the streets of the old Jewish quarter. Dumped it there among the ghosts. Hendrik
had kept his face uncovered, half-hoping he'd be recognized. Not caring. But there was no one there anymore to
know Hendrik de Geer and what he'd done. So many of
the Jews were gone; a hundred thousand dead, it was said.

He believed it. A dozen were on his conscience.

I didn't mean for them to die!

But they did.

He poured another glass, drank it down, then another.

Bloch will go after the Minstrel. Ryder won't stop him.

It was none of his concern. Samuel Ryder was a coward and a fool, and to save himself he would have to appease Phillip Bloch. For him, there was no other choice. *He's like me, this senator,* the Dutchman thought. *He would involve people he cares about in his schemes to save his own skin.*

Now that Bloch knew about the diamond, he would never be satisfied until it was in his possession. Ryder would help if necessary. Bloch would know that.

They'll go to Catharina...to her daughter...to Wilhelmina.

Willie, the wily old bitch. There was no forgiveness in her stone heart. She could always see through him. For a time, she'd been excited by what he was. Now she'd kill him without a thought.

You must stop Bloch. You know how he thinks. You can do it.

No, he couldn't. Phillip Bloch had a stockpile of weapons, he had men who were well trained, if loyal only to themselves, and he had contacts, like Senator Ryder. He was tough, deliberate, cautious, and very dangerous. Hendrik was too old to take him on. Too tired.

And if Catharina dies?

Then she dies.

And he thought, as he refilled his glass, *I'm already damned.*

They took Matthew's car, a black Porsche, to the airport. "A German car?" Juliana said. "Aunt Willie would be disgusted."

Their shoulders almost touched in the cozy confines of the sportscar, and Matthew saw that she was still pale from her ordeal on his front steps. He glanced down at the slender, blunt-nailed hands folded on her lap. Her wrist was swollen, but she'd refused his offer of ice, assuring him and, he thought, herself that the injury was only minor. He hadn't told her what it was like to stand there and watch her tough it out with two of Bloch's men. Hadn't told her how the anger had ripped through him; how he'd had to fight the impulse to go after the goddamn cowards. They wouldn't deliver Bloch's message to him personally but had waited for an unarmed piano player. She'd handled herself well under the circumstances.

But Juliana Fall was getting to be one hell of a distraction.

"Why would Aunt Willie be disgusted?" he asked.

"She has this thing about Germans."

"You sent her back to Rotterdam?"

Juliana turned and looked out the passenger window. "No one sends Aunt Willie anywhere." Then she turned back to him. Her cheeks had regained some of their color. "You know, Matthew, I keep telling myself if you'd gotten yourself throttled on *my* doorstep, I'd have insisted you return home, as well. But then again, I wonder if I might understand your need to see this thing through."

"It's not your fight."

She looked at him, icy and smart and nuts and beautiful. Matthew didn't know why the hell he hadn't kissed her by now.

Because, jackass, you won't stop with a kiss. And then where would you be? Stay away, my man. Stay away.

She said coolly, "Bullshit."

"I don't want you around."

"And I make my own decisions."

"Not used to considering anyone's opinion but your own, are you?"

She gave him one of her distant, mysterious smiles. It warned him away and made him want to come closer. It made him realize how much he didn't know about Juliana Fall, and how much he wanted to know everything. For the first time, he saw her self-awareness—her understanding of who she was and what she was.

The mystery went to her dark eyes. "An only child in a solitary profession, a woman of some means who lives alone? Of course I'm accustomed to doing as I please. And you should talk. When I left the newsroom, your editor said, and I quote, 'Tell that independent pain in the ass to keep me posted.' We're not so different."

"We are," he said. "I know what I'm getting into. I've been there, Juliana."

She scoffed. "Why is it that men who've been to war always think they know more than people who haven't?"

"How the hell many 'men who've been to war' do you know?"

"Your view of the world is just as skewed as someone who has never seen combat," she said, not backing down. "We all state our convictions from within our convictions."

"Jesus Christ."

She lifted her small round shoulders and gave him another of her cool smiles, but said nothing.

"I don't think I've ever heard anyone accuse a Vietnam vet of being smart. We fought and died and were heroes and cowards and everything else in a war most people hated, not least of all us, in a war we didn't win. Not smart, wouldn't you say?"

"I wasn't implying you were smart. I was implying you thought you were smart."

"Just experienced." He gave her a sideways glance. "You can be an irritating woman."

"It's the Peperkamp in me. The Falls are all so civilized. But never mind. Tell me about Phillip Bloch—and your friend, have you heard from him? Weaze, is it?"

"Otis," Matthew said, a sudden feeling of hopelessness

washing over him as he envisioned the emaciated former gunner, his friend. "Otis Raymond. We called him the Weasel in 'Nam. I haven't heard from him. But, Juliana, I was wrong to suggest that you should feel responsible for anything that might or might not happen to him. I was hot. I needed someone to lash out at."

"That's okay. Musicians always have people screaming at them. We get used to it. You and Otis Raymond and Phillip Bloch were in Vietnam together?"

"We were there at the same time—I wouldn't say together. Bloch was a platoon sergeant, I was a helicopter pilot, and Weasel was one of my door gunners. We transported troops into and out of combat."

Juliana waited, but Matthew didn't go on. Finally, she said, "You're not a talkative person, are you? You say what you have to say and that's it. I can see why you haven't done much since *LZ*. When you have something else to say—something that you haven't said in any of your other work—you'll do another book. But not another *LZ*, even if that's what your public wants. Anyway, what does a gunner do, exactly?"

"Kills people."

Juliana smacked her mouth shut.

"That wasn't fair," he added quietly.

"No, maybe it was. I don't like to be forced to talk, either."

"So I've discovered."

"I don't know anything about the military. At best, my memories of Vietnam are dim. I remember catching scenes of the war on television, between homework assignments and practice sessions, and I remember debates in school about whether the U.S. had any business being there. But I was more interested in analyzing Bach cantatas." Her expression was grimly self-critical. "The Vietnam War's another huge gap in my knowledge."

Matthew hadn't expected her to be so perceptive, about

herself, or, certainly, about him. He pulled back into himself, and when he went on, his tone was less personal, almost clinical.

"My first tour of duty, I flew the Bell UH-1 Iroquois in its transport role. Hueys were the warhorses. The UH-1Bs were the primary transport helicopters. We called them slicks. The UH-1Cs were fitted with armaments—they were the gunships—the hogs, we called them. As pilot, my job was to get us in and out of LZs safely. The slick itself was unarmed, but it could move faster than a gunship. I had a copilot up front with me. In back were the crew chief and door gunner—we communicated with them over radio. They both were armed with M-60 machine guns to protect themselves, the passengers, the crew, and the ship. If we came down in a hot LZ, we could expect plenty of fire. We were all vulnerable, but gunners were the most exposed. A lot of them didn't live long."

"But Otis Raymond survived?"

Matthew looked straight ahead. "Yeah, he survived. He was good—and he was lucky. We both were. When I went to LOHs for my second tour, he transferred with me." He glanced at Juliana and gave her a small smile. "An LOH is a light observation helicopter. We'd draw fire to locate the enemy, and the gunships would come in and do their thing. By then the snakes had replaced Hueys as gunships."

"Snakes?"

"The Bell AH-1G Cobra. It was heavily armed and a hell of a lot faster than the hogs. Part of the strategy behind the hunter-killer teams was to reduce troop losses. It was a numbers game."

Juliana nodded, not so much understanding, he thought, as acknowledging that she was both interested and listening. "Why did you stay in for a second tour?"

He shrugged. "Somebody had to do the job. By the time we'd stayed in a year, Weasel and I figured we knew what we were doing and maybe could keep somebody else who didn't have our experience from getting killed."

"As a pilot, did you feel responsible for the men who flew with you?"

"Yes."

"And you still fee responsible for Otis Raymond."

He sighed, saying nothing. What the hell *could* he say?

"I won't pretend I can even imagine what you went through," Juliana told him quietly. "I'm sorry—"

"No, you're not, Juliana." He looked at the pale, beautiful face. "You're damned lucky."

Disgusted, Wilhelmina sat on the chair at the dusty Steinway concert grand in her niece's quiet living room. The bright winter sun streamed in through the big windows, and she could hear the traffic down on Central Park West. She was tired. She had just spent the last three hours searching every corner of her niece's monstrous apartment for the Minstrel's Rough. Wilhelmina herself had never seen the Minstrel, but she knew enough about diamonds to feel sure she'd recognize the world's largest uncut diamond when she saw it.

But she'd found neither the Minstrel nor any indication that Juliana had stashed it elsewhere or had even heard of the legendary stone. All she'd found of interest, minor interest at that, was a gigantic closet full of old clothes and a half-dozen different kinds of colored mousse—and cosmetics! Wilhelmina had never seen so much face paint! Such colors! And she didn't for a moment believe they belonged to a friend, as Juliana had suggested. Juliana was too solitary a person, and somehow the things reminded Wilhelmina of her niece. Whatever the case, that was her business and of no consequence to her aging aunt.

Yet Wilhelmina was still positive that Juliana had the Minstrel's Rough. It would explain so much. It was also logical, and the old Dutchwoman was not one to back away prematurely from what made sense.

At any rate, it had been a frustrating morning. The man posted outside the Beresford continued to stand in the cold, but Wilhelmina paid no attention to him whatever. But better to be aware of him than not.

She had made a cup of café au lait and now was tempted to play the piano. Would any of Juliana's monumental talent seep from the ivory keys into her old bones? Bah, she thought, I must be more tired than I feel.

The Chopin Piano Concerto No. 1 was open on the rack. Wilhelmina knew it to be a difficult piece, but she'd never played it. She wondered if she should give it a try now, to clear her mind.

She pressed middle C very slowly, and no sound came out. *Hendrik...*

Yes, he was in her thoughts. Catharina had called, tearfully telling her older sister about seeing him that morning. Wilhelmina wished she'd been able to speak up and ask Catharina to relate every detail of their conversation...how he'd looked, sounded, must have felt. Everything.

Not that she cared, of course.

"You're kidding yourself, Willie," she muttered. "You still care. You always will."

Suddenly she felt eerily alone amidst all that space, with so many people in the city around her. At home in Rotterdam, she never thought about being alone.

"Liar," she said aloud, with vehemence.

She jumped up, suddenly spooked, and ran around into all the rooms, pulling drapes, checking the locks on the doors and windows, and then came back to the living room, shaking. She turned on the stereo. She didn't care what she listened to. Anything besides the cries and the screams and the prayers and the loneliness that too often whispered to her in the night.

Hendrik...may God damn you to hell!

And not just for what he'd done—but for showing her what might have been.

"You're being unfair," Juliana informed Matthew as he walked with her to the shuttle gate. "Unfair, unreasonable, and damned provoking."

He grinned. "Damned provoking, huh?"

"Yes."

"Well, so are you, sweet cheeks."

"Me?"

"Uh-huh. You're holding out on me."

She didn't say a word.

"Maybe not much, maybe a lot. With you, it's hard to tell. But whatever you're not telling me, I figure I don't need to know. It's just not worth pulling you deeper into this mess. Whether by accident or design, two people are dead. As far as I'm concerned, that's enough."

"I think we should work together," she told him as the announcement came for her flight to begin boarding.

"God save me."

"You have no right to tell me what to do."

"I have every right to keep you from bird-dogging me—and I can do it."

Her dark eyes gleamed with frustration and excitement, which both worried and pleased him. But the paleness was still there, the bruise on her wrist. He admired her for not wanting to run, but he couldn't let her determination undermine his own common sense. Having a piano player strutting around behind him wasn't going to accomplish a damn thing. And there was no guarantee she was ever going to get around to telling him what she knew about the Minstrel's Rough. She didn't believe in tit for tat.

Not, of course, that he'd told her everything.

"Matthew, listen to me," she said, "I'm involved in this whether or not you like it."

"That's my point. I don't like it. Get on the plane, Juliana. Go home, go to Vermont, go to the Club Aquarian, go any goddamn place you want to—just stay the hell away from me."

"Maybe I'll go see Sam Ryder and find out if he's more cooperative."

It was the wrong thing to say. Matthew jumped forward and pulled her around by the shoulders so she faced him. "Don't screw around with Ryder." The words came out dark and angry, but he didn't raise his voice and his mouth hardly moved. "He'll eat you alive."

His tone, his expression, his firm grip on her would have intimidated the hell out of anyone else. He knew it. But Juliana just wrinkled up her face. "That's not your problem."

"I'll make it my goddamn problem."

"I'm not your concern," she said.

"The hell you're not."

She was as worn out as he was, as testy, as independent, as used to getting her own damn way. She was never nice for the sake of being nice. It wasn't necessary in her world. Wasn't necessary in his, either. He looked at the uncompromising set of her jaw and her lovely mouth, and he said the hell with it. He pulled her even closer and kissed her hard, briefly, tearing himself away before the warmth of her penetrated too deeply.

Just as he'd wanted himself, a kiss wasn't enough. It wasn't even close.

"I don't want to see you zipped up in a body bag," he said.

She teetered a bit, and he was pleased to note he'd had the same dizzying effect on her that she'd had on him. But she recovered. He could see her kicking herself back into gear. "So that's it, right?" she said hotly. "You kiss me and pack me off like you're Davy Crockett off to the Alamo or wherever he was off to."

"That's right," he said.

She tossed her head back, insulted.

Stark laughed. "You liked the kiss, sweetheart, and don't try to pretend otherwise. You kissed me back."

"A reflex. Like playing arpeggios."

"I don't think I've ever had one of my kisses compared to playing arpeggios."

"Well." She fell into the long line for the shuttle to New York. "If Aunt Willie and I are followed again, I'll know who *not* to call."

Matthew's thick black brows drew together in a deep frown. Christ, if he only knew when to take her seriously. Her high cheekbones were pink, the rest of her face dead white. What the hell was she talking about this time? Followed— *again?* Bullshit. It was just a ploy. But Aunt Willie…

"Is that woman in New York?"

Juliana just smiled and waved.

Matthew swore, but she continued to ignore him. Finally, swearing some more, he scrambled for a ticket and got in line, at the end because she refused to let him cut in front of her.

She did, however, arrange to have him sit next to her. Their shoulders brushed lightly. Arpeggios, he thought, Jesus. She looked at him up close, her eyes sparkling. "I have an ulterior motive for permitting you to sit beside me," she said.

He was thinking she meant their kiss had knocked some sense of fair play into her and she was going to tell him about Aunt Willie and being followed and maybe even something about the Minstrel's Rough. She might even want another kiss.

But she went on, matter-of-fact, "Now I know about helicopters. So tell me about platoon sergeants." She smoothed her skirt and looked over at him. "What exactly is a platoon?"

Nineteen

Catharina was impatient for the last of her customers to leave so that she could close up the shop. Over and over again she had berated herself for not telling Hendrik she had the Minstrel. That way, she could have protected Juliana—and even Wilhelmina. She could lead Hendrik away from them, just as Johannes had tried to do. It was a good plan; anyway, good or not, it had to be done.

If only she'd thought to do it when Hendrik was there. But she would have another chance. She would *make* one.

The cleanup crew already had the kitchen spotless, and there was just one trio of friends lingering over a pot of tea and a tray of butter cookies. Catharina didn't rush them. She laid six miniature cream puffs in a box to take home to her husband; they were his favorite. He was urging her to go to their country house in Connecticut for a few days and make wreaths, gathering the pine cones, sprigs of evergreen, and perhaps some grapevines from their own woods. She remembered herself urging Juliana to go to Vermont. Was there really anywhere they could hide?

The little doorbell tinkled, and two men entered the shop. The trio had split up their bill, and each young woman was counting out her money; they had on their

coats already. Catharina started to tell the men the shop was
closed, but she stopped herself, staring at them instead. One
was perhaps in his early fifties with a blunt, mean face and
iron-gray hair. He wore a navy blue sweater that emphasized the breadth and strength of his shoulders; she thought
the sweater was intentionally snug. She noticed the bulge
of his thigh muscles beneath the sturdy pants. The second
man was perhaps twenty, rangy and dark, wearing a jacket
and baggy jeans. Catharina didn't think they had come to
buy cream puffs.

"Afternoon," the older one said, nodding in greeting.

Catharina nodded back, holding her head regally, and
when she spoke, her Dutch accent sounded exaggerated,
even to her. "Good afternoon. Can I help you?"

The older man laughed, a twangy snort that she found
disturbing. "Now that's the kind of talk I like. Yeah, you
can help me—Mrs. Fall, right?"

"Yes, that is correct." Again, the heavy accent.

"Sergeant Phillip Bloch."

She closed up the white box. "What is it you want?"

"The Minstrel's Rough."

Matthew had reluctantly agreed to split up with Juliana
at the airport so she could fetch her mother, mostly because
he wanted to have a word alone with Wilhelmina Peperkamp. She pulled open the door wearing an apron that had
sixteenth-notes across the front and fit rather cozily around
the old Dutchwoman's ample middle.

"You Peperkamps get around," he said.

Wilhelmina was in a no-nonsense mood. "Come in, Mr.
Stark."

He did.

"Where's Juliana?"

He explained as he followed the old Dutchwoman down
the hall to the kitchen. He remembered her story about

feeding her brother's cat, but she showed no indication the silly lie embarrassed her. She just seemed peculiarly glad to have some company. She was an independent, stubborn woman—a Peperkamp.

"You two are being watched, I see," he said. He'd compelled Juliana to describe the man who'd followed them and had spotted him outside the Museum of Natural History. He'd stopped himself just short of going over and pounding the bastard into the pavement.

"Yes, but he's not an expert. We have our ways of dealing with him."

J.J. Pepper, for one. Juliana hadn't mentioned her on the plane, but Matthew had no doubt her services were called into use to handle her Burberry man.

The kitchen was a large, airy room, its faded elegance in need of remodeling, and Stark wondered how Juliana fit in with the rest of the crowd in the prestigious Beresford. Knowing her, she probably didn't care one way or the other—or even notice such things. She had any number of small, upscale appliances, but they looked relatively unused. Wilhelmina had already started cleaning the place. There was a mop standing in a bucket of sudsy water, and the counters were sparkling.

"I thought apartments were small in New York," Wilhelmina said as she squatted down and worked at a spot on the floor with a fingernail, "but this place! Did you see that giant green something in the entry? I can't decide what it is. I've watered it, but who knows. Maybe it doesn't need water. How is your investigation coming?"

Stark debated grabbing a sponge but leaned against a counter instead. Yes, a woman of action was Wilhelmina Peperkamp. "Facts seem to be coming my way instead of me going theirs."

"Ahh, yes. I know what you mean."

He had a sneaking suspicion she did. "I'm glad to see

you're just washing floors, but I have a feeling that isn't all that you're up to. Look, this thing's getting serious—"

She glanced up at him, annoyed. "My brother's body is being cremated, Mr. Stark. He died of a heart attack, but who's to say what brought it on? You don't need to tell me about danger, I assure you. I was in the Dutch Underground Resistance during the war. I know danger."

Properly chastened, Stark watched her get up and swish the mop around, then wring it out. She attacked the floor under the table, complaining because Juliana had such a big kitchen for one person and so many gadgets and who knew how to work such things and there was no food in the place. No cheese. She'd already cleaned out the refrigerator, apparently, and thrown out everything that didn't look right to her. What it might look like to Juliana didn't seem to matter a whole hell of a lot. She finished up with the floor, dumped out the water, and proceeded to scour the sink, working fast and furiously.

Matthew found her opinionated and critical, but she also seemed to practice her own brand of tolerance: you could do as you goddamn well pleased, just so long as you didn't expect her to approve. Hell, maybe he didn't need to worry; the old battleax could probably handle Phil Bloch.

"Tell me, Mr. Stark," she said, drying her hands with a linen dishtowel, "are you planning to write another book on these past few days?"

"Did Juliana tell you about *LZ?*"

Again annoyance flashed in her plain, square face. "No, I read it when it came out—in English, of course. I avoid translations whenever possible. It was an excellent work, but naturally with a book like that, there's always the danger it's the only one you have to write. Either you wrote that book over and over—under different titles, of course, and perhaps the readers don't mind, but still it's the same—or you just stop. If a new idea comes, it comes. If not, at least you won't starve." She nodded at his feet, adding, "You have good boots, Mr. Stark. I'd say you're doing all right."

"I'll tell my editor. Judge me by my boots, not my lack of production."

"You're lazy?"

A sin in Wilhelmina Peperkamp's world, to be sure. She scowled at some expensive European hand cream Juliana had on the sink but squirted some out and rubbed it into her tough old hands.

"*Unmotivated* might be a better word," Stark said. "But never mind. You and Juliana are being watched—"

"Catharina, too," Wilhelmina added perfunctorily.

"I suspected as much. I think it's because someone thinks one or all of you can lead him to the Minstrel's Rough."

Wilhelmina put the cap back on the hand cream and looked at him, her stony expression matching his. "You know, Mr. Stark, if one looks closely, one can see how your eyes tell what is in your heart. It's not easy to see, perhaps, but it's there. You're not so tough." She smiled at his look of surprise. "Why don't you just tell me what you know?"

"I haven't made all the connections yet," he said, determined not to let the old Dutchwoman get to him. "I'm trying. But you put me at a disadvantage by not leveling with me. What do you know about the Minstrel?"

She shrugged, but he didn't for a second believe her look of nonchalance and ignorance. "It's a legendary diamond. I've never seen it and have no proof it exists, but I grew up in the diamond business. I've heard stories. If it could be located and successfully cut, it would be worth millions."

And what would Phillip Bloch do with that much money? He was a retired army sergeant. "Why do people think you have it?"

"I don't know that people do think that. Do you?"

"It's a damn good guess." He saw that his dark looks weren't inspiring her to talk. Another Peperkamp trait. "What about your sister?"

"Achh, she bakes cookies. She always could cook. In the war, she would come up with so many ways to stretch what food we had. Here, I've some coffee made. I don't know why Juliana doesn't have a regular coffeepot, but—" she shrugged "—one adapts."

"Your sister doesn't like to talk about the war, does she?"

"No."

Stark nodded. "I can understand that."

"Yes," Wilhelmina said, "I believe you can. For me, it's more difficult to understand, because I think we cannot afford not to talk. But Juliana's never pushed."

"Good for her."

The coffee maker, Stark noted, was top-of-the-line. He took a seat with her at a high-gloss rectangular oak table and watched without expression as she added two tablespoons of canned evaporated milk to her coffee. Aunt Willie's coffee was strong enough to kill a horse, but he drank it anyway.

"Do you want to tell me about Hendrik de Geer?" he asked.

She shook her head. "No."

"You knew him during the war?"

"Yes, but that's of no consequence."

"At this point, probably not," Matthew agreed. "What's important right now is getting you three out of the reach of the man I think de Geer's been working for. I'll help you get somewhere safe, then I'll figure out a way to stop these guys."

"Is this man someone you know?" Wilhelmina asked, interested.

Stark grinned. "Tit for tat, Ms. Peperkamp. You tell me about de Geer and the Minstrel, and I'll tell you what I've got on my end."

"Maybe you have nothing," she said with a grunt, drinking some of the coffee, "and then where would I be?"

"Whichever way you want it. I have a call to make. Mind if I use the phone?"

"And if I do mind?"

Stark laughed at her combativeness. "Hell, Juliana can afford it."

"Who are you calling?"

"The *Gazette*." Wilhelmina Peperkamp followed him into the living room, making no attempt to give him any privacy, but Matthew didn't care. Ziegler picked up on the first ring. "Working hard, Aaron? Good. Got anything for me?"

"Zip," Aaron said, sighing. "I got in touch with most of the men whose names you gave me, but none had heard from or about Phillip Bloch in a number of years—or were too keen to hear his name. They also hadn't heard from Otis Raymond. I checked the wires, too, and the morgue, but no luck."

"Stay on it, see if anything comes up," Stark said and, before hanging up, he gave Ziegler the number on the telephone next to the goldfish tank. Given the general disarray of the rest of the place, it was cleaner than he'd have expected, but he had to admit to a certain satisfaction that beautiful, talented, wealthy Juliana Fall didn't worry about maintaining the standard Central Park West opulence.

"Did he have anything?" Wilhelmina asked, her frustration with her own inactivity mounting.

"No."

"Bah. I hate waiting."

"Ready to knock heads together, are you?" Matthew grinned. "We could have used you in 'Nam."

"A terrible war," she said.

"Name me one that wasn't."

She pursed her thin lips thoughtfully. "A good point. Where are you going?"

He was zipping up his coat. "See if I can find some heads to knock together. Sit tight, Aunt Willie. I won't be long."

Catharina pulled out a length of delft-blue ribbon; it was real ribbon, not paper. The Minstrel. Of course. She wasn't surprised—or, after forty years, frightened. She'd known someone would come, not this man, perhaps, but someone.

"And why do you want the Minstrel?" she asked, nominally curious.

"I don't like to waste time, Mrs. Fall. The stone, please."

"As you wish."

With a few deft movements, she tied the ribbon around the box, which she tucked under her arm, nodding toward the kitchen. They would use the rear exit—less likely to run into any well-intentioned rescuers that way. This, Catharina thought, was what she had to do—and it was going to be easier than she'd envisioned. She hated only to worry Adrian, to sadden him…

No, she wouldn't think of those things now.

"Come with me," she said, hearing the resolve in her own voice.

The two men followed her into the kitchen as her mind raced. Where should she take them? Johannes had led his merry chase to Amsterdam. She considered Rotterdam, the Hague—no, she thought. Switzerland. She would tell them the Minstrel was in a safe-deposit box in a Swiss bank. Her husband being a banker and herself a member, if a somewhat eccentric one, of the Park Avenue elite, she could name several. She would pick one, and they would go.

In the front of the shop, the doorbell tinkled again, and Catharina held her breath.

"Mother?"

No! "Juliana—no. Get out! Quickly!"

But Bloch was already swinging back around toward the kitchen.

Muttering in Dutch, Catharina grabbed a knife and sent it slicing toward the big gray-haired man. He dodged, swearing, as the knife stuck in the doorframe inches to his left. The younger man lunged toward her. Catharina began pulling pots and baking pans off their hooks and throwing them in their path.

"Juliana," she screamed. "Run! I don't need you!"

Catharina kicked a stack of baking trays onto the floor, blocking the younger man's path, and snatched up another knife, an eight-inch Sabatier. She flung it at the sergeant, who was circling around the cooking island toward her. The blade nicked his wrist as he put up a hand to keep the knife from striking his neck. Catharina felt herself going wild, as her wispy white-blond hair hung in her face. She'd never before felt as if she could kill someone.

"Feisty, aren't we?" Bloch said, grinning as he carelessly shook a spurt of blood from his hand.

"If you touch my daughter, Phillip Bloch," Catharina yelled hoarsely, "I'll kill you. Nothing will stop me!"

"Get the girl," Bloch said calmly to the younger man. "I'll take care of this one."

Juliana appeared in the doorway, her face pallid with fury and terror as she held a wooden shoe above her head as a weapon. Catharina felt a surge of pride at her daughter's courage, but also a sinking sense of despair.

Doing as he was told, the younger man kicked his way over the baking pans, pulling out a gun in a holster over his kidney. Juliana wasted no time. As he swung toward her, she lunged at him and smashed the wooden shoe down on the side of his neck, clearly not expecting to have a second chance. The impact of the shoe on flesh and bone made a sickening sound. The man sank to his knees. His gun flew out of his hand and skidded across the floor.

Catharina was sobbing, adrenaline pumping painfully

through her. "Good for you, Juliana! Now for God's sake, *run!*"

But the blow had only stunned the younger man, and he recovered enough to whip around and grab Juliana by the knee, toppling her over. Her head struck the door-frame, and she landed awkwardly, in a sprawling heap. Catharina saw that her daughter had instinctively protected her hands.

"Juliana!"

Catharina reached for another knife, but Bloch bounded over to her and smashed it from her hand, ignoring his flesh wound. He grabbed the baker's wrist and twisted it behind her, and she cried out in agony as she heard the snap of her own bone.

"You sonofabitch," Juliana yelled, trying to pull herself up.

"Don't move or I'll snap another bone," Bloch said.

Through her blinding pain, Catharina saw the young henchman strike her daughter across the side of the head, knocking her back to the cool tile floor. Catharina began praying in Dutch for strength and forgiveness. Her help-lessness was the worst pain she had ever experienced.

"I should learn not to underestimate you Peperkamps," Bloch said. He was breathing hard and bleeding signifi-cantly, and he coughed and snorted, catching his breath. "God*damn* women. Still, ain't this convenient? We got us two little birdies with one stone, don't we? Pick up the girl, Peters. We'll go out the back."

Juliana's Burberry man had moved across the street to Central Park, where it was dark and getting very cold. Matthew trotted across the street and before the guy could do anything had him pinned against the tree, with a fore-arm pressed against his throat. "What's your name?" Stark asked.

"Paul—"

"Hello, Paul. I'm Matthew Stark."

"Jesus Christ." The bland eyes widened. "Steelman? Weasel's told me about you— Shit. Look, I'm just following orders."

"Bloch's."

It wasn't a question. Paul tried to nod but couldn't. "Hey, look, he's okay. Just trying to get it together to go after some commies, that kind of thing, no big deal."

"Then what's he doing have piano players and old women followed around?"

"He's just looking after his own interests. I got orders not to hurt nobody."

"You haven't got the talent to hurt anybody," Stark said mildly. "Those women have been running circle around you. What about me? Got any orders?"

Paula licked his fleshy lips. "Truth is, I can do anything to you. I mean, Bloch don't care what happens to you. But Weaze says you're okay."

"Tell me about Weasel."

"I ain't seen him in a while, I been up here."

"Where'd you see him last?"

"I *can't...*"

"Where?"

Stark didn't raise his voice. He didn't have to. Weaze had been telling stories about Steelman, some of them probably even true. "Florida. Ryder's place on the Dead Lakes. Bloch knows I told you, I'm dead."

"Is he there now?"

Paul didn't say anything. Matthew repeated the question. Paul licked his lips some more; they were purple in the cold. He looked like the kind of guy who considered standing in the cold watching a ritzy apartment building on Central Park West hazardous duty. "No." It came out as a whisper. "He ain't there."

Matthew waited.

"Man, I can't—"

"You'd better. I can think of lots of things I could do with you if you don't."

"He's here in New York, okay? I think he's going after the women, first the baker, then these two, just to ask them some questions. They deal with him straight, he'll let 'em go."

"You dumb fuck," Matthew said, but he didn't waste any time or energy explaining to Paul that it didn't matter if you dealt straight with Sergeant Phillip Bloch. If you were a loose end, he cut you off.

He ran out into the street, and a cab screeched to a stop in front of him. It was occupied. He didn't care. He tore open the door and flashed his press badge. "It's an emergency—please," he said, climbing in.

The woman already occupying the cab decided she wouldn't stay in for the ride and shot out. The driver, a fat, slow gentleman from Brooklyn, insisted on checking Stark's press badge before he went anywhere.

"Okay, fella," he said, "where to?"

It sounded ridiculous, but Matthew said it anyway, "Catharina's Bake Shop on upper Madison."

Phillip Bloch's henchman Peters bent down to haul Juliana to her feet, but she was ready for him. Ignoring the shooting pain in her head and the muted cries of her mother, she kicked out viciously, one of her three-hundred-dollar black Italian shoes landing squarely in his face, knocking him backward. He grunted in surprise and blinding pain, and Juliana seized the opening, scooting backward as far out of reach as she could and scrambling agonizingly to her feet.

Bloch growled. "Fuck it, do I have to do everything?"

From the front room came a crashing sound and, absurdly, the tinkling of Catharina's little doorbell. Matthew,

Juliana thought wildly, hanging on to the doorframe, it's got to be him!

A stout, fair-skinned older man jumped behind the counter, brushing her aside as he went into the kitchen.

"Hendrik—help Juliana!" Catharina was sobbing as Bloch twisted her good arm behind her back and pushed her toward the storeroom and rear exit. "Never mind me— *for God's sake, never mind me!*"

"Don't follow me, de Geer," Bloch said. He had pulled out a monstrous gun and looked ready to call the whole thing a wash and kill everyone in sight. Blood poured over his hand. "I'll kill her right now—and the girl. I'll cut my losses. You know I will."

The Dutchman took a short breath and halted, his cold eyes giving Juliana a quick, appraising glance. The young henchman was coughing, climbing slowly to his feet. Juliana could see his eyes focus on his gun and shot out one foot, kicking it farther away. De Geer folded his hands together and brought them down on the stumbling Peters, hitting him almost exactly where Juliana had gotten him with the wooden shoe. He fell unconscious.

Phillip Bloch had seized the opportunity and had disappeared through the storeroom with Catharina.

"Come, you must get out of here," the Dutchman said in a low voice, "before he changes his mind and thinks he can handle us both after all."

Juliana lunged blindly toward the storeroom. *"Mother—"*

"Bloch will kill her, and you, if we don't leave now. He means what he says."

"Damn it, I'm calling the police!"

Hendrik de Geer grabbed her by the shoulders and held her, not ungently, against the doorframe. "No. Understand me, Juliana. He will kill her."

She nodded dully, hurting everywhere, gulping for air as she tried to still her pounding heart and concentrate…

Mother. But she knew the Dutchman was right. "He wants the Minstrel," she said.

"Of course he does. Now come. I will get you somewhere safe."

She looked at him. She had never seen eyes so piercingly blue. "You're Hendrik de Geer."

"Yes," he said, without pride. "I'm the man who betrayed your family and the Steins—*my friends*—to the Nazis. And, of course, you're wondering whose side I'm on." He gave her a thin, wretched smile. "But that's very simple, Juliana. Everyone knows whose side I'm on—my own. Right now it suits me to help you. Now come."

Betrayed…my friends…Juliana held back another wave of shock. She couldn't think about the past and all she didn't know right now. *Stay within yourself.* Shuji always said. "Wait—it's all right. I can find my own way."

"Your mother told me—"

"I know, but go after her. You can do it." She had the feeling he had to. "I'll be all right."

The smile grew less thin, less wretched, and the cold eyes moistened and became almost warm. "You're a fine woman, Juliana Fall," he said.

He waited until she'd gotten safely out to the street, past the unconscious Peters, the fallen gun, the fallen knives, the pots, the baking pans…the smashed box of cream puffs. The glass door was smashed, but she seemed hardly to notice. She was a strong girl, Hendrik thought. He reminded her of Catharina—and Wilhelmina. He watched her stumble out into the street and flag a passing cab and waited until she'd climbed in, safe.

Then he went silently through the storeroom.

"Juliana." Shuji opened the door to his Upper East Side town house. "You look like hell."

She managed a weak smile. "Jazz'll do that to you."

"Bullshit."

"I need help, Shuji."

He sighed. "Get in here."

Shuji's town house combined a Japanese sense of negative space with his flair for the opulent and dramatic. The entire fourth floor was his music studio. Juliana knew; she'd spent countless hours there. A warmth came over her, a nostalgia for those days, their security. She almost cried.

"What do you need?" he asked.

"A car and some cash."

He managed a small smile. "The *New York Times* find out what you've been up to?"

"No, my mother's been kidnapped."

He looked at her, uncertain that she was in fact serious. For almost twenty years he'd listened to her problems, excuses, fears, exaggerations. He knew her better than he knew anyone. Loved her in a way he could love no one else—as, he realized, she did him. She was unpredictable and outrageous, and he knew he was lying to himself if he believed he could ever walk out of her life, J.J. Pepper or not.

He handed her the keys to his Mercedes and all the cash in his wallet. "I presume you're in too big a hurry to answer any questions."

"Later," she said, throwing her arms around him as she felt the tears hot on her cheeks, and then she fled.

It must be a man, Shuji told himself, heading back upstairs to practice. Now at least he could. Since their argument he'd been able to do little more than stare at the keyboard, something, of course, he would never admit to her. He hadn't understood what happened to her. J.J. Pepper, dyed hair, turbans, outrageous clothes. Jazz. He shuddered. Yet now, while he still didn't understand, he did know it wasn't something he needed to address. It was Juliana's problem—something she had to confront and decide what to do about on her own. If she wanted his counsel, she would ask for it. The student-teacher relationship they had had for so long was over. It was one of those things that had been ending for a long time, gradually fading, not like a sunset into the night, but like the colors of dawn into a bright, beautiful day. Yes, that was how he would think of it.

They'd become friends, he thought with satisfaction. Equals.

The cabdriver obviously felt vindicated when he pulled up in front of Catharina's Bake Shop and the place was crawling with police. Blue lights were flashing, in contrast to the festive holiday lights lining the street. Stark passed him a twenty and didn't wait for change as he got out, dropping his mask in place. Inside he was empty and stone cold. He flashed his press credentials and talked to the cop in charge, listening without comment. It seemed to be a simple break-in; they'd found a guy unconscious in the kitchen claiming he was smacked on the head while buying cream puffs. Guy's name was Peters—Alex Peters. They'd tried to reach the owner.

Just then Adrian Fall walked up and introduced himself, but Stark had already guessed who it was, not so much by his resemblance to his daughter—although it was there, in the coloring, the bones, the sensitive mouth—but by his look of terror. Stark knew something of how he felt.

Bloch had struck it rich, Matthew thought bitterly: Juliana and Catharina in one fell swoop. But if Matthew mentioned his name now to the police, Bloch would just dump them the first chance he got. That was the sergeant's style. No deals, no loose ends. His chief strength, his only weakness.

"Goddamnit," he muttered. *Wilhelmina...*

He thanked the cop as he heard Adrian Fall say his wife had called from her shop two hours ago and hustled down the block to the first pay phone he came to. He dropped in some coins and dialed Juliana's apartment, and Wilhelmina answered on the first ring, saying, "Allo."

"It's Stark." He looked up at the milky-dark sky above Manhattan. "A man named Phil Bloch has Juliana and your sister. He'll come for you next. Then he's going to find out which one of you has the Minstrel's Rough. If he gets to you before I do, *don't tell him*. Stall him. I'm on my way."

"Who is this Phil Bloch?"

There wasn't an ounce of fear in her solid, accented voice. "A real shitkicker, Willie. Lay low."

He hung up, thinking Ryder, you sonofabitch, you put this in motion. This is all your fucking fault, and if anything happens to the Peperkamps or Weasel, I'm coming after your ass the way I should have twenty years ago.

He flagged a cab and headed back to the Upper West Side. He passed the bakeshop. Adrian Fall was standing outside, his hands thrust deep into the pockets of his conservative cashmere overcoat, his handsome patrician face white and gaunt in the harsh light of the police car. Matthew felt for the man. It couldn't be easy to be in love with a Peperkamp.

Her hands were all right.

It was Juliana's first coherent thought as she drove north along the Hudson River Parkway, staying within five miles of the posted speed limit. Traffic was heavy. Cars passed her with ski racks on their roofs; there'd been snow in Vermont and the Berkshires during the week and another couple of inches was forecasted. Skiing would be excellent. Juliana didn't ski. She'd never taken the time to learn and she'd always been afraid for her hands. That wasn't why she went to Vermont. It wasn't why she was going now.

The initial shock of pain had subsided, and now she felt a dull throbbing at her side where she'd fallen against the door. She wanted to hear her mother's voice tell her to drink some warm milk lightly flavored with cocoa and go to bed…her mother, whose pain had to be—

"Oh, God," she mumbled, hearing again the snapping of her mother's arm.

Her father would be frantic, but she didn't dare call him—couldn't. He would demand that she come home; he had a right to know what was going on. But she couldn't explain, not now, and she had to live up to her responsibilities. If only she'd known seven years ago that Uncle Johannes wasn't half-kidding or half-nuts. Her father would blame Aunt Willie, whom he'd never liked. He called her a troublemaker.

Aunt Willie…

If she couldn't call her father, Juliana felt she at least had to give her aunt some kind of explanation—tell her what had happened at the bakeshop. *Matthew…* She owed him something, too, although she was no longer sure what.

She began looking for an exit.

The old aunt was having a goddamn cup of tea when Matthew pounded into the apartment. "Get your things," he told her. "I'm getting you out of here."

He thought rapidly, where the hell can I stash her? In a hotel. The Plaza. She could complain about how fancy it was, and he'd send Feldie the bill. Jesus. *Hey, don't worry about it,* Weasel used to tell him, *guys with no sense of humor're the ones who get aced.*

Weasel. Juliana. Catharina Fall.

If only he'd taken Weasel's tip more seriously and put the screws to Ryder at Lincoln Center when he'd had the chance.

If only. His goddamn life was filled with if onlys.

Wilhelmina got up slowly, dumped out the rest of her lukewarm tea into the sink, and rinsed out her cup. "I will not run," she told Stark.

"Don't argue with me. I'll haul you out of here on my back if I have to."

She raised her thick eyebrows. "Imagine what the door-men would say. They do have their uses, don't you think? Mr. Stark, I appreciate your protective impulses, but I cannot permit myself to run to safety while those I love are in danger." She placed the cup on the counter and turned back to him, her plain face racked with worry. "They're all I have left."

He nodded curtly, realizing he had no right to order her around—not that she, like her lovely niece, would pay a damn bit of attention if he did.

"I don't expect you to take me with you. I'd slow you down, and you seem quite competent. You don't need me. Just leave, and let me do what I must."

The telephone rang, and Matthew pounced on it.

"Matthew—"

His stomach twisted together at the strain he heard in her voice. "What happened, where are you?"

"Your damned Phillip Bloch took my mother. I met the Dutchman, Hendrik de Geer. He's gone after Mother, I think. I don't know, I— He said we shouldn't call the police."

"He's right. Tell me where you are, Juliana. I'll come for you."

"There's more between you and this Phillip Bloch than you told me, isn't there?"

"Yes."

"Tell me now."

"Did he hurt you?"

"No, I'm okay. My mother threw a knife at him. It just knicked his wrist." She sounded breathless, just skimming along the surface of her emotions, not diving in too deep. "Tell Aunt Willie, won't you? She always thinks Mother's such a wimp."

"Where are you?" he asked again, his voice burlap-rough.

"Does Senator Ryder know Bloch, as well?"

"Yes, goddamnit. Where are you?"

"He wants the Minstrel. He'll come after Aunt Willie, too. He'd have taken me, but I hit his man Peters and then Hendrik de Geer helped me because Mother yelled for him to…" She broke off, her voice choking; she coughed. "Bloch broke my mother's arm, just snapped it like kindling. He's a terrible person, isn't he? I—" She cut herself off. "Matthew, tell Aunt Willie I'm okay."

Stark gripped the phone. "Juliana, let me come for you—"

"It's all right," she said dully. "Really. This isn't your problem, Matthew. I don't want you hurt, too."

"I can handle it. Juliana—"

But it was too late. She'd already hung up.

Aunt Willie was standing next to him. She handed him a set of keys. "They're to Juliana's Nazi car," she said. "She may have another set and be in it herself, but I don't think so. I found these in her room. She's gone to Vermont."

"How do you know?"

"Because I know."

"The Minstrel?" he asked, with a flash of his brown-black eyes. "I'll be gone to hell. Juliana has it, doesn't she?"

I don't even like diamonds. Right, *sweetheart.*

"Go to Vermont," Wilhelmina said.

"How do I know you're not just trying to get rid of me?" He was remembering the cat in Antwerp.

Wilhelmina sighed, a touch of emotion coming into her unremarkable eyes. "You're in love with Juliana, aren't you?" she asked, without surprise. "A man like you wouldn't have many women. He would wait, and when the right one came along, he would know it."

Every fiber inside him told him the old woman was right, but he only hissed impatiently. "Jesus Christ—"

"You don't know that I'm not just trying to get rid of you," she said. "But, understand me, Matthew Stark, I know you care deeply for Juliana—and nothing must happen to her. She's the last of the Peperkamps. It's not you who must trust me—I must trust you."

"And I'll bet there aren't many people you do trust."

She shrugged impassively. "That is so."

Matthew quickly told her about the knife and de Geer, and if either surprised her, she didn't say. She just produced addresses for her niece's garage and Vermont house—Stark guessed she'd only started mopping the floor *after* she'd given the place a thorough shake down—and hurried him out the door. She told him to mind the man across the street watching the building.

Stark assured her he could handle the situation.

"You would have survived the occupation, I think," she said.

From Wilhelmina Peperkamp, Stark knew that was a supreme compliment.

"I will get you the Minstrel," Catharina said, leaning forward toward Bloch as the car in which they were riding turned into Central Park West. She cradled her broken arm as best she could, but the pain was excruciating. It had already begun to swell badly. *Ah, Mamma,* she thought with tears in her eyes, *I remember your strength.* Bloch was in the front seat with one of his men; she was in the back with another. Neither was as young as the man Peters, and neither offered to help with her arm. "There's no need to involve the others."

His cold, clear gray eyes fastened to her. "I make the decisions."

"If you touch my daughter or my sister, I won't get you the Minstrel." She blinked past the pain. "I won't care what you do to me."

"But you'll care what I do to them." He turned back around, still furious with himself for not having pushed it to the limit with de Geer. He should have killed the Dutchman and taken the girl and never minded the crazy, ugly look in de Geer's eyes. Maybe he still could get the diamond, maybe not. Either way, he had to go through this; he had other matters to consider, namely covering his ass. Without looking back at the baker, he added, "I'm through taking chances."

Catharina's heart beat rapidly, and it was difficult to control her breathing. But she refused to faint. They would be at Juliana's apartment soon. She had to trust that Hendrik had gotten her to safety. Hendrik…once more she was trusting him with her loved ones. What choice did she have?

What choice did you have then?

She looked out at the lights in Central Park. Juliana and Wilhelmina would not be at the apartment. She had to believe that. Still, she said once more, "You're wasting time, Sergeant Bloch. We can just go now for the Minstrel."

"Yeah, we could," came the hard, mean voice. "But we ain't going to."

Wilhelmina prepared herself a snack of bread and butter. Not butter, really. Juliana used some kind of low fat, low salt, no cholesterol margarine the old Dutchwoman thought disgusting. She found a piece of semisweet chocolate in the cupboard and broke it up onto the bread. Much more palatable.

The doorman had called up, saying a Hendrik de Geer was downstairs asking to see Wilhelmina Peperkamp. Of course he would know she was there, of course he wouldn't bother with a fake name or trying to sneak in. He knew her too well. He would know she would let him in, that she had no choice.

The doorbell rang, and she went into the foyer, opening the door. She made herself not react to the sight of him. Stocky, rugged, the same. His blue eyes held hers a moment. Then she gave him a condescending smile as she noticed he was puffing from exertion. "Getting old, Hendrik?"

He replied in Dutch. "You grate on a man's nerves, Willie."

He still called her Willie. He'd started it, almost sixty years ago. "I grate on everyone's nerves. Come in."

She turned her back to him and went into the living room, pretending not to care what he did. Johannes was dead and now her sister was missing. And Juliana was going for the Minstrel. Nothing useful would be accomplished by looking backward. She must look ahead.

Hendrik had followed her into the room and was looking at Juliana's fish. "She's a strange one, isn't she? Unpredictable, but tough." He turned to Wilhelmina, who was standing at the piano, not too close. "The Peperkamp in her, I suppose."

She put down the last of her bread and chocolate, unable to eat.

"You always did have a sweet tooth," Hendrik said.

"One of my indulgences."

"That and your flowers."

She shrugged, but his words made her think of home, her little apartment, her routines. Her plants would probably be dead when she returned home. She'd neglected to have anyone come in to water them while she was away.

Hendrik was looking at her. "We would have had a nice life together, if the war hadn't come along. We would have kept each other in line."

"I can't see you living with me in a little Delftshaven apartment growing begonias."

"Maybe we wouldn't have. Maybe we would have had a yacht and be out sailing the seven seas."

She scoffed. "Always the dreamer."

"And you, Willie? Haven't you ever dreamed?"

"Only of what was, never of what might have been. Now enough of this nonsense." She gave him a hard look. "What do you want here?"

"To take you away," he said simply.

Her heart leaped stupidly, an echo of the girl she'd been, but she'd learned long ago not to rely on anyone to take care of her. She would take care of herself. She always had.

"I'm going after Catharina," the Dutchman went on. "I promised Johannes nothing would happen to her—or to you and Juliana. I meant what I said."

"And Johannes didn't believe you, of course," Wilhelmina said with a snort. "We've all heard your promises before—and believed them. You'll see to your own skin before anyone else's."

"Perhaps I've changed."

She only laughed. Promises meant nothing to her, only actions. Still, a small, rebellious part of her hoped Hendrik wasn't lying this time, or even kidding himself. He'd always been so optimistic, so filled with high hopes and grand ideas. He thought he could do anything. Wilhelmina had always been attracted to that side of him. When he was young, it had made him seem so alive, so filled with energy and hope that they all had believed he could accomplish the miracles he bragged about. He hadn't been obnoxious so much as refreshing.

He hadn't changed. Wilhelmina had no intention of giving him the opportunity to prove himself; she preferred to be master of her own fate. Yet she supposed there was a glimmer of desire to see him this once seize the opportunity, not wait for it or back away from it, but act out of conviction, not necessity.

"Catharina doesn't have the Minstrel, does she?" he asked, going to the windows over the couch.

Wilhelmina made no answer.

Hendrik glanced at her, smiling. "It's all right. You don't need to tell me. If Johannes had given Catharina the Minstrel, she'd have tossed it into the Hudson River. You and I know how she hates it—but Bloch doesn't. But when he discovers she doesn't have the stone, he'll kill her and come for Juliana and you, too, Wilhelmina. He may even come before he knows for sure which of you has it. That's his way."

"Let him come. Juliana isn't here, and I have no fear."

"You may get your wish," Hendrik said grimly. He'd been peering out the window down at the street, and now he nodded to Wilhelmina. She came over and stood next to him. Two men were moving quickly toward the entrance. "That's Bloch and one of his men."

"There are doormen—"

Hendrik laughed, and she regretted her lapse into naiveté. He went on, "If Bloch finds me here, he'll kill me. Then I'll hardly be in a position to help."

Wilhelmina shrugged. "It seems to me he'll kill you anyway at some point."

"Maybe so." He grinned at her. "You'd like that, wouldn't you, Willie? But revenge never feels so good as we think it ought. Hating me keeps you alive."

He started toward the door. Wilhelmina touched his arm, but not to stop him. He seemed to know this. His eyes were as blue as she'd remembered and had seen in the dreams she'd never been able to control and will away. Who was she to change what had been? He was a devil, yes, but she'd not always thought him so. That, too, was a part of what had been.

She asked quietly, "Did you ever touch her?"

"No," he said. "Never."

Then he ran. As before.

The old Dutchwoman spoke no English, which pissed

Bloch off, but he figured the younger sister could translate—and he had no trouble getting through what he wanted her to do. A .357 Magnum reduced the need for a common language. He waved it around and told her to get her fat ass out the door, and, sure enough, she did.

He let himself relax, cutting down slightly on his guard—and that was when she whipped around with a goddamn knife that could have sliced an elephant in two with one swipe. She had it at his throat before he could shoot the silly bitch. Like a damn fool, he'd hesitated that fraction of a second because he didn't want to cause any more ruckus than he already had in busting past the doormen. Now if he fired, the old woman's last act would be to shove her fucking knife in his throat. And even if it weren't and he could manage to blow her fat butt across the hall, there'd still be the noise and the mess.

There was also the chance she had the diamond. He wanted Wilhelmina Peperkamp alive.

"Achh," she grunted, cursing him in Dutch. She threw down the knife and proceeded to the elevator.

Jesus Christ, Bloch muttered to himself, glad none of his men had been around for this one.

He refused to meet her eye on the ride down in the elevator. He decided she'd made her point.

They collected his man in the lobby; he'd done a fair job of convincing the doormen they shouldn't call in the cavalry just yet. Their car slid up to the Central Park West entrance, and they jumped in, Bloch giving the stout old Dutchwoman a good shove. Henson, the guy posted across the street, had joined them. He didn't look too happy, and within a block, the sergeant found out why.

"Stark was here," Henson said.

Bloch swore. He should have taken care of Matthew Stark himself when he was in Washington. Hell, he should have taken care of him twenty years ago in 'Nam.

"Tell him anything?"

"No."

Bloch didn't believe it. Time he and Matt Stark finished things, anyway.

"Think the doormen'll call the police?" Henson asked.

"Worry, worry," Bloch said derisively. "What do you care if they do? We're free and clear."

But Henson sat back, not reassured, and Bloch wondered if the guy had scruples or was just scared. Either one didn't sit too well with him. Mostly his men were shit. Not all of them, but enough. But that would change soon, and it was another problem for another time.

He told the driver to speed it up, he wanted to be at Teterboro Airport in New Jersey as soon as possible. Then he told the two women, who were yapping in Dutch, to shut the fuck up. The younger one was a nice-looking woman with real manners, but pale and sweating from her busted arm—and Jesus Christ, did she hate his guts. The old one called him a Nazi. Bloch was just as glad she hadn't known about her sister's arm before she'd thrown down her knife.

"Well, ladies," he said, downright jovial, "I hope to hell one of you can lead me to the Minstrel's Rough. Otherwise I'm going to have to find where de Geer stashed pretty little Juliana Fall. Then we can have a nice family reunion."

He knew he'd have to find Juliana Fall at some point, regardless of what her aunt and mother did. She knew too much as it was, and she could identify him. A loose end. But he saw nothing to be gained from telling them that, and at the moment he thought the best strategy was to get back to camp and reassess exactly where he stood. If he were lucky, the girl, the Dutchman, and Steelman himself would come to him.

If not, he'd go to them.

Twenty

❦

The tiny, antique cape house stood on a hillside over-looking the winding Batten Kill River in southwestern Vermont. Three inches of light, dusty snow glistened in the moonlight on the gravel driveway. Juliana plowed Shuji's Mercedes right through it and went in through the back, into the country kitchen, turning on lights and ignoring the pounding in her head and the tugging at the back of her eyes that told her she needed sleep. She stumbled into the common room and started a fire in the huge center chimney fireplace, using more matches than usual because her hands were shaking with cold and fear. Finally, it caught.

The crackling of the flames and the soughing of the wind were the only sounds. She listened to her footsteps on the wide pine floor as she went into her small bedroom off the common room and found some warm corduroys and a sweater and heavy socks and put them on. She left her city clothes in a heap on the floor.

The fire didn't take long to get going, and Juliana soon added another log. Then she sat cross-legged on the round hand-braided rug in front of the hearth. Everything about the house was soothing. There was a basket on the floor filled with the needlework she only did when she was here;

for the past four years she'd been working on a sweater made with wool from a farm nearby. There was a stack of unread books on the Shaker candle table. Bundles of herbs she'd dried last summer. Reference books on bird watching, gardening, jam making. The women who came here and exulted in simple domestic chores, she thought, was as different from the Juliana Fall who had just completed another highly acclaimed European tour as she was from J.J. Pepper.

She rested back against the Duncan Phyfe sofa, trying to ease her tension, to think. Just a few minutes, she thought. If she just closed her eyes and emptied her mind for a little while, she would be better able to deal with the problems of her mother and the Minstrel's Rough. She could feel the fire warm her feet. The Chopin sounded in her head. She listened to it, hearing it in a way she'd never heard it before. Closing her eyes at last, she let the sounds envelop her, then seep in, becoming a part of her.

After a while she became aware she was no longer alone in the house. She hadn't heard anyone come in. Although preoccupied, she hadn't been asleep and was certain an unusual sound—a door, a car—would have alerted her.

Very close to her a sandpaper voice said, "I don't know why I don't just wring your neck and be done with it."

She opened her eyes, and when they fell on the solid figure of Matthew Stark, her heart skidded; she'd been missing him, she realized, wanting him here while she was hurting in so many different ways. "Matthew." Could he hear the longing in her voice? "How did you get here?"

He glared down at her, his dark face lost in the shadows of the room. "I came through the goddamn kitchen door that you left unlocked."

"If I hadn't," she said noting the socket wrench in his right hand, "you'd only have broken in. Then I'd have had to buy a new door. How did you find me?"

"Your Aunt Willie. She guessed you'd come here."

"She did, did she? I didn't think she had that much imagination. I've just been sitting here humming Chopin," she said. As if to prove it, she hummed some for him. "That's the one I'm supposed to be working on. Frederick Chopin's Piano Concerto Number One. My uncle's dead, Rachel Stein is dead, my mother's been kidnapped, my aunt's muttering about *onderduikers* and Nazis, I've been knocked around and have met a Dutchman who betrayed my family and the Steins to the Nazis—and I'm humming goddamn Chopin."

Matthew let his gaze fall on Juliana and saw the wild, scared, determined look in her dark eyes, and he felt his heart leap as he thought, this lady's getting to me. "So you ran into Bloch," he said.

"Yes. A charming individual. His man Peters flattened me, but that's okay because he didn't hurt my hands. When I was in junior high and high school, I'd go to fine arts camp, and the keyboard people would all be on the same volleyball team. We consistently had the worst record because we were all so terrified of hurting our hands. We'd hit the ball with our forearms, elbows, shoulders, heads—anything but our hands. This was probably about the same time you were trying to stay alive in Vietnam. Silly, isn't it?"

"Jesus Christ," Matthew said, and couldn't help himself. He was envisioning a bunch of piano players on a volleyball team, and it was so damn crazy, so ridiculous, that he started to laugh, Bloch or no Bloch.

"Damn you—"

Juliana reared back to smack him one, and he caught her hands and pulled her to her feet. Then she was in his arms and he stopped laughing and his mouth was on hers. They just couldn't stop. She had on a gray turtleneck sweater that had come untucked from her pants, and she reveled in the feel of his hands on its softness, her softness. She slid her arms around him and brought him even closer.

"I'm becoming very attached to you, you know," she whispered, her mouth close to his, and she wondered if she'd started this or if he had, but she didn't care.

"Feeling's mutual, although if anybody had told me a month ago I'd be in Vermont kissing a crazy, internationally famous pianist and chasing the world's largest uncut diamond…" He grimaced at the thought. "Jesus."

He let her go and watched her stumble back on the couch, and suddenly in the firelight he could see the swelling along the side of her neck, below her jaw. Bloch's handiwork. Matthew felt a hollowness inside him—and a seething anger. "Tell me what happened."

At first she said nothing.

"Juliana." He spoke her name softly. "Talk to me now or I'll leave you here and go find Bloch my own way."

"You'd do that, wouldn't you?"

"Yes."

"I wouldn't blame you," she said. "I'm not trying to be an ass—but it's difficult to talk… My mother…"

"Tell me, Juliana."

It wasn't a command, but more of a plea, not to tell but to share, not to throw the burden onto him but to transfer some of the weight of it to him. Juliana nodded, and in a surprisingly clinical manner recounted what had happened in Catharina's Bake Shop. She held together because she had to. If she was going to help her mother, there was no choice. She couldn't fall apart.

Matthew stood through the whole thing, pacing in front of the fire. When she'd finished, he said, "That's not everything."

Her ice-emerald eyes widened as she glanced up at him. "What do you mean?"

"The Minstrel's Rough," he said. "You have it, don't you? That's why you came here."

"Is that why you did?"

His eyes held hers. "No. I came because of you."

Looking into his face, reading what perhaps no one else could see, she believed him. "What about Aunt Willie? What have the two of you been up to?"

Matthew dropped the topic of the Minstrel for the moment and without preamble or sugarcoating told her. "We should give her a call," he said.

"Can't. I don't have a telephone here."

"Charming, but I doubt it'd make any difference. She feels a responsibility toward your mother, I gather, and if it comes to it, she'll go with Bloch."

"Are you going to tell me about him?"

"Are you going to tell me about the Minstrel?"

She jumped up, going into the doorway to the bedroom. They were at an impasse, she thought. Up against a brick wall. She wasn't sure she was ready to tell him about the Minstrel. Four hundred years of tradition were at stake. She tucked in her sweater, wincing at the sudden stab of pain down her neck and into her shoulders. She felt woozy and confused, fleetingly guilty. She didn't like stonewalling Matthew, didn't like his black gaze on her like that, searching, wanting. It'd help, she thought, if he took off that damn leather coat.

"There's a bed upstairs," she said. "The room's unfinished, but you'll survive. It's ridiculous to think either of us will be able to accomplish anything tonight." Her entire body felt as if it were ready to turn to liquid and seep into the cracks in the floor. "Good night, Matthew."

She went into the bedroom and, although she never did when she was alone, shut the door behind her.

The fire had died, and she hadn't turned up the thermostat. It was chilly in the house as she padded upstairs in her bare feet, guided only by the starlight and the reflection of the night sky off the snow outside her windows. The stairs were as old as the house, and they creaked. Her parents didn't like her coming here alone. If she didn't have a husband, they thought she ought at least to have a dog.

She came to the upstairs landing. The ceilings were low, lending to the cozy atmosphere. On stormy days, she liked to flop in the bed up here and curl up under the quilts and read while listening to the pitter-pat of the rain on the roof. Sometimes she just liked to lie and daydream about not always being so alone. And yet she didn't mind solitude. At least, not always.

There was no door to the small bedroom on the right. The old plaster walls had crumbled, and the floors were covered with layers of ugly linoleum, and there were no curtains on the one small window. Restoring the room was in her "one of these days" plans; it wasn't something she worried about. She'd picked up an iron bed at a flea market, several quilts, and a big old trunk, and that was the furnishings.

She could see only the foot of the bed from the door, a darker outline against the general darkness. Holding her breath, she took a step into the room.

An iron shaft clamped down around her middle and catapulted her across the room onto the bed. The old springs creaked madly, and she bounced hard, the wind knocked completely out of her. Adrenaline flooded into her bloodstream in such a rush it hurt, and she gulped for air as the weight came off her, slowly, as if not quite sure it was the proper thing to do.

The dark, male silhouette stood upright. "Hell of a time to be sneaking into a man's room," Matthew said.

She sat up halfway, leaning back on her elbows. "I thought you might be awake."

"I was."

"What the devil did you think I was?"

"Act first. Then find out."

As her eyes adjusted further to the darkness of the room,

she realized he was in nature's best. Quite nude. And magnificently so. "I didn't expect… I thought you'd be…"

"Didn't think to pack my jammies," he said sarcastically, making no attempt to cover himself.

She herself was clad chin-to-toe in an L.L. Bean flannel nightgown. "Well, you could have worn something."

"I wasn't expecting company."

"I guess I get what I deserve."

"I guess you do."

"Matthew, I—" She stopped herself. "I can't very well talk with you standing there like that. Aren't you cold?"

He grinned. "Freezing."

There were no heat vents upstairs, and it was even colder than downstairs. Even with her flannel nightie, she was chilly herself. But instead of putting on his clothes, Matthew pulled back the covers and climbed into bed. He stretched out, forcing her to sit up straight, but even so she could feel his calves through the quilts, touching her behind.

"Not what you imagined?" he asked at her stricken look.

"I thought we could go downstairs. I have some instant cocoa I could fix."

"Perish the thought. No brandy?"

She shook her head. "No alcohol whatsoever. I hate to drink alone."

"A nasty habit. But I'm afraid instant cocoa isn't worth the effort of putting on my pants and traipsing through this refrigerator of a house. Is your room nice and cozy?"

"Well, it's better than this."

"At least there's no damn hay up here." He leaned back against the pillows, a shaft of moonlight catching his dark chest. She noted the muscles, the scars. "What did you want?" he asked.

She curled her feet up under her in a tailor squat and covered them with the flannel nightgown and, facing him, leaned back against the footboard, its iron bars frigid.

Matthew laughed. "Don't you want to crawl under the blankets with me?"

"No, thank you."

"Freeze, then."

"I came to tell you about the Minstrel's Rough."

That cut off his laugh. He said seriously, "Go on."

She shivered; it was so damn cold. But she knew if she went under the covers with him, she might not come out again. "I'm so used to not talking about it—to pretending it's just another hunk of rock and not the Minstrel. Uncle Johannes brought it to me in Rotterdam seven years ago. I never took him seriously. In fact, I thought he was a little crazy. I discredited his story because it was easier that way."

"Where is it now?"

She shrugged. "I've been using it as a paperweight."

"Jesus."

"For jam recipes," she said.

"Why not? It's only the world's largest uncut diamond."

"If you'd seen Uncle Johannes that night, you might have done the same."

"I don't make jam."

Ignoring him, she recounted the night at the little stone church in Delftshaven, when her uncle had presented her with the crumpled bag and the stone wrapped in faded velvet.

When she'd finished, Matthew asked, "How did the Minstrel come into your family?"

"According to the legend, the Peperkamps provided safe haven in Amsterdam to Jews driven first from Lisbon, then Antwerp. Those were the major diamond centers at the time. The Peperkamps helped them settle into Amsterdam, where they were able to establish themselves as diamond merchants. They were always voices for tolerance and religious freedom."

"Were they in the diamond trade themselves?"

"No, they were simple merchants. It was a turbulent

time in Holland. Throughout the century, they were fighting off the Spanish—particularly after Philip the Second came into power in 1556. He was extreme in his anti-Protestant views and enacted a number of vicious edicts, instigating revolt in the northern provinces. There were uprisings and atrocities on both sides until Philip was dead, the Spanish Armada defeated, and the Spanish finally routed from Holland by 1609, I believe it was. Anyway, the Peperkamps became known for their advocacy of what we now might call human rights, but they paid dearly for their positions: several family members were tortured and executed by the Spanish *and* extremist Protestants, neither of whom appreciated their views.

"Rumors about the Minstrel's Rough had existed for some time, and it came into their hands in 1581, three years before the assassination of William of Orange by a Free Catholic for a reward offered by Philip of Spain. It was presented to them anonymously, for their sacrifice, and ultimately led them into the diamond business themselves. They were curious about the stone and had no idea of its value. They decided among themselves that it would never be cut, in remembrance of those who'd been lost and those who'd been left with no choice but to accept their help. It would not belong to them. It would belong to no one. They would be the caretakers. No one would know for certain the stone existed, its grade, its potential value. In each generation, there's been one primary caretaker, one person trusted with the tradition. Only he—until me, it's always been a he—has control over the stone, whether it's finally to be cut, what becomes of it. Everything—the legend, the tradition, the mystery—rests with that one person."

"Hell of a responsibility," Matthew said.

Juliana was shivering uncontrollably. She nodded, saying nothing more.

He gave her a small grin. "Some advantages to having

a family that goes back to about the Depression. Juliana, you're going to freeze. Come under the blankets a minute and warm up—or here, take one." He peeled off the top quilt and flung it down to her. "You should get back to sleep. You'll need it."

"I know, but I can't. Mother—"

She broke off, shutting her eyes and putting her thumb at the top of her cheekbone and her forefinger at the inner corner of her eyebrow and pressing down hard, as if that would help hold back the anguish. Matthew slid forward, the quilts dropping to his waist, but he seemed unaware of the cold as he took her in his arms. She felt herself go limp as she laid her head on his shoulder, absorbing his warmth.

"Oh, hell," he breathed, and kissed her hair. Unable to fall asleep, she'd taken a shower after he'd gone to bed, trying to wash out the pain and the frustration and the worry and watch it go down the drain. She'd wanted him to come to her. But he hadn't.

"I know Bloch," he said. "He'll figure out you have the Minstrel and use your mother and your aunt, if he can manage to grab her, as bait for you. He won't kill them, Juliana."

"Until he gets the Minstrel or realizes he can get it," she finished, knowing Matthew wouldn't. "Then he'll kill all of us."

"We don't know that."

But she could see he did.

"For now, they're safe."

She turned her face to him, her hair falling against the warm skin of his shoulder and her eyes as luminous and unreadable as the stars. "Who is he?"

In the dim light she could see the blackness of his eyes, but she didn't turn away. She pulled the quilt up over her, staying in his arms instead. For the first time that night, she finally felt warm.

"Phillip Bloch is a retired army sergeant—"

"And he was a platoon sergeant in Vietnam, and a platoon's made up of three ten-man squads. I mean, who is he to you?"

"Sam Ryder was his platoon leader. We were in the central highlands at the same time—those two, Weasel, a pilot named Jake MacIntyre, a crew chief named Chuck Fisher, and me."

"When you were flying a Huey?"

"Yeah."

"As a slick?"

"That's right. Ryder's was one of the platoons we transported. Bloch was in for his third tour. Ryder was as green as they come, but indecisive as well as incompetent. The army has a nice way of weeding out the dumbasses. If you're no good, you get killed in combat. Sometimes you had to hope they got killed before they killed you just by being dumb. Sometimes you had an experienced platoon sergeant who could keep things from getting out of hand, keep guys alive where the lieutenant, the platoon leader, couldn't."

"What did Bloch do?"

"He had the experience and the knowledge to get around Ryder, and sometimes he used them, when it suited his purposes. Mostly it didn't. I knew platoon sergeants who died saving their men, who rubbed green lieutenants' noses in it to make them learn fast or find a way out. Bloch looked after himself, period. He wanted Ryder to survive, and he wanted him to come out of Vietnam a hero, so he covered for Ryder and cushioned him and his commanders from the results of his incompetence. Because of that, guys who should have made it out didn't."

"And now Bloch is using what he knows about Ryder's true role in Vietnam against him—as collateral for blackmail," Juliana said, understanding. "Matthew, what about Jake MacIntyre and Chuck Fisher?"

He looked away from her, but their bodies still touched. "Their names are on the wall."

The Vietnam Memorial. "Was Bloch responsible for their deaths?"

"They were in my ship. I was responsible."

"You're hard on yourself, Matthew."

"Not hard," he said. "Honest. At least I try to be."

"I like that."

"Do you?"

He seemed to want an answer, and she nodded, not taking her eyes from his, wanting to know everything about him—and him to know everything about her, the bad as well as the good.

"Yes," she said finally, with certainty. "Integrity, compassion, intelligence, courage, sensitivity—they're not easy to find in ourselves, much less anyone else. But they mean more to me than money, power, success, any of that stuff. On paper, I guess people don't come any more different than the two of us, but I don't think we're all that different, not where it counts." She smiled, a little taken aback with herself. "Anyway, I should get back downstairs."

With his fingertips, he brushed a few stray hairs from her forehead. "Do you want to?"

She shook her head. "No."

"You're tired."

"I know, and I hurt. No one's ever hit me, Matthew, until today. I've never felt so—small. I—I wanted to be big and strong enough to scare those men off. I've never even *thought* about my limitations in that way. Do you know what I went after them with when they had my mother? A wooden shoe. A goddamn wooden shoe."

"Darling, you're tough in all the ways that count."

She laughed bitterly. "So put that on my mother's tombstone."

"Darling—"

"I want to forget for now, Matthew—I just want you to hold me…" She caught his fingers in hers. "I'm so glad you're here, Matthew. I don't think I could have stood being alone, not tonight."

She lifted her face to his, and his mouth was there, warm and soft and everything she needed. His arms went around her, his lips opening, and she closed her eyes as his tongue slid between her teeth. It was a different kind of burning she felt now, not the burning of tired eyes and sore muscles and unanswered questions. She wrapped her arms around him, pressing herself into him, and they fell down onto the pillows together, a tangle of quilts, sheet, and nightgown.

"I don't want to hurt you," Matthew whispered.

"Don't worry, please."

"I've never met anyone like you. Never."

She smiled, wishing she could laugh. "Don't think I stumble on Matthew Starks every day."

He kissed her again, a deeper, harder kiss, and when it was over, he'd pulled the nightgown over her head and tossed it onto the floor. They climbed under the quilts, pulling them all on top of them, their cool, naked bodies intertwined. They didn't speak. Juliana didn't want to break the spell with reminders of death and betrayal and diamonds and all they would have to face. The now, the present, the moment, was filled with need and passion. She ignored the pain of her bruises and her terror and focused on the stirrings that had been thee inside her ever since Matthew Stark had darkened her dressing room door at Lincoln Center.

He smoothed his hands over her breasts and stomach and followed with his mouth, arousing her with nipping, wet kisses. Soon they both got so hot they had to throw off a couple of the quilts. She touched his hard muscles, rubbed her fingers through the dark hairs on his chest, let them examine the scars he had yet to explain. But what she still had to learn about him no longer mattered. She felt a part of him, felt him a part of her.

"Are you sure?" he asked again, sliding her on top of him, so it wouldn't hurt so much. He kissed her bruised wrist, gently.

"Yes. More than anything, you're what I need right now. Don't stop."

Even in the dark, his smile was gentle. "No problem, darling."

Whatever else she felt took second place to the mounting, insatiable longing that welled up inside her as she lay on top of him, his hands moving over her hips and bottom and legs. He lifted her up slightly, and when she came down, he was in her. She cried out when he came into her, but so did he, and they made love explosively, tenderly, and she hoped, *knew,* this wouldn't be the last time.

"Matthew!"

She groaned, feeling the spasms, and his arms tightened around her as he shook and moaned with her, until there was silence and stillness, the snow falling lightly outside and no place warmer than beneath their tattered quilts.

Twenty-One

During the past few days, Wilhelmina had discovered she hated to fly. In her mind, it was unnatural. God meant for birds to fly, not people—and, besides, the motion, the *unnatural* motion, upset her stomach. The plane she'd taken across the Atlantic Ocean had been her first, and she'd considered the entire experience oppressive. It had been one of those monstrous things with an upstairs and innumerable comforts to make the passengers forget they were in the air when they weren't supposed to be. Think of yourself as an eagle, the man sitting next to her had advised, seeing her look of distaste and mistaking it for fear. She'd felt more like one of the fat pigeons in the park who never looked as if they'd get very far when they tried to fly.

As unpleasant as that trip had been, it was more like a stroll to her neighborhood grocery compared to the flight to which she and Catharina were now being subjected. They bumped along in the air like a bad driver on a rocky road, and there were many strange noises and creakings that Wilhelmina refused to tell herself were normal. Catharina had told her the plane was small and that was why the flight was so much rougher. Wilhelmina had responded, yes, that was exactly her point.

Bloch had separated them in the passenger compartment, putting a man with a gun on each of them and telling the one on her to "watch the fat ass, she's a sneaky bitch."

Wilhelmina held her tongue, but only because she thought her pretended ignorance of English might still be useful. Had it not been for the danger Catharina was in, Wilhelmina would have slit the coward's throat when she'd had the opportunity and damned the consequences. If he shot her with his filthy gun, so be it. She was too old to take him as a hostage, not that that would have produced an acceptable outcome. Given the looks of this man, Wilhelmina had suspected his men wouldn't be terribly loyal and would likely enough have simply let her have him and cut their losses, which could have proved disastrous for Catharina.

She glanced at Catharina, who smiled wanly. She was holding up well—better than Wilhelmina would have expected. Juliana was not with them. That was something to bolster the spirit. Wilhelmina remembered during the war, when she'd sat in the dank, horrible Gestapo prison listening to them torture her father, how she would think of her little sister and be thankful that at least she was still free.

The plane landed with a series of bumps and rattles, and she and Catharina were herded out into a ridiculously small airfield that smelled like gasoline and rotting vegetables. The air was moist and warmer than in New York, although by no means summerlike.

With her good hand, Catharina pulled on the arm of the sergeant. "Why don't we go directly to Switzerland and get this over with?"

Wilhelmina admired how clear and strong her sister's voice sounded, in spite of the pain she suffered. She'd gathered Catharina was trying to get him to believe she had the Minstrel in a safe-deposit box in a Swiss bank. It was a gamble, but better than putting him on to Juliana.

"Just do as I say," Bloch replied.

Nazi, Wilhelmina thought. He was too accustomed to giving orders and having them obeyed. Expecting people to be afraid of him.

He ordered them to get into a helicopter. He called it a bird.

Wilhelmina looked around with a sense of foreboding she hoped she masked, but in the eerie light of the airfield she saw the silhouette of a helicopter. To her it looked nothing like a bird, but more a dead spider on its back. When the propellers began to twirl, it looked like a dying spider on its back, which in Wilhelmina's opinion wasn't any better at all.

Whispering in Dutch, Catharina explained she thought they were in Florida or southern Georgia, near a swamp, that's what the smell was, and did Willie think they should continue to cooperate? *Dag,* she whispered. Yes. For now.

The man Bloch told them to shut up and get in the chopper, the fat ass first.

Wilhelmina got the idea.

Matthew awoke at dawn, the light streaming through the window as pale as the soft hair spilled across his chest. He had willed himself to awaken before Juliana. She was lying on her side in a dead sleep, her smooth back to him, snuggled up close, the quilts pulled up to her chin. He could feel his own warmth on her skin. A part of him told him to kiss her and love her and maybe later call the police and let them handle everything while they just stayed in bed together.

But then he saw the bruise along her jaw, and he stopped the wishful thinking. He knew Phil Bloch. The sergeant would get the Minstrel on his own terms, not anyone else's.

Taking care not to let the cold in under the covers, Matthew extricated himself from the bed. The room was freezing. He could see his breath in front of his mouth, and the last thing he wanted was to wander around buck naked. He gathered up his clothes and his boots and tiptoed out of the room, cursing silently as the goosebumps sprang up all over him. For no reason at all he thought of the Weasel and how he'd laugh his ass off right now, seeing Matt Stark tiptoeing out of a warm bed, with a woman in it no less, turning purple, all so he could go finish up what Otis Raymond had started him on. *A piano player,* the Weaze'd say, grinning that ugly, yellowed grin. *Jeez'm, Matt.*

Jeez'm indeed. He got down the stairs and jumped into his clothes and rubbed his hands together, trying to get warm. He checked the thermostat: fifty-five degrees. Good Christ. And it was colder than that upstairs. With a growl, he turned the heat up to all of sixty-two. He wouldn't be around to enjoy it, but what the hell.

Juliana would. She could afford the damn oil bill.

He snuck around in the kitchen and got the keys to the Mercedes. The keys to her Audi were already in his pocket. Then he went outside. It was cold out but breathtakingly beautiful. Three inches of snow—a mere dusting around here—had fallen during the night, and the view was as picturesque as any he'd ever seen. He could understand Juliana's attraction to this place. But he didn't linger. The Batten Kill River, with snow-covered branches hanging low on its banks and its clear, cold waters running past patches of ice, wasn't going anywhere. He'd be back to see it. He glanced up to the side window and in his mind saw Juliana snuggled up under the blankets, and he thought, Damn right I'll be back.

Unless after this she didn't want him. But that was a chance he'd have to take.

He opened up the hood of the Audi and pulled out the spark plug wires, just in case she had a spare set of keys in the house or in her purse. Then he got in the Mercedes. It started right up and handled the snow in the driveway with hardly any trouble at all.

But, apparently, the noise was just enough to awaken his sleeping beauty.

Juliana leaped out the front door with nothing but a ratty quilt over her and yelled, "You sonofabitch," as she pounded through the snow after him. Good thing there weren't any neighbors, Stark thought somewhat grimly, or they'd talk. World-famous pianist trots naked through snow after has-been reporter. Well, not quite naked. But that'd kill her reputation a hell of a lot quicker than J.J. Pepper could.

As the Mercedes hit the plowed and sanded main road, he left her standing there, cursing him. He took some consolation in knowing he'd turned up the heat. At least he wouldn't have to worry about that lovely behind of hers getting frostbite.

He doubted she'd see it that way.

Bloch pulled the phone toward him in the handsome study of Senator Samuel Ryder's fishing lodge on the western edge of the Dead Lakes. As a military compound, it worked out okay, but not great. He and a couple of his most trusted men occupied the lodge, while the others were tucked into the fishing shacks around the perimeter. Ryder had been properly horrified when Bloch had called him up and said, Hey, Sammy-boy, guess where I'm hanging out? But it was only a temporary arrangement. Bloch had himself a *real* camp in the works.

He nibbled on a handful of sunflower seeds and carob chips. If he ate any more than that, he'd feel too full, and then he'd want to sleep. Couldn't afford to sleep right now. He'd blown it. An A-plus shit-ass job he'd done. The two women were stashed in one of the unoccupied shacks. The old one still wasn't saying anything, and the young one was still saying the Minstrel was in Switzerland. Christ! How stupid could he be? Ryder must be rubbing off, he thought, dialing the senator's Washington number with a steady hand.

The aunt hadn't slit his throat, which he had deserved to have slit for letting a goddamn seventy-year-old woman get in that kind of position over him. She'd only let him off because she wanted to be with her sister.

The mother was protecting the daughter. Jesus, did it piss him off for forgetting how sentimental and dumb people could be about their relations. He had a brother; hadn't seen him since before Vietnam. He hadn't wanted to sign up. "I don't believe in this war," he'd said. Bloch felt a war was a war, and one was pretty much the same as another. When you were a soldier, you were paid to kill, not to think.

Yeah, he thought with a spasmodic laugh, you leave the thinking up to idiots like Sam Ryder.

The senator answered on the twelfth ring. Bloch kept count. "Knew it was me, didn't you?" he said.

He could hear Ryder's fear just in the way he breathed. "What do you want?"

"Juliana Fall."

"What?"

"She has the diamond."

"That's ridiculous, Sergeant, she's a concert pianist! She knows nothing about diamonds, I'm sure. Why would she have it? Look, why don't you just give it up? I'll see what I can do about getting you some stop-gap funds to help you vacate the camp and start over elsewhere—"

Bloch ignored him. "The Dutchman helped her get out yesterday. Sammy, Sammy, you're not helping me. Why don't you go and find out where she went."

"Sergeant, I can't help you! Don't you understand?"

"Yeah, I do." Bloch ate some more sunflower seeds. "I understand I'm sitting down here in your goddamn fishing camp with a couple tons of illegal weapons and ten men who probably ought to be in jail, and how sweet that'd look splashed across the front page of every goddamn newspaper in this country."

Ryder coughed, spitting with anger, but that, Bloch knew, was the most he could ever do with his anger—just spit and sputter with it. Made a good politician, Sammy-boy did. "Where am I supposed to find Juliana Fall?"

"Don't whine, Lieutenant. You'll think of something."

"Sergeant—"

"And keep an eye out for Stark, let me know if he comes your way. I don't like it that he's messing around out there and I don't know where he is. I've got a man at his house, but he hasn't showed. You keep in touch, Lieutenant. And Sammy? I can use you in Washington."

Ryder sputtered, and Bloch laughed, hanging up.

Then he got his number-two man into the office and told him to start packing up. "When I give the word," he said, "I want to be able to abandon camp within thirty minutes."

"Will do," his man said.

Bloch grinned. Now that was what he liked to hear.

Juliana had put on clothes—heavy corduroys, turtle-neck wool sweater, socks, boots, deerskin gloves with her spare keys, and parka—before trying her car. It didn't start. She didn't know a damn thing about engines, but she opened up the hood anyway and had a look.

She knew enough to spot pulled wires.

"That bastard."

He'd made damn sure she couldn't follow him—not that she had the slightest idea where he was. Going after Phillip Bloch, undoubtedly, but where was he? If she had a telephone, she'd call the police and have Matthew Stark arrested for stealing Shuji's car. But she didn't have a telephone. She couldn't even call a damn garage to come fix her car.

"Aunt Willie would say I'm soft," she told herself aloud.

Aunt Willie, she thought, would be right.

Slamming the hood shut, she went inside for a scarf.

Cashmere. It was softer on her neck and mouth. Then she went into the kitchen and looked on the pine shelf where she kept her jam recipes.

The Minstrel's Rough sat there collecting dust.

Why hadn't Matthew swiped it along with Shuji's car?

"Because," she said, "he knows Bloch is going to get rid of everybody whether he gets the Minstrel or not."

Get rid of everybody. What a quaint little euphemism. Phillip Bloch would kill everybody whether or not he got the diamond. Matthew knew this, and so hadn't bothered with it.

But maybe she could use it as a bargaining chip, if not to make a deal, at least to buy some time—for her mother, her aunt, even for Matthew.

She snatched up the huge rough, shoved it into her inner coat pocket, and headed back outside. Her head was pounding, and she was stiff and sore and hungry, but she trudged outside. The sun was blinding on the snow, and the wind had picked up; it was bitterly cold. Walking was difficult and, because she couldn't see the patches of ice under the freshly fallen snow, treacherous. If she fell and broke a wrist or her hands got badly frostbitten, her career would be over.

Some things, she told herself, you just had to chance.

The nearest house was a mile down the road and belonged to a dairy farmer who brought her surplus tomatoes and summer squash during the summer and sometimes fresh, raw milk that tasted wonderfully unlike anything she'd ever bought in New York. His son was outside shoveling the walk. She explained her problem, and he put down his shovel and drove her back over to her place in his truck. He said it'd take some time to fix her Audi, he wasn't used to working on foreign cars, would she like to ride someplace?

"Yes, the airport, if possible. There's—there's been a family emergency."

"Albany?"

She nodded. Albany was about forty miles away, but it
had regular flights to New York—and probably Washington, too. She was thinking Washington might be her best
bet. Senator Samuel Ryder, Jr., was a part of this mess. He
was to have met Hendrik de Geer at Lincoln Center, she
remembered from what Matthew had told her, and he had
been in Vietnam with Bloch and Otis Raymond and Matthew Stark. Perhaps, with proper motivation, he could tell
her where to find Phillip Bloch. She was ready to kick ass
and take names; she'd give him proper motivation all right.

"Albany's fine," she said.

"Okay, get in."

Matthew spotted the skinny man who'd held the gun on
Juliana sitting across from his town house in a rented Pontiac and had his cab drive around the block and back again,
letting him off below his house. He'd left the Mercedes at
the Albany airport and taken a flight to Washington, all very
quick and clean. Discipline had helped him put Juliana Fall
out of his mind. Helped him, he thought, but without a
whole lot of success.

The guy flipped to the sports section. Even at a distance,
Matthew recognized the four-inch bold type of the *Gazette*.
He might just be watching his place—or waiting for Matthew to return so he could take him out, although in that
case he'd have expected to find him inside rather than out
and sure as hell not reading the damn paper. Knowing
Bloch as he did, Stark knew killing him wasn't something
the sergeant would want to delegate. He'd prefer to save
the pleasure for himself.

But best not to take chances.

Taking the direct approach, Stark tore open the driver's
side door, grabbed the guy by his shoulder and wrist, and
ripped him out of the car, shoving him down on the hood

and twisting his arm behind his back. He'd left a Colt .45 on the console next to his Styrofoam mug of coffee. He was curly-haired, rail-thin, and probably twenty years younger. Stark felt like an old man.

"You're Bloch's man?" Stark asked quietly.

"No."

"Your orders?"

A woman with a baby in backpack halted fifteen yards down the brick sidewalk, turned white, and quickly crossed to the other side of the street.

Stark jerked the guy up and slammed the car door shut with him. "Talk."

"Bloch'll kill me—"

"Bloch isn't here. I am."

"Jesus Christ, I knew I didn't want this job. Look, man, I'm just supposed to keep an eye on the house, 'case you or the girl shows. If I'd known that was her yesterday—" He seemed to realize it wasn't a good idea to finish his thought and shut up.

The girl. Juliana. Not a girl, he thought, remembering last night. "Then what?"

"She shows, I grab her—not hurt her, okay? Man, I got special orders *not* to hurt her, so you don't have to worry about that. You I'm supposed to report back where you go, what you do, stuff like that, take you out if I can but not get killed trying to do it. I been warned about you. I mean, Weaze—"

"Weaze's got a big mouth."

"Yeah, right."

Stark could see the kid idolized Otis Raymond. Weaze must love that, he thought, and loosened up his grip. "What's your name?"

"Kovak. Roger Kovak."

"You're a stupid shit, Roger Kovak. Weasel and Bloch go back to a day before you were even born. Weaze has got an excuse for being dumb. You don't. You want excitement, go climb Mount Everest. All Bloch's going to do for you is get you killed or jailed."

Roger Kovak looked terrified. He was the kind of kid, Stark thought, who would have gone to Vietnam thinking he was going to come home John Wayne and found out way too late all he was going to do was come home dead. Matthew opened up the car door. He got out the Colt, then shoved Roger Kovak back in the front seat and left him there with his newspaper and his cup of cold coffee. He could call Bloch if he wanted. Stark didn't care.

Bloch already knew he was coming.

The Pontiac roared to a start and screeched down the street. Stark didn't even glance back as he went inside. His house was toasty warm. He remembered his cold walk down Juliana Fall's steep stairs, how warm it was under the stack of quilts with her, warmer, he thought, than he'd ever been. *She shows, I grab her.* He wondered if leaving her in the middle of goddamn nowhere with a disabled car and no telephone had convinced her to stay the hell out. Something cold and empty inside him told him it hadn't.

He tucked the Colt in his waistband and headed upstairs, where he got out the SIG-Sauer P-226 9mm automatic he kept around because he knew people like Phillip Bloch. He strapped on the hip holster and then put on his leather jacket and went back downstairs. He didn't feel good, and he didn't feel confident. He just felt armed.

The light was blinking on his message machine. He pressed the button and played back the messages. There were two. One was from a buddy who wanted him to go to the Caps game that night. The other was from Alice Feldon.

"Otis Raymond is dead," she said. "Call me."

Twenty-Two

S am Ryder settled back in the leather chair at his desk, with his back to the half-smiling, half-knowing face of his father. He had come to his office because it seemed the right place to be—cushioned from men like Phillip Bloch, Hendrik de Geer, Matthew Stark. Here process was important. The rule of law. There wasn't just power here, but tradition, and when his footsteps echoed in the wide corridors, he felt himself a part of that tradition, not just of his father, but of the men before him. The United States Senate. This, he thought, is where I belong.

But Phil Bloch and Matthew Stark were trying to pull him back to the central highlands of Vietnam, to a time and place where he didn't belong. Had never belonged. He had done his duty, and more. It was over. Finished. If Bloch and Stark couldn't accept that, then so be it.

Bloch would eliminate Hendrik de Geer. Then he and Stark would eliminate each other. It was the only way, and it had to work. Otherwise they would all be there forever, hovering in the shadows with their accusing eyes, their knowledge, and their threats.

One of his aides, also working on this chilly December Saturday, announced that Juliana Fall was there to see him.

Ryder shot forward in his chair. *Juliana!* But how? Why? She had the diamond, Bloch had said. *Find out where she went.*

She's come here, Bloch, you stinking slob, he thought. She's come here to me. *I* didn't have to go looking.

He told his aide to send her in at once.

Juliana rushed in, pushing back her hair as she said breathlessly, "Senator Ryder, thank you for seeing me."

He nodded, unable to speak. If possible, she was even more beautiful now. He was stricken by her look of vulnerability; her pale face made her eyes seem even darker, more hauntingly beautiful.

"I hope you'll be willing to help me," she went on, obviously agitated. "I—I need to find Phillip Bloch."

"Juliana…" Her name came out as a whisper, a breath, and he was on his feet, unsteadily moving toward her. *No, not her! She can't be involved in this!* He took her arm. "Here, sit down."

She pulled away, more assertively than he would have anticipated from someone of her background. Her dark, beautiful eyes riveted on his. "Please don't tell me you don't know what I'm talking about because I know you do."

"Don't be silly. But, of course, if I can help you—"

"Tell me where Bloch is!"

"I haven't the slightest idea," he said, cool and patrician, wanting desperately to touch her and kiss away her fears, but disturbed by the aggressiveness she was exhibiting. Had he misjudged her? There was no reason for her to be involved—why was she? "Sergeant Bloch was my platoon sergeant in Vietnam, but that was twenty years ago."

"You were at Lincoln Center with Rachel Stein. She'd learned of your involvement with de Geer and was trying to get you to bring him to justice for his betrayal of her and her family and my family to the Nazis during World War Two." Juliana paused, no longer gulping for air but regarding him with a cold, determined eye. "That alone, Senator Ryder, ought to interest the *Post* of the *Gazette* or any number of news organizations. Once they start to dig—"

"Don't threaten me," he said icily, despising the willfulness he now saw in her delicate face. Beautiful, yes, and vulnerable, too, but also tough. Inappropriately tough, in his judgment.

She choked back her frustration. "Do you want me to plead? Help me, for God's sake!"

"You're not the woman I thought."

His words were simple and pained, but Juliana seemed unmoved by the sadness and disillusionment he felt. She'd destroyed his image of her, the woman he'd thought he could love. They'd spent only minutes together, but he'd sensed she possessed the level of sensitivity and femininity he'd found lacking in most women. She'd failed him.

"We hardly know each other, Senator, but that's not the issue. Please help me."

"What do you plan to do once you locate Bloch?" he asked, trying to sound disinterested. *Did she have the Minstrel?*

"I can't explain."

She did. Dear God, she did!

"Senator, where is he? I mean what I say. I'll take everything to the press if you don't help me. Don't you see? I don't know what else to do!"

Ryder shuddered with indecisiveness. From long, terrible experience he knew Bloch didn't make deals. If Juliana tried to exchange the Minstrel for her mother and her aunt, he would take it and get rid of all of them. *He'll kill them— say it.* But not necessarily. There was no reason she should be hurt, provided Stark and Bloch got to each other first.

"I don't want anything to happen to you," he said.

"Thank you, I don't either, but some things you just have to do."

Yes, he thought, that's right. If he sent Juliana down, Bloch would look upon Ryder favorably, and, should things *not* work out by some chance, that would be helpful. But why shouldn't things work out? Telling her Bloch's location wasn't putting her into any more danger than she was already in. No matter what he did or didn't do, Bloch *would* catch up with her. This way, he was giving her the advantage. That was how he had to look at it.

"He's taken over my fishing camp on the western edge of the Dead Lakes. It wasn't my idea. I had no knowledge of what he was doing—he presented me with a *fait accompli.*"

Juliana obviously didn't care about his problems. "Where are the Dead Lakes?"

He hesitated.

"Tell me, damn it!"

"Fly into Tallahassee," he said stiffly, pretending it was someone else doing the talking, as he did when he had to leak information to the press about confidential Senate matters, as he had twenty years ago when he'd told Bloch that he wanted Matthew Stark and his crew to fly into their LZ. "You can rent a car and drive out there. Stop at a gas station or a grocery. Anyone can tell you where the camp is."

Bloch's men had shoved Wilhelmina and Catharina into a one-room shack with a small three-quarter bath and kitchen facilities that consisted of a sink, a two-burner heating unit, and a small portable refrigerator, which was empty. The shower was mildewed. The walls were rough boards, uninsulated, and the damp, chilly wind off the lake blew in through the cracks. There was no heat. For furniture there was a studio bed, a couch that pulled out into a bed, a vinyl-covered La-Z-Boy, a small table covered with a red-checkered vinyl cloth and two folding wooden chairs. The back exit was securely locked. The front entrance was guarded by a man in a khaki shirt and trousers who'd told the women to get some sleep.

They'd taken turns dozing on the studio bed, only because they were older than they'd once been. Forty or fifty years ago, Wilhelmina thought, nothing could have made her sleep. At ten o'clock, the guard had brought them a repulsive meal of plain yogurt, granola, and grapefruit juice. Wilhelmina had reminded herself of the days of eating tulip bulbs and fodder beets; she was surprised to see that her sister didn't seem to mind the food. They'd done what they could to splint her arm, binding it with a handtowel, but it needed proper tending. Catharina never complained, although she had to be in agony.

Now they were both up, Catharina posted at the front window overlooking the strange, dark lake, Wilhelmina posted at the side window looking out at the cypress trees laden with what her sister told her was Spanish moss. Beyond was a handsome rustic lodge made of rough uncut pine. A screened porch ran its entire length, and a well-kept gravel walkway led to a boathouse and dock. The helicopter pad where they'd landed was a good distance behind the lodge, but exactly how far was difficult to say. Wilhelmina had still been so preoccupied with the terrible ride and her sister's pain that she didn't trust her sense of distance.

"Our sergeant lives well," Wilhelmina said, speaking still in Dutch. It was natural for her, and Catharina had made no objections.

"I don't think this camp belongs to him," Catharina replied, not looking from the window. Her color wasn't good; Wilhelmina was worried. Neither woman was as resilient as they'd been forty years ago. "My guess is it belongs to Senator Ryder."

"And Bloch has his fingers in his pocket—a nasty business."

"He's called my bluff," Catharina said despairingly.

"So it would seem," Wilhelmina said, solemn but not dispirited. "I'm sorry, Catharina. But I don't think we should underestimate Juliana. She has a good mind and courage. She'll do what's necessary."

"What's necessary to her will be saving us, Willie."

"Then so be it."

Catharina made no answer, sinking into the silence that had overtaken her since arriving at the camp. Wilhelmina was worried about her sister and wished she could do something to take away her pain, to ease her sense of despair.

"I know how desperately you want Juliana just to hide herself away," Wilhelmina said quietly. "I understand. But Catharina, she must make the decision herself."

"I don't want her to suffer!"

"Of course you don't. You want to protect her, just as all of us wanted to protect you during the war. But tell me, Catharina, haven't you always wished we hadn't? You've tortured yourself for years because we all did everything within our power so that you wouldn't be taken by the Nazis, too."

"You and Johannes sent me to Hendrik with the Minstrel because you knew he would never hurt me," Catharina said suddenly, half to herself. "If he were to betray us, as he did, you knew he would keep me safe."

"No, you were the logical choice—"

"Don't lie to me, Willie. Please."

Wilhelmina sighed. "None of us wanted anything to happen to you. If you survived, a part of us would survive."

"Mamma and Papa didn't survive. They died for me."

"No, Catharina. They would have died for you, make no mistake about that, but they didn't. They died because they were knowledgeable, active members of the Dutch Underground Resistance. They knew names and places. They were filled to the tops of their heads with information the Germans wanted. The Nazis weren't interested in you. You were safe in hiding, but they didn't torture Mamma and Papa to find out where you were. That's youthful self-centeredness, Catharina. They died because of their convictions."

Tears had spilled from Catharina's soft eyes, and she pushed them away angrily. "I've always wanted to be as strong and unshakable as you, Willie—and look at me! Did you... Were you there when Mamma and Papa died?"

It was a question she'd never asked, and one Wilhelmina, although she'd known her sister must have thought it, had never tried to answer. She nodded, feeling so tired, so alone. "I was brought out to watch while they were executed—shot. Papa was nearly dead from the torture."

"Mamma?"

"She was tortured as well, but not as much. They made me watch to weaken my resolve."

"They didn't know you very well, did they?"

"No," Wilhelmina said. Her resolve had been strengthened. After that moment, she'd never feared pain or death.

Catharina was sobbing openly now, her entire body shaking uncontrollably. "All my life I've thought I should have been there."

Wilhelmina shook her head. "I'm so glad you weren't—and that was the best gift you could ever have given Mamma and Papa, not to have been there. Think if it had been you and Adrian, Catharina. Isn't that what you'd have wanted for Juliana?"

"Yes." There was no doubt in her tone. "Yes, it's what I'd have wanted."

"Then let us put the past aside for now, shall we? We must concentrate on the problem at hand."

Catharina smiled through her tears. "You're a tough old bird, Willie," she said in English. "I'm glad we're together."

Wilhelmina nodded, deeply moved. "I, too, Catharina."

"His body turned up on a beach in Florida," Alice Feldon said, giving Matthew the straight facts on what had come over the wire on Otis Raymond. "Apparent suicide. He was shot in the head. Usual burned-out Vietnam vet crap. Only reason it hit the wires is because he was found by a socialite on a fancy private beach on the Gulf of Mexico near Apalachicola. She promptly fainted. Anyway, that's it."

Stark nodded slowly, his thoughts drifting back twenty years.

"Beg pardon, sir," Otis Raymond had said, sidling up to him with that deceptive ambling gait the first day they'd met, "but I want to tell you, you and me, we're getting out of this shit alive. I ain't planning to get aced in no goddamn jungle."

He'd given Lieutenant Matthew Stark a crooked, yellowed grin that strangely lit up his face, made him look almost innocent. He was skinny and ugly, and he still had pimples.

"Hate snakes, you know?"

But it was bullshit, and they both knew it. Otis Raymond hadn't expected to live.

"I'm making sure the *Gazette* carries the story," Alice Feldon said.

"Thanks." There was no emotion in Stark's voice. "Weaze would appreciate that."

"I'm sorry."

"Yeah."

"Ziegler's seeing what more he can find out."

"He doesn't have to. I know what happened."

"Matt—"

He looked at her, his eyes unfocused. "Weasel had an instinct for survival that he couldn't suppress, but it didn't make him cowardly. In fact, he'd do the craziest damn things and still live. But when Jake and Chuck got aced, Weaze figured it should have been him."

He stopped, and for once, Feldon didn't press him for

more. She just stood there and waited for him to go on—
or not.

"Jake MacIntyre and Chuck Fisher," Stark said. Saying
their names still hurt. "Jake was a pilot and Chuck was our
crew chief. They died when a chopper I was flying went
down. Chuck took three bullets and died on the ground, before the search and rescue team could get us out. Jake lived
a while longer. Weasel held onto him all the way back, and
he screamed the whole time, there wasn't anything anybody could have done, but Weaze felt he should have been
able to do something, that it was his fault, that because he
didn't mind dying he should have."

"Maybe it wasn't anybody's fault," Feldie said.

"No, it was somebody's fault all right. It was Sergeant Phillip Bloch's fault and Lieutenant Sam Ryder, Jr.'s—and mine."

"Stark—"

But he didn't listen, walking over to his desk. He pushed
back the memories and picked up the telephone and dialed
his attorney. "Dave, Stark here. I want you to do something
for me."

"You don't sound too good, Matt. Everything all right?"

"Just listen. A man named Otis Raymond was found
dead this morning on a beach on the Gulf of Mexico in
Florida. They say he committed suicide." Bullshit, Stark
thought. Bloch had killed him, and Bloch had put him there
because he knew it'd hit the wires and Stark would find out
and come after him. Finally. "He was a Vietnam vet. There
won't be an investigation. I want you to arrange for his
body to be brought back to his family in Valdosta, Georgia.
Wire them the money for funeral expenses. Got that?"

"Raymond, the Gulf, Valdosta."

"You know my iron box? Inside are some medals." *You
keep 'em for me, Matt, okay, 'case one day I feel like wearing them again, like maybe I deserve 'em.* "Get them to Valdosta, too. They go to his parents."

"Matthew, Jesus—"

"Do it, Dave."

"If it's what you want, but, Matt, are you sure his family can handle it?"

Matthew had met the Raymonds once, when he'd delivered Otis to them half-dead from drugs and alcohol and nightmares. They were hard people, weather-beaten and uneducated, and to this day they wouldn't be able to find Montana on a map, much less Vietnam. But they'd loved their son. They hadn't known what to do with him when he was a restless kid, and they hadn't known what to do with him when Stark had dumped him on their front steps. But their impotence and his weaknesses didn't matter anymore. Otis was dead.

"Yeah," Matthew said, "they'll handle it."

Twenty-Three

∾⤙⤚∾

Juliana stopped at a pay phone at Washington National Airport and got the Palm Beach number of Abraham Stein from Florida information. She had called her apartment from Albany, getting her message machine, and she'd known then that Bloch had Aunt Willie, too. Or Aunt Willie was after him. She'd considered calling her father but had rejected the idea, simply because she couldn't bear to hear the terror in his voice, to lie to him and tell him she was fine and everything would be all right. Instead she'd flown straight to Washington and taken a cab to Capitol Hill, hoping, praying Ryder would be in his office, that he could be compelled to help her. The impulse was there—still—to try the *Gazette* and his house for Matthew. She ignored it. Even if she found him, he would only ditch her again.

She dialed the Palm Beach number. When Abraham Stein answered, she remembered his sister had just died, and she felt like an intruder. But she was running out of options.

"Hello, Mr. Stein, this is Juliana Fall," she said, not knowing where else to begin. "I'm Catharina Peperkamp's daughter, and I need your help. I don't have time to explain everything, but—"

Abraham Stein didn't hesitate. "Just tell me what you need."

"I need you to meet me at the Tallahassee airport in four hours."

"I'll be there."

"And—and I'll need the quickest transportation you can arrange to Senator Ryder's fishing camp on the Dead Lakes. If you could rent a car, that would be fine, I'm sure."

"Not to worry, Juliana."

"I can explain then."

"You can tell me whatever you want to tell me. But you don't need to explain."

When she'd hung up, she didn't move for a moment, and suddenly she swore and snatched up the phone again, dropping a quarter into the slot. She got the number for the *Washington Gazette* from information. Her call was routed to Alice Feldon. She quickly identified herself, asking for Matthew.

"He's not here," the editor said. "You mind telling me what the hell's going on?"

"Has he been in?"

"Yes. He left a few minutes ago. His buddy Otis Raymond is dead."

Juliana doubled over, falling against the wall. *If the Weaze ends up on a board because you wouldn't talk, count on seeing me again.* "Did Matthew say where he was going?"

"No, but if you have any idea, I'd like to know."

"Thank you," Juliana said hollowly.

"Wait a second—"

She didn't. Her flight for Tallahassee had been announced.

Matthew intercepted Sam Ryder as the young, good-looking senator left his town house, where he'd stopped briefly on his way from his office to his club. He planned to spend the rest of the afternoon playing tennis, to lose himself in the sweat of physical exercise and competition. Whatever happened to Juliana Fall—whatever she chose to do—wasn't his responsibility. He could have earned himself points by calling Bloch and telling him she was on her way, but he'd resisted. He was proud of himself for that act of will.

But now his heart thumped wildly in his chest as he looked at Stark, leaning insolently against the wrought-iron rail on the bottom step in front of the senator's town house. "Thought you'd end up slithering back here," Stark said.

Only once before had Ryder seen Matthew Stark's eyes so black and distant. "I'm not in the mood for your insults, Matthew. If you'll excuse me—"

"No excusing you, Sam. Not anymore."

Ryder straightened up, perspiring heavily. "What do you want?"

"You're going to take me to Bloch and help me stop him."

"I can't possibly—"

"You can and you will, buddy. You know as well as I do the sonofabitch is going to pull up, cut his losses, and disappear. He'll kill Catharina Fall and Wilhelmina Peperkamp and Juliana Fall if he can catch her, and he'll dump their bodies on some beach the way he dumped Weasel's."

Horrified, Ryder grabbed the rail. "Weasel? My God, Matthew, are you serious? Otis is…" He couldn't say it.

"Otis is dead. This time he did manage to die trying to save your sorry ass."

"I never asked him—"

"That doesn't make you less responsible. Bloch killed him, and you're part of it."

"How—"

"Blew his goddamn brains out. I'm going to find out why, *Senator,* and I'm going to find out exactly how you're tied into it, and I'm going to see to it you take the fall this time."

"Stark, for God's sake, calm down. You don't know what you're talking about. Look, I know Weasel was a friend of yours. I tried to help him out, remember, when he got out of the army, but he went his own way. I'm sorry he'd dead."

"Sorry doesn't cover it, Golden Boy. You fucked up twenty years ago, and I let it go. I won't this time."

Ryder was panting, trying to catch his breath. "I didn't want anything to happen to Otis!"

Stark's gaze was unrelenting. "You didn't want anything to happen to your father, either, but it did." He pulled himself off the rail and stood up straight, feeling hollow and old and angry. "Let's go. You've got your own private plane. We'll take it."

"No, I won't do it."

"I'm carrying a Colt and a SIG-Sauer. Commercial airlines are pretty touchy about folks taking weapons aboard their planes. I need a ride, Sam—and even if I didn't, I'm not letting you off this time."

Ryder gulped for air. "You can't coerce me, Matthew."

"I can talk, buddy. I can talk about Weasel, Rachel Stein, Hendrik de Geer, Phillip Bloch—and I can talk about Vietnam. My editor's on my ass for a story. I'll give her one."

Ryder gripped the rail; he was shaking and sweating and hating himself for his terror, but hating Matthew Stark more, blaming him. "Matthew, be reasonable."

"I am being reasonable. If I weren't, I'd have beaten you to a pulp by now. Coming?"

His legs feeling weak beneath him, Ryder stumbled down the steps, and Matthew moved smoothly in beside him, cool, remote, steady. Ryder tried to straighten up, tried to be as strong. But terror and indecision ate away at his muscles, and he despised Matthew for his control, his capableness—for his insistence on blaming Ryder for things that weren't his fault. Didn't he understand? Damn him, *didn't he understand?*

"Don't blame me for this, Matthew. It's Bloch… I couldn't refuse him. He'd already set up at my fishing camp when he contacted me. There wasn't anything I could do. He demanded money, thousands and thousands of dollars, and I did what I could, but then he wanted more. Rachel Stein came to me in the midst of all this, she'd seen me with the Dutchman, and I found out about the Minstrel, thought there'd be a possibility I could get it for Bloch and get him out of my camp and stop him from bothering me. But I tell you, Matthew—*believe me!*—I didn't want anything bad to come of this."

Stark grunted. "Didn't your mother ever tell you, Sam? The road to hell is paved with good intentions."

Hendrik de Geer lit a cigar and rested back in the fishing boat. It bobbed silently in the cold, dark water, hidden among some cypress knees. He'd stolen it from one of the public camping areas along the Dead Lakes and had cautiously made his way here, careful not to get lost among the many channels and coves that had misled even the most experienced fishermen.

Dominated by the lodge and surrounded by several smaller buildings, essentially shacks, the Ryder camp was perhaps a hundred yards from Hendrik's vantage point. A guard posted at the dock observed the lake through binoculars. Hendrik wished himself fortunate to have a pair He wasn't worried about being discovered. He was well hidden among the cypress, and he'd stolen the fisherman's cap and vest, thus disguising himself to some extent, although the cigar would probably give him away to anyone who knew his habits. But it was an excellent cigar, and he needed to think.

Sergeant Bloch was preparing to abandon his camp. Hendrik could see that from the activity around the lodge, and it was something he would expect Bloch to do. He would wait until the last moment, but he would cut his losses when he knew he'd run out of options. Even if he could continue to control Senator Ryder, others—the American reporter, even Juliana—could find out where he was and bring the authorities down on top of him. The sergeant had broken innumerable laws, not the least among them murder. Now, obviously, he wanted to be ready to move. It only made sense. In his position, Hendrik would have done the same.

The Dutchman put out his cigar and looked again toward the fishing camp. Did Bloch know Wilhelmina and Catharina would never lead him to the Minstrel? Would he kill them before he abandoned camp—or wait and try one last time for the stone by using them as bait with Juliana? She had the Minstrel's Rough, of course. Hendrik was annoyed with himself for not having seen that sooner, from the beginning even. He'd been so sure Johannes had the stone.

He should never have gone to Antwerp. He should have gone back to Florida, killed Bloch, then, if necessary, killed Ryder. He should never have talked himself into believing that he could accomplish everything. Keep the Peperkamps free from harm. Keep the Minstrel out of Bloch's hands. Keep himself alive, too.

Always the optimist, he thought bitterly.

He watched the guards change in front of the shack where he guessed they held Catharina and Wilhelmina. It was where he would have put them, in Bloch's place.

He's waiting for the daughter and maybe still half-believes they can lead him to the Minstrel's Rough... That's why he doesn't kill them.

But he would. There was never any question of that. And he could wait. Who was there to stop him?

The Dutchman sighed heavily. Well, he thought, perhaps with a little cleverness on his part, he could upset the sergeant's carefully laid plans.

Bloch will kill you, as well.

Yes, he thought, that was a possibility. Even a likelihood. Much simpler, of course, just to row silently away and disappear. He was alone, an old man facing an armed camp. What could he do?

He smiled to himself. "What, Hendrik," he muttered, "are you being a pessimist after all these years?"

Bloch nodded with satisfaction as his number-two man left the lodge office. Things were going his way. When he gave the order, they could be out of camp within half an hour. A cargo plane was waiting, gassed up and ready to go, at the small private airstrip in Calhoun County, about twenty miles north, near Blounstown. His new base in the islands was all set. Even had flush toilets, showers, and fresh coconuts and grapefruits there for the picking. A-plus. He wasn't in this business to operate out of a goddamn hellhole. No need.

Had to pay for the place, that was all. The boys he was dealing with had taken his last dime and said not to worry about the rest just yet, they'd get it before he moved in, if they didn't, they'd come for that little ol' arsenal he'd gotten together during his army years. Guns and ammunition were always good collateral, they said.

Bloch wasn't going to give up his weapons. Twenty years he'd been getting them together, and without them, he'd be sitting with nothing, just a crummy Army pension. He'd have to go work for the postal service or something.

Well, hell, he thought with the Minstrel he could buy and sell those dudes. No more stepping and fetching. He'd be right in there with the big boys.

"I want that stone," he said aloud, rising from the desk.

His man on Ryder had reported in. Juliana Fall had gone to see the senator at his office, and Matthew Stark had grabbed him outside his town house, they'd left in a cab, but the guy had lost them. That was okay that he'd lost Stark and Ryder. Wasn't any real mystery where they were going.

"They're coming right here," Bloch said, laughing hoarsely. "Ain't that just loverly? We can take care of unfinished business, and then I can sit and wait for pretty Juliana Fall to come see me with the Minstrel in hand."

Because he was betting—hell, he *knew*—that Ryder had told her where to find her mamma and her fat-ass aunt. She'd be along, too, in good time.

Funny how things sometimes just worked themselves out.

"The guard thinks we're two old women," Catharina said. She continued to speak easily in Dutch, surprised at how good it felt. "He's very confident, perhaps too confident. If we can surprise him, perhaps we can escape. Bloch is preparing to abandon camp, and I don't think he plans to take us with him. If he does, it only means he thinks he can get Juliana, too, and the Minstrel. But if we can escape, we can lose ourselves out there in the forest and find help."

Wilhelmina grunted. "We can also get eaten alive by snakes and crocodiles."

"Alligators," Catharina corrected. "Better than shot here like mad dogs."

Her older sister was surprised and impressed by Catharina's display of nerve. "Or used to lure Juliana?"

"Yes, but as you've been trying to tell me, Willie, I think she'll know how to handle herself."

"You should tell her that."

"And many other things, too. I hope I'll have the chance."

Wilhelmina nodded, understanding. "Well, we might as well try to get out of here. Another meal like this—" she glanced distastefully at the remains of something the guard had called tofu burgers "—and I'll be looking for the snakes myself. They say many are good eating. What's your plan for getting past the guard?"

Catharina beamed; Willie was asking her opinion, expecting she had a plan. "Paring knives," she said victoriously.

"Paring knives?"

"Yes, you didn't notice?" She went over to the small kitchen area and with her good hand pulled open a creaking wooden drawer, pointing to the array of utensils, among them two paring knives. "It's not the best-equipped kitchen, and the knives are hardly Sabatiers, but I believe they'll suit our purposes. I think I can manage despite my arm."

Wilhelmina had risen and was behind her younger sister, peering at the cache of ready weapons. "Obviously these are not the kind of men who think about what might be in kitchen drawers."

"And with a baker and a former fighter for the Dutch Underground Resistance in their midst! Shame on them!"

Catharina laughed, looking as beautiful as Wilhelmina had ever seen her, and the older Dutchwoman thought, if I die today in this strange, swampy place, then at least we'll have had this moment, far too long in coming.

Twenty-Four

Abraham Stein wasn't much bigger than his sister and looked twice as old. "I called some friends," he was telling Juliana as he led her with surprising agility through a glass door, "and they know someone who knows someone who knows someone who was friends with the father, the first Senator Ryder, who was killed, you know, in Vietnam. They've been to the fishing camp, which is more for entertainment than for fish, and it has a helicopter pad. Isn't that beautiful?"

Juliana looked at him, baffled. The old man spoke very rapidly, his accent more noticeable than his sister's, and she wondered if she'd misunderstood. "The *father* was in Vietnam? But I thought it was the son who'd gone."

"Yes, yes, as a soldier. The father was a senator then. Of course, I forget how young you are, you might not remember. He was killed during a fact-finding mission to Vietnam, when his helicopter was caught in a battle of some sort. It was a terrible thing. Quite a scandal. The son was with him and himself was nearly killed." Abraham Stein looked at Juliana, his lively dark eyes suddenly grave and filled with sorrow. "It's a terrible thing for a son to have to watch his father die. From cancer and old age, yes, then there can be no regrets, but at the hands of others—" he shook his head "—that never leaves you. No matter how we pretend, it's always there."

"You speak from experience?" Juliana asked, not sure she should.

He smiled sadly. "Do I need to? But enough of this. Come. I have a helicopter waiting for you. The pilot knows how to get to Senator Ryder's camp. I told him there might be some danger involved and he said good, he hasn't had any excitement in a while. Helicopter pilots tend to be this way, I think."

Juliana thought so, too. She could just bet who'd been piloting the helicopter in which the senior Senator Ryder had been killed. During the flight to Tallahassee, the thought of Matthew had never left her; she wondered where he was, what he was doing. She hadn't stayed put in Vermont as he'd obviously intended her to. She wasn't sure how that would sit with him. But he'd let her know.

She'd thrown her parka over her arm and now reached into the inside pocket and pulled out the paper bag in which she'd placed the Minstrel's Rough, inside its faded velvet. "I have another favor," she said, embarrassed.

Abraham Stein was delighted. "Yes, what is it?"

She thrust the bag at him. "Take this. I can't tell you what's inside, and I'd like to ask you not to look—for your own sake, no other reason. If you don't hear from me within twenty-four hours, take a boat out into the ocean where the water's very, very deep and throw the bag into it. Then call in the National Guard and tell them to come get me. Will you do that?"

"Of course." He tucked the bag into his suitcoat pocket, with no indication whatsoever of curiosity.

"You don't have any questions?"

"No," he said. "I have no questions."

They were outside now, and Juliana couldn't suppress a rush of excitement liberally mingled with fear as she saw the helicopter standing out on the landing pad, warmed up and ready to go. "Aunt Willie, Mother," she whispered, "hang in there."

Then she heard a familiar rough, deep voice. "What the hell do you mean this is the last goddamn helicopter and it's unavailable?"

She looked around and saw him. Matthew. Samuel Ryder was standing next to him, Matthew's intense dark looks, black leather jacket, and Gokey boots in contrast to the fair, patrician handsomeness of the senator. Juliana took a sharp breath, wondering if there was some way she could just sneak into the helicopter.

The unhappy official tried to explain there was nothing whatever he could do, the helicopter was already spoken for, but Matthew wasn't listening. His gaze had fallen on Juliana. He ignored the official and Ryder and the little old man standing next to her and walked up to her.

"I should have tied you to the goddamn bedpost," he said. "My mistake."

"What are you doing here?" She could see plainly enough he wanted to ask her the same question. Abraham Stein was watching the proceedings with interest.

"Damn it," Stark said.

"If you don't behave," she said, "I won't let you ride in my helicopter."

"I ought to steal the thing right out from under you."

But she grabbed his wrist and held him back. "Don't, Matthew. Neanderthal tactics aren't going to work with me. I'll just find another way there."

"You know, lady, you may be generally uninformed about life in the twentieth century, but—" he paused, grinning "—you've got guts. Let's go."

Juliana and Ryder rode in back, Matthew up front with the pilot, who'd also flown in Vietnam and had heard of

Steelman Stark—and sympathized with his feelings toward the junior senator from Florida. Matthew had told the pilot Ryder wasn't going to enjoy the trip: "He won't know if I'll try to toss his butt out of the chopper or not."

"Wouldn't blame you if you did," the pilot had replied. "The way I hear it, he was responsible for what happened back in 'Nam."

"Matthew," Ryder croaked, his face ashen, "don't do it."

"Why not, Sam? I've been waiting twenty years to get back into a helicopter with you—"

"For God's sake, that's over and done with! It wasn't your fault, and it wasn't my fault. It was just one of those terrible things that happens in war."

"No, it wasn't. It never should have happened, Sam. Your father, Jake, and Chuck could all be alive today if you hadn't lied about that LZ—or maybe if I'd been a better pilot or just smart enough to know you were lying."

"Matt, don't. Jake and Chuck were good soldiers. They knew the risks. And my father—he would have forgiven you. *I* forgive you."

"Jesus Christ, Sam, it just might be worth the consequences to toss your goddamn dumb ass out of here. But it's not." Matthew saw the confusion in Juliana's eyes and grinned at her. "More history for you to learn, sweet cheeks. We'll talk later, okay?" She nodded, and he turned back to the pilot. "How far to the Dead Lakes?"

"Maybe twenty minutes."

Behind them, Ryder said, "Bloch will kill you the minute you land."

"He can try."

"Damn it, Stark, I wish you wouldn't talk like that! We need to consider alternatives to violence."

Matthew looked over at the Golden Boy senator with the wide, terrified baby blue eyes. "I'd love to, Sam. Got any ideas? You think Bloch's going to want to deal? The sonofabitch killed the Weaze, and he probably killed Rachel Stein, and he's going to kill those women—unless old Aunt Willie gets loose first and kills him."

Ryder licked his lips. "You could at least try to make a deal—"

"Jesus, you're a card, Sam. Don't you remember 'Nam? Phil Bloch doesn't deal. He's very good at killing people, and he's very good at taking care of himself. Look, if it helps, I have no interest in killing the man. I just want to stop him, which is what you should have done to begin with. Of all people, Sam, you know what he is."

"How could I have stopped him? He was threatening to tell people I was the one who told you to fly into a hot LZ, that I got my own father killed! How could I function with that kind of rumor hanging over my head?"

"Not rumor," Stark said. "Fact."

"That's not true! The LZ was secure as far as we knew, but there was a war going on, for God's sake. There were VC and NVA all over that valley."

"Sam," Matthew said without emotion, "that LZ was never secure, but the information I got was that it was cold—safe for a goddamn United States senator to have a visit with his son the lieutenant. But you wanted your daddy to see you in action, and what should have been a routine resupply mission turned into a firefight."

The young senator stared straight ahead as they flew over the Dead Lakes region. It was almost nightfall. "If that's what you want to believe, Matthew, go right ahead. I suppose we all have to have our delusions."

And none is bigger than yours, Sam, Matthew thought. But he didn't pursue the subject. In a way, it was his own fault Ryder had never owned up to what he'd done. The commission that investigated the death of Senator Samuel Ryder, Sr., during a fact-finding mission to Vietnam had pinned the blame squarely on the shoulders of the helicopter pilot who had "stumbled" into the hot LZ, resulting in the deaths of the senator and one copilot, Jake MacIntyre, and one crew chief, and the wounding of one door gunner, Otis Raymond, and of himself. What should have been a routine VIP tour, a cushy mission for a top-notch pilot like Stark, had turned into a disaster.

Stark, Otis Raymond, and Phil Bloch had all kept their mouths shut about what they knew: that the senator's son and namesake had wanted to impress his father so much he'd deliberately lied about the area where his company was on patrol. Nothing bad was supposed to have happened. Matt Stark was supposed to be a good enough pilot to pull them out in case they were fired on. For his part, the senior Ryder had demanded that Stark go into his son's landing zone if at all possible, telling the young pilot he'd fought in the Pacific during World War II, which had been a real war, and he wasn't afraid.

At the time, Matthew had tried to spare the green lieutenant any further suffering. His father was dead. It seemed like enough. But by taking the blame himself, Matthew had helped Sam Ryder, Jr., convince himself that he hadn't been in any way responsible.

"Okay, Sam," he said, "have it your way. Just tell me one more thing. Do you know how she—" he nodded to Juliana "—found her way down here?"

"Well, I…" Ryder sputtered, lifting his shoulders helplessly.

"You told her." Matthew didn't raise his voice; there was no point. "You figured you could throw her to Bloch, which he would see as a gesture of good faith on your part—and the hell with what happened to her?"

"That's not true. I don't want anything to happen to her!"

"Let's put it this way, Sam," Stark said, turning around and looking not at Ryder, but at Juliana. He'd never known anyone like her. Never. "Nothing had better happen to her."

* * *

The one part of him that had never failed Hendrik de Geer were his eyes, and yet now he could not believe them. From his position in the fishing boat, he saw two things happen almost simultaneously. One, a helicopter kicked up dust and wind as it came down for a landing behind the lodge, creating a good deal of excitement among Bloch's men. Two, Wilhelmina and Catharina had surprised their guard as he went in to check on them while the helicopter was landing, and had battled him out onto the porch with what even from a distance looked suspiciously like kitchen knives.

Hendrik quickly started the engine of the boat. It would have been simple—and very wise—for him just to get out of there as quickly as possible. In all the chaos, no one would even notice.

You're a coward, he told himself silently.

Yes, and cowards often died fools' deaths.

He gunned the engine and sped toward the dock. Another man had seen the difficulties the guard was in and was moving toward his aid. Hendrik leaped from the boat with the assault rifle he'd stashed outside the camp, when he'd first started dealing with Bloch. He'd picked it up after stealing the boat.

"Good evening, Michael," he said calmly. "I wouldn't go any further if I were you."

"De Geer." The boy eyed the rifle. He was no more than twenty-one, lured into this life by false tales of adventure and romance. All he'd experienced so far, Hendrik knew, were the bites of insects and the discipline of a man he could neither respect nor admire. "What're you doing?"

"If you're going to stay in this business and live, you're going to have to learn to cut your losses, Michael. Bloch has tread where he never should have. He's abandoning camp, but it'll be too late. He's not a hero, Michael. He's a murderer."

"You're crazy, de Geer. Bloch'll kill you."

The Dutchman shrugged, impassive. "In this life, death is always a possibility. Drop your weapon, Michael—or we can begin the evening's body count with yours."

Michael paled, eyeing the rifle, and nodded, slowly dropping his automatic.

"Get out," Hendrik said. "This isn't your fight. If you have a buddy, take him with you. Take as many as you can."

The boy just swallowed and began to run, and Hendrik picked up the automatic and moved quickly toward the shack. Catharina had been thrown to the ground and was awkwardly climbing to her feet, holding her injured arm, her color terrible. Wilhelmina held a paring knife to the throat of the now very still, very terrified guard. She was bleeding and winded, but undaunted.

"Ahh, Willie," Hendrik said, laughing in spite of himself. He took Catharina by the shoulder, steadying her. She smelled of sweat and dirt and a light, fading perfume, none of which, he thought, he would ever forget. "Are you all right, Catharina?"

She nodded. "Hendrik—I didn't think…"

"You didn't think I'd come? Neither did I, I suppose. Forty years ago I wouldn't have. Make no mistake about that, my sweet Catharina." But he didn't waste time on sentiment. Pointing his rifle at the man on the porch, whose name he'd forgotten, he said, "Come, Willie, you and Catharina have done your job. He won't move—will you, my friend?"

The guard seemed almost pleased to be held off by an FN NATO assault rifle rather than an old woman's kitchen knife. A man's pride, Hendrik thought, disgusted and amused.

Wilhelmina climbed stiffly down from the porch, ruing the loss of her youth. When one reached the age of seventy, she thought, one should plant begonias. She gave Hendrik de Geer a stony look. "Did you forget something? Is that why you returned?"

"Yes," he said. "I forgot how much I care about you two. Now come, both of you. There's a fishing boat down at the dock. It's a simple engine, you can manage it. I'll get you to it. Then take it and get out of here. Look for another fishing camp. Get help."

"What about you?" Catharina asked.

Hendrik let his gaze linger on her soft green eyes. "I have always been good at taking care of myself, Catharina."

"No question of that," Wilhelmina muttered.

He gave her a thin smile, remembering how they'd always sparred with each other, even when they were teenagers and Catharina was still but a baby. "Mind the alligators, Willie."

"I'm not afraid of alligators."

"No," he said, "but they may be afraid of you."

Twenty-Five

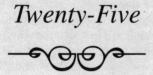

"Wait for me if you can," Stark told the pilot. "If you can't, get the hell out." He nodded to Juliana and Ryder. "Take these two with you."

"Will do."

Matthew turned to Ryder. "Keep her here. Understood?"

He was half-waiting for Ryder to tell him Juliana could stay with the pilot, that he was a veteran combat soldier and would be willing to help Matthew with Bloch. But the senator from Florida only nodded, white-faced.

Juliana was closer to purple-faced. "What if 'her' doesn't want to stay here?" she demanded, her tone scathing as strands of pale blond hair flew across her face. Stark thought she looked gorgeous.

"Look," he said, "you know Eric Shuji Shizumi. I know Phillip Bloch. I won't interfere with you and Shuji, you don't interfere with me and Bloch. Okay?"

"He's got my mother and my aunt."

Stark hadn't thought his logic would work with her. "Here." He pulled back the slide on the Colt, lowered the hammer, and handed it over. "It's an automatic. To shoot someone just flip off the safety, cock it, point and pull the trigger. It's an old Army gun. Ryder knows all about it, but

I think right now I trust you more." Then he leaned over and kissed her hard. "Be good."

He jumped down from the helicopter and disappeared into a darkened stand of yellow scrub pines just beyond the landing pad. Juliana watched with concern and fury—and relief, at least for herself. The knots of tension all through her told her to curl up in a ball inside the helicopter where no one could see her and just wait for everything to be over. She didn't want to be in the way. A liability. A potential victim. But she didn't want to do nothing, either.

"Matt went through advanced infantry training," Ryder said, almost tenderly. "He knows what he's doing."

"You could help him," Juliana said.

"I can't—"

"Won't. You don't want to." She looked at him levelly, seeing what he was, knowing what he was thinking. "You want him to die, and you want Bloch to die. That's it, isn't it? Then neither will be around as a threat to expose you to the world. But I want you to know, Sam Ryder. The threat won't die with them, do you understand? *I'll* expose you."

"You're wrong," he said.

"Then get your butt out there and help him!"

Ryder started to say something, but he jumped suddenly from the helicopter. Juliana thought she might have gotten through to him. She watched him run across the clearing behind the lodge, but then he veered over to an open Jeep. He didn't have a chance to start it up. One of Bloch's men was there with a gun. Ryder looked a combination of scared and indignant as he went with him into the lodge.

"I've got to tell Matthew," Juliana muttered, and started to jump out herself.

The pilot caught her by the arm. "Sorry, lady. Stark can handle the situation—and don't bother waving that gun at me because I know you're not going to shoot me."

But Juliana was looking past him, stricken. "Mother!"

The pilot whipped around, and while he was momentarily off-guard, Juliana seized the opportunity and jumped from the helicopter, keeping her head down as she dove under the rotating propeller, plunging wildly toward the lake, holding on to the heavy Colt.

Hendrik de Geer was helping her mother and Aunt Willie into an aluminum boat. He was armed with something that looked like it could kill a tiger, but it wasn't going to do him a damn bit of good if he didn't see the man sneaking toward them from behind a rustic-looking shack. He carried a rifle that was insignificantly smaller than the Dutchman's.

Juliana slowed down as she flipped the safety on the Colt, worried the thing would go off, but it didn't, and she moved steadily, ducking onto a path flanked by scrub pine. Her mother and Aunt Willie were in the boat now. De Geer looked around but couldn't see Bloch's man, who had stopped at the corner of the shack and was raising his rifle, obviously planning to pick off the Dutchman and maybe the two women, as well.

"No," Juliana yelled, *"don't!"*

The man swung around, trying to find her with the rifle, and her mother screamed. *"Juliana—leave us!"* But Juliana didn't and blindly pulled the trigger on the Colt. Sound exploded all around her, and the recoil from the firing jerked her arm up and back. She yelled out, pain and numbness slicing through her hand, and flashing before her was Shuji's face when she told him she'd ruined her career fighting bad guys in a goddamn Florida swamp. It all seemed so crazy and silly she wanted to laugh even as she more or less fell, jumped, and was hauled backward into the trees.

A series of loud cracking sounds around her and Matthew's hot breath on her face chased away the vagueness. "Jesus H. Christ," Matthew said. "Living with you is going to be something else."

She realized she was still holding the Colt, but her hand was so numb she couldn't feel it. "My hand…"

"Lady, you'd better worry about your neck because I think I'm about to strangle you."

"Did I get him?"

"No, you didn't get him, goddamnit, how the *hell* do you think you can hit someone when you shoot with your damned eyes closed?" Matthew hissed angrily, dumping her down among the prickly pine needles. "But you distracted him," he admitted, "and de Geer got him."

"Mother—"

"Aunt Willie bopped her one and got her out of here in the boat. She must have realized that was the best thing she could do since they're unarmed and could serve only as potential hostages."

Only then did Juliana look down toward the lake. There was no sign of the boat. Everything was strangely quiet. "Where's Bloch?"

"Inside pulling up anchor, I suspect. Most of his men have hit the road. They don't mind playing war with him, but they don't want to die or go to jail for him. I had a chat with a few. They decided they didn't want to hang around for the FBI."

"Are they coming?"

"Sure."

"But how—"

"I had Feldie give them a buzz. Called her from the airport. They'll want to be damn careful about putting an assault on a camp owned by a United States senator, but I suspect they'll be along."

"One of Bloch's men has Ryder. He was trying to run and got caught."

"Oh, terrific. Now Bloch has himself another hostage." Matthew suddenly went still. *"Damn."*

Juliana followed his gaze to the back of the lodge and

didn't have to ask him what was wrong. She could see. Phillip Bloch was making his way toward the helicopter, armed with a rifle.

"The pilot'll just take off—"

"He can't. Bloch'll shoot him, and he knows it."

Without a word, Matthew slunk off into the shadows, leaving Juliana where she was. Trusting her. She thought of the Minstrel and wondered if she could delay Bloch with the promise of it but knew they were beyond all that now. Bloch would just shoot her and get the hell out. At best he'd grab her and take her with him. So running out into the open wasn't going to do any good. But neither was staying where she was.

She crept off after Matthew. Feeling had returned to her hand; it was strained but not broken. If she had to shoot again, she would expect the recoil and steel herself for it.

"I'll cover you," she said, coming up behind Matthew. He gave her a dubious look, and she managed a smile. "I may not hit anything, but Bloch won't know that."

"All right. Just try not to hit me."

She nodded gravely, and Matthew just grinned and started out from within the brush.

Juliana grabbed his shoulder. "Wait—look."

Sam Ryder was being marched to the helicopter at gunpoint. He and Bloch's man joined the sergeant as they moved toward the landing pad.

"The dumb son of a bitch," Stark muttered. "Bloch'll kill him."

"Isn't there anything we can do?"

Before Matthew could answer, Hendrik de Geer bounded from behind the lodge. He called something in Dutch, and the man on Ryder whipped around, firing a burst. De Geer returned fire, and both went down. Even from where she was, Juliana could see the blood spreading over the Dutchman's chest. Ryder stood frozen, staring down at the dead man at his feet.

"Sam," Matthew yelled, jumping out from the brush, "drop and roll, goddamnit!"

Ryder didn't move. Bloch had turned and, seeing what was happening, hesitated momentarily. If he went and grabbed Ryder, the chopper would take off without him. If he didn't, he'd lost his hostage.

He raised his rifle.

"Shit," Matthew muttered as he fired twice, but Bloch was too far for Stark's aim to be effective. He dove out of the brush, staying low as he catapulted into Ryder and knocked him down. Bloch's bullets thudded and kicked up clouds of dust as both men rolled behind a Jeep. Juliana couldn't see if either had been hit, but she used all her self-control to keep quiet. Bloch didn't know she was there.

Staying within the protection of the stand of pines, she made her way cautiously but quickly toward the sergeant. He was keeping an eye on the Jeep and had fired at the helicopter, a warning shot for the pilot to stay put. Juliana felt she'd gotten the poor guy into this mess and couldn't abandon him. Except for watching a few television detective shows, she had no sense whatever of tactics. She only knew she wasn't going to let Phillip Bloch get into that helicopter.

"Stop," she yelled over the whirring roar of the propeller, and fired the Colt in Bloch's general direction. The kickback hurt like hell, but she was prepared this time. She missed, of course. Hitting a moving target wasn't as easy as it appeared. But she did succeed in slowing Bloch and diverting his attention from the chopper, Matthew, and Ryder. He paused and fired blindly into the brush, preventing Juliana from getting off another shot as she dove to the ground. Then Matthew was there, coming at Bloch from an angle, surprising him. He fired once, hitting Bloch high in the chest. Bloch jerked, dropping his weapon as he fell. He clutched his right collarbone with both hands. Matthew walked closer and kicked the rifle out of reach, just to be safe.

There was a sudden silence as the helicopter propeller went still. "Good going, Matt," the pilot said, climbing out. "I radioed for help, pronto."

Matthew was breathing hard as he stared down at the writhing Bloch. "I should kill you, Bloch. You killed Weasel and you killed Rachel Stein and you made sure a lot of guys died in Vietnam who didn't need to die. You let Ryder get in over his head and you let him stay there."

"Ryder was my commanding officer—"

"Ryder was a jackass and you knew it. But you let him keep fucking up—you kept him alive when anyone else that green and that stupid would either have learned or been killed. You encouraged him to believe his father would be impressed by seeing his unit in action. You knew he was giving me bad information, that the area was still hot, but you didn't stop him, you didn't report him, you didn't tell me what the fuck was going on. So we came in unprepared, and his father got killed, and Jake and Chuck got killed."

"Sam figured everything'd work out." Bloch's voice was raspy; he was wincing with pain but not yelling. He'd never been shot before.

"It didn't."

"I was following orders."

"You were already looking toward today."

Bloch snorted. "So what're you going to do about it?"

"Nothing," Matthew said. "Not a damn thing but stand here and wait for the police to haul your ass out of here."

Juliana had made her way to the prone figure of Hendrik de Geer. He was lying on his back, bleeding heavily. She knelt in the sand beside him and touched his shoulder. Warm blood had seeped everywhere. "Don't try to move," she said needlessly, taking off her sweater. "I'll see what I can do about the blood." He lifted his hand and covered hers, his skin clammy and purplish. "Don't bother," he whispered, weak. "I've seen many wounds, Juliana. This one…" He smiled a little, shook his head slightly. "Catharina and Willie?"

"They got away."

"Good, that's good. You must tell them…" He winced, shuddering with pain, and swallowed. His mouth and eyes looked sunken. Juliana tried staunching the blood anyway with her sweater. He went on, his voice even weaker, "You must tell them I'm sorry for Amsterdam. Tell them I was afraid, and I thought too much of myself. I know… I know it makes up for nothing. Being sorry doesn't help."

Juliana nodded, shaking all over. "I'll tell them."

"And tell them, too…" He smiled, clutching her hand with more vigor, and for a moment the piercingly blue eyes focused. "Tell them I did love them both."

Twenty-Six

Alice Feldon was standing at her desk Monday morning when Matthew Stark strolled in with a cup of coffee in one hand and the *Post* under his arm. She slammed down her phone and stalked over to him. "I'll warn you right now, Stark, I am one furious editor. I've got the big guns all over me because they okayed trips to New York and Antwerp, hotel fees, a concert ticket—all because I promised them a page-one story. And what happens? *I read the whole goddamn thing on the fucking wires!* Senator's fishing camp used to stockpile weapons, two men dead, retired army sergeant arrested, senator denying he knew anything about what was going on, world-famous piano player hugging her mother knee-deep in some godforsaken place called the Dead Lakes—Jesus Christ! There's even a photo of you, you sonofabitch, punching out Sam Ryder."

Matthew drank some of his coffee. "Yeah. Felt good, too. Should have done it years ago." He grinned. "Relax, Feldie."

"Relax!" She was indignant. "I'll *relax,* you lazy shit, when your butt's out of here!"

"Get yourself a cup of coffee, a pencil, and a pad of paper and pull up a chair."

She dropped her glasses on the end of her nose and narrowed her eyes at him. "You've got something."

He laughed. "Facts, Feldie, just facts." He yelled across the newsroom. "Ziegler—get your butt over here!" He looked back to Feldie and grinned. "I think it's time he made some points around here. He can help you write the story."

"Help *me?*"

"Yeah. You remember how, don't you?"

"Stark—"

"Quit dawdling, Feldie."

"Damn you, I'm your editor—"

"Fact one," he said, starting across the newsroom to his desk. "Senator Samuel Ryder, Jr., not only knew about Sergeant Phillip Bloch's activities but approved them and helped him buy some of the arms and set up his new base in the Caribbean. Fact two. He did so because Bloch was blackmailing him because he knew Ryder had directed the helicopter carrying U.S. Senator Samuel Ryder, Sr.—his own father—into an area he knew still to be hot. The chopper was shot down, and three people, including his father, died. How much Sam, Jr., was actually responsible for may be debatable, but Bloch exploited Ryder's unadmitted guilt over the incident. Fact three. Otis Raymond was the door gunner in the helicopter in which Ryder, Sr., was killed, and he saved Ryder, Jr.'s life. Bloch found out Otis was snitching to me in order to get Ryder's butt out of trouble one more time. Bloch will be indicted for his murder."

"Jesus Christ, Stark, I get the picture."

Matthew grinned. "And I haven't even gotten to the part about the world's largest uncut diamond."

"Let me get coffee. Why don't you just start writing?"

"I can't, Feldie. I'm part of the story."

She looked at him. "Okay. Give me a minute."

She and Aaron Ziegler pulled up chairs and took notes as Matthew gave them everything he had—except one tiny fact.

"You never saw this diamond?" Feldie asked.

A paperweight for jam recipes; only Juliana. "No."

"Then there's still no proof it exists?"

"That's right."

"What about the Peperkamps?"

"Call them. They'll tell you what they told me. It's a myth."

"So Ryder was wrong?" Alice shook her head. "So all that scrambling for nothing."

"For a chance, Feldie. For a chance."

"I guess. Ziegler, get going and type up these notes."

Aaron looked at Matthew. "Are you sure you want it this way?"

"I'm sure," Matthew said. Zeigler nodded and headed for his desk, moving fast; he knew what he had. Matthew handed his editor a neatly typed sheet of paper.

"What's this?"

"My resignation."

"Matthew, don't be a jerk. You know I was—"

He held up a hand, stopping her. "I know you were."

She sighed. "What are you going to do?"

Rising, he put on his leather jacket. "Become a music critic."

"That's not funny. Stark, stay," she added. "Do this story."

"Thanks for arguing, Feldie, I was hoping you wouldn't let me go without a little bit of a fight. But it's okay. Time to move on. Hell, I've even got a glimmer of an idea for a book."

"About Vietnam?"

He grinned. "No."

"We won't run the story," she said suddenly, "not as you gave it to us. We'll just present the facts. You do up the rest for some big fancy magazine. It doesn't belong in the *Gazette*." She gave him a devilish smile. "Too goddamn long."

"The boys upstairs'll throw you out."

"The hell with them. They fire me, I'll swallow my pride and move over to the *Post*."

"Alice—"

"Get out of here. You heading to New York?"

He looked at her, surprised. "How did you know?"

"A woman who'll paint her nails African Violet has an instinct for these things. Just invite me to the wedding, okay? Every now and then I like to have an excuse to wear high heels."

"What are you talking about?"

"Your piano player. Marry her, for God's sake."

"Feldie, I've known the woman for two weeks."

"Yeah," Alice Feldon said, "but the way I see it, you've been waiting for her for thirty-nine years."

Catharina smiled at her daughter, sitting on the edge of her mother's bed in the huge, elegant master suite of her Park Avenue apartment where her doctor had insisted she remain for a couple of days. An infection had started in her arm, but they'd given her antibiotics and put on a cast and everything would be fine soon. She only regretted not being able to roll out her *speculaas* for the holidays.

"Hendrik de Geer was a friend of ours—Johannes, Wilhelmina, myself—for many years, since he was a boy," she said, speaking quietly. "During the war, he became an informant for the Underground Resistance, sharing information he'd learned from his contacts with the NSB, the police of the Dutch Nazi party. We despised them even more, I think, than the Germans, because they were Dutch, our countrymen. Hendrik played a very dangerous game, but no one made him. It was his choice. He knew the risks."

"Was he actually on the Nazis' side?"

Catharina shook her head sadly. "He was on no one's side but his own, Juliana. During that last, terrible winter, we were all suffering terribly, none more than the *onder-*

duikers, and our resources were stretched to the limit. Hendrik came to us and said he believed the Nazis were suspicious of us, but that he could keep them away and get us food and some coal if only he had something to bargain with. Father and Johannes decided to tell him about the Minstrel. Wilhelmina was against it, of course, but they were desperate to help those in hiding. We were all starving—and so cold! We were desperate, and we trusted him."

"You couldn't have known," Juliana said.

"Perhaps. What Hendrik didn't tell us was that the Nazis suspected *him* and he was going to use the Minstrel to save himself. Well," she said, "it didn't work. Johannes and my father gave me the stone to bring to him, knowing, I think, that he'd never harm me, but it was too late. The officer who'd suspected Hendrik of playing both sides against the middle had pressured him, and to save himself he told them everything—about Mother and Father's work with the Resistance, Willie's, where Johannes was hiding, Ann, the Steins. His plan was to get back to them before the Nazis could and warn them, but he couldn't. They were all arrested, and here we were, Hendrik and myself, 'free.' He could have taken the Minstrel and left me, too, to the Nazis, but he chose instead to get me safely into hiding and disappear, without the Minstrel."

Catharina stopped, unable to go on. Juliana touched her mother's hand. "Was anyone killed?"

Her mother nodded, tears streaming down her cheeks. "Nine members of the Stein family were murdered in the concentration camps. Rachel and Abraham were the only survivors. Willie was imprisoned until the end of the war. Johannes was sent to a labor camp."

"His wife?"

"She was deported to Auschwitz, but she came back. However—" Catharina held back, unable to go on. How could she tell her daughter? *How?* "However, her son was sent with her, and he was gassed. It's something I've never been able to bring myself to talk about. I— It's as if I've blotted him from my memory, but, of course, I haven't. He was your only cousin on my side of the family. His name...his name was David. He was six years old."

"Dear God," Juliana whispered, "I had no idea—"

"I should have told you, I know."

"No, Mother. A month ago, I might have said yes and been furious, but not now. You weren't ready to talk. I understand. What about your parents? What happened to them?"

"They were executed," she said. "Shot by the Gestapo after being tortured for information. They never broke. I've always thought they should have gone to Hendrik with the Minstrel, and if they had—but they guessed what he might do, you see, and they wanted to protect me."

Juliana smiled through her tears. "But now you understand, don't you, about protective parents?"

"Yes," she said, grasping her daughter's hand with her thick, strong fingers. "They did what I would have done."

"What about the Minstrel?"

"I returned it to Johannes after the war, when he was released. He was the rightful caretaker. The stone was his to do with as he felt necessary. I begged him to throw it into the sea, but obviously he didn't listen. In all these years, I never thought you would have anything, ever, to do with the Minstrel's Rough. I expected the tradition to die with him. But we're a family of tradition, aren't we? You were the last Peperkamp, and Johannes felt it his duty to pass the stone to you, no doubt. He did it in Delftshaven, at the concert?"

Juliana nodded. "He told me not to mention it to you."

Catharina smiled, still crying. "Yes, I can see why. But it was his right—I don't question that—and he must have thought Hendrik was dead since he hadn't come for the

Minstrel in all that time. And who else knew about it? Only us. Juliana—what Hendrik told you, before he died…"

"Mother, please, you don't have to explain. That's none of my business. I understand that I don't have to know everything about your life."

"I want you to know, Juliana—he was my first love. I adored him—idolized him. He was what all men should be, and when he betrayed us… I thought I could never love again. But when your father came to Holland as a graduate student, he was so different, so good." She lifted her shoulders, uncertain how to explain. "He taught me to laugh again."

He came in then, Adrian Fall, tall and so enduringly patient. For two days now he'd been turning away reporters and telling Catharina and Juliana that yes, he would forgive them, but never, never again were they to put him through such horror. While they were in Florida fighting Bloch and his men, he'd been in New York screaming at the police to find his wife and daughter.

"Wilhelmina called," he said. "She informed me she's bringing supper."

"What?" Catharina laughed. "She's a terrible cook!"

Adrian looked at her, his eyes crinkling at the corners as he smiled at his wife. "Better than you, I should think, in your condition. She said she's discovered Zabar's and was delighted to see they had smoked eel. If you both don't mind, I think I'll send out for a sandwich."

Catharina assured him that Wilhelmina wouldn't be offended, and when he left, Juliana looked at her mother. "Does he—"

"No," Catharina said, "he doesn't know much more than you did. Juliana, do you want to tell me about Matthew Stark?"

"Not now," she said. Matthew… How many times had she picked up the phone to call him? How many times had she remembered how he'd lifted her up into his arms and kissed her, right before he'd turned around and landed his fist squarely on Sam Ryder's jaw, just as the FBI and God knew who else had arrived? They'd practically ended up arresting him! He was in Washington, she knew. She smiled at her mother. "But would you like to hear about J.J. Pepper?"

Wilhelmina had transplanted four begonias into fresh, clean pots and put them in the windowsill in her living room. The sun was shining. It was a fine day in Delftshaven, and she was content. She had arrived home the day before and would go to Antwerp in the morning to settle her brother's affairs. She missed him. She had seen so little of him over the years, but she'd always known he was there in Belgium with his diamonds, with the memories of their shared past. Now he was gone.

She had spent her last night in New York with Juliana, and they'd had dinner with Catharina and Adrian and learned more about J.J. Pepper, whom Wilhelmina found quite reassuring. A needed presence in her niece's life, to be sure. At least this J.J. explained all the old clothes.

Juliana had come to her before dawn and awakened her, sitting on the edge of her bed. "Were you and Hendrik de Geer lovers?" she asked directly.

"You're impertinent," Wilhelmina told her.

"He loved you first, and then my mother started to mature, and he fell in love with her, too. That's what he meant, isn't it?"

"Go back to bed."

"I can't sleep." She sighed, her eyes shining even in the dark. "I feel like playing the piano."

"At three o'clock in the morning?"

She nodded.

"Well, then, let me get my robe. We'll play a duet."

"*You* play piano?"

"I used to. Lately it keeps coming back. I don't know why. I sometimes play at the church. During the occupation, when times were particularly difficult or frightening, I would sing sonatas to myself, to occupy my mind so I wouldn't worry so much about what would happen to us all, about failing my responsibilities. Rachel and I would sing all the time. She had such a wonderful, clear voice, Rachel did. We didn't have a piano. I'd pretend to play on the table, and Rachel would pretend to catch my missed notes. Your mother thought we were so crazy! She was always cooking. She could lose herself in her cooking at any time. She never complained about hunger of anything else as long as she had something to cook, if only potatoes and seeds and beets."

They'd played for hours, and Wilhelmina made no apologies for her missed notes, her awkwardness. Juliana was delighted. "You should get a piano!"

"Bah. The neighbors would complain."

But now she almost wished she did have a piano. She never fell asleep when she was the one doing the playing!

At the airport in the morning, Wilhelmina had kissed Juliana goodbye and told her, "Yes, Hendrik and I were lovers, but only for a little while. I always suspected what kind of man he was—I just didn't think he could ever hurt us. If I could have seen what he'd do, I'd have slit his throat in the night. After what happened, I tried to find him and kill him, but now… I think he suffered more by living."

"And you, Aunt Willie? Are you lonely?"

"I've had a good life, Juliana. No, I'm not lonely. But you must come visit me." She smiled. "Bring your mother."

"Oh—I almost forgot. Mother sent these."

It was a box of butter cookies. Inside was a note. "Willie, Adrian and I talked last night. I told him everything. It felt so right! I've been crying ever since; for his goodness, for Mother and Father, and little David, and Mr. and Mrs. Stein, the children, even for Hendrik, for everything…at last. The burden of guilt isn't gone, but it's lessened. I know Mother and Father wanted me to live, as I would do anything—too much?—to protect Juliana. Dear sister, forgive me. You never drove me away. I left because I couldn't stay; that's all. And because of Adrian. He's made me so happy. Enjoy the cookies. C."

Wilhelmina had enjoyed the cookies tremendously. She'd eaten most of them on the plane; there was only one left.

She went to the wooden box she kept on the hearth and dug out an old black-and-white photograph. The edges were crinkled and yellowed, the quality of the photograph not terribly good, but she didn't care. She balanced it against a lamp and looked at it a long while.

It was of Rachel and Abraham, Johannes and Ann, Hendrik and herself, and Catharina, a mere child, at a skating party before the war. She'd once considered cutting Hendrik out of the picture, but in so doing she would have cut out a part of herself.

She went into the kitchen and made herself a cheese sandwich and a pot of tea and ate the last butter cookie.

Twenty-Seven

"Get your butt down here."

It was four-thirty on Wednesday afternoon, and Juliana had picked up the phone on the first ring, dazed and filled with compulsive energy. She'd had a monumental day of practice. The Chopin had jelled in her mind, and she regretted having to let it go, even for a second, and yet she knew she needed the break. She'd be better off for it, and so would her music. Although she was pleased to hear Len Wetherall's voice, there was another voice she'd have rather heard. She wasn't sure when she would. Or if. But she tried to understand. He'd been through a lot; he needed to be alone.

"Len—what do you mean?"

"I mean you're already thirty minutes late, babe."

She was surprised. "I'm not fired?"

"Hell, no. You've got an audience, angel. Folks've been reading the papers. World's most beautiful concert pianist rescues mother and Dutch aunt from the clutches of killers." He laughed. "I like that. You're a curiosity. Now you got to wow them so they keep on coming back."

Wow them. Juliana smiled: the world of J.J. Pepper wasn't so different from her own. "Who should I come as?"

"Come as yourself, babe. That's all you can ever be."

She tinted her hair green and put on J.J.'s white organza tea dress, circa 1919, and her own full-length white mink coat and hat, white boots and white gloves, and she took a cab.

Len met her at the door. "Whoa," he said, grinning.

"I wouldn't show up at Symphony Hall in Boston looking like this, but here, it feels right. I've got a lot to learn about jazz and pop," she said, "but one day soon I hope to record some of my favorite—" she grinned "—tunes."

"You going to stick to early evenings and catch-as-catch-can between concerts?"

She nodded. "But I'm cutting back on the number of concerts I do a year. I don't want to do so many any longer—but I can't give this up, Len."

He let his relief show. "That's great, babe, because I don't want to have to give up J.J. Pepper, either. She's fun and spacey—and talented as all get-out. I'd like to keep her around, so long as that's what she wants."

"It is."

"What's Shuji say?"

"It's not up to him. He knows that. He doesn't understand, and he'll never like jazz, but he's not going to abandon me because of it."

"That's okay, then. You don't need him to understand?"

"No, I don't," she said. "It's okay."

When she'd finished her first set, she knew she'd wowed the crowd because Len told her when she came to the bar for her Saratoga water. Only then did she notice the applause and whistles and hoots of appreciation—and that she'd kicked off her shoes. She'd let go in a way she never did when playing Carnegie Hall.

Len nodded toward the other end of the bar. "You've got company."

Sipping her water, Juliana looked down the bar and became very still.

Matthew Stark.

"Say the word, I'll toss him."

"No, I'll take care of him."

Len grinned. "Thought you might, babe, thought you might."

She ambled down and leaned against the bar next to Matthew's stool, feeling the sweat trickling between her breasts. She could almost talk herself into believing it was his fingertips.

"Hey, toots," he said with that slight, unreadable grin, his dark eyes on her. "Nice hair—same color as your eyes, isn't it? Better watch out nobody comes along and hangs candy canes on your ears."

"Matthew," she said, hearing the hope and hollowness in her voice. Did he know? Could he hear how much she wanted to be near him? Almost four days without seeing him and it seemed an eternity. Their night together in Vermont had changed everything. Knowing him had changed everything. "I thought you'd still be working on your story."

"Feldie's sticking to the facts, which were straightforward enough. She isn't printing a thing about the Minstrel's Rough." He grinned, loving the way she couldn't keep still, the way she blinked, the way she stood there, gorgeous and green-haired and the only woman he'd ever want again. "So you're safe from the IRS for now. Any plans for the stone—or don't you want to tell me?"

She shrugged. "I think it should fade back into the mist of legend."

"Back to being a paperweight for jam recipes, is it? Tell me, J.J.-slash-Juliana, what are you doing for the holidays?"

"Going to Vermont—finally."

It was the truth, although she had hoped not to go alone. She'd considered various ways to get Matthew back up there with her, including letting *him* deal with the matter of Shuji's car. "You *lost* my car!" he'd raged. "Is this what happens when Jelly Roll Morton gets in your veins? *Get it back!*" But he'd headed to his house in California, trusting her. Abraham Stein was sending her a package to Vermont via courier. The Minstrel's Rough was being returned to its place with her jam recipes. She'd considered various alternatives. Donating it to a museum, throwing it into the ocean, giving it to her mother or Abraham Stein or even Aunt Willie. But she'd decided to keep it. Only the Peperkamps knew for certain it existed...and Matthew.

That was the tradition, for four hundred years.

"Vermont, huh?" Matthew said. "Well, isn't that a coincidence? I'm heading that way myself." There was a tiny drop of perspiration on her right temple that he wanted to brush away with his thumb, but he resisted—for now. "There's this little house I know overlooking the Batten Kill, it's the coldest damn place you've ever been, but not when you're under layers of quilts with a beautiful green-eyed blonde. She plays piano—classical—but I think she sneaks off and messes around with jazz once in a while. I don't have any real proof. I haven't known her all that long, but it doesn't seem to matter. I'm in love with her."

"Matthew, are you serious?"

"Of course." He smiled. "There's only one little problem. I'm not sure she likes my boots."

"She loves your boots," she said, suddenly breathless, "and your black leather jacket. She thinks they're sexy. She thinks their owner's sexy, too, and she's in love with him."

He laughed, looking at her. "I think some of your weirdness has rubbed off on me. Would Len throw me out if I kissed you?"

She grinned at him. "Do you care?"

"It's worth the risk, but I'll make it quick."

He kissed her, but it wasn't quick. They both saw to that.

"What about the *Gazette?*" Juliana asked. "Isn't Alice Feldon expecting a story from you?"

"Not anymore."

"Are you quitting?"

"No, my love," he said, kissing her again. "I'm starting."

New York Times
bestselling author

HEATHER GRAHAM

On a weekend vacation, Beth Anderson is unnerved when a stroll on the beach reveals what appears to be a human skull. As a stranger approaches, Beth panics and covers the evidence. But when she later returns to the beach, the skull is gone.

Determined to find solid evidence to bring to the police, Beth digs deeper into the mystery—and everywhere she goes, Keith Henson, the stranger from the beach, seems to appear. Then a body washes ashore, and Beth begins to think she needs more help than she bargained for....

THE ISLAND

"Another top-notch thriller
from romance icon Graham."
—*Publishers Weekly*

*Available the first week
of March 2007, wherever
paperbacks are sold!*

REQUEST YOUR FREE BOOKS!

2 FREE NOVELS
FROM THE ROMANCE/SUSPENSE
COLLECTION PLUS 2 FREE GIFTS!

YES! Please send me 2 FREE novels from the Romance/Suspense Collection and my 2 FREE gifts. After receiving them, if I don't wish to receive any more books, I can return the shipping statement marked "cancel." If I don't cancel, I will receive 4 brand-new novels every month and be billed just $5.49 per book in the U.S., or $5.99 per book in Canada, plus 25¢ shipping and handling per book plus applicable taxes, if any*. That's a savings of at least 20% off the cover price! I understand that accepting the 2 free books and gifts places me under no obligation to buy anything. I can always return a shipment and cancel at any time. Even if I never buy another book from the Reader Service, the two free books and gifts are mine to keep forever.

185 MDN EF5Y   385 MDN EF6C

Name	(PLEASE PRINT)	
Address		Apt. #
City	State/Prov.	Zip/Postal Code

Signature (if under 18, a parent or guardian must sign)

Mail to **The Reader Service:**
IN U.S.A.: P.O. Box 1867, Buffalo, NY 14240-1867
IN CANADA: P.O. Box 609, Fort Erie, Ontario L2A 5X3

Not valid to current subscribers to the Romance Collection,
the Suspense Collection or the Romance/Suspense Collection.

Want to try two free books from another line?
Call 1-800-873-8635 or visit www.morefreebooks.com.

* Terms and prices subject to change without notice. NY residents add applicable sales tax. Canadian residents will be charged applicable provincial taxes and GST. This offer is limited to one order per household. All orders subject to approval. Credit or debit balances in a customer's account(s) may be offset by any other outstanding balance owed by or to the customer. Please allow 4 to 6 weeks for delivery.

Your Privacy: Harlequin is committed to protecting your privacy. Our Privacy Policy is available online at www.eHarlequin.com or upon request from the Reader Service. From time to time we make our lists of customers available to reputable firms who may have a product or service of interest to you. If you would prefer we not share your name and address, please check here. ☐

BOB07

CARLA NEGGERS

32237 BREAKWATER	___ $7.99 U.S.	___ $9.50 CAN.
32205 DARK SKY	___ $7.50 U.S.	___ $8.99 CAN.
32104 THE RAPIDS	___ $6.99 U.S.	___ $8.50 CAN.
66972 THE CARRIAGE HOUSE	___ $6.50 U.S.	___ $7.99 CAN.
66971 THE WATERFALL	___ $6.50 U.S.	___ $7.99 CAN.
66970 ON FIRE	___ $6.50 U.S.	___ $7.99 CAN.
66969 KISS THE MOON	___ $6.50 U.S.	___ $7.99 CAN.
66923 STONEBROOK COTTAGE	___ $6.50 U.S.	___ $7.99 CAN.
66845 THE CABIN	___ $6.50 U.S.	___ $7.99 CAN.
66684 COLD RIDGE	___ $6.99 U.S.	___ $8.50 CAN.
66651 THE HARBOR	___ $6.99 U.S.	___ $8.50 CAN.

(limited quantities available)

TOTAL AMOUNT	$ _____
POSTAGE & HANDLING	$ _____
($1.00 FOR 1 BOOK, 50¢ for each additional)	
APPLICABLE TAXES*	$ _____
TOTAL PAYABLE	$ _____

(check or money order—please do not send cash)

To order, complete this form and send it, along with a check or money order for the total above, payable to MIRA Books, to: **In the U.S.:** 3010 Walden Avenue, P.O. Box 9077, Buffalo, NY 14269-9077; **In Canada:** P.O. Box 636, Fort Erie, Ontario, L2A 5X3.

Name: _____
Address: _____ City: _____
State/Prov.: _____ Zip/Postal Code: _____
Account Number (if applicable): _____

075 CSAS

*New York residents remit applicable sales taxes.
*Canadian residents remit applicable GST and provincial taxes.

MIRA®

www.MIRABooks.com

MCN0307BL